GIRL GONE VIRAL

GIRL GONE VIRAL

Arvin Ahmadi

VIKING

VIKING
An imprint of Penguin Random House LLC
375 Hudson Street
New York, New York 10014

First published in the United States of America by Viking,
an imprint of Penguin Random House LLC, 2019

LIBRARY OF CONGRESS CATALOGING-IN-PUBLICATION DATA IS AVAILABLE.
ISBN 9780425289907

Printed in USA   Set in Dante   Book design by Mariam Quraishi

10 9 8 7 6 5 4 3 2 1

I can't stand this terrible uncertainty.

—Ursula K. Le Guin

"Schrödinger's Cat"

My dear family:
I must leave you.
I don't wish to be found.
The world is complicated,
The future even more so;
I don't wish to complicate it further.

Yours,
Aaron Tal

PART ONE

GIRL EXPOSED

Chapter
One

I swear, I'm not usually this creepy. I'm not the kind of person who gets off on eavesdropping, and I can count on one hand the number of times I've stalked a crush on social media. But right now, I'm sitting next to a celebrity couple at an expensive Manhattan restaurant, and it's impossible not to stare.

The afternoon hangs still. No breeze, just the faint heartbeat of the city around us. If you didn't glance up at the glimmering skyscrapers, you would think we were having lunch on a sidewalk in Paris. You would think nothing could go wrong.

I turn toward Hailey Carter, the star of the hour. Her face practically demands attention: flushed cheeks, messy golden-brown curls, those curious blue eyes. I'm surprised she's not wearing sunglasses. It's the kind of painfully bright day where nothing can hide—not the loose thread in Hailey's whimsical sundress, not the puddle of blood beneath her filet mignon, and especially not the fact that her boyfriend has no interest in being with her. As my gaze drifts to him, he manages to slouch even deeper into his wicker chair and focus even more intently on his phone's screens.

Hailey's lips move, though I don't hear what she says. Whatever it is, Timmy doesn't reply. His jaw tenses, and he runs a hand through his perfect brown locks, but he doesn't offer her any real attention.

Everyone says Hailey is lucky to be dating Timmy. She's a constant fixture in the tabloids, the love child of two washed-up pop singers, and he's the young Grammy winner with a fan base so rabid it sometimes feels like a parody. She dropped a tennis shoe from her balcony last year and almost killed a man; he drops platinum albums.

Hailey Carter pipes up again. This time it's not her lips but her throat. A deep and demanding "ah-*hem*." Timmy finally looks up from his phone, his face peeking out from the shade of the large overhead umbrella, and his eyes narrow on the nervous girl across the table. I hear their next words clearly.

"What?"

Hailey frowns. "Are we really doing this again?"

As I stare, a paparazzi drone swoops down and flies past my nose. More of them descend like vultures, smelling the blood of a juicy tabloid story, just like they swarmed me seven years ago when word had gotten around that my dad was missing.

"Get out of my face!" Hailey says, swatting one of the drones away. "Out!"

"Hailey, stop it," Timmy hisses. "You're causing a scene."

"Oh, I'm always causing a scene, aren't I, Timmy? You get to be the calm, cool, collected one, and I'm just *crazy*."

Once, I broke down in front of those flying cameras outside our home. I poured out my ten-year-old heart to them, and my mother ran and grabbed me by the wrist, pulling me inside and slamming the door shut. She told me my father was gone. That there was no point in looking for him after the police found that cold, heartless note. I told her the drones could help, because if he was out there, he needed to know we were hurting.

When you're desperate, you'll do whatever it takes to be heard.

"You *are* crazy, you know that?" Timmy spits at Hailey. He looks nervously in my direction. "You'll never change."

My dad never did turn up, and eventually the drones outside our house moved on. On to the next girl's tragedy. The next juicy headline.

I wish I could say I moved on too, but certain memories are like shadows. You catch one glimpse, one fuzzy reminder of your dark past, and you realize it's been following you this entire time.

"*Get out!*" Hailey Carter screams. She leans across the table and shoves Timmy with her ring-studded fists.

Timmy stumbles out of his seat. A waiter rushes from inside the restaurant, though he stands a safe distance from Hailey. She picks up the steak from her plate and looks like she's about to hurl the slab of meat at Timmy, whose delicate fingers are curled around his chair like it's a shield. The waiter gasps, extending an arm toward poor, beloved Timmy.

"GET *OUT*," Hailey screams again. The veins in her neck pop.

Timmy doesn't move. He glances out of the side of his eye at the whirling drones, his chest rising and falling. He can't come off like a coward when he's being recorded. His fans think the world of him; they're expecting him to be brave. I look down at the piece of steak in Hailey's hand. I can see every detail. The crimson streaks running through the pinkish brown meat. Hailey's fingers digging deep into the flesh.

I look back up. Hailey's face and mine are so close we could melt into one. I'm looking inside her, and I see a girl who can't show the world her multitudes because it refuses to see more than one dimension.

She says it once more, with absolute finality. *"Get out."* This time, Timmy listens—he jumps over the sidewalk fence and takes off down the street. That's when Hailey begins murmuring to herself, *"Get me out of this world."* Over and over and over. Whether she means her personal life or her mental health struggles, or this modern world where the lines between reality and fiction are blurring every day—it doesn't matter. Because everything freezes, and the Manhattan streets dissolve before my eyes.

I'm not really there.

Chapter

Two

I rip off the headset.

I can't tell which is beating harder, my head or my heart.

It takes a second for my eyes to adjust from pixels to reality. From the mess of Hailey Carter's life to the spotless white halls of the Palo Alto Academy of Science and Technology. From her floral-printed sundress to the track sweatshirt in my lap . . . and Dr. Travers's brown loafers right in front of me.

Given the fact that Dr. Travers doesn't usually leave his desk when he lets us work outside the classroom, this is less than optimal. I look up at Dr. Travers. His arms are crossed.

"You're supposed to be on Instagram, Ms. Hopper."

You'd think the sudden presence of my History of Social Media teacher would freak me out more, that the slow *tap, tap, tap* of his foot would intimidate me into getting back to working on the assignment. Instead, my heart calms down. Hailey Carter's voice drains out of my head. I'm back.

"Sorry," I reply sheepishly. Dr. Travers gestures at my headset. I slip it into the pocket of my hoodie. He gestures again, this time to my side. I pick up the class-issued iPhone.

He smirks. "Back in my day, if we wanted to be delinquent, we just checked that little phone under our desks. Headsets weren't quite in vogue yet."

A few of the other kids in my class are scattered throughout the hall, holding back snickers.

"Now, I know it's smaller, heavier, and much slower than what you're used to," Dr. Travers says, "and it only has one screen. But I thought the experience of scrolling through Instagram on an *iPhone* would make the assignment more authentic."

"Mhmm."

"Like digging up fossils, or setting foot in the Colosseum."

"Just like that."

I'm waiting for Dr. Travers to leave, but as if he's just seen my private thoughts, he crouches and lowers his voice. "Your mind's stuck on that contest, isn't it?"

My eyes jump and meet his square glasses.

"I swear that's not what I was doing—"

"Of course it was. You were on WAVE. Besides, I've seen you and your friends with your cameras, filming Ms. Lee around campus." Dr. Travers chuckles, and I realize he might actually be watching our channel. "You know, Opal, I fully expected some of our students to enter. Kara Lee, absolutely. We have so many ambitious minds at this school, and where better for lofty dreams than virtual reality? But I never would have expected *you*. You're taking quite the risk, aren't you?"

My breath tightens, like someone's gripping my lungs. Dr. Travers isn't knocking my ambition; he's acknowledging my past. Because if there's one thing I've learned in high school, it's that people talk. And when it comes to my attempt at winning Make-A-Splash, there's plenty for people to talk about.

"Now get back to work."

Dr. Travers disappears into the classroom. If we went to a normal high school, my classmates would take his departure as a cue to ditch the iPhones and mess around. It's a Friday afternoon, after all.

But nothing is normal at PAAST. Everyone gets back to work.

I swipe to unlock this ancient phone, astonished at how tiny the screen used to be before they made them retractable and foldable. I open Instagram. Our assignment is to look at formerly popular accounts and identify patterns in how they posted: time of day, ratio of selfies to non-selfies, frequent themes. Dr. Travers likes to joke in class that if he'd been born with six-pack abs instead of early onset male pattern baldness, he could have used those tactics to be "Insta-famous." Instead he settled for Twitter and teaching.

But I can't focus on the assignment. My mind is still lingering on that viral Hailey Carter breakdown. That line. It's ringing in my ears. *Get me out of this world.*

Maybe that's why it caught me off guard when Dr. Travers brought up the contest. I mean, everyone at school knows I'm entering—but they also know better than to bring it up around me, because winning would mean returning to a world I was supposed to have left behind.

My senior year was all set before this contest. I'd worked hard these last three years at PAAST, piling on extracurriculars and good grades to get into Stanford. The plan was to apply early decision and create new memories there. But then I heard about Make-A-Splash. *Join the WAVE*, I read on the official page after I'd come out of the shower, my hair dripping over my shoulders. *If you've ever thought about hosting your own channel, now is your chance . . . The winning team will be rewarded with $1 million, flights to Palo Alto Labs' headquarters, and an exclusive meeting with Howie Mendelsohn . . .*

Seven years ago, when I needed him most, Howie Mendelsohn couldn't give me the time of day. News of the contest brings all those memories flooding back, a wave of emotion crashing into my perfect sand castle of stability.

At the end of the period, I mosey into the classroom to drop the iPhone back in the bin on Dr. Travers's desk.

"Earth to Opal? You look like you saw a ghost."

It's Moyo. His puffy vest jacket brushes the back of my hand, and he smells faintly of autumn leaves. I turn around.

"Oh, wow." Moyo's eyes pop. "I amend my statement. You look like you asked the ghost to prom and it turned you down."

I muster a playful smile. "Ghost prom sounds a lot more interesting than the crap we've been airing on WAVE."

"Just wait until you see what Kara asked me to design for Monday's episode. You'll *wish* we were doing ghost prom."

"I swear, if it's another shopping trip to Paris . . ."

"Mon chéri! Un béret, s'il vous plaît!"

My expression sours as I think about how badly I'd misjudged

Kara's star power. I learned the hard way that just because she's been a fixture on Zapp since the days when it overtook Instagram on multiscreen phones, it doesn't mean she's any good in VR. Kara's Zapp brand is best described as Lifestyles of the Rich and *Almost* Famous. (Sample caption: "Another trip to St. Barts, *ugh*.") I never bought the whole rich-kid self-deprecation act, but plenty of other people did. I assumed her two hundred thousand followers would appreciate a fully immersive look into her life, so we started *Kara Lee: Behind the Scenes* on WAVE. But three-second snippets don't translate into full episodes. Kara's clunky. She's awkward. She said "such that" twenty-seven times in one half-hour episode. I counted.

I nearly tore Kara's hair out last weekend. She's driving our chance of winning Make-A-Splash into the ground. I keep trying to bring up data—what do her fans want, what are they clamoring about in chat rooms—but Kara's convinced she knows her brand better than the numbers do.

I should have known she wouldn't listen. Kara's the star, and I'm essentially tech support. That was the arrangement. She gets her way.

History of Social Media is our last class of the day, so Moyo and I head back to the dorms together. He tells me about some of the absurd Instagram captions he saw during the assignment, and when I bring up a particularly bad pun involving Middle Eastern food, Moyo hunches over and pretends to vomit. "I falafel," he groans. In the senior hall, we pass his soccer teammates, who raise their eyebrows and nudge elbows like they always do whenever they see us together, even though Moyo and I have been friends, *just* friends, since freshman year. We stop outside my door.

"What are we doing this weekend?" Moyo asks. "There's a new taco place on University Avenue I kind of want to check out."

"I'm staying in," I say.

"Again?" Moyo lets out a disappointed sigh. We spent all of junior year dreaming about senior off-campus privileges, and so far, I've spent the first three weekends holed up in my dorm room.

"I want to see if I can do something to pull our numbers up. You know the contest ends next week, right? Monday's episode is our last chance."

Moyo shrugs. "Won't do any good with Kara treating us like we're invisible. But your call. Let me know if you need a break."

I enter my dorm room, which is even messier than Hailey Carter's life. The school year started barely three weeks ago, and my floor already looks like a post-apocalyptic war zone, complete with Red Bull shrapnel and dirty laundry debris.

My walls are checkered with glowing "You May Also Enjoy" tiles from WAVE, years' worth of Hailey Carter meltdowns in XP form, ready for 360-degree consumption. Because WAVE wants you to *experience* as much as possible in their world, anytime, anyplace. "If you liked Hailey's epic lunch meltdown, then you'll love the time she threw a hissy fit in the middle of Times Square!" I've experienced them all, though. Hailey's bizarre antics are virtual reality gold. She's the joke that keeps on giving, and there are rumors that she's been so good for WAVE that they're going to sponsor her rehab.

Get me out of this—

There's a knock at the door.

"Come in!"

As soon as the voice-activated lock pops open, Shane barges into my room. He's wearing a white undershirt that looks like it hasn't seen a washer in eons. His brown hair is chaotic, even messier than it was on the first day of classes, when Dr. Travers called him out for having "Bieber hair." No one really understood what that meant, but it annoyed Shane enough that he dropped the class.

"We miss you in HSM," I say.

"Whatever. Dr. Travers is lame." Shane's bouncing on his feet, grinning widely. "I have something you'll like."

A stranger might raise a brow at Shane's lack of hygiene and his spastic energy, but I've known him for too long to worry. He traces a long stroke over the tablet he brought with him, finishing with a flick, and my walls suddenly fill with endless lines of data. When I process the glowing text, my jaw drops. This code is more beautiful, more detailed than Michelangelo's Sistine Chapel—and more revealing than his *David*.

"Shane." I gawk. "How did you . . ."

"Don't ask questions," he says, pinching my lips closed. I haven't seen Shane so drunk with pleasure since we actually went drinking off-campus last year. "Consider it a gift."

"There's no way you got all this data—" I lower my voice. "Legally."

"And there's no reason anyone should find out," Shane says, grinning slyly. That smile combined with his giddy drunkenness takes me back to our awkward kiss freshman year, and how I probably shouldn't let him pinch my lips in the future. I raise a brow, and Shane rolls his eyes. "Come on, Opal. After that showdown with Kara last weekend, I thought you could use some ammunition. I mean, screw Kara—you understand WAVE better than any of us. Now you have the numbers to prove it."

"Even if this wasn't impressively sketchy, I don't know how we're going to analyze all this data in one weekend."

"*We* can't, but *you* can. My parents are dragging me with them on one of those 'device-free' retreats in Monterey this weekend. Which reminds me—I should probably go and, like, shower and hug my laptop goodbye."

Before I can open my mouth to object, Shane shoots off one last grin and leaves.

I stare at the writing on the wall. Snippets of numbers, letters, and symbols ripple before my eyes, and slowly, Hailey Carter's wounded voice becomes an afterthought. I'm comforted by code. After my dad disappeared, I didn't touch a command line for an entire year—but the first time my fingers plucked out the words hello, world again, it was like a rope pulling me out of my pit of depression. Sometimes I wonder if I followed in my dad's footsteps as a coder because I had something to prove. But I've always loved numbers. They were my way of making sense of the world before he left, and I've only needed them more since.

But what Shane's given me—these aren't just numbers. They're people's lives.

Imagine someone watching you when you think you're alone. Imagine them recording your face's every move: every time you laugh or cry, every flinch, every blink. That's what WAVE started doing last week in an effort to "provide users with the best, customized experience." The idea is that the data is for internal use only, and for XPs that explicitly ask for permission.

Unless you're Shane. Because somehow, my friend has hacked into millions of headsets and stolen that data. And that data has found its way to my walls. I stare the way you can't help but stare at the hot neighbor through the window taking his shirt off.

Then I get to work. I would never release people's private data, but it doesn't mean I can't study it. For the next forty-eight hours, I'm plugged in. Headphones. Liquid meals. Allergic to sleep and showers and other bodily needs. I'm swatting bugs in my code, getting loopy off *if* loops and *for* loops and, Jesus Christ, it's like a roller coaster.

But toward the end of this blurry trip, I discover a secret in the numbers. It's the kind of discovery that would get all the internet trolls talking—that could win us the attention we need to win Make-A-Splash.

I discover that everyone is lying.

Chapter
Three

By Sunday night, I want nothing more than to reunite with my pillow—but instead, I put on my headset one last time.

The cold goggles push lightly into my skin, and headphones come out the sides and hug my ears. The plexiglass visors lock into place over my tired eyes, making a powerful *thunk*, like a heavy vault door being closed. Sometimes I imagine Howie Mendelsohn, WAVE's reclusive inventor, swallowing the key himself and trapping me inside his virtual universe, a devilish grin smeared across his face. I met him once seven years ago, when he and my dad were up late working on their stealth-mode start-up at the marble island in our kitchen—and that's all I remember. His smile. Like he knew exactly how my life was about to change.

If we win this contest, I'll meet him again.

WAVE makes a high-pitched *ding* when my friends accept my chat request, and within seconds, we're standing inside our favorite chat room, Pete's Arcade. My eyes skate over the coin-operated machines like Star Trek and Wheel of Fortune glaring their tacky blues and reds, and land on my two best friends.

"Seriously, Opal? It's one a.m. I'm exhausted," Shane groans. He drops his gaze below the snakeskin joggers and designer sneakers his mom almost certainly bought for his avatar.

I gesture at the brand-new clothes. "I see Mrs. Franklin really took the device-free weekend to heart."

Shane snorts. "She barely lasted five minutes in the car ride home before another shopping spree."

"Greetings, night owls!" Moyo bellows as his avatar materializes. He dishes me a side-eye. "A text would have done the job, I'm sure. But that wouldn't have been your style. All hail Queen Opal Hopper! Interrupter of late-night activities, demander of attention!"

"Don't pretend you weren't already up," I chide. Neither of them goes to bed before three a.m., ever.

"Well, I was engaged in very important business," Moyo says.

Doodles. I'd bet my new haptic gloves Moyo was drawing at his makeshift studio. Curfew in the senior dorms is midnight, which happens to be when Moyo's fingers start itching for pencils over stylus pens. His parents wouldn't buy him art supplies this year—they wanted him to focus on digital design, for his college applications—so Moyo built himself a drawing board out of scrap cardboard.

"Sure you were, Picasso," I say. "And what's your excuse, Shane? Some late-night Rubik's Cube action?"

Shane jerks his head up, but his arms stay at his side—which means he's turned off limb control.

"Oh my God, you really *are* solving a Rubik's Cube."

"How exactly does one solve a Rubik's Cube with goggles on?" Moyo asks, his playful eyes meeting mine.

"He can feel the colors," I say, smirking. Moyo and I share a special language, and making fun of Shane is our favorite dialect. "Naturally. It's like synesthesia in your fingertips. Though I don't understand why you can't just buy haptic gloves off WAVEmart. We get that sweet PAAST discount, and you'd still feel the synesthetic"—I flutter my fingers in front of his face—"tingles."

Shane looks peeved, but he doesn't swat my hand away. I bet he's still twisting little squares. "Wait," he says, and his jaw clinches the way it always does when he's snapped the last square into place. "You're calling about the contest, aren't you? What ever happened with that data?"

His eyes brighten. Shane wants to win Make-A-Splash just as much as I do, though for him, it's kind of a shotgun effort. He realized over the summer that the extracurricular box on his MIT application was about as empty as a quantum vacuum, and even for a double-legacy applicant, that's not a good look. I convinced Shane that he could use a quick, shiny résumé padder like Make-A-Splash.

"That's exactly why I'm calling," I say, smiling.

Moyo's expression slumps. He got roped into all this—the three of us have been a unit since sophomore year, and Moyo wasn't about to go breaking the rule of three. Or any rule, for that matter.

"Have you guys seen the latest Hailey Carter meltdown?" I ask.

"I saw the holos," Moyo says. "Someone photoshopped her into a snake suffocating Timmy. His fans went nuts. They think she's the devil."

"You know she was born on leap day," Shane says.

"What does that have to do with it?" Moyo asks.

"It means she won't ever grow up. Remember that XP you showed me last year, Opal, where she threw a hissy fit in an ice cream shop?"

I'll admit, I had always accepted the "Hailey Carter is a train wreck" narrative. She's an internet martyr—a fixture on Zapp and Livvit boards, an easy target for holographic memes.

"I'll never understand all the online hate for her," Moyo says.

I grin widely. "Oh, yes you will."

I walk over to the Pac-Man leaderboard in the back of the arcade and erase the top scores so that I essentially have a blank slate. A whiteboard.

"What if people don't actually hate Hailey Carter the way you think they do?" I ask. "What if we could stir up our own drama on the internet and prove that we're all rooting for her?"

"Rooting for her?" Moyo repeats. I can almost feel his curiosity hanging in the air. That's what I love most about Moyo—he's the open-minded, artsy, philosopher type, without any of the usual douchebaggery. I wave my hand over the screen, and it fills with a line graph.

"The comments on Hailey Carter's latest meltdown were overwhelmingly negative. From start to finish. That's this red line. But the thing is, that dialogue was dominated by Timmy's fans.

Anytime someone tried showing an ounce of support for Hailey, they got shut down." I tap at the board, and a cutout of Timmy's face appears every time the red line dips. I tap it again, and a green line appears. This one doesn't dip but rather rises gradually, shooting up near the end. "The first line was everyone's public reactions. This second line is how they reacted privately."

Moyo doesn't notice the giant difference between what people write in the comments and how they actually feel about Hailey Carter.

He doesn't notice the jump in sympathetic gestures after Timmy runs off and you're left alone with Hailey. More winces, more whimpers, more hands clasped over mouths. How the vast majority of viewers—even Timmy's biggest fans—actually feel for this girl in pain.

He doesn't notice that people aren't as cruel as you'd think from the comment section.

Or maybe he does. But instead of acknowledging my breakthrough, he homes in on one specific word: *"Privately?"*

The data. Right. That's how I came to these conclusions, isn't it. Meekly, I turn to Shane, who's drifted to the corner of the arcade.

"Shane, over here—" I linger as I read the terror in Moyo's eyes. "He may have stumbled upon some helpful data."

"And you struck gold," Shane says, his eyes leaping. "Imagine Kara calling out one of those trolls on her channel tomorrow. Like, 'NOPE, even you have a heart, troll. In your face!' Literally! It would be huge."

"She'd look like a mind reader," I say. "It takes 'behind the scenes' to another level."

Moyo draws a deep breath. His avatar's arms swing steadily by his side, but I don't need WAVE to tell me where his real arms are. I know from his silence that he has one hand cupped under his chin, conflicted about what to say next. I shift my attention from his face to his shirt, an oversized Nigerian button-up that he designed himself. I examine the patterns carefully, searching the blotches of red and green, focusing on the bright shade of yellow he copied straight from the sun.

Having access to the private emotions of every person on WAVE makes nerds like Shane and me giddy with possibility. It's a rare patch of spring flowers in Antarctica, or Moyo's colorful shirt against the retro arcade background. But Moyo's different. He sees the weeds that grow underneath the flowers: difficult to pull out, maybe even poisonous. He sees his Nigerian mother clucking her tongue, disappointed in her son's loosened morals, his disregard for privacy.

When Moyo doesn't respond, I finally say, "It's just facial expression data. The new tracking feature they added last week."

"I didn't even know they were letting XPs track that," Moyo sputters, somewhat angrily.

"You gave WAVE permission," Shane says. "You checked a box."

"I check a lot of boxes!" Moyo huffs. "Besides, no one checked a box letting *us* look at it."

"Moyo, it's not a big deal—"

"What if they start letting XPs track more than your face?"

Moyo says incredulously. "Would you want strangers looking at that?"

"Like what, when I'm in the shower? When I'm naked in bed stuffing my face with potato chips?" I say with a laugh.

"This isn't a joke," Moyo says.

I'm getting exasperated, but I should have expected as much. Arguing with Moyo is like refracting sunlight to make a fire: it's all about finding the right angle.

Shane stares at Moyo from over in the pinball corner. "You do understand that no one would find out about the hack," he says, his eyes bulging. "It just lets us know how people will react. It's like a cheat sheet."

"What do you mean?" Moyo asks.

"We'll be collecting our viewers' data during the show, and we'll use *that* as our evidence. Which we're completely allowed to have. This collection of data just shows us what we're going to find there."

"Doesn't make it right," Moyo replies.

"Look at it this way," I say. "You had no idea you were giving XPs permission to track your face until I told you, right? If we spread the word with our channel, we'd be doing a public service for all the Moyos out there."

"We'd be taking advantage of them!" he barks back.

"All right, Moyo, then look at it *this* way: Shane's already hacked the data. We want to win this contest. Not a single one of Kara's XPs has broken ten thousand views, and if we don't hit it big with this next one, we're done. So there's really no point in arguing with me right now," I fume. Screw refraction—I'm lighting a match. "If you want to go and turn off facial recognition on *top* of limb control, be my guest. You can be one of those static blobs floating pointlessly through WAVE. But the rest of us are on board with all this benign tracking if it means we get a better experience. And speaking of, did you even consider what this discovery could mean for Hailey Carter? Doesn't she deserve to know there are people out there, millions of people, who actually care about her?"

Moyo goes quiet, and I assume I've either broken him or gotten through to him. All of a sudden his shoulders wake up with life, and then his arms and legs; he's turned on limb control. His whole body seems tense at first, but then he relaxes.

"Fine," Moyo sighs. "As long as no one finds out about the data hacking." His muddy brown eyes are distant and defeated.

I fill up with warmth. "Of course."

"But do you think—"

"Dude! Just chill," Shane bursts out from his corner.

I raise a brow at Shane. *Chill.* Every once in a while, Shane actually lives up to his jockish looks. He might have decently toned arms from the pushups he performs every morning and wear the fitted shirts his mom buys him, but in reality, he's neither jock nor prep nor apathetic bro. He's the nerdiest of our nerdtastic unit, an honor we liken to being the tallest giraffe.

Moyo gives Shane a look. "I was just going to ask about Kara," he says. "She wanted to preview her Halloween costume options tomorrow. I don't see how we're going to convince her to air a Hailey Carter PSA . . ."

We decide our best chance at getting through to Kara is with Peter Isaacson, her drama department confidant, who's been feeding her scripts for *Behind the Scenes*. I used to help him with his calculus homework, so he owes me. I agree to meet with him in the morning, and we say good night and exit the chat room. I don't take off my headset, though. I bury my face in the folds of my bedsheets and twist my head, high-def 3D icons whirling before my eyes like a carousel floating in outer space. Each one invites me inside for a ride. This time of night, I always pick the same pony.

I extend my hand to seize a green scribbled-tree icon, and in a quick flash, I'm dropped into an old Jeep rumbling down a bumpy dirt path. The Tahoe basin glimmers a perfect blue. Yellow leaves dance over the road. The California sun sinks behind pine trees of every variety, and the familiarity of this simulation puts me at ease. Campfire is a simple XP with many paths, but they all lead to the same place.

I know with razor precision when he'll appear at the clearing on the left, and I always savor the moment in slow motion. The Jeep crawls down the road, inch by inch, and I turn my head, rubbernecking without shame. There he is. My dad, waiting for me by our campsite. His green eyes twinkle just for me, and I smile, irresistibly soaking it all in: Abba's gawkish frame, his salt-and-pepper hair, the way he waves his hand like an overeager kindergartener. A fire crackles behind him. I used to get out of the car and join him, back when I first created Campfire, but I can't do that anymore. Now I keep driving, thinking about how I used to hold that soft hand the entire drive home.

That was just before things got "complicated." Before Howie

Mendelsohn convinced my dad to leave Stanford, before Abba grew cold and distant and spent all his time with Howie, before he left that note and never came back.

I take off my headset. "Lights out," I instruct, and my dorm fades to black. *"Alarm set for six fifty-five a.m.,"* purrs M4rc, my voice assistant.

Then the wall facing my bed illuminates, and the sound of audience laughter fills every corner of the room. M4rc's gotten to know me well over the years—he's like my secretary, nanny, and parent all wrapped in one. He reminds me to take my vitamins. He listens in on my conversations. He plays soothing music when I'm studying for exams. And on nights like this, when I've got a lot on my mind, he knows I can't fall asleep without the lullaby of some late-night talk show host.

JIMMY FALLON

And how about Hailey Carter? Man, I know she goes AWOL all the time, and I wish her all the best. But Timmy? Did she have to bring our sweet, sweet Timmy down with her?

[Laughter from the audience. Giggles from Jimmy.]

JIMMY FALLON

Team Timmy specifically requested I say "sweet" twice. They're very demanding folks.

[More audience laughter.]

JIMMY FALLON

In fact, they're backstage right now and holding
me hostage. Guys, I'm Jimmy! You're looking for
Timmy!

[The laughter from the audience swells, almost drowning out Jimmy's giggles. Almost.]

JIMMY FALLON

One thing's for sure: Howie Mendelsohn lives for
drama like this. Hailey Carter, out in the real
world, racking up hits for his virtual empire.
I bet he's throwing a huge party under his
rock! The biggest rock party ever. Maybe if I
stop talking to people, I'll be worth a cool
hundred billion too. Maybe then they'll call me
the next Steve Jobs.

If you ever find yourself with a missing business partner,
here's what you do: Go back to your old company. Go quiet. In-
vent a headset and build an empire.

Most of all, ignore his daughter's countless emails asking to
talk. Shut the door on her when she shows up at your doorstep,
begging you for clues—what her dad had talked about those last
few days, where he might have gone.

One minute you're a suspect; the next minute you're Steve
Jobs.

Silicon Valley moves quickly. People have mostly accepted the narrative that I've moved on from my dad's disappearance: I focused on school, got into PAAST, became your typical Palo Alto overachiever. And for the most part I have. But this contest has opened up those old wounds: the possibility that my dad is still out there, that Howie Mendelsohn knows more than he let on, that he might have played a part in his disappearance.

Howie Mendelsohn took my dad away from me during his last months. Maybe he didn't take his life, but he took his time. They worked together around the clock, morning to night, until that very last evening when Abba left their office and never came back. Howie's the one person who can help decode the great mystery of my life.

Chapter

Four

The next morning, I'm stepping out of my dorm when I realize something. If I want to be treated like more than tech support, I need to dress the part.

I turn around and hunt through my closet. I change into a light-blue crepe blouse and spend an extra minute in front of my Picasso Mirror. The augmented-reality feature overlays different makeup options on my face, and I swipe through some of the classier looks. Peach blush, copper tones. Rainbow eye makeup, heightened cheekbones. Thin eyeliner, thick eyeliner, eyeliner that curves beyond the edges of my eyes. I settle on an option called Boldly Simple Contour and carefully follow the mirror's instructions.

The world would be a better place if appearances didn't matter. If I could confidently say that Peter Isaacson was going to judge my idea on its merits alone and not, say, the frumpy sweatshirt I was wearing earlier. But as I cut across the emerald lawn that separates the dorms from the main building, I notice people are already looking at me differently. Rosalind Wu, who decided this year that winking was going to be her new thing, winks twice. Jez Marshall, the class creep, bugs his eyes before croaking a nervous "hello." Even some of the underclassmen stare for just a second too long.

If I'm being honest, I kind of like the attention.

I meet Peter in the Sphinx during morning announcements. The Sphinx is the entryway to our school, a three-story atrium erected out of steel bars and large glass panels—a shining feat of interior design but a colossal waste of vertical space.

"Goooood morning, students! Another sunny day at the Palo Alto Academy of Science and Technology! The time is little-hand-eight, big-hand-twenty on—ready for this one?—the TWENTY-NINTH day of the NINTH month of the . . ."

The morning announcement bot makes M4rc sound like the hot guy on the football team. At least it's not broadcasting the date in binary this time.

"So what's this big favor you need?" Peter asks, his backpack overflowing with physical textbooks. He's the only person I know who hasn't gone fully digital. He's a weird kid.

PAAST's campus is tucked away behind soaring sequoias and endless home renovations, just a stone's throw away from Stanford. From above, the main building is shaped like a blunt arrow, with the Sphinx as the head. Most of my classmates are sprawled on the marble floors in small circles, scarfing breakfast and cramming for quizzes. Peter and I are over by the slanted glass window wall, towering over them. We stand out like sore thumbs.

"Let's walk toward Hell," I tell him quietly.

Our state-of-the-art classrooms, faculty offices, shiny research labs, and voice-activated lockers live in one hallway that makes up the shaft of the arrow. Officially, it's called the Main Hall, but everyone calls it Hell.

"How was Kara's party?" Peter asks out of the blue.

I jerk my head. "What party?"

His whole face goes red. *Oh.*

My lips tense. "Never mind." I extend all the screens on my phone and tell Peter about facial recognition, and how it's basically mind reading, and none of the other Make-A-Splash entries have taken advantage of it yet. He suggests, completely seriously, that we hold a staring contest on the channel because "Kara's really good at them." I smile charitably. Then I tell him about Hailey Carter.

"Whoa," he remarks when I finish explaining. "You want Kara to call people out for lying in the comments? How can you be sure?"

"I processed external and internal data from the latest Hailey Carter XP"—I quickly flash the graph with people's public and private reactions—"which would suggest a random sample of WAVE users should react accordingly."

Peter hesitates. "Um, right. Yeah."

"It's all inferential statistics. If you ran a Bayesian analysis and translated the facial gestures into human emotion, you could predict with a decent level of certainty that the future events would reflect the prior ones."

"Uh huh. Of course."

It's bullshit, is what it is. But I can't let Peter in on the data hack—and besides, he barely scraped by calculus. I knew he'd buy my jargon. He's a theater kid, like Kara.

We keep shuffling along as I pull up another chart on my phone screen. Outside the Geosystems Lab a group of under-classmen explodes into over-the-top laughter; I recognize some of them from last year's school musical, *Dear Evan Hansen*. I have no doubt in my mind that Kara invited them to her party. I hate that I care that she didn't invite me. That she didn't invite Shane or Moyo, either. We're the ones making her show happen.

"Did she invite you?" I ask Peter abruptly. "Kara. To her party."

"Yeah," Peter says. "Couldn't go, though. My mom took away my off-campus privileges since I flunked the first phy-sucks quiz. Heard it was wild."

"Oh."

Look, I get it. Kara's just as pissed off about her low numbers on WAVE as I am. But that means we should be spending *more* time together, not less. I'd never seen someone wrinkle their nose with as much revulsion as Kara did the other weekend when I sug-gested she take her fans on a tour of her giant home. She wasn't always this insufferable; back in middle school, we spent an after-noon on the swings in her backyard, after we'd finished working on a group project, and I told her my theories about my dad. I could tell she believed the Silicon Valley rumor mill, but at least she listened.

Girls like Kara belong in the spotlight. They wear expensive clothes and stunning smiles and read scripted lines. They have fathers who provide and pamper endlessly. Girls like me with broken histories and hidden agendas, we help them get there.

"Don't take it personally," Peter says, giving me a sideways glance. "Aside from the theater department, she only invites other billionaire-spawn."

"Internship season is under way, and Silicon Valley wants your talents more than ever! Lori Sandberg in the career center is extending her office hours . . ."

PAAST is one of the most elite institutions in the world, but our high school nearly went bust after Silicon Valley almost crashed and burned. The hardware revolution was in full swing when I was a kid; billions of people who couldn't afford expensive gadgets before now owned smartphones, headsets, personal AIs. But the problem with record-low prices was record-high malfunction rates, which often resulted in nasty human injuries. This really angered a lot of folks and hurt the industry for a couple of years. Kara's father, Sigmund Lee, was one of the entrepreneurs who managed to weather the downturn. It turns out even when people are protesting explosive headsets, they're all right with drones delivering their pad thai. His company is worth a cool $20 billion dollars now.

I'll never understand why my dad left his tenured Stanford job to work on a start-up during the tech downturn. And I'll never understand why Howie Mendelsohn left Palo Alto Labs, his first start-up, to join him. After Abba disappeared, Howie boomeranged back to PAL, which had survived by churning out addictive phone apps, and they did something unusual: they saved PAAST. To show its commitment to the next generation of entrepreneurs, PAL made the single-largest donation to a high school in history.

Slowly, the pieces fell back into place. People put their faith in Silicon Valley again, and the industry delivered. Smarter homes. Smarter cars. Screens everywhere. Congress revitalized virtual reality by loosening copyright and privacy laws, which helped PAL launch WAVE. Hollywood was even behind it at first, thinking the widespread growth of this new entertainment platform would fuel a renaissance for their industry. By the time they realized Howie's invention was eating their lunch, it was too late.

"So what do you think?" I finally ask Peter.

"This is good," he says, nodding. "Really good. People would freak if we told them they actually care more about Hailey Carter than Timmy." He looks away and runs a hand through his shaggy black hair.

"But you don't think Kara will bite."

"You know Kara Lee."

I groan. "She's *beyond*."

We reach Peter's physics classroom. "Listen. I'll work on a script Kara might get behind and try convincing her at lunch. I can't promise—"

"That's all for today, folks. And remember. The past may be behind us, but the future is PAAST. Go, Calculators!"

Peter rolls his eyes. "I hate that stupid catchphrase."

"I kind of like it," I say. "So you think there's a chance?"

"A non-zero chance, yes."

I have a tough time focusing in my classes throughout the day. The knot in my stomach tightens with the crippling pressure of Make-A-Splash: whether Kara will listen to Peter, whether Hailey Carter will actually get us the kind of attention we need, whether we'll win . . . It gets even tighter between periods as I squeeze through the pressure cooker of Hell, a dimly lit tunnel that oozes more stress than a petri dish overflowing with agar.

"Bump me your physics notes."

"Can I copy your homework?"

"Are you ready for that test?"

"I'm going to fail."

"My dad is going to kill me."

"I want to kill myself."

"I heard the sushi at Kara's party was beyond expensive."

"I heard Mrs. Fischer is actually voting for Gaby Swift."

"I heard Jacqueline Sharif is applying early decision to Harvard. That makes twenty-two of us, right? They never take more than five."

After my last class, I trek down to the Media Room. I still haven't heard anything from Peter, so I can only assume Kara didn't bite and that we'll be filming her usual monologue and green screen segments.

The Media Room sits at the very end of Hell, crammed between the Oceanography Lab and the Robotics Lab. As I pass the voice-activated lockers, it strikes me how these lockers, like so many of the devices in our lives, are always listening.

"Spencer's a total shoo-in for MIT."

"Cassie has no chance."

"I was up till three last night. Stupid multi-var problem set."

"I was up till four."

"I'm *still* up. All-nighter, baby."

At three p.m., the doors to the Media Room burst wide open. I'm expecting it to be Kara with one of her Category Five hurricane entrances, but instead, Moyo stumbles in. He runs to the center of the titanium chamber, panting heavily, and rests his hands on the back of a metal chair. The steel doors clamor shut behind him. Shane and I exchange confused looks before turning back to our friend's panicked eyes.

Moyo takes a deep breath. Relaxes his muscles. Lets his jaw hang for a second before he finally speaks.

"Kara got food poisoning."

Chapter

Five

My fingers freeze over the keyboard. Shane, who's hauling a heavy cart of equipment, skids as he fails to bring it to a full stop. The wheels squeak, and one of the monitors nearly slides off.

"What?"

Our phones buzz. Shane pulls his out first.

"Not food poisoning," Shane says, skimming the text. *"Norovirus.* Principal Frasier just sent out an alert. Most of the theater department is sick."

"I bet it was the sushi at Kara's party." I jump out of my chair in the control room and start pacing in front of the green screen. "Shit."

My hands are shaking at my side as I feel this contest slipping out of my grip—my chance to meet Howie Mendelsohn and get the answers I've wanted. After all this time. All those unanswered emails.

But I'm also battling with the sinful satisfaction of schadenfreude. I'm so unexpectedly struck with pleasure at Kara's misfortune that I can't bear to look Moyo in the face, so instead, my eyes jump from panel to panel until they reach the blinding lights above the green screen.

And then, a profoundly obvious realization: Kara's out of the picture. She doesn't control the show today. For the first time, I'm not invisible, but essential.

"What are we going to do now?" Shane says, hunched over the cart. He looks like he's going to hurl.

"We could call it off," Moyo suggests.

"Are you kidding?" Shane snaps. "You might have your stellar college portfolio, Moyo, but for some of us, winning Make-A-Splash would make a huge difference on our applications."

"Okay, fine. We could ask one of the theater girls who, like . . . lived?" Moyo offers nervously. "I saw Priyanka and Alyssa around the dorms Saturday night. I bet they're fine."

"And catch them up to speed? Yeah, right. We might as well just livestream Kara from her bed, vomiting into a bucket. I'm sure her fans would love that."

"That's literally sick, Shane," Moyo says.

"I was joking, dude!"

As they argue, I'm turning my idea over in my head. Inspecting it from every angle. Because it's the only way I could still meet Howie Mendelsohn.

"I'll do it," I blurt out.

Moyo twists his head toward me.

"Absolutely not," he says. He latches his eyes onto mine and doesn't let go, like he's pulling me back from the edge of a cliff.

I look for Shane to back me up, but he's already escaped to the control room. His swishy hair peeks out behind a line of computer screens.

Moyo opens his mouth to say something but stops himself. The muscle in his jaw flares through his flushed cheek, and I'm convinced he's about to call this whole thing off. Instead, he puts on a reluctant smile and says, *"I'll do it."*

I stare dumbfounded at Moyo. Surprised and unsurprised. If you asked me to close my eyes and picture my best friend, sum him up in one expression, I'd see that tight-lipped smile he's wearing right now. It's the face he makes every time he gives in and lets Shane copy his homework at lunch. It's the way he says yes when yet another person asks him to design a T-shirt for their school club. It's the warmth on the other end of the line when he calls me on Father's Day and asks how I'm feeling, and instead of opening up—instead of acknowledging that he's calling because he cares, because that day, like Abba's birthday and so many others, is another reminder of my loss—I simply reply, "I'm fine."

Moyo smiles because he's doing me an unspoken favor.

I recognize the sympathy behind that smile, and it kills me.

"No," I insist.

"But Opal—"

"I'm the one who wanted to enter this contest in the first place," I say firmly, though my head feels woozy. "I'm the one who creeped on millions of private user accounts and discovered that everyone is lying about Hailey Carter. I know exactly what buttons to push. In fact, this could be a good thing—Kara was never going to get behind another rich girl stealing attention away from her anyway. She would have wanted all the sympathy for herself. She would have managed to make it all about her."

"But what if they make it about *you*?" Moyo asks.

"Excuse me?"

Moyo clamps his mouth shut. His gaze tiptoes around me like I'm a thin sheet of ice that could crack at any second. "All I'm saying is you'd be putting yourself out there, and there's no guarantee it would work."

"Putting myself out there with whom, exactly?" I demand. He doesn't answer. "Ah. Howie Mendelsohn."

Moyo looks at me like I've committed an unspeakable crime.

For as long as we've been friends, Moyo and I have never talked about my complicated past. But I know without the slightest bit of doubt that he's filled in the gaps—from his buddies on the soccer team, from whispers in Hell, from the internet. Right now, we don't have time to skirt around the obvious. Right now I want to wring the fear out of Moyo like water twisted from a wet towel.

Shane pokes his head up from behind one of the screens in the control room. When we make eye contact, he ducks like a whack-a-mole. I turn back to Moyo. He's gnawing the inside of his cheek now.

"Shane told me everything," Moyo blurts, staring at the floor. "The theories. The files. The trip. That stupid comment. I know it was a long time ago, but I don't want you getting hurt like that again."

I'm not so much pissed at Shane, who's cowering behind a

computer screen, or Moyo, who recognizes that our perfect, uncomplicated friendship has gone crashing out the window, as I am shaken by the reminder of that comment. The one from the video the paparazzi drones had recorded when I was ten. I kept it to myself for a long time, until the summer before eighth grade, that summer when every little thing reminded me of my father—the smell of burnt toast, literally any passerby with an accent. That's when I shifted my detective work from Howie Mendelsohn to Tahoe, our mecca of memories. That's when I decided to run away. The morning of my bus ride, I met up with Shane in the cold movie theater in his basement to finalize how he would cover for me. As we were hugging goodbye, I confessed to him that I was worried. Not about the trip, but about that single comment that had stuck with me.

Poor girl. I hope she doesn't let this ruin the rest of her life.

There were other comments that tossed around detailed theories of suicide or foul play, ones that praised my dad's brilliance or questioned his sanity—but those weren't the ones that lingered. It was the one about my future. How it would forever be cloaked in the shadow of my past.

"You know," I say now, "when I first heard about Make-A-Splash, I half considered getting on WAVE myself. *Hello, world. I'm Opal Hopper, but I used to be Opal Tal, and that's precisely why I'm entering this contest. My dad was Aaron Tal, the professor who worked with Howie Mendelsohn until one of them disappeared and the other became a bajillionaire, so needless to say, I'd like to have a word with Mr. Mendelsohn. If you wouldn't mind helping a girl out, just watch my channel and give me views so I can win this damn thing.* Would have saved a lot of time, don't you think?" My voice is shaking. I'm ambling through unchartered territory, words I didn't dare say out loud these last three years, let alone around Moyo. "But I was afraid. I don't want to be afraid anymore."

Moyo looks at me with frightened eyes, because he knows.

Everyone knows.

Here's what I know: Seven years ago, my dad left his office on a chilly September evening and never returned. Howie Mendelsohn claimed to be home that night, reading some business book in the hammock in his backyard. But no one saw him there. What they did see were Howie Mendelsohn's regular late-night walks with my dad along the San Francisquito Creek—at least three people had seen them on different nights. Howie didn't answer any of my emails.

Five years ago, Howie Mendelsohn's company, Palo Alto Labs, launched WAVE. My first reaction was rage. My next reaction was to build. I built Campfire. And I never stopped coding after that.

Three years ago, I enrolled at PAAST. A few kids looked at me funny, mostly locals, since the school is funded by Palo Alto Labs, but most people figured, "She's a nerd." I legally changed my last name. I met Moyo. I started over.

And now, I'm risking it all. My privacy. This life I've created for myself, separate from my past. That's what Moyo is suggesting.

But maybe I never really left that part of me behind. Maybe I'm like Schrödinger's cat, existing simultaneously in a state of Opal Hopper and Opal Tal. Focused on school, but still wondering about my dad. Invincible, but still vulnerable. Ready to get on WAVE and talk about Hailey Carter, but scared as hell.

A flat screen above the control room keeps the time to a hundredth of a second, and it jumps to the next minute: 3:07.

Shane leaves his hideaway in the control room and approaches me in small steps, and I swear, if he's going to try and apologize about telling Moyo something I would have expected him to tell—

"You look nice today, Opal."

Those five words plunge my cheeks into a warm, glowing bath of blush.

Maybe I'm just delirious, but a sense of duty stirs inside me, spreading from my feet all the way into my chest. I need to step up. A sacrifice on this level is the only way the rest of my sacrifices will pay off.

"We have twenty minutes," I say. "Let's move."

Twenty minutes quickly blur into twenty seconds, and before I know it I'm standing in front of the green screen. I scrutinize the cramped Media Room. Thick, tangled wires snake along the ceilings and walls, and the same electric current running through those wires somehow finds its way into me. I feel alive, but programmed. I clench the notes I furiously scribbled, knowing I have to toss them aside now. I've got every line, every cue memorized. The time has come to run the code, but my system overheats. The harmonies of the other machines begin to taunt me: the spotlight hanging overhead, the cameras peppered throughout, their buttons flickering—

Moyo puts up three fingers.

"Three . . ."

I scan my surroundings one last time. Behind me, a wall painted green. Directly in front, three flat-screen monitors that will show my audience.

"Two . . ."

There's nothing special about the space where I'm standing. Moyo's design coupled with Shane's setup will make it special.

"One . . ."

Moyo balls up his hands and clamps them together, like an imaginary clapper board.

He mouths: "Action."

Episode 005

OPAL

Hello, world.

I'm completely frozen from head to toe. My body is stuck. But like an old faucet that hasn't been turned in years, I yank myself into motion and look closely at the screens mounted on the wall in front of me. And there they are.

Four hundred people. Live. Every single one of them is staring at me with their perfectly rendered avatar eyes gleaming like crystal orbs. It's one thing to watch the show from the control room, aware that there's an audience but primarily focused on audio mixing and digital effects. It's another thing to be front and center. I swallow the walnut-sized lump in my throat as I inspect the sea of avatars. They're looking at me with confused, almost angry expressions, like I've already deceived them.

OPAL

I'm sorry to announce that Kara Lee is out sick today.

It takes a second for them to register, but soon, they begin zapping out like flies. *Zap, zap, zap!* The studio echoes with the sound of popped bubble wrap until I'm left with only ten audience members.

I hiccup, and another avatar zaps out.

Out of the corner of my eye, I see Moyo waving his hand. He's motioning for me to move left. I must be dangerously close to bumping into a curtain or stumbling off this tiny black stage that's supposedly beneath my feet.

Kara would always open with a monologue on this stage before jumping into her immersive XPs. I look up at the screens. Moyo really designed the studio to perfection, all the way down to the gum underneath the seats. He also designed the studio to shrink and expand based on how many people are in the XP, and right now, it's like a small black box. Three rows of four seats each—and only nine of those twelve seats are filled. We've never had an audience this small.

OPAL

Well, that was fast. Those of you who stuck around are in for a treat, because we're really going "behind the scenes" today. But first, I have a question for you. Do you think you're an honest person?

One of the avatars in the front row jerks his head back, his eyebrows raised so high I think they might float off his face. I take a closer look and . . . shit. It's Peter Isaacson. I bet now he thinks our meeting was all a ruse, that I poisoned the sushi at Kara's party just to steal her thunder. Wonderful.

> **OPAL**
>
> Are you honest in real life? Like, when you tell your best friend you like her boyfriend, but he's actually kind of annoying, and you laugh at his jokes, but there's seriously *nothing* funny about them?

More heads twist and turn from the audience.

> **OPAL**
>
> It's the same thing on the internet. It's the same social pressure. Because let's be real, you're not really "lol"-ing at those debauch-erous XPs.

A subtle jab at the Andover bros. They're a group of lacrosse players from one of those private boarding schools in New England. Somehow DeBrochery, their WAVE channel filled with misogyny, homophobia, racism, and fart jokes, has them in the lead to win Make-A-Splash.

> **OPAL**
>
> Everybody lies. Especially online.

I look directly at the hollow glass ball of the camera over the middle screen.

OPAL

Let me show you.

It's time for the immersive segment. The nine remaining avatars shrink smaller and smaller before me as the studio grows vaster, wider, emptier. Desperately, I make eye contact with Moyo and Shane over in the control room. I almost wish Moyo had been serious when he offered to draw up a few avatars in their underwear and plant them in the seats.

But then, I notice Moyo ball up his right hand and burst his fingers in Shane's direction. He mouths: "LiveTags."

Of course. How could I forget about LiveTags? I'm over here drowning under the weight of this pathetically small audience when there's a lifeboat right above my head. Kara never liked the idea of floating blocks of text—she said they felt like clutter, and she had disabled the feature on her own WAVE. She was certain we'd lose her core fans if we messed with her clean-cut brand. But like them or not, LiveTags are personalized to users who might be interested in your content; in other words, they attract new viewers.

#THETRUTHABOUTHAILEY
#MAKEASPLASH

#LIARLIARLIAR

#GIRLGONEVIRAL

(I thought the last one was kind of cheesy—more Lifetime special than LiveTag. But Shane said it would be algorithmically effective. Must be the "girl" part. That word's been a crowd pleaser for decades.)

Adrenaline shoots through my body as new avatars appear and the studio expands. There's a pair of redheaded twins in the third row, their expressions wide-eyed and fresh like a limitless summer day. Behind them, a goth middle-aged gamer type, and next to her a man whose hair stands up like a pine tree. It looks like his face is being tugged by some invisible force, and I wonder if this man is lying upside-down against his bed in real life. Altogether, about forty new people have joined.

OPAL

Welcome to our newest audience members. Now, check this out.

I nod at Shane to make sure he has everyone's opt-in for biometrics. *Do you give this XP permission to observe your facial expressions?* Most people tap yes without even thinking about it. Shane nods, and then motions to Moyo, who flips the switch.

The audience's eyes roll back, like they've been possessed. It's the default stance for when an avatar is immersed in an XP *within* an XP. And that's what we've done here—we've thrown them into Hailey Carter's breakdown all over again.

Maybe it's the whites of their dead eyes staring back at me, but I begin to sense their visceral discomfort before Hailey has even snapped. And then she does. I know exactly when it happens because one of the twins jumps in his seat, and his brother squirms. The rest of the audience turns squeamish in some way or another, and I shoot my attention over to the biometrics that Shane has projected on the far monitor. I smile, knowing that things are going as planned.

Then they're back.

Some of the avatars literally have to shake off the discomfort they felt at the end, when it's just them and Hailey at that restaurant table, and she's murmuring, *Get me out of this world*. They try to look unfazed. A few of them even brush it off with half-hearted chuckles. Eye rolls.

OPAL

> Yeah, you're right, she's a *total* laughingstock.
> That's the impression you would get from Zapp,
> Livvit, all the forums and holo pages.

I lift a finger and point at a girl in the front row. Her fiery hair cuts across her shoulders in a short, straight bob, and her eyes bug out as if in a constant state of shock.

OPAL

> Right, Stacey?

She keeps her focus locked on me. Her back perfectly straight. Lips pursed coolly. She doesn't respond, just waits intently for my next move.

> OPAL
>
> What were your initial thoughts?
>
> STACEY
>
> I think Hailey Carter is absolutely nuts. It's a shame we keep giving her attention when she keeps screwing up like this.
>
> OPAL
>
> And Timmy?

Stacey's cheeks burn bright red, almost inhumanly so. From her avatar, you'd think she was in her twenties. Elegant, Audrey Hepburn–esque. But her profile says she's actually fourteen. That's three years younger than me.

> STACEY
>
> Timmy is a pure and precious cinnamon roll.
>
> OPAL
>
> You didn't once stop and wonder if maybe he did something wrong? Maybe he was unfair to Hailey in their relationship.
>
> STACEY
>
> Timmy shouldn't have been dating her in the first place!

Stacey bites her lip.

STACEY

Timmy is a *perfect peach* who must be protected at all costs. Every word that comes out of his mouth brightens my day. He's a gem.

OPAL

You've now referred to Timmy as a dessert, a fruit . . . and a rock.

STACEY

You're the rock!

For a second, I think Stacey has recognized me, but I quickly remember she's just being sassy and defensive. She's a Timmy fan. It's in their blood.

Thank God I'm not wearing haptic gloves, or else the audience could zoom into my clammy hands. I clap them together and prepare mentally for the big reveal—for the moment I'll prove once and for all that Hailey Carter's suffering matters.

OPAL

So you don't feel sorry for Hailey Carter?

STACEY

Not one bit.

Her eyes narrow, demanding that I get to the point.

                              OPAL

          That's a lie.

My breath tightens as Stacey stares me down even harder with
sharp eyes that aren't used to being corrected. I wave my arm in
the air, and Shane, as planned, pulls up Stacey's biometrics on a
hovering screen behind me.

                              OPAL

     At first, yes, you didn't give a crap about Hailey
     Carter. About ninety-five percent of your atten-
     tion was on Timmy during the first half of the XP.
     You're understandably obsessed. But right when Hai-
     ley snaps, something inside you snapped too. You
     flinched. Your eyebrows arched ever so briefly in a
     manner typically associated with sympathy. You'll
     see here—follow the dotted line—that your attention
     quickly went back to Timmy. And when Hailey lifts
     the steak and threatens him with it, you physi-
     cally gasped. But at that point—see this chart over
     here?—at that point, your eyes flickered back and
     forth, back and forth. Confusion. Concern.

Stacey's eyes rocket like she's swallowed a hairball, but it
doesn't faze me. I'm on a roll. I have data on my side. Data makes
me confident.

And here's where it gets interesting. Each time
    Hailey says "get out," you make this face at
    Timmy. Like "Come on, Timmy. Leave." And then
    when he finally does, you're still holding
    your breath.

The entire audience leans in, their own expressions a whirl-pool of wonder and horror.

OPAL

And finally, you're alone with Hailey. Your heart
    is racing. And your face exhibits every single
    predictor of crying short of tears. You wanted
    to. But you didn't let yourself.

Silence. I let Stacey process the fact that none of this was illegal, that she let me into her head, essentially. I let her process the cold, hard facts.

STACEY

That was—I—

Zap. Stacey has abruptly left the XP.

I glance across the Media Room at Moyo and Shane, their smiles glowing behind computer screens.

> **OPAL**
>
> I apologize if I caught Stacey off-guard. If
> I made her feel exposed, like a zoo animal,
> just now. But you know what? Welcome to Hailey
> Carter's world.

Just before she bailed, Stacey's avatar's face turned the same cherry shade as her lipstick. It reminded me of my freshman bio teacher, Dr. Difulgo, after Jacqueline Sharif called her out on mixing up the Krebs cycle with the Calvin cycle. PAAST students are notoriously ruthless when it comes to correcting teachers.

> **OPAL**
>
> Who else in this room thinks Hailey Carter de-
> serves better?

Slowly, a couple of avatar hands go up. Then more. Until every hand in the room is raised.

> **OPAL**
>
> We're better than the comment sections make us
> appear. Most of us are decent humans. The prob-
> lem is, that's not the kind of narrative that
> lends itself to scandalous headlines. It's not
> what the internet trolls want. Sympathy doesn't
> make for entertainment: the memes and spoofs
> and simulations that attract millions on WAVE.

I check the screen and wait—for people's heart rates to calm down, for their eyes to soften, for the biometrics to level out for my grand finale. I stand a little taller and smile, because for the first time all afternoon, I'm commanding my own stage.

OPAL

But it's worth talking about here.

Chapter

Six

As I'm wrapping up the XP, I notice one viewer leave his seat early. Just one. A twerpy kid who looks like a puberty-stricken version of Stuart Little. His avatar fades to nothingness like a dying star in the sky, and my heart all but dies with it.

Because that's when reality settles in. Fifty viewers. Even if I made a splash in their eyes, it's nowhere near what we need to win the contest.

Moyo rushes over and grabs me by the shoulders. Usually, his warm touch brings a smile to my face instantly, but not today.

"Aaaand we're back to reality!" Moyo booms.

I muster up a smile that probably resembles a two-year-old's attempt at drawing a straight line.

"Yeah. Reality. What a treat." I roll my eyes and zip across the Media Room, pick up my backpack, and leave. Moyo and Shane are protesting behind me, but I ignore them.

My vision blurs as I walk quickly through Hell, descending the stairs into the Sphinx. School let out over an hour ago, but the place is still buzzing with students who stuck around for Chess Club, Aviation Club, track, rowing, swimming, water polo, SMEER (Student Movement to Elicit Empathy in Robots), whatever looks good on a college application. And of course, Cyber Club—which I'd been a loyal member of for three years. I pass my old teammates Cy Draper and Timothy Hackney, who are leaning coolly against the space-gray façade of the main building, duffle bags at their feet.

"The regatta's on the same day as Cyber nationals."

"You can't do both, bro?"

"One's in LA and the other's in SF. Even with Hyperloop . . ."

Before I can eavesdrop further, I feel a tap on my shoulder. It's Jez Marshall, eager as ever, eclipsing my view of Cy and Tim. He's got these buggy eyes that latch onto anything in their path, and his head seems to be in a perpetual state of bobble.

"Greetings, young grass*hopper!*" Jez's breath smells like cheese pretzels dunked in ramen noodles. I turn my face away. "I was thinking of you today. Are you still doing that WAVE channel with Kara?"

"Yeah," I say.

"Must have been a heck of an XP today. *Behind the scenes with norovirus, this year's hottest plague!*"

"Yeah," I say, distracted by the conversation behind him. It sounds like Tim Hackney is going to skip out on Cyber nationals.

"No offense, but I never understood why WAVE wanted more creators in the first place. Who wants to sit and watch a glorified talk show," Jez says, his face plastered with a pervy grin, "when there are so many epic games you could XP instead."

"Don't want to hear it, Marshall," I say, walking away.

"The other day, I spent, like, fourteen hours in this—"

"Shut up, Marshall."

"I'm just trying to be helpful!"

People like Jez are never trying to be helpful. They're always asserting their superior ideas, their superior intellect, the superior way they spend their time. But that's not why I'm livid. If anything, I feel bad for Jez, who's known around school for his addiction to Half Month, the most popular game on WAVE. What I can't believe is that Cyber Club picked Tim Hackney, jock extraordinaire, for nationals. And now he's not even going to show up! It's the first time I regret quitting Cyber Club this year. I thought if I had more time . . .

God. All that work for just fifty viewers?

Back in my dorm room, I ask M4rc to project the stats for our entry and some of our competitors' entries up on my wall.

I scroll.

And I scroll.

And I scroll.

It's unhealthy how much time I've spent these last few weeks obsessing over this contest, watching clips from the Andover bros and strangers across the country, analyzing every detail of every experience they've created. I can't stop myself. Even now that we've aired the last episode, my natural compulsion is to compare. Ogle. The Andover bros are leading, with nearly 450,000 views for one of their earliest XPs, in which they dressed in drag and screamed nonsense at each other. It wasn't even interactive; you're just standing among them, watching them act like insensitive buffoons.

I know the other Make-A-Splash entries like the back of my hand. There's the dating game XP. The XP where you race against pink chinchillas. The one that placed body cams on identical twins who trade places and play tricks on their friends.

The critical voice in my head comes out in full force.

We didn't have any special effects, it says.

We weren't silly enough, it prods.

The interactive portion was weak.

It was too serious.

Too cookie-cutter.

Too boring.

Too invasive.

That voice sinks deeper and deeper, twisting through my throat, my belly, my heart, until it's corrupted every fiber of my being.

A part of me hopes replays will save us, and to an extent they do. I sit at the edge of my bed and watch obsessively as our view count creeps up, little by little, until it tapers off at three hundred. Three-oh-one. Three-oh-two. I'm staring at my wall for hours; every now and then I practice one of those breathing exercises my mom tried teaching me back when things got really bad. Three seconds in, three seconds out. Straight back. Arms dangling, brushing the fabric of my new sheets . . .

I dig my bare fingernails into the comforter. I half expect my bed to bleed cotton.

At this rate, we're not getting anywhere close to 450K. I hang my head for a sober moment, wondering what went wrong. My one chance to break free from Kara Lee's mind-numbing programming, and we probably would have been better off with those peeks into her closet and theater rehearsal after all. Kara, with her Hollywood aura and hordes of friends. Kara, whose father kept promising to fire off a tweet about our WAVE channel through his company account with millions of followers.

Kara, who has a father.

Three seconds in, three seconds out. I catch my reflection judging me harshly from the corner of my Picasso Mirror—annoyingly rosy cheeks, Jolly Rancher lips, muddy brown curls to top it all off—and I glare back at this girl as if she's committed some vague act of betrayal against herself. I shift my glance and notice the school track outside my window, glimmering orange and pink under the sunset. It's been months since I've gone running. This would have been my fourth year on the cross-country team, but I thought my time would be better spent focused on the contest.

I'm tired, yet somehow I leap out of bed and change into my old uniform. Before I know it, my feet are pounding against the spongy gravel. I don't know how many laps I run; all I know is it's a lot more effective than those stupid breathing exercises. I'd forgotten how much I needed running for my mental health. For the first time in weeks, I'm relaxed. I feel sweat against my pores instead of goggles. My eyes aren't glued to a screen. My mind slows down and my heart beats strong and my fingers slice through the air.

I have no desire to deal with people in the dining hall, so I pick up a Soylent from the dorm vending machine. I chug it in two gulps, wincing as the sour goop slides down my throat. You'd think after all these years in business, Soylent would have come up with a tastier meal replacement. Nope.

When I get back to my room, I tell myself I'm going to shower first before checking any of my gadgets or stats, but of course that doesn't happen. I swipe my phone off my desk—and I see it's exploded.

"Holy shit," I whisper under my breath.

I've never seen so many notifications in my life. I extend the screen so it becomes the size of a tablet, but even as I scroll, new notifications keep cascading down and I can't get them to stay still.

The view count appears on my wall: 862. It's barely tripled. All those notifications are for individual views and engagements—WAVE's way of making creators feel special when they're not getting any real traction. A couple of them are for comments, mostly Luddite trolls decrying the death of privacy. There seem to be more and more of them on WAVE these days, which is ironic, because the whole point of the Luddite Party is that they're opposed to technology.

I take off my sweaty clothes and march into the shower to get ready for bed. I have so much sleep to catch up on. That's how sleep works at PAAST—you deprive yourself of it for days before disappearing on a roller coaster of REM cycles.

But instead of shutting my eyes when I sink into my sheets, I instinctively reach for my WAVE headset.

The day has come. Are you ready, Victoria? It is
    time . . . Drumroll, please . . . For the four
    hundredth edition of "Carpool Karaoke"!

VICTORIA BECKHAM

God, you're getting old, James.

CORDEN

Four hundred times I've made a fool of myself.
    And I've lost half my accent in the process.
    Can you even tell I'm British anymore?

BECKHAM

You're a "Wannabe" Brit at best these days.

A familiar beat blasts in my ears as James Corden and his co-host
flail their arms in the air and sing along to the music. They're going
back and forth, asking each other what they want, what they really,
really want. His co-host is dressed in all black, with super slick hair
and intense cat eyes. I feel like I recognize her from somewhere.

CORDEN

Now, I know I'm getting old, but Victoria, you
    are looking younger than ever. Absolutely stun-
    ning. What's your secret?

BECKHAM

Oh, the usual suspects. Exercise. Skincare.

CORDEN

All the little things that "Spice Up Your Life."

BECKHAM

I see what you did there, and I must say, you're incredibly cheesy.

CORDEN

Why thank you, Victoria. In fact—

Suddenly the car jolts to an abrupt stop. It nearly gives me a heart attack, until I remember I'm not actually in the back seat of James Corden's car, but lying down in my own bed.

CORDEN

Ohhhh boy. Did you feel that? The speed bump back there? Fun fact, it's one of the last remaining speed bumps in LA. Self-driving cars don't need that [bleep]!

I rip off my goggles. Screw it. I don't want to zigazig ha with James Corden anyway. Tonight, I'm dozing off on my own terms—not with the lullabies of another talk show host. I can jump-start my own dreams.

****

Someone is calling me at three in the morning. At first, I think the ringing noise is in my dream—that there's something wrong with the Jeep as it's rolling down the Tahoe trail. Or that my dad is calling from the campsite. But when I open my eyes, I'm blinded by the glare of the emerald telephone icon on the wall in front of my bed. M4rc asks if I want to answer. Although he's been given explicit instructions not to disturb me while I'm sleeping, there are a few exceptions.

"Moyo?"

"You won't believe what happened."

Moyo shares a screen with me. It's our WAVE stats, and one number in particular pops out.

"Shit."

I cut off the feed and pull up the stats on my own screen.

"Holy . . . Moyo. What the—I can't believe it. MO-YO!"

We had hit 450K all right. And then some.

452,603.

"The craziest part is that I wasn't even checking," Moyo says. "One of my friends in Lagos texted me the LudUnderground post. He's always sending me stuff like that, since they can't believe the Luds are a thing here—"

"What does any of this have to do with the Luds?"

"Don't freak out," he says quickly. "Believe me, I was worried at first too. But it's less about you and more of a flame war about privacy and the future—their usual crap. We just happen to benefit indirectly, since we sparked it."

"Moyo, what are you talking about?"

"One second. Shane is dialing in."

The green phone icon on the wall splits and multiplies like cells during mitosis.

I sit up against my headboard and clench a handful of my sheets. Shane's presence suddenly makes this all the more real.

"Shane, did you hear—"

"Yes. I wrote a conditional statement in the code that notifies me if we get more than one hundred simultaneous views. It went berserk a few hours ago. I've been following the redirects, and while it originated on LudUnderground, we're getting viewers from all over—"

"Guys," I interrupt, "what's going *on*?"

Shane and Moyo talk back and forth, explaining how one of our early commenters was a prominent mod on LudUnderground. He posted about our episode with the headline "WAVE IS WATCHING YOU." The site is basically a watered-down version of a nineties internet forum, entirely text-based. A harkening back to the good old days before websites started tracking cookies, let alone facial expressions on virtual reality.

"It turned into your usual Lud debate about the downfall of privacy in the internet age and all that crap," Shane says. He sends us one of those holos with a Lud holding a PETA sign in one hand and a burger in another. "Hypocrites. Anyway, the best part is our XP got shared, and people watched MOM I'M BUSY CAN'T YOU SEE THIS IS IMPORTANT?"

The sound of a door creaking open signals that Mrs. Franklin has entered our phone call. She's given herself free rein to interrupt all of Shane's online activities. Each time Shane tries blocking her with a hack, Mrs. Franklin just summons Mr. Franklin, a prominent coder-turned-founder-turned-philanthropist, to undo it. "One sec," Shane says, and he mutes his end of the line.

We've heard the dialogue for this movie so many times we

can picture it: Shane twisting his neck to yell at his mom's faceless icon on the wall. Mrs. Franklin demanding to know why Shane is awake at three in the morning. Shane chewing out his mom for setting alerts or whatever she did to figure out he was still awake. Her going, "I just—" and Shane throwing his Rubik's Cube at the wall. One time he chucked it so hard it cracked the school-issued PolyWall. The new one must have cost a fortune, but the Franklins have no trouble affording expensive things.

When Shane unmutes his line, there's a husky groan followed by a long, drawn-out sigh. Then another door-closing sound.

"Like I was saying. Luds and techies started sharing our XP, and it turned into this perfect storm of viewers that made us go—"

"Viral," I whisper.

"Precisely," Shane says. He shares another screen with hour-by-hour stats. "#LEAVEHAILEYALONE is the number one trending LiveTag on WAVE."

There's a long pause on the line.

"What do you think, Moyo?" I ask.

He clicks his tongue. "I think this is what drugs feel like."

"I swear, if you're going to lecture us—"

"And I *like* it," Moyo finishes proudly. "Seriously. Who would have thought going viral would feel so thrilling? Instead of heroin, we're injecting ourselves with views and comments. We're overdosing!"

My back melts into my headboard as Moyo laughs, and I smile, because I can actually picture Moyo delighting in his newfound badassery. Maybe it's my brain this late at night, but I have the clearest memory of his eyes. The way the dark edges crinkle when he laughs like this. I remember it from last year, when we snuck off campus—there's something about rule-breaking Moyo that imprints itself in my mind.

"The real drug is the data we hacked to get here," Shane says, interrupting the cozy silence between us.

My smile fades. "Are you saying . . ."

"No, no. No one suspects anything. I'm just saying, we should be careful now that we have all this attention," Shane says. "Keep it under wraps."

"Let's hope it *all* stays under wraps," Moyo adds.

The shiver down my spine reminds me of what I'd forgotten so quickly—why I entered this contest in the first place, what I risked by going on WAVE. My avatar profile may be set to private, but let's be real—it's all out in the open. My intentions. I didn't want to be afraid again, yet here I am, my body tightening at the thought that someone could leave a comment like that again.

I hope she doesn't let this ruin the rest of her life.

Not tonight. Tonight, I'm not thinking about anonymous strangers and their unsolicited opinions about my life. Tonight, we celebrate.

"Four hundred and fifty-four thousand views," I read off the screen. I was waiting for the figure to tick up to the next thousandth place.

"Fiffffffffttttttyyyyyyy-five!" Moyo exclaims very slowly as the view count creeps higher. "Unless someone swoops in with a million views, we've won."

"Gentlemen, I'll see you at lunch tomorrow," I say before hanging up.

Notifications flood my front wall in some M4rc-determined order of priority. It's times like this when I'm convinced he's not just my secretary or my DJ but my conscience, because one text in particular floats to the top:

> Hi, darling, I was twirling through WAVE before bed and noticed your little show about Hailey Carter. I didn't watch, I promise. I know you don't like it when I pry. But just be careful putting yourself out there. Privacy is hard to get back.
> XO,
> Mom

It turns out Shane isn't the only one with a nosy parent. The difference is, my mother might lurk, but she knows better than to push me too hard, or else I might run off to Tahoe again.

And of course she was "twirling" before bed. It must be part of her new evening routine: five minutes of meditation, ten minutes of reading, a face mask, and a quick *twirl*. Just the way she says it reminds me how my mom has always been betrothed to routines and plans. That's why her and Abba's relationship crumbled the year before he disappeared, because he sold his soul to his lab at Stanford and then revealed next to nothing when he quit.

None of that was part of the plan when they got married. Not the fights. Not the secrets. Certainly not the way he disappeared.

I feel like I should respond. Before I can make a decision, though, another text appears beneath her last one. Why is she up at this ungodly hour?

> Opal, I just woke up and saw that your XP has gone viral. I'm reading through these comments and people are talking about . . . a contest? I know you don't usually respond to me, but I'd really appreciate an answer right—

So much for avoiding the comments tonight.

An animated windshield wiper slides across the text, indicating that she's hit Delete. Mom isn't exactly tech savvy—it's one of so many ways she was different from Abba and me—and she hasn't turned off Text Preview, the feature that shows the other person what you're typing as you type.

> I just don't see what a million dollars—
> A meeting with Howie Mendelsohn? Honey, let's not go down that road again—
> When will you—
> Why won't you—
> Sweetie, please don't—
> Opal, please, enough is enough. Stop wasting your time trying to understand a man with more issues than we knew, who never had time for us—

I stare, transfixed, as the half sentences appear and disappear. It's like I'm hearing her old lectures all over again. Back then it was about grief and resilience, taking control of my life, focusing on the positive aspects. She stopped in middle school when she finally realized her lectures were pushing me further from her, because the more she refused to entertain my hunt for answers, the more I'd chase after them.

Finally, she types slowly:

> Congratulations, honey. I love you.
> Just please, be careful. I don't want to see you getting hurt.

Those words cut over the old wounds. I'm already hurt, Mom. I was hurt when you forced me to take painting lessons and modern dance classes, attend therapy, participate in anything that might steer me away from math and science—make me less like my father. If you wanted to help me heal, you could have listened instead of lectured. You could have asked me why I believed Abba was still out there, instead of scolding me for "rejecting reality." You could have covered up your bitter resentment of Abba instead of letting it bleed underneath the surface of every birthday, every memory, every mention of his name.

If my hurting had actually mattered to you, Mom, you'd have attempted to understand it instead of trying to make it go away.

I'll never forget the ways my mother tried to control my pain back then. But I'll also never forget how I hurt her too. It took three days for the police to find me in Tahoe and drive me back to Palo Alto. I remember the way my mom's lips quivered when she opened the front door, like the last petal hanging from a rose, and in that moment, I knew she couldn't live with losing another person she loved.

Ever since Tahoe, she's given me space.

I'm not going to reply. It's better for both of us.

I abandon my upright position against the headboard, crumpling my spine and slipping completely under the folds of my sheets. With one hand on my stomach, rising and falling as I breathe in hot air, I ask M4rc to project Campfire on my walls. Green light pours in through the covers. I close my eyes and listen to the wilderness, the rumbling of the Jeep along dirt roads, the rustling of tree branches.

Tonight, when the Jeep rolls past Aaron Tal, I don't see a cluster of images I stitched together in three-dimension, but for the first time in years, I see real flesh. I see the thin frame of a man who's still out there. A man who got overwhelmed, overworked, had all the life in him sucked out by this town, and ran off—but who misses his daughter deeply, and would be proud of what she's accomplished tonight.

Aaron Tal worked his entire life on code just like mine, on worlds just like WAVE. Now, his daughter is making her own splash.

Chapter

Seven

The tapping sound is coming from outside.

At first, I tell myself it's the tree branch that sometimes scratches at my window. But the taps are too clipped. Too evenly spread out.

Too persistent.

I rise up in my bed, clutching a pillow near my racing heart. "M4rc, raise the blinds," I say, the words quivering with caution.

What time is it? I peer around my room but can't see a thing. As the blinds rise like stage curtains, early morning sunlight washes over the dark space. I see blades through the thick glass windowpane, four of them, spinning in a fast horizontal blur.

Then I catch sight of the body, and I know.

It's a delivery drone. I've never seen anything like this before—a drone so close to the dorm building, let alone tapping on my bedroom window. They're supposed to drop off at the PAAST Post Center. Maybe this one is just lost, but a thrill in my belly urges me to let it in, this real-life Hedwig. The drone's body is about the size of a shoebox, beautiful titanium with a curved guard for protection. It levitates along an invisible axis, tapping the window at three-second intervals.

I ask M4rc to open the window.

The drone flies into my room. Its path is straight and precise— more refined than the drones used by USPS and other delivery services. The shoebox body splits open to spit out a single package. I wait for the drone to whiz out of the room before I go to pick it up. The package is heavier than I was expecting. Its rectangular container is made of tin, and the morning sunlight reflects off its magnificent shade of navy blue. I unlatch the lid, which is marked only with the letters *P.A.L.V.*

Inside the box, beneath a flat strip of cardboard, I find a pair of goggles unlike anything on the market. I graze my fingers along the smooth edges, careful not to smudge the lenses. These goggles feel less metallic, more plastic than my WAVE. And they're fully transparent, like scuba goggles.

Invisigoggles. I recognize them from Livvit, where an anonymous Livviter recently posted a holo of the not-yet-released headset. If they really do work, then I wouldn't need Shane's three-screen set-up anymore. I could simultaneously exist within the studio while moving around freely in front of the green screen.

There's a note inside:

Opal,

Followed your overnight success. Brilliant. Truly brilliant. Thought you could use these. You're an entrepreneur now.

Neil

I have so many questions. Who is Neil? How did he get ahold of Invisigoggles? And the one that worries me the most: how did he know where to find me?

****

As I enter the Sphinx, most of my big concerns—mysterious packages, anonymous commenters—vanish when I notice my classmates are staring at me. A new fear creeps in, that Kara Lee is going to appear out of nowhere, full of rage and jealousy. I breathe a sigh of relief when I remember she's still out sick with norovirus.

Hell feels warmer than usual today. I float down to my locker, clinging to the Invisigoggles box with both hands, thinking about the last line of that note.

You're an entrepreneur now.

Entrepreneurship in Silicon Valley is like static electricity: rub up against enough Zuckerberg wannabes and you're bound to catch the spark. That's what happened to my dad. Sparked and burned. It's how Kara evolved from just another awkward theater kid in middle school to queen bee at PAAST; as her dad's net worth grew, so did her social status. It's how Moyo and I got close. We met in freshman calculus—the only girl and the only black kid in a nine-person class—and became fast friends. One day while we were working on a problem set in class, Moyo looked around the room of white and Asian boys, sighed, and turned to me. "You know it's on us to flip the script," he said. That's when we promised ourselves that someday, we would build an empire together.

Are we on the cusp of that empire?

"Let me in," I mutter at my locker. The door swings open and I carefully place the Invisigogs on the top shelf, nesting them between an old track sweatshirt and my emergency Red Bull stash. I grab a can and stuff it in my pocket. I stare inside my locker, blink a few times as the exhaustion washes over me, and grab another.

Maybe I deserve to feel like an entrepreneur. But for now, I just want to meet one.

Win the contest. Meet Howie Mendelsohn.

****

"I don't get it," Moyo says. "Why would this Neil guy single you out?"

I already regret telling Moyo and Shane about the mystery package. All through first period, I went back and forth about what it might mean while Dr. Difulgo lectured on cancer DNA mutations, and I decided it was nothing to worry about. But Moyo doesn't think the diagnosis looks so good.

"You think he's some creepy fan?" I ask.

"I think he knows exactly where you live," Moyo says, pacing the narrow control room. The Media Lab director lets us hang out here whenever we want, since Moyo designed his wedding invitations free of charge last year. "He might even know about the hack. I mean, 'truly brilliant'? There's something creepy about that line."

"Don't be ridiculous," I say. "He could be on the school board. Or some weird freshman. I wouldn't worry about it; you know how strict they are with deliveries here. Remember the pizza incident?"

Shane once tried to have gourmet pizza delivered for his birthday lunch, but the school blocked the delivery drone because it was unauthorized. We ended up feasting on Moyo's double chocolate chip cookies.

"Who cares," Shane says absently. "God, even when you're calling them out on their shit, the trolls still piss all over the comment section. Not that they're saying anything about you, Opal. I mean, they're not *not* talking about you, but—"

I shuffle behind Shane, whose eyes are glued to the flat screen in the back of the room. Carousels of stats spin around in a steady, three-dimensional flow. Shane flicks a finger along the trackpad, sending the objects spinning faster, and then swipes more slowly to pull up the timeline of comments.

> 0:43: Lol I just told my best friend his girlfriend's hot
> 0:44: But she's disgusting
> 0:46: Guess this chick's right i'm a liar

0:46: Did you really lol when u wrote lol

0:47: Lol

0:47: I wish this chick was my gf

0:48: ikr?

0:48: She looks like a young Natalie Portman.

0:48: Trembling

0:48: Trembling

0:50: Even her boobs are trembling. B or C cup??

0:50: Natalie who?

0:51: Anyone have a tape-measure from WAVEmart?

0:53: C

"Ew," I say, grimacing. I pull up the neckline of my shirt. "They were barely showing."

Though some twisted part of me is relieved those perverts were drooling over my breasts and not my backstory.

Moyo nudges Shane, and he blazes through the next five minutes of comments. The words blur until he slows his fingers and swipes up.

5:45: WTF WAS THAT

5:46: is this xp tracking our facial expressions

5:46: shit

5:47: trembling

5:47: trembling

5:47: u idiots u gave it permission

5:48: Technology is meant to function for human-
kind, not against it. We live in a society where our
personal freedoms are eroding like sand beneath
our feet as we allow this evil to spread into every
facet of our daily lives. Act now! Rid yourself of
this cancer before it is too late!
5:51: Gtfo lud you've been posting that on literally
every xp
5:51: friggin lud
5:51: Who's this Stacey chick?
5:51: Stacey vs the host, who's hotter?

I brush Shane's hand off the trackpad and close the carousel window. "Shane, these comments are gross."

If we learned anything from Hailey Carter, it's that the comment section isn't representative of an overall audience. It's always the trolls and lonely virgins who leave disgusting messages, who zoom into girls' breasts, pulling out their measuring tapes purchased off WAVEmart to . . . Anyway. I know how the game is played. Comment sections are less playground, more kiddy pool of pee, and maybe deep down, that's why I never check them anymore.

"There's always at least one hypocrite Lud trolling around the comment section," Shane spits, as if the Luddite Party and his family have been sworn enemies for centuries. They might as well be. Shane comes from a long line of MIT grads, and he's expected to follow in their footsteps.

"What if this Neil guy is a Lud?" Moyo asks. "What if a bunch of them got talking on one of their forums and planned to send you those Invisigogs?"

"And what? They're going to explode when I put them on?"

Moyo stares at me, wide-eyed.

"You can't be serious, Moyo. You think those tech-illiterate dimwits got ahold of a pair of self-exploding Invisigogs *overnight*, figured out who I was and where I live, and wasted it on *me*? Instead of Howie Mendelsohn or Kara's dad or one of the dozens of other techies who are actually creating the future they're trying to destroy?"

My friends' glances drop to the ground when I utter Howie Mendelsohn's name, and I realize we're all asking ourselves the same question: now what? Shane's fingers twist around an imaginary Rubik's Cube. It's abundantly clear that when the contest ends at midnight, we'll win. But that's when things get complicated. Shane wins bragging rights for his college apps, Moyo wins money that can go toward his future business, I win my meeting with Howie Mendelsohn—but what about Kara?

I remind Moyo and Shane that Kara joined our team for attention. We're not entertainers; we're nerds. The XP was just a means to an end. So I propose we make a point of giving the show back to Kara Lee before she gets nasty.

Shane shakes his head. "No, no, no."

"Why not?"

"Come on, Opal. We're onto something here." His ears turn red, a surefire sign that Shane Franklin is excited. "We can literally see inside people's minds. Understand how they feel. When does that ever happen?"

"Not often . . . because it's illegal."

"Oh, *now* you care about the law."

Moyo chuckles, and he crosses his arms. He watches this rare argument between Shane and me.

"What about the seven hundred thousand people who watched?" Shane says. "And counting. Are we just going to leave them hanging? They don't want *Kara Lee: Behind the Scenes*. They want *Behind the Scenes with Opal Hopper*."

"Um . . ." I bob my head back and forth. "Technically we never changed the show title. It's still *Kara Lee: Behind the Scenes*."

"Kara." Shane snorts. "Look at this." He pulls up one final chart on the computer screen. "Have you looked at your stats?"

"Didn't you just say we had seven—"

"No, I mean *your* stats."

My eyes graze over the rank chart, and they fixate on the word at the very top.

LIKABILITY

"Having access to our viewers' deepest feelings means we know how they felt about you," Shane says. I hold my breath, prepared for the next missile strike of internet troll hate. "For reference, Kara's replay XPs put her at sixty percent likability. But you? Eighty-five percent."

If eyes could turn inward to examine our deepest thoughts,

that's where mine would have gone, when in reality, they went blank as I wondered . . .

Likable? I've seen myself painted in plenty of strokes throughout my lifetime. Coder. Daughter. Good with numbers. Bad with people. Even worse with boys, except for Moyo and Shane. Night owl. Despiser of mornings. Red Bull addict. But *likable* has never been one of those strokes. It was never a quality I strove for—at least, that's what I tell myself. Nobody at Stanford liked my father very much, and yet Aaron Tal still managed to get ahead. With numbers. But these numbers from WAVE tell a different story, and for a second, my face lights up with a thousand watts of validation.

"If Opal doesn't want to do it," Moyo says, "we can't make her."

He rests a strong, sensible hand on my shoulder, and my heart rate slows down.

I smile graciously. "Thanks, Moyo. We can talk more tomorrow, after we've officially won the contest."

That dopamine rush of fame, of being "liked"—I remind myself it's artificial. My problem has never been a lack of attention from hordes of strangers, but rather, one stranger in particular. Besides, I know firsthand I can't handle the spotlight. It's only a matter of time before people get nasty again. I can't risk it.

Chapter

Eight

We've officially lost.

It's midnight, and I've refreshed the Make-A-Splash home page no fewer than five times. There they are, the Andover bros, their meaty arms spread wide, whooping and celebrating like fools, in a three-second holo. I'm convinced my eyes are tricking me. It's supposed to be us, our names, our avatars; we should have won by a landslide.

Instead of calling Moyo or Shane, I pull up the rules page. Surely it has to be a mistake. Maybe WAVE is announcing the winners backward . . . starting with second place? I scroll through the legal jargon until my eyes land on one line: "The prize money will go to the team with the highest total number of views."

Total. Mathematically, that means the sum of all parts. Realistically, that means the Andover bros knew exactly what they were doing by posting every day. We weren't the ones gaming the system. They were.

I see on my wall that my friends are calling me, but I don't answer. I go back and do the math myself, adding up the views for every damn XP they posted over the last thirty days. I check on our latest numbers.

We lost by 511 views.

While my fingers shake over my keyboard, M4rc alerts me that the Andover bros are going live on WAVE. I pick up my headset in a daze and enter the XP. The flashing red view count is in the tens of thousands, but I'm alone in a vast black space lined with curtains that shine like the night sky. No, like shooting stars dripping straight into the ground. From behind one of those curtains, a twiggy brunette in a fiery red pantsuit appears with four boys.

"... On behalf of all of us at WAVE and Palo Alto Labs, we'd like to congratulate you gentlemen right here in our imagination center."

"Whoop whoop!"

"Aaaandover's legiooons—"

"Now, a million dollars is quite a lot of money for people your age."

The Andover bros look at each other and smirk like the rich bastards they are. That money means nothing to them. It's their weekly allowance.

"But I wanted to focus on the truly extraordinary reward, your upcoming meeting with Howie Mendelsohn. As you know, Mr. Mendelsohn lives a very private life within the walls of Palo Alto Labs. Part of the reason he agreed to this contest is because he sees young people such as yourselves as the future."

"Haiiilll to the Royal Bluuuuue."

"What are you most looking forward to asking Mr. Mendelsohn?"

The boys look at each other again, shrugging. One of them pipes up.

"Where's he hiding the chocolate factory?"

They burst into laughter that punches so hard, so aggressively, that I mute my microphone, convinced I'm going to scream . . . but instead, I talk to myself.

These are the model citizens you've agreed to meet with, Howie? A group of hooligans? You're telling me that you have time for *them* when you can't be bothered to answer the emails I've been sending you since I was a little girl?

The Andover bros and the PAL spokeswoman, Monica, continue making chitchat as if I'm not there. Even if they can't hear what I'm saying, I know WAVE can. It's always listening. Always watching. And you know what? I'm happy to be recorded, because then, at least, there's a chance my rage will reach Howie Mendelsohn.

I mean, really, Howie. According to Abba—back before he stopped talking—you courted him for nearly three years. What did you need him for so badly? Why did you need one hundred percent of his time and energy?

None of this is fair.

I learned a long time ago that I couldn't count on fairness. Not me, not Hailey Carter. Fairness is a rubber band, and the longer you stretch it—the more you rely on its elasticity—the more it stings when it snaps. I've learned that instead of wrapping my life with rubber bands, I'd have to use twine. Rigid, sturdy twine.

A moment of weakness. That's what this last month has been. I let myself get caught up in my old ways, my fight for fairness.

Monica announces that the XP is coming to an end, but I stay in this dark and empty room. Standing under the shooting stars, this downpour of imagination. I'm done imagining. I'm done trying to come up with theories and answers when the man on the other side of this wonderland is my missing variable. My chest tightens under the weight of all the questions I've been trying to ask for years, and so I rip them out, one by one. I'm not leaving until WAVE kicks me out. I want Howie to hear me, even though I know he won't.

What was Aaron Tal like during those last few months?

What did you talk about during those late-night walks?

Did he ever say anything about wanting to harm himself?

Did *you* harm him, Howie?

Did you disappoint him?

Did I?

****

The next morning, I wake up feeling so numb I can hardly get out of bed. Moyo and Shane find me in the Sphinx and complain over each other about WAVE, how the rules should have been clearer, and how Palo Alto Labs is sketchy to begin with. I brush it all off. I spend the day not in mourning for the loss but instead bemoaning my own stupidity.

In first period, I clumsily work on carving notches into my wooden clock. Mrs. Fischer, our shop teacher who just transferred to PAAST this year, notices my mediocre job and hawkishly comes up to my station.

"You call that a clock?" She's not one to mince words. People say Mrs. Fischer got fired from her last school in Nevada for cursing out the principal. We may have geniuses with PhDs teaching us math and science, but convincing someone to teach woodworking at PAAST is like convincing an imam to move to Las Vegas.

"Sorry," I say, dropping the X-Acto knife to the steel welding table. "I didn't get much sleep last night."

Mrs. Fischer moves to the side of the table and inspects my eyes. They were pretty bloodshot to begin with—from the exhaustion, from the tears—but they sting even more as she stares me down intensely. Her breath is foul.

She shakes her head. "Too much time on WAVE. That's the problem with your generation. You need to spend more time on things that are *real*." She points a thick finger at my Frisbee-sized analog clock. "And less time in that damn pixel world."

As Mrs. Fischer walks away, some of the other kids at my station roll their eyes. Everyone knows she's a Lud. The shop teachers at PAAST are always notoriously anti-technology, coming from places like Alabama and Ohio—ground zero for the movement. None of them ever lasts more than a year here.

The rest of the day, people are more forgiving. Two freshmen in my Future of Morality class come up and tell me they admire my balls, and in Bots and Big Data, Amit Reddy randomly turns around in the middle of Dr. Ezersky's robotic arm demo and says, "You're going to be a big deal someday." Thankfully all of Kara's friends are still out sick with norovirus, so I don't have to field any attacks on her behalf.

As I'm leaving History of Social Media at the end of the day, Dr. Travers calls my name and asks me to stay behind.

"I was rooting for you, Ms. Mind Reader," he says. Dr. Travers's eyes twinkle behind his old-school spectacles, and for a moment, he reminds me of Abba.

"Thanks," I whisper. I bite my lip. "We still lost, though."

"You can't get caught up in numbers, Opal."

"But don't you say that on social media—"

"People fall prey to patterns, yes. We are driven by numbers and comparisons, but often, it's to our detriment. There's always going to be someone more successful than you, someone more liked than you, with more views than you."

"The Andover boys had the *most* views."

Dr. Travers smiles meekly. "Technically, Hailey Carter received many more views."

"She didn't want those views," I say.

His smile fades.

"If you take away one lesson from my class, let it be this. Humans are experts in sharing. It started with cave paintings and evolved into books, tweets, virtual reality—who knows what's next. But the pieces of ourselves that we share are just that. Pieces." Dr. Travers walks me to the door, his gentle hand resting on my shoulder. "We're complicated beings who hardly understand our own selves, and that's precisely why we put those experiences out into the world. To find our place in it."

Outside the classroom, Moyo's waiting for me against the wall of lockers, his hands deep in the pockets of a smooth crimson fleece.

He looks at me with that tight-lipped smile.

"I'm fine, Moyo."

He bites his lower lip. He doesn't believe me.

"I've dealt with worse," I remind him. He shrugs, and we walk quietly together through Hell, which has cleared out after the last period. The ceiling tiles glimmer with shards of light poking in from the rooftop greenhouse.

"I know how much you wanted this," he blurts as we walk out the doors of the Sphinx. "How much winning the contest meant to you."

"Yeah, sure," I say, forcing a smile.

"And I want you to know you're incredible," Moyo says. "With or without Howie Mendelsohn. With or without any man."

"Moyo." I blush, and a real smile wiggles its way into my lips.

"I'm serious." He steps to the side and holds an arm out to let me enter the residence hall first. "I've never been more impressed with you than when you got on WAVE like that. I was wrong. You knew exactly what you were doing."

I jab him lightly in the rib as I pass through the door. "Well, let's hope Stanford finds it just as impressive."

****

Just like that, my focus takes a ninety-degree turn. October picks up where September left off, and the chilly air of college admissions season descends upon Palo Alto. With November 1st just a month away, every senior kicks into high gear. We empty the floors of the Sphinx and rush to our dorm rooms to fine-tune every last line of that Ivy League early decision application. God knows the rest of our lives depend on it.

I've dreamed of going to Stanford since I was a little girl. Of course it's not that simple anymore, with my mom's constant presence on campus as dean of freshmen and my dad's infamous legacy. But I still remember the happy times, when the three of us would stroll through campus together on Saturday mornings. I remember relishing the precision of my mom's step, or the way Abba's emerald eyes glimmered as they grazed over the sprawling lawns of this university that claims its own zip code. Nothing can stain those memories. Stanford means to me what marriage and children mean to some people my age: a lofty dream that, while not quite in my control, I refuse to imagine my future without.

It's better that we lost Make-A-Splash, I convince myself. I haven't so much as looked at my Stanford application since I became obsessed with winning this contest. Right now, getting into college is the most important thing—and my essay's not going to write itself.

Describe a problem you've solved or a problem you'd like to solve.

Five hundred words? I only need three.

This stupid essay.

I imagine the admissions officer opening my file, expecting to find a juicy, dramatic personal statement from Opal Hopper, Palo Alto martyr. A searing account of how I've moved on from my dad's death. Just to find those three words. The fantasy alone cheers me up a little.

But then I get to work. I'm up all of Thursday night, writing and deleting sentences. Early Friday morning, I bitterly trot over to the computer lab before class, hoping maybe a change of scenery will fix my writer's block. As I'm crossing the wet lawn, I stomp into a dark puddle and splash water all over my fox-print leggings. Nope. There goes my optimism.

The computer lab is unsurprisingly empty. Since we all have laptops, headsets, and PolyWalls, hardly anyone uses the lab except to discreetly copy homework between classes. There's one other student here—a freshman or sophomore boy who probably hates his roommate—and we work in silence.

Until my phone chirps loudly and startles us both. I'm reaching into my pocket to silence it when I read the alert.

My name has shown up in a weekly *Scalleyrag* roundup.

> Another week, another invasion of privacy. Because if it wasn't enough to creep on our emails, texts, location, shopping habits, and porn preferences— the tech gods have decided our bodies are next.
>
> By now you've surely heard about the young WAVE host who used facial data to "out" the Hailey Carter sympathizers among us. She enraged Timmy fans! She enraged Luds! She forced us to examine how we lie, in real life and online.
>
> But this young host hasn't been completely

honest herself. We were intrigued why such a truth seeker would set her own WAVE profile to private. So we did a little snooping and learned that our anonymous host isn't just another teen with an avatar; she's **Opal Hopper**, a senior at the Palo Alto Academy of Science and Technology.

And get this: Hopper has a secret past life. You might remember her as Opal Tal, daughter of Stanford professor Aaron Tal, who disappeared under strange circumstances seven years ago and set Silicon Valley ablaze with rumors and gossip. At the time, he was working on a stealth-mode start-up with none other than Howie Mendelsohn. Hopper—according to legal records, she changed her name three years ago—was entering **Make-A-Splash**, a contest where the winners would receive one million dollars . . . and a meeting with Howie Mendelsohn himself. I wouldn't call that a coincidence, would you?

No word on Aaron Tal's whereabouts, though according to my older colleagues, most of the rumors at the time of his disappearance involved either suicide or running away. At Stanford, Tal was known for being exceptionally brilliant, but hot-tempered and unfriendly. Few were surprised that he took off in some form or another. Though many felt sympathy for his wife and daughter.

A sad story indeed, which is why we can't help but wonder about Hopper's intentions about getting on WAVE. Whatever they are, at the very least, we hope this Princess of Palo Alto is satisfied with her fifteen minutes of fame.

If the computer lab walls weren't made of liquid crystal, I'd be slamming my balled-up fist through every single one of them by now. I spring out of my seat and pace the area around my workstation, my hair a mess of cotton candy curls that I'm twirling tight to keep from throwing something.

The Princess of Palo Alto is pissed.

The other student in the lab eyes me nervously, so I turn around and face the wall. I cross my arms and dig my elbows into the crystal ridges, press my forehead against the cold glass, squeeze my eyes shut, but it's no use. The hyena in my heart won't stop howling. I leave the computer lab.

The lawn between the main building and the residence hall feels wetter this time around, but maybe I'm just stomping my feet harder—the puddles splishing and splashing and going "screw you" beneath my feet.

I settle in my room. Roll off my wet leggings.

So close, I whisper to myself. I'd come so close to moving past this episode of my life, this reboot nobody had asked for. But there's no doubting it anymore: I'm back. Not just with Howie Mendelsohn, but with the whole freaking rumor mill.

Imagine finding out your perfect dad was actually a monster. The police tell you they can't go looking for a grown man who doesn't wish to be found, so you take matters into your own hands, and slowly, the truth comes out. Not the truth you were looking for, but one that had been hidden from you your whole life. You dive into his online professor ratings for the first time and discover a different version of your dad—angry, temperamental, known to throw chalk at his students. You start to see why he never talked about teaching. You email his former students and colleagues, and your blood broils even more when they reply with bullshit kindness—like the grad student who offered to take you out for ice cream and never did, or the young professor you discover your dad had fired. "Your father was a good man, Opal," he replied to my email. "He always spoke his mind." Maybe I should have been more suspicious, but the guy had left academia to teach yoga in Brooklyn.

It's hard, gathering facts about a missing person. It's even harder when people just tell you what they think you need to hear, shining a rose-tinted light on the past—when in reality, you just want the truth.

At the same time, you create your own truth. Your own narratives. You get suspicious of the one man who won't talk to you, because maybe his truth is so hard to swallow he can't even bear to sugarcoat it.

My hands are shaking. I remind myself that I've been through all these emotions before, every single one of them, and I made it out alive. Still, what kind of insensitive "journalist" would write something so blatantly mean-spirited? And to follow it up with that stupid princess comment . . .

"What the actual fuck," I snap. "What the actual—"

Actually, I have an idea.

"M4rc, who wrote this post?"

"Matthew Seamus, editorial assistant at *Scalleyrag*."

"And where is *Scalleyrag*'s office located?"

"Thirteen fifty-five Market Street, fifth floor. San Francisco."

I hurricane toward my wardrobe, flinging it open and ignoring the automatic outfit suggestions. Instead, I reach for the bottom-most drawer, one that I have to manually open and that contains just one outfit.

My Undetectable.

At the beginning of each school year, a sort of frenzy occurs when students check into the residence hall. We surrender our bags and suitcases onto a conveyer belt, and a large, shining machine swallows them up, like at airport security. Except this machine doesn't X-ray for liquids or explosives. Instead, it unzips every bag and suitcase and embeds into every article of clothing a tiny Bluetooth chip, no bigger than a single staple. These chips chirp a low-frequency signal that is unique to each student.

The school maintains it's not for tracking or discipline but to "enhance the student experience." It's the reason we don't have room keys—our doors swing open for us when we're outside. It's why the screens around campus are constantly changing, customized for each student or cluster of students around it. Rowers get the latest regatta schedule. Cyber Club members get code. Drama kids get jazz hands.

Even if we were being tracked . . . Most students at PAAST are goody-two-shoes types; they would never risk their spot at this institution. The administration has an honor system for bringing in new clothes, and it seems to work just fine, with most students willingly giving over their new clothes for chipping.

Moyo, Shane, and I are not most students.

I reach inside the bottom drawer for a black jacket and army green khakis, slipping them on in two sweeping motions. They feel lighter, freer than my other clothes. Last year, my friends and I decided on a whim that we wanted to drink alcohol for the first time in the historic Hewlett-Packard Garage. Shane's family owns the building, and he was sure that his parents hadn't set up any monitoring there. It's a relic of Silicon Valley's roots, where the tech industry was born. They wouldn't dare ruin the historic space with surveillance cameras. And even if they did, Shane gets a special kick out of disobeying his parents.

So over Thanksgiving break, we visited a local thrift shop in downtown Palo Alto. We bought an outfit each, stuffed them into our backpacks, and brought them back to school. It was as simple as that. The following Monday we snuck off campus and drank cheap lemon-flavored vodka with warm Coke, dozing off on the dusty couches.

I've kept my clothes in this drawer in case I might need them again someday.

Today.

I splash a handful of warm water across my face and tie my hair into a tight ponytail. My cheeks burn as I rush off campus. Within ten minutes, I reach my house in Palo Alto, an exquisitely designed stack of wooden boxes that looks like the aftermath of a game of Tetris. Our sleek black Tesla is parked in the driveway, just as I'd expected, even though Mom would have left for work by now. She always preferred walking.

I press my thumb to the car door lock, get inside, and tell it to drive.

"Destination?"

"San Francisco," I reply. "*Scalleyrag* office." Staring back at me through the reflective windshield are my stormy green eyes, my dad's eyes, brimming with rage that I haven't seen in years.

****

The Model Z trails three other Teslas up 101. When we reach the exit for San Francisco, we veer off together like a flock of birds dipping in perfect synchronization. My car breaks from the pack on Market Street and drops me off in front of a large building. I tear through the tall doors, my shoulders grazing the golden edges as they swing open. A passerby gives me a look. You're supposed to pause to let the self-activating sensors register your presence. Not me. Not today. Today, I'm doggedly determined. Today, I'm a human bulldozer.

I fly past the empty security desk and take the elevator straight to the fifth floor.

"I'd like to see Matthew Seamus," I say to the receptionist. I surprise myself with how calmly I'm able to speak while I catch my breath.

The receptionist, of course, is not human but an artificially in-telligent dummy. Literally. They've planted a computer and speakers inside a pale, thin, blond mannequin whose face moves like she just got Botox injections. I find the entire experience pretty creepy and annoying. Most corporate offices make do with reception screens, but San Francisco always finds new ways to out-weird itself.

"Do you have an appointment?"

"Did Mr. Seamus have an appointment to write that bullshit post about me?"

So much for calm.

"I'm sorry to hear you're angry. My name is Amy."

"Sure it is."

"Do you work in public relations?"

"Excuse me?" My face sours. "Do I look like I work in PR?"

Amy does not respond.

Of course. She's pattern-matching. Every other young woman who visits *Scalleyrag* works in PR, so Amy has to assume . . .

"I was the *subject* of an *article* that *Matthew Seamus* posted this morning," I say, making sure to speak very clearly and emphasize hard facts, "and I would like to speak with him. Please tell Mr. Sea-mus that I am here."

"May I ask—"

"Oh, for the love of God!"

"You know, she's useless if you don't have an appointment."

I turn around. Somehow I had missed the one other actual

human in the *Scalleyrag* lobby. She's wearing a tight white skirt and cream blazer with metallic stilettos, the neutral tones blending in with the room's overwhelming hospital aesthetic.

"The first time I came here, Amy just goes, 'Excuse me, are you on the wrong floor?' Like she'd never seen a black woman at *Scalleyrag*. Pattern-matching, right?"

I shrug shyly and laugh, unsure of what to say. I like this woman. For some reason, I feel like I know her from somewhere.

"In Amy's defense, I *was* on the wrong floor. I was supposed to meet with a VC up on nine. This was back before I was making *Scalleyrag* headlines myself."

Suddenly, I recognize her.

"You're Nikki Walker!"

Nikki Walker snaps up from the sofa and approaches in three precise, parkour-like strides. She sticks out her hand. Her expression radiates the confidence of a woman who's hit numerous "Most Influential" lists, who became the first black female tech billionaire, and who is known for her vicious business tactics. It's a good thing they don't run public opinion polls on entrepreneurs, because Nikki's numbers would get her impeached.

I'm not surprised to see her friendly side, though. A while ago I watched an interview she did with Jimmy Fallon. It was the only time Nikki Walker seemed to let her guard down, although the commenters wouldn't let you believe that. "Totally scripted," one wrote. "I didn't realize you could rehearse personality," another snarked.

"Pleasure to meet you," Nikki says. She clasps my hand, and with two decisive shakes, I feel better already, like I can fight the world.

"My friends and I use Zapp all the time," I blurt. "The new video roulette feature, totally genius, it's like—"

"I've heard it all."

Nikki's face deflates at the mention of Zapp, as if it's the last thing she wants to hear about right now.

"What's a young woman like you doing at *Scalleyrag*?" she asks. "Nobody ever shows up at this place under . . . ideal circumstances."

"It's a long story," I say.

"Give me the elevator pitch."

"Um, okay. My friends and I made an XP where we used the new tracking feature, and it pissed off some Luds and went viral. *Scalleyrag* wrote—"

"You're Opal Hopper."

"Yeah," I say flatly.

I let my eyes meet hers, expecting a nasty edge of executive realness, but instead, Nikki Walker emanates compassion. Just for a moment. She quickly purses her lips and asks, "What business do you have here then?"

I look at her as if the answer is obvious. Nikki throws the knowing look back at me, and I flinch, my clammy fingers fumbling at my sides.

"I mean, I assume you read the article."

"Yes. And?"

Nikki gives me a hard stare.

"Opal." It's Amy. Her prosthetic head swivels ninety degrees, catching us in the corner of the lobby. "Matthew Seamus is ready to see you."

"How did . . ."

"You said his name. She probably gave him a view of the lobby."

I swallow what feels like a fat lump in my throat.

"Do I go?"

Nikki Walker cocks her chin in the direction of the newsroom. She's thinking. Her gaze levitates between Amy and the stark whiteness of the lobby ceiling.

"Look," she says, her direct tone at odds with her ambling stare. "You have two options at this point. Leave, and this reporter knows you showed up. Chances are he'll slam you with another ruthless hit piece."

"And option two?"

"Meet with him, say hello, and figure it out from there." She leans in closer and whispers into my ear, "Whatever you do, be strong. Women like us have no other choice."

I bite my bottom lip and nod. I turn to face Amy, fastening my eyes on the receptionist's long neck. As I approach the pearly desk, I breathe steadily, my hands balling up clumps of jacket from the inside pockets.

Suddenly, a short man appears next to Amy. He has a curly tousle of ginger hair and a wide, freckled face. A soft blue floor light saturates his ironed slacks and tucked-in dress shirt, and his wire-frame glasses glimmer with specks of color. The man adjusts his glasses and clears his throat.

"How lovely to meet you in person, Ms. Hopper."

Chapter

Nine

Matthew Seamus moves fast. We've hardly said hello when he blazes through the entryway behind the reception desk, his mahogany loafers slapping the polished concrete with each step. I follow him, struggling to keep pace.

"That was quite the conversation you had with Ms. Walker back there."

I freeze. I feel exposed, like he's just ripped the clothes off my body. He was listening? Before I can say anything, I realize that I've lost Matthew Seamus. I find myself standing alone in a long hallway beside a transparent cube with a frizzy-haired woman inside beating its thick walls with a bludgeon. I would be more worried if the lady wasn't laughing manically and recording the experience with a drone.

Before I can search my surroundings, I feel a tap on my shoulder.

"We have cameras in the lobby," Matthew explains, preempting my inevitable *what the fuck* reaction, "and whenever one of us has a visitor, we're shown a live stream. They installed them after our editor, Sam, wrote about a group of urban hackers from Los Angeles and they drove up here armed with . . . God knows what. Anyway, Sam handily dealt with the hackers with *words*, what she knows best, thankfully. Tennis rackets, I think they were? Nothing dangerous, but it caused quite a ruckus. It's perfectly safe here, I assure you. Especially now with LobbyStream—we can just escape through the emergency stairs. But I promise you, we've had no incidents since the racket ruffians. Ha! Unless you're carrying some lethal tennis paraphernalia on you, Ms. Hopper?"

"Um, call me Opal, please."

"*Opal*. Of course."

The hallways are packed with neutral black and gray cubicles, though surprisingly devoid of people. We've turned at least three corners and are still walking at a brisk pace. I wonder where Matthew Seamus is taking me.

"How old are you, Matt?"

"Please, call me Matthew. And twenty-four. I graduated from Stanford last year. Linguistics and creative writing major. Editor of the *Daily* too."

We pass a brightly lit micro-kitchen, and without slowing down, Matthew sticks an arm out and swipes two green bottles off a counter. He hands one to me.

"Drink this. It'll drown your blood with electrolytes for days."

I open the bottle and take a sip. I have so many questions. What is a Stanford grad doing at *Scalleyrag*? Why does this drink pinch the inside of my cheeks like sharp little fingernails? Why was there a woman in the other hall bludgeoning the inside of a cube?

"Matthew, I, um—I came here because your article . . ."

"Pinnacle."

"What?"

"For legal purposes, we're required to call our stories *pinnacles*," he says. "Some kerfuffle over fake news. The powers that be decided it would be best to use a portmanteau for 'opinion' and 'article' to describe our particular style of reporting. Though I assure you, we are still the Valley's most respected news source."

"Uh, yeah, of course," I reply sheepishly.

What am I doing? I've never been the type to beat around the bushes. For all I know, Matthew Seamus could have been one of those pathetic message board freaks who posted theories about my dad's disappearance between Netflix binges and jerking off. They seemed like the kind of people who would grow up and work for *Scalleyrag*.

Something is throwing me off in here. It could be the obscene hospital lighting. My vision's getting blurry, like I'm walking through the gates of Heaven—if Heaven had digital screens and hallways that snaked in every direction.

I can't believe we're still walking.

"Honestly, Opal, I'm *curious*, what did *you* think of the pinnacle?"

I also can't believe this man is only twenty-four. There's a shrill quality to the way Matthew Seamus speaks. On one hand, it explains how he could be so oblivious to the cruel effects of his writing. On the other hand, he comes off more like an old man from a cartoon who's missing his pipe and monocle.

"I think you know how I feel about it."

"Do I?" he asks rhetorically.

"Umm . . ." My voice keeps choking. I want to tell Matthew Seamus how I really feel, that he's an asshole for bringing up my dad like that, but I can't. I can't draw any more attention to myself.

Or can I? Nikki Walker did urge me to be strong. It wouldn't be the first time in my life I was given that advice.

Balsa, my father used to call me. *"Do you know why I call you that?"*

"My friend at school says it means 'purse' in Spanish," I'd tease.

"That's 'bolsa,' my girl."

"That's how you say it!"

"Now you are making fun of my accent," Abba would tease back. *"You are strong and mighty, my beautiful daughter, like balsa wood. You are light as a feather, and people will underestimate you for that. But balsa is strong. Balsa always floats."*

"You called me a princess of Palo Alto," I snap at Matthew Seamus. "You brought attention to my past, knowing very well it would hurt me. You made assumptions about my intentions, spread old rumors, and in the end, you just figured, *Hey, she got her fifteen minutes of fame!* Does that make you feel good about yourself?" My heart is pounding. My stomach whirls. It's like that woman with the bludgeon is inside my chest, slamming every wall.

Why am I going off on this journalist? I should have known better, but that entire walk I was winding up my arm, preparing for the pitch . . .

"Just so we're clear," I lash out, my mouth dry. *Breathe, Opal. Breathe.* "I intend on getting a lot more than fifteen minutes."

Matthew Seamus pinches his lips. He raises his stubbly chin ever so slightly, and I wonder if I've actually chipped away at some essential part of this young journalist's ego. When he finally speaks, he lets out a high-pitched *harrumph* sound, as if someone had plopped down on a squeaky old chair.

"Well, perhaps we *will* see more of you, Opal Hopper."

I look around and notice we're back in the lobby.

"What was that?" I ask.

"That was a lap. I'm surprised you didn't figure it out yourself, considering your superb mind-reading skills," he says, grinning. "If I didn't know better, I'd think you've been inside our heads this whole time."

We lock eyes, and instead of wavering—instead of letting Matthew Seamus jerk me around like he's done this entire lap around the office—I hold my ground. I stand tall, feet planted like the roots of a tree.

Matthew Seamus breaks eye contact, and before I can react, he takes off through the entrance and turns the corner with the crazy cube lady.

What just happened?

And was it good . . . Or very, very bad?

FROM: nw@zapp.com
TO: opal.hopper@paast.edu
SUBJECT: [empty]
O,
Just had a thought. Matthew Seamus, he's

an editorial assistant. Bottom of the pecking
order at *Scalleyrag*. It means he's hungry for
a stepping-stone, anything that'll get him hits.
Take advantage of that.
NW

****

I don't fully process what just happened until I'm back in the Tesla,
resting my head against the edge of the open window.

Then it hits me, the impulsiveness of my morning. Just like
the day I burst out of the house and begged the paparazzi drones
to bring back my dad, I've let myself act on pure emotion. I didn't
for one second stop to think what my desired outcome might be.
And this time, there was no one to run out of the house and pull
me back.

The wind tickles and tousles my hair over the highway. I'm
tired. I take out my phone and notice Moyo and Shane have texted
me, but instead of responding, I decide to check my Zapp profile.
I'd sort of lied when I told Nikki Walker I was obsessed with the
holo-based social network. Until I started working with Kara, I
didn't even have a profile. I'm not much of a phone person, and
holos kind of suck when they're not in VR.

"Open Zapp," I mumble.

My phone rumbles, and I flinch. I flatten my hand and let the
extendable screens do their dance, stretching to maximum size.

There must be a mistake.

I have fifteen thousand followers on Zapp.

My hands quiver as I set the phone down on the dashboard. Matthew Seamus did this. When we went viral, my name did pop up in a couple of comments, but people were too busy arguing over the privacy issues to care. But now that it's out in the open, there's no telling what people might do. Like the Luds. Just last summer, thousands of them descended on a small town outside St. Louis to protest the latest robot farm that replaced an abandoned steel mill. I wouldn't put it past them to troll my Zapp account.

And the Timmy fans. God. They might as well be a political movement. They mobilized hardcore after Hailey Carter, bombarding her with digital tomatoes and nasty messages.

This is all Matthew Seamus's fault.

I grab my phone off the dashboard and tap a Zapp at random. The extendable screens curve into a bowl, and it's like I'm reading my tea leaves, ominous and foreboding.

I'm looking at myself. Specifically, my eyes. They duplicate on every screen until I'm holding a bowlful of peas. They split open and closed, and my car fills with a young boy's voice: *The truth is eye-opening.*

That wasn't so bad.

I go through more Zapps.

Sucks what happened to her dad.

She should have won that contest.

Pretty awesome how she stood up like this.

I'm ten years old. Everyone at school bullies me for my frizzy hair. But this week, one of the boys in my class stood up for me. He said he

*always wanted to but didn't think he could. Two other girls said the
same thing at recess. Thank you, @OpalHopper. Bullies suck and it can
be hard to stand up to them. But now I know I'm not alone, and there
are more good people than bad people in the world.*

A chorus of thank-yous.

My lungs fill with the gobsmacking thrill of the moment.
The car picks up speed—at least, it feels like we're moving faster—
and I lift my gaze up to peek at my reflection in the windshield.
I exhale, and very quickly, like a sled starting down a hill, I fly
into the possibility that all this attention could be a good thing.
A fresh start. A rebrand. I'm not a loser, not a victim, but a girl
with a voice.

I'm also drowning in private messages—most of them a
stream of emojis or images I don't care to open. But there's one
that's actually addressed to me.

Dear Opal,

Sorry if this is super random, but I grew up
near you in Mountain View and my dad was
friends with your dad at Stanford. My dad died
by suicide two years ago, right after I went off to
college, and I always assumed it was because
of his depression. But that post in *Scalleyrag* got
me thinking. Can you talk?

Amber Donahue

Huh. I didn't think my dad had any friends at Stanford. Part of me thinks this is a joke, but my fingers ignore the logical part of my body, quickly hit Reply, and type out four words: *Yes. Next week. Anytime.*

I navigate back to the main Zapp page and watch as the screens adjust over and over, moving like a spider that's fallen on its back. My phone spazzes, surfs, curves, and twists its tentacles with the energy of thousands of strangers who have joined together in my little corner of the universe.

Strangers who might even have answers.

I text back Moyo and Shane:

We need to air another episode. Next Monday.

****

After dropping off the Tesla, I weave through the tree-lined streets of my old neighborhood and arrive back on campus. I slip into the residence hall, change out of my Undetectables, and wait until the break between periods before entering the main building. People look at me differently in the Sphinx, but no one says anything. It's more crowded today. As I make my way toward Hell, Kara Lee appears.

"Kara! Glad you're feeling better," I say. I mean it.

Kara crosses her arms.

"I am, and I'm sure you're feeling great."

She glares at me. Passive-aggressive isn't a good look for Kara. It brings out her flaws. Her typically unblemished skin boils with redness, and when she scrunches her nose, I imagine a baby carrot in the middle of her face. One of the oddly shaped ones you leave at the bottom of the bag.

"It's overwhelming, that's for sure."

"Oh, I'm *sure*," Kara quips. "Anyway, I just wanted to say congratulations, and I appreciate you filling in for me at the last minute."

"Of course."

Kara flips her glossy black hair in a big, circular gesture. Most of it falls behind her shoulders, but a few strands get caught in the spikes of her leather jacket.

"And that I look forward to taking over next week—"

"Taking . . . over?"

"Well, of course. It was my show to begin with. It's not like we just wanted to win the contest, take the money, and forget about the millions of people who—"

"*Millions?*" I haven't looked at our stats since last night. But now that I think of it, the extra attention from *Scalleyrag* could have been just what we needed.

I'm trying to break free from the chains of Kara's jealous sweet-talk, but she's trailing behind me. She smiles, tight-lipped.

"I'd just like to make it abso-tively, *beyond* sure that I'm all set to take over . . ."

I pick up my pace.

"Let's talk later," I say. "I just need to—"

"Opal Hopper, you know I can pull in millions of—"

"Like I said, talk later!"

I take one last look at Kara and notice that the girl who is used to getting everything she's ever wanted, who never breaks a sweat, looks agitated. Vulnerable.

"I'll see you in Hell!" Kara yells from the edge of the Sphinx.

I know what she means, but the other interpretation makes me giddy with pleasure.

Maybe even power.

****

It turns out I'm not the only one who's giddy on this wild Friday, because after History of Social Media, Shane practically prances into my room.

"Uh, *déjà vu*," I say.

"Literally." He grins. "Opal. I did it again."

"Uh-huh. Okay, Britney."

Shane doesn't get the reference, but he swipes a finger over his tablet and splatters code all over my walls. Code that befuddles my sense of what's real and what's not. My head spins as I consider one of two possibilities: either my friend has cracked the secret to time travel and taken us back exactly seven days—in which case, I'd ask him to take me back seven years—or, somehow, Shane has hacked into WAVE again and stolen more data.

"Shane . . ." I gawk.

"It was right there!" He paces around my bed, where I'm sitting cross-legged and staring at him with my mouth open. "I'm serious, Opal. This is kind of weird. I think there's a bug at Palo

Alto Labs with the new tracking feature, because I just hit Refresh, and boom. The data appeared."

"What if it's a trap?" I ask. I grab a pillow from behind me and clutch it in my lap. More attention means more reason to be paranoid.

"Don't be such a Moyo," Shane groans.

It's not like Moyo is around to steer us in the right moral direction anyway. He's busy with his art school applications this weekend.

After Shane promises me that he's covered his tracks, I get to work sifting through this fresh batch of user data. I'm crunching numbers all through the weekend. I run a linear regression model while mixing cinnamon oatmeal for breakfast. I check the response variables while I'm in the girls' bathroom during Blast from the PAAST, the mandatory senior class mixer in the gymnasium each month, where they play music from previous decades. As far as school-sponsored events go, it's actually pretty fun, though I really wish it wasn't mandatory.

Kara pesters me again at the dance. She sidles alongside me during the "Electric Slide," as if we're boogie-woogie besties, and when I not-so-accidentally kick my foot into her heel, she just bites her tongue and smiles. After the song is over she asks what the plan is for Monday's episode, her voice all squeaky and nervous, and that's when it hits me: Kara Lee doesn't even know the login to her own WAVE channel.

"Finders keepers," I tell her.

Kara immediately drops the nice act. "Fine. Fine! I'm sure

you'll drive it right into the ground, Opal Hopper," she spits.

Late Sunday night, I pull up Shane's dashboard on my Poly-Wall. I scroll through the grid of audience members slowly, taking comfort in the fact that behind each avatar head shot is a living, breathing human being. A person who, for thirty precious minutes last week, appreciated my existence. A person like me, holed up in their room, looking to feel a little less lonely in the world.

Episode 006

> **OPAL**
>
> Hello, world.

Holy hell! These Invisigoggles work wonders. I actually feel like I'm inside the studio Moyo designed—as if I'm standing upon the brilliant black stage and before the twenty-nine thousand avatars in plush velvet seats.

I squint and cup a hand over my eyes, looking out at rows upon rows of avatars. It reminds me of the March on Washington. It reminds me of Carnegie Hall. It reminds me of commencement at Stanford.

And yet I'm still worried. All it would take is one person to heckle me, to scream "Opal Tal!" or some nonsense about my dad.

> **OPAL**
>
> Welcome to *Behind the Scenes*. Unless you've been living under a rock, you know the upcoming presidential election could be a turning point in American history. In just one month . . .

Out of the corner of my eye, I notice a moving figure. He's running down the aisle, his avatar covered in a black ski mask. My heart stops.

> **OPAL**
>
> Um, excuse me, sir . . .

The man sprints closer, leaping up on the stage, and even though I know he can't actually harm me, I scream. The audience gasps.

Holy shit.

I didn't feel it, but I felt it.

"B Cups! I told you, Zander!"

My body shakes, and I rip off the goggles. Moyo's and Shane's eyes are exploding. Stunned. *"Microphone?"* I mouth, tapping my ears. Shane toggles a switch.

"It's off."

"Did he just grope you?" Moyo screams.

The WAVE comments about my cup size were bad enough, but for someone to come out here and feel them?

I shut my eyes.

Calmly, I say, "Shane, create a fence around the stage. *Now.* And kick that user's ass out of the studio."

"I've already—"

"And his jackass friend Zander. I don't care if every man in that audience is named Zander, kick them all out."

"They're gone."

I can already see the trolls commenting on how I can't take a harmless joke. I can already see the viral holos. Those three seconds on loop. "You know what? Screw it. Anyone whose biometrics feed shows them laughing or in any way pleased with that stupid stunt, get rid of them too."

"Opal, if you don't want to—"

"I'm going back in."

OPAL

Sorry for that interruption.

A violent sound cracks through the studio like thunder, indicating that Shane has bulk-expelled a good chunk of people. The ones who remain sit painfully silent. Even with the loss, the view count is five thousand higher than it was before. I look at the avatars in the front row, and every shining eye is fixed on me.

As I bite my lip, hold my breath, dig my toes into the insoles of my shoes—I ask myself: *Why did I come back? Why am I constantly trying to be stronger than I am?*

My eyes sweep over the sea of witnesses awaiting my next move. One more episode. That's it. After this, I'm signing off WAVE for good. I let myself get carried away with the positive response on Friday, and look where that got me—sexually harassed within seconds. God knows what else might happen if I keep getting in front of all these strangers.

One more breath. That's all I need.

OPAL

As I was saying. The presidential election is a month away, and this year's race is heating up with the rise of the Luddite Party. They're the new kid on the block, the fever your doctor told you not to worry about. At first it was just old people barging into Best Buy and smashing the laptops. *Oh no!* you thought. *Grandma forgot to take her meds!* But then Congress bailed out Silicon Valley and left Middle America hanging. And those hissy fits turned into protests, and those protests became a revolution.

Now the Luds are legit. One of them, Gaby Swift, the daughter of a steel mill worker in rural Pennsylvania, is running for president. And she's expected to win twenty percent of the vote—more than any third-party candidate in American history. Turns out this fever is an all-out influenza, and our country is faced with a sickening choice: between the past and the future, between a backward society and an advanced one.

Let's take a look inside one of her campaign events.

In a flash, the avatars sitting before me all roll their eyes back, revealing nothing but white.

I've transported them to an all-American cookout. The idyllic yard is bursting with kids running around, spraying hose water at each other and tossing Frisbees. Smoke rises from the grill along the white picket fence, and beside it, Gaby Swift is chatting up the grill master. She's wearing an airy, bright-yellow pantsuit, and she slaps the back of his sweaty shirt while laughing at his joke. The man claws a charred hot dog off the grill and puts it in a bun for her. She smiles. Takes a bite. Smiles again.

The XP goes on like this. Virtual footage from one of the fifty cookouts she held this summer—one in every state. Gaby Swift may be old-school, but she's smart; she would never let her campaign post an XP on WAVE. It's widely rumored that she hired the "mole" who showed up at this particular cookout in South Carolina, armed with a 360-degree camera that somehow nobody noticed.

After a few minutes, I pull the audience out. Understandably, thousands of them left while immersed inside this Luddite propaganda. Of the thirty thousand or so remaining, I choose Zach.

                           OPAL

Thoughts, Zach?

                           ZACH

You couldn't pay me to spend another second inside that experience.

                           OPAL

You're not a Gaby Swift fan.

                           ZACH

Not in the slightest.

                           OPAL

And yet you connected with her message of nostalgia.

I hear gasps throughout the audience.

                           ZACH

Wh—what? No way. Didn't you hear what I said?

OPAL

I heard what you said, but I was also paying attention to how you reacted. Your biometric scan shows that every time you let your stare linger—

ZACH

I'm on WAVE, for Christ's sake! I work in tech!

Whatever LiveTags Shane and Moyo are shooting out seem to be working, because I notice out of the side of my eye that the red view count ticker is skyrocketing. Fifty, fifty-five thousand live viewers.

OPAL

You're saying you don't have *any* qualms about the future of technology? About the rapid development of robot farms, drones, artificial intelligence . . . even virtual reality?

ZACH

I mean, it's not without it's problems.

OPAL

Those are the problems Gaby Swift is talking about.

ZACH

Yeah?

OPAL

So maybe your biometrics are telling a different

story. One you don't want to admit. But one you
connect with.

Just like when Stacey cowered in her seat last week, Zach sits
there stunned. I'm honestly impressed he hasn't popped out of the
XP like she did.

An ominous wind of fear ripples through the audience. Avatars begin to chatter among themselves, but most of them seem
to be deep in thought. Looking inward. Asking themselves: *Am I a
Lud?* Some of them look left and right, and I wonder if I've made
them paranoid about their neighbors. Skeptical of every person
who's brushed off Gaby Swift as a joke, a nut job. Every friend
who assured themselves, "She'll never get elected" or "Her America isn't the progressive America I see every day."

What if her America is sinking in, and we just don't see it?

What if we're lying to ourselves?

Chapter

Ten

Moyo and Shane rush up to me right after the broadcast, still reeling about the man who violated me on stage. I say I don't want to talk about it. *Later.* Later never happens, because things take off right away.

The Lud message boards go nuts, except this time, they're torn over whether I'm the devil for stealing personal data, a saint for giving Gaby Swift a boost, or a sex icon for reasons I'd rather not get into. I'm most offended by the Gaby Swift accusation. The point of my broadcast was exactly the opposite of that. I wanted to caution people on WAVE—people who should believe in a techie future—that they're falling for her propaganda. Unlike Hailey Carter, lying about who you support for president could be dangerous.

After the episode, I message Amber Donahue and let her know I'm not really up for talking this week. I'm not really up for anything else WAVE-related when I feel like the entire platform has violated me. The Carter family sends me an email about collaborating with Hailey, but I ignore it.

The next night, M4rc plays a late-night interview with Mr. and

Mrs. Carter on my PolyWall. They have dark, heavy bags under their eyes, and there's a tired drawl in their voices as they thank viewers for their empathy and understanding. I swear they're talking directly at me.

And then they do.

MR. CARTER

You know, young women like Hailey—they get lifted up just as quickly as they get crushed. We're thankful that, for whatever reason, Opal Hopper objectively *proved* the emotional whiplash our culture puts them through.

MRS. CARTER

We couldn't be happier that Opal Hopper is shining a light on the truth.

Shined. Past tense. Mrs. Carter's point is exactly why I'm not getting back on WAVE. Too many ups and downs. Too much to risk.

****

The next morning, I'm savoring the sun-kissed view of the school track outside my window, thinking about how I'll finally have the time to go running again, when M4rc alerts me of an important email. It's from Neil, my mystery Invisigog donor.

Another stellar job. Let's meet for coffee this week. Thursday? 4:30? Philz?

I'd set up an email filter over the weekend to block all the spam I started receiving after my name became public. How did Neil manage to get past it? How did his drone manage to tap on my window?

I notice the email address: Neil@waveverse.com.

No one I know has a four-letter WAVEverse username. Not even Kara, who surely would have paid for the status symbol. I look up this man's profile on WAVE and learn that his avatar is pimped out in all the latest gear, he graduated from Yale, and he's an investor.

A venture capitalist. Of course. I know all about VCs, the deep-pocketed wizards of Silicon Valley. I remember meeting one with my dad outside an ice cream shop on University Avenue when I was really little. Abba spoke faster around him and was simultaneously interested and dismayed when the stodgy man offered him his card. It reminded me of how I act around people like Kara—people in your world with power, whose attention you're almost ashamed of wanting to win.

Even though I'm done with WAVE, I hold off on responding. Later that day, I'm extracting DNA from bacteria cells in biotech when my phone buzzes in my pocket. I ask my lab partner to take over for a second. It's another email from Neil:

> Sorry if I wasn't clear in my first email. I'd like to discuss opportunities with you. Already cleared with Principal Frasier for you to leave campus Thursday. See you then.

So much for holding off. When I tell Moyo about the meeting, he bursts like a teakettle—but then he simmers. I knew he would be conflicted. When we dreamed up ideas for our start-up, we always considered that we would need investors like Neil.

Moyo insists on coming with me. Not because I'm a girl, he adds quickly, but because I'm a girl people have their eyes on.

Thursday afternoon, I'm running to meet Moyo when I bump into Kara Lee. She's standing at the same spot in the Sphinx, next to the hydration station, tapping her deadly stilettos.

"Opal!" Kara yells.

"Kara, I'm so sorry, but I'm in a hurry, I'm going to miss—"

"No, wait, I just want—"

"I have to meet this . . ."

"It'll only take a second, I wanted to say—"

I realize my wrist is being clenched tightly. Nervously. The inside of Kara's sticky hand reminds me of my own palms during that first episode on WAVE, less than two weeks ago. I yank myself free.

"I have to go."

Moyo and I meet up outside the residence hall, and together we gallop down Bryant and Forest, our backpacks tap-tap-tapping the back of our spines like reins on a horse. Within minutes, we reach Philz. It's an outdated coffee shop with hipster-jungle decor, but what was I going to do, question the VC's choice of location? We order mint mojito iced coffees and find a table outside, next to the entrance. Despite having emailed Neil an id.me pin with our exact GPS coordinates and a description of what we're wearing—

black blazer for me, beige bomber jacket for Moyo—I'm hoping we spot him first.

Just when I take a second, maybe less, to check my phone, I feel a tap on my shoulder.

"Opal. Freaking. Hopper. We've been waiting for you."

****

Neil Finch. He drops his name nonchalantly, like a pat on the back or the casual way he chugs his large iced coffee while replacing his chair with one from nearby. Apparently, the first one was too wobbly for his liking.

"But enough about me. *You're* the star of the moment." Neil leans closer, and it strikes me that this man has an optimal face. It isn't flawless, necessarily, but each feature is in perfect sync with the others, as if his crooked nose coordinates with his delicate lips, and the gray fringes of his sideburns have daily meetings with his slick salt-and-pepper hair. The only part that seems to march to its own drumbeat is his eyes. There's something wolverine-like about them, constantly narrowing in on a target. Me.

Moyo sits there, fumbling with his fingers. Neil's made a big deal of introducing himself to me, asking if I wanted any more coffee or food, but he hasn't said a word to Moyo.

"We're very impressed with your success on WAVE so far," Neil says. "You know, those boys from Andover haven't made a peep since winning our contest. For all we know, they've gone and spent the prize money on kegs. Now if only they would live stream their silly keg stands on—"

"I'm sorry," I interrupt. "Did you say *your* contest?"

Neil nods affirmatively, and I look at Moyo. He pipes up.

"We thought you were an—"

"Investor. Yes. With Palo Alto Labs Ventures, the venture capital arm of Palo Alto Labs." *Which owns WAVE.* Moyo and I exchange looks—but while Moyo's eyes fill with deep fear that we've been misled, mine are more curious. I take a long sip of my coffee, wondering if Neil Finch was sent here by Howie Mendelsohn.

"We're sorry, Mr. Finch," Moyo says, "but we're not airing on WAVE anymore."

For some reason, it bothers me that Moyo would go ahead and say that. Even if it's what I decided at the end of Monday's episode, we never discussed it explicitly. I slam my cup down on the table. Neil seems to pick up on our unspoken disagreement.

"Oh no! No, no, no." Neil Finch looks at me like we're old friends. "Your channel, Opal. It's simply . . . *disruptive.* It challenges the status quo in ways I've never seen on our platform. I must say, you remind me so much of your father."

My pulse freezes.

"You knew my dad?"

Neil raises his chin dubiously, and for a split second, I see a different face. He's ruined the perfect geometric balance.

"I started my career at Palo Alto Labs as Howie Mendelsohn's assistant, so I met your father a couple of times. Though I wish I could say I knew him better. Brilliant man." He sighs. "Such a shame, what happened."

What happened. People always use that phrase around me, coddle me with it, but I know what they really believe. I see through their "ums," their puppy-dog eyes. They think my dad killed himself. Especially tech folks like Neil Finch, who are all too familiar with the pressure to succeed.

He flattens the front of his tight long-sleeved shirt. It's charcoal gray and made of some sweat-resistant mesh fabric, with matte tape layered over the chest and shoulder areas in futuristic swirls. I'm almost certain the shirt is tracking Neil Finch's physical activity, probably a fitness start-up he's invested in. Judging from how his biceps ripple under the sleeves, that activity is probably significant.

I want to find a way to ask Neil Finch about his former boss without seeming obvious, but Moyo takes obvious to the next level. He pushes his chair back and says, "It was nice meeting you, Mr. Finch, but we should get going."

Neil ignores Moyo and looks at me.

"There is one tiny issue I meant to discuss," Neil says, running his fingernails along the lattice metal of the table. "One regarding data theft."

I drop my cup to the table. Blood comes rushing through my head. I try to maintain some semblance of composure, of balance, but I can't find the anchor within me.

Neil Finch knows about Shane's hack. He'd been buttering me up just to take me down. I process every single word that follows in one swoop; I don't think I even blink.

"One of our backend engineers noticed an unauthorized account accessing our systems last week," he says, flattening his hand on the table. "Nothing changed, nothing stolen. It was quite bizarre. Even more so because this account was masked as a Palo Alto Labs employee. It had its own unique ID, profile, building number, employee dorm assignment. The account made it past dozens of layers of security. But there was one glaring omission. When Sri, our applications manager, ran a routine diagnostic test on our employee intranet, he noticed one account was not properly configured. See, he'd just added an extra field to every employee account last quarter specifically for his diagnostics. You wouldn't know if you were cloning, say, a PAL employee account from last year."

The sun shifts away from our table, leaving us under a chilly shadow. I pick up my drink to take a nervous sip, and the table wobbles. Neil frowns.

"We traced this fictitious account back to the lat-long coordinates for PAAST, and the data viewed seemed to be entirely biometric."

I haven't peeled my eyes away from Neil Finch, but I hear Moyo gulping loudly. I'd kick myself for putting him in this position, if I could move.

"It's no coincidence you went viral," Neil says, "for revealing how people lie, is it? For showing the difference between what they say and how they truly feel?"

A deep, pounding chill settles into my bones.

Shane should have never hacked into WAVE.

We should have never used that data.

Moyo was right. And now, he's suffering because we didn't listen.

Palo Alto Labs could threaten everything we've worked so hard for. They control our school. They control this industry. And they all but control my past. That connection should have been reason number one for stopping Shane from pulling that stunt. We'll be lucky if we only get kicked out.

Neil Finch scans our faces for what seems like an eternity. He's reading us, waiting for us to burst at the seams, when he finally speaks.

"We can only hope you'll take the same ability to think *outside* the box with you as you continue to grow your channel, Opal."

"Wh—" I stammer. *"What?"* My fingers fumble in my lap, almost dancing. "Are you saying we're not in trouble?"

Neil considers his next words carefully. "I'm saying Howie and I discussed your case, and he believes your XP elevates WAVE in profound ways. It's struck a chord. It does something the dating games and skydiving simulations can't and won't ever do."

I'm overcome with relief, like the moment a painkiller finally sets in, but also a mixed dose of euphoria and suspicion. Howie Mendelsohn knows who I am. He's thought of me. Talked about me. Might even think highly of what I've done.

This is too much to process.

"Though if you choose not to continue on our platform . . ." Neil lets out a long, drawn-out sigh—the kind that makes it very clear who's in charge. "We'd have to reconsider the consequences."

As I'm trying to sort out my feelings, Moyo blurts, "And what if we did keep airing episodes? Where do you see this going?"

Neil grins.

"Have you two heard of WAVEcon?"

Everyone with a headset has heard of WAVEcon. At the beginning of each year, our home screens get inundated with updates from the annual gathering of virtual reality creators. It's when all the big stars gather in the San Jose convention center and throw giant parties, announce new programs for the upcoming year, and show what a tight-knit, quirky, fun-loving community they've become. The whole spectacle is kind of vomit-inducing for the rest of us who possess normal amounts of energy.

"We haven't announced yet, but Howie will be attending for the first time this year. He believes it's time for the creator of WAVE to meet the creators who make it happen," Neil says in a boardroom sort of way. "He wants to get to know people like you."

Neil Finch has me in the grip of his hands. Before I can let my bewildered heart bleed through my mouth, Moyo makes sense of what he's saying. "Howie wants to meet us?"

"If you reach a certain level of success, yes."

Poseidon status. Howie's only making time to meet with WAVE's most elite circle, the channels marked with a golden trident. It's the ultimate status symbol in his virtual playground. Poseidon channels are known for pulling in millions of live viewers—"five million at minimum," according to Neil—and for their quality content. That little trident is as coveted as an Academy Award.

Neil goes on with tips for growing our audience, ideas for future shows. He promises to put us in touch with an app that automatically leaves comments. This man is larger than life, like a

Jackson Pollock painting, just splattered in the most peculiar ways.

"We realize how all this may be awkward," Neil says as he stands up to leave, "given your history, Opal. But trust me, Howie is willing to put everything aside and *chat*. For the sake of WAVE."

He wraps his untouched scone in the flimsy wax paper and stuffs it into his paper coffee cup, handing the trash to the young woman who walks out the door.

The woman looks at Neil Finch with a confused expression. She's in her late teens or early twenties, with a tight, slick black ponytail and light brown skin.

"I don't work here," she says in an annoyed tone.

Neil shrugs, and I take the trash from the woman he mistook for a Philz employee.

Chapter
Eleven

There's a bench on campus in the narrow pocket where one of the corners of the Sphinx clips the residence hall. It's where Moyo and I used to meet freshman year. I learned everything about Moyo on this bench. He told me about life in Nigeria, because even with California's many wonders, he missed home so much. He loved talking about his mother, a civil engineer who left her dream job to focus on raising him full time. She took him to art classes and let him scribble all over their walls in Lagos—not only that, but she eventually carved out the drawings and had them framed, drywall and all. I loved hearing those stories.

After our tense meeting with Neil Finch, we naturally gravitate toward our old bench. I used to worry that Shane would discover us there, even though it's near the senior wing of the residence hall. Funny how three years later, I ended up living in the room directly above it. Three years later, I'm still nervous that Shane might discover us and get jealous.

Or perhaps, it's a different kind of nerves.

"I've never been so scared in my life," Moyo says, digging his knuckles into the dark wood of the bench. "Neil Finch knows exactly why we were able to make such a big splash, and he's not afraid to use it against us."

"They couldn't implicate you, Moyo," I assure him. "Shane hacked the data. I'm the one who used it. It's been all over my PolyWalls. But you're fine."

"We don't know how much they've been watching us, Opal. Palo Alto Labs practically built this school."

I turn to face Moyo, and for the first time today, I notice just how shaken he is. His lips are quivering. When I glance down, I catch him thumbing the zipper of his jacket.

"How are you not afraid?" he asks softly.

I want so badly to set Moyo free. To tell him I'll take it from here, that Shane and I can continue airing episodes on WAVE. But I can't let him go; I need Moyo the way humans need air and plants need water. He's the reason I'm not afraid. Because I'm not alone.

"WAVEcon could be cool," I say after a long pause, my eyes distant. I muster a smile. "Think about it. They wouldn't have invited us if they weren't on our side."

"But think of what it'll take to get there," Moyo presses. "We . . ."

"We'd have to grow bigger."

"We'd have to hit *Poseidon status*. People who grow that big get consumed by WAVE. It becomes their life."

We get quiet. I peer over at the Chinese yo-yo club that's gathered nearby. I watch as the performers toss their brightly colored yo-yos high in the air, bending to catch them and send them spinning. I distract myself with the intricate acrobatics, the blur of it all.

"Do you remember when we looked at those comments?" Moyo asks. "The morning after your first episode. The disgusting ones about you."

I ignore him, choosing to follow one of the yo-yos instead. The red one. It seems to hang in the air forever, like a floating drop of blood.

"Because there's more where that came from," Moyo says. "I'm worried about you. We never talked about those comments. Or the guy who rushed the stage and groped you. And while we're talking about numbers, have you looked at *all* the biometric data? Because there's a small pool of viewers, mostly men, whose eyes blink rapidly during your performance, their faces shake, and their headsets are zoomed into your—"

"Moyo. Stop it," I hiss.

"The internet isn't a kind place, Opal."

I shift my attention from the yo-yo performers to the sharp corner of the glass Sphinx. I see it all come crashing down. I see the glass cube from the *Scalleyrag* office, and I see Moyo inside it, bludgeoning the walls of this dangerous world we're entering.

I see Mrs. Fischer, the shop teacher, approaching from the Sphinx.

"Ms. Hopper," she says in her shrill tone. She's wearing a disgusting brown overcoat and long black boots. There's something twisted about the way she singles us out. "What a nice little hiding spot. If I didn't know any better, I'd think you and Mr. Adeola were plotting murder."

Moyo flinches.

"*Oh*, I'm sorry," Mrs. Fischer says, her eyes digging right into mine. "Sore subject, isn't it?" The harsh lines on her face are nastier than anything I've ever etched into my wooden clock for her class. If Moyo looked horrified before, it's nothing like how I look now, I'm sure. I stare bitterly at Mrs. Fischer.

"Fuck you," I whisper under my breath.

Mrs. Fischer's eyebrows shoot up. "Excuse me?"

"Go ahead. Report me," I fire back.

"Opal. Stop it." Moyo nudges me with his knee.

Like a snake with its grip around its next meal, Mrs. Fischer holds my gaze. But then she lets go. "Lucky for you, Ms. Hopper, I don't record every interaction with students. Let alone strangers," she smirks. "Back in my day, people would be up in arms if Face-book so much as tracked your text messages. Now you kids are taking data from our *faces*, and they're just shrugging."

I bite my tongue, the way I'm sure Moyo's been biting his this entire time. Her lips curl into an unpleasant smile.

"Well, not everyone. You made that clear with your latest viral stunt," Mrs. Fischer says, eyeing me with satisfaction. "In fact, I meant to say thank you! Ever since you brought up Gaby Swift, I've learned that I'm not the only teacher at this school worried about the woeful state of technology. Some of the humanities teachers feel they're treated as second-class citizens here."

It's taking every ounce of self-control within me not to stand

and spit in Mrs. Fischer's face. Thick skin. I've worked too hard for it.

A soft breeze passes, and Mrs. Fischer buttons up her coat. "Well, you kids turned awfully quiet. I just came by to remark how wonderful it is that you're living in the moment. Life without gadgets—it's not so bad!" She shoots off one last devilish grin. "Just try and look a bit happier about it."

My eyes sting as they follow Mrs. Fischer. She walks off campus, across the street, into the town of Palo Alto. It gets windier, colder, and I move closer to Moyo, as if he's capable of radiating warmth.

Moyo wraps an arm around my shoulder. That's when I lose it. I crumple completely into his arms and sob uncontrollably, blubbering about how I'm afraid, how I can't pass up this opportunity, how I've wanted for so long to meet Howie Mendelsohn and get these answers about my dad, and besides, I have no choice in the matter, so I might as well play along.

It occurs to me at some point that people may be watching, that the Chinese yo-yo team may still be there. But I feel safe in Moyo's arms. Protected. He takes my insecurity—maybe even revels in this side of me I've hidden for so long. He doesn't judge, he doesn't chime in with his opinion. Moyo just comforts me. He rubs my back. Brushes his finger through my wavy hair.

Bleary-eyed, I look up at my friend's profile. I can see, from just inches away, that Moyo is struggling. I've never opened up to him about my dad and Howie Mendelsohn like this before. I notice the tenderness in his pressed, pink lips, and the questions in his distant eyes, their edges crinkled like raisins.

But in the same face, I see Moyo grappling with the rawness of the decision I've just made. For better or worse, we're going back on WAVE.

****

. . . Our intrepid reporter's experience inside the cube may have proven that while violence is never the answer, at zero gravity, it might just be enough to spice up your love life.

And finally, number five on our Friday Five.

Another week, another XP from our Princess of Palo Alto. Now, allow us to give credit where credit is due. This girl is on fire, and she's gunning for more than fifteen minutes. Why else would she have skipped class last week to stomp down to the *Scalleyrag* offices, delivering yours truly a piece of her mind?

Perhaps we can expect another visit from Her Highness? Afternoons would be best, Ms. Hopper, around two or three p.m.

We must admit, we're just as shocked as the rest of you with Opal Hopper's constant accusations. "You're a liar! You're a liar!" Surely some of us tell the truth online, don't we? We in the journalism industry would like to think so.

And Ms. Hopper: in what imaginary universe do you consider Gaby Swift a serious presidential candidate? Maybe you're misinterpreting the facial data. Maybe a "smile" here and a "gasp" there don't indicate support. Who knows, someone could have just sneezed with their headset on. The polls are clear—Gaby Swift has no chance of getting elected.

Though we understand if you're less than pleased with Silicon Valley these days, Ms. Hopper, it makes us wonder: What are *you* thinking behind that headset? What are your true intentions? We only wish we had as much access to you as you do to us.

Nevertheless, we persist. If Opal Hopper is in for more, so are we. We'll catch the Princess of Palo Alto next week, as she hacks into the deepest, darkest corners of our minds . . . on *Behind the Scenes*.

****

Discipline is more of an art than a science at PAAST. Rather than explicit rules and consequences, our school operates like the startups on Sand Hill Road, with "core values." Principles like *integrity* and *personal responsibility*, the usual suspects. Apparently, you can remember the whole list with an acronym that sounds a lot more like an infectious disease, but it boils down to this: don't fuck up.

When I see that Matthew Seamus has exposed me for sneaking off campus, I'm not sure exactly how much trouble this annoying journalist has gotten me into, if any. Disciplinary issues are usually taken care of behind closed doors. Like freshman year, when Art

Agarwal was mysteriously expelled just days after he was elected student body president. One minute he was everyone's favorite band geek, the next minute—gone.

But nothing happens. I go about my classes like any other Friday. No one calls me into the principal's office or knocks on my door or demands that I pack up my things.

Maybe Palo Alto Labs really is on our side. Maybe they put in a good word with Principal Frasier.

That's what scares me.

****

The thing about getting off the hook is that karma always finds another way to screw you over.

Our next two episodes of *Behind the Scenes* suffer badly. We're almost back to Kara-level numbers, even after incorporating the growth tips Neil recommended, like a bot called Conch.io that leaves positive comments as soon as you go live. We turned it off after Moyo objected on moral grounds, but what does it matter? Lightning might have struck twice, but it feels like we're never going to see another flash again. And if there's no lightning, there's no Poseidon.

It doesn't help that we can't hack the user data anymore. Trying to figure out what people want without knowing what they're thinking . . . it's like being a magician and losing your power. I used to have this awesome wand, and now the only thing coming out is smoke.

My mind keeps drifting to one piece of advice from Neil Finch.

Think outside the box.

"We need to give the people what they want," I tell Moyo and Shane. "Right now it's just me talking at the camera. Maybe we need more action. Like those video games Jez Marshall is so obsessed with playing. Or we could make it a dating competition, like that old TV show our parents watched."

It's a few minutes shy of nine p.m., when the Media Room is supposed to shut down. We've been there for almost six hours since class let out, and Moyo and Shane are both slumped on the couch in the back corner, their arms draped over the sides.

"How about we call it a night?" Moyo says, stretching his neck. "You know we're losing steam when Shane's fingers aren't all up on a keyboard or Rubik's Cube."

Shane lets out a deep and glorious yawn.

"Noooope. I can't be tired."

"That's the spirit!" I cheer.

". . . because I have to finish my MIT app tonight," Shane says. "My dad wants to review all my essays before I click Submit next week. How are you guys doing on yours?"

"Already turned mine in," Moyo says.

"Going fine," I mumble.

Fine. That's one way of putting it. I still haven't touched my Stanford essay since the week of our first episode. How could I? I'm spending every waking minute sifting through our stats, thinking about WAVEcon, worrying that Matthew Seamus might find something else to write about me. And now with this dip in views, it's only gotten worse. I've slept five, maybe six hours this week. Do the math and that's less than two hours a night.

The last thing I want is to head back to my dorm room alone. I feel outside myself, like my mind has spread into the rest of my body and is clawing to get out. If I go back, I'm sure I'll lose myself to sleep; I'm hitting my limit with caffeine.

I need to stay awake. Moyo and Shane, their jobs are finished. Moyo stitched together an amazing new studio, grand as a Broadway theater but with the intimate warmth of a small-town living room, and Shane upgraded our graphics and hacked together a bot that would incorporate terms from our most popular LiveTags. But me . . . my job is never done.

Think outside the box.

Maybe we just need a change of scenery.

"Hey. Do you guys remember that time we spent the night in the HP Garage? When we put on our Undetectables and—"

"Such a fucking fun night," Shane says abruptly.

Moyo and I look at each other nostalgically, as if we're the parents and Shane our son who just took his first step.

"What if we went tonight?" I blurt. "For old times' sake. I'm still looking at numbers for next week, and Shane, you can finish up your MIT app. And Moyo . . ."

"No way," Moyo says, sitting up straight. We enter into an intense stare-off, and Shane sits up slowly, his eyes ping-ponging between the two of us.

"Moyo."

"Opal."

"Guys," Shane snaps. He looks at Moyo, whose eyes bug out

in that responsible-parent sort of way. "Oh, come on, Moyo. I've snuck out to the Garage a bunch of times since that night, with Heather Lowenstein."

Moyo and I could not react more differently to this announcement, which I had already guessed and Moyo wouldn't have dared to believe. The details of our expressions don't matter, only that they're as polarized as two ends of a magnet.

"What?" Shane says, defensive, leaning in closer to Moyo. "You really think I haven't had a drink since that night?"

Moyo manages to croak out, "I just . . ."

"You know what? Let's do it." Shane looks to me. "For old times' sake."

With a cluck of the tongue, Moyo signals both his moral objection and his concern that we'll get caught. Then, with a shrug, he raises a white flag and surrenders to peer pressure.

"Perfect. Two to one. Democracy wins, as always," I smirk proudly. "I hope you didn't get rid of your Undetectables, Moyo."

****

Shane puts on a loose black turtleneck and ink-stained jeans that hug his quads. Moyo and I look equally shady in dark blue and musty brown. *GQ* would definitely accuse us of clashing, but for tonight's activities, it'll have to suffice.

We meet in the grand entryway of the residence hall. A group of underclassmen watches us from the boxy couch by the door as we leave; they probably think we're headed to the dining hall for a late-night bite.

I'm the first to zip across the schoolyard and cross the border, without a worry in my step. Whether that's from genuine confidence or sleep deprivation, I can't be sure. Shane follows closely behind, with Moyo trailing by fifteen or twenty feet. We make sure to cross through the dark part of campus, where the powerful streetlamps struggle to reach.

"Did you hear—"

"Shhhh."

"I just thought—"

"SHHHHH."

"That shadow, did you see that—"

"Moyo. Seriously. Shut up."

As we scuttle down Waverley, alternating positions as leaders of the pack, I can't help but feel like we're being watched. I've been extra paranoid since meeting with Neil Finch, shooting glances over my shoulder more than usual and looking out for surveillance cameras. That's all it takes, isn't it? Get people to think they're being watched and they'll act differently.

It doesn't matter if these towering lampposts contain light bulbs or cameras. It doesn't matter if we're actually being watched. Paranoia and surveillance are cut from the same cloth.

Finally, we tiptoe up the driveway of the HP Garage. Shane fishes a ring of keys from his jean pocket and wiggles the largest one into a rusty latch.

"When was the last time you needed a *physical* key to enter a building?"

"Shhhh."

Moyo shoots me a wicked smile. At least, that's how it seems from his eyes, which is all I can see in the darkness.

"You know, we don't have to be quiet anymore. We're off campus."

Before I can protest, the Garage doors let out a groan. Shane motions for us to get out of the way as he swings them open.

The space looks like it should smell musty. Decrepit. Like a corpse might be hidden under the cracked concrete. But the only smell is that of pristine cleanliness—the waft of disinfectants and chemicals used to preserve this museum of a shed. It looks like it's been frozen in time, this one-room garage with wide, wooden wall panels and outdated machinery scattered around on peeling tables and upside-down buckets. A single light bulb hangs at the center of the ceiling. Its soft nectarine glow illuminates the whole room.

Shane flips one of the rusted metal buckets right side up to reveal a bottle of Jack Daniel's whiskey duct-taped inside.

I smile. "Well, that's a throwback to junior year if I ever saw one."

Shane unscrews the cap and takes a swig of the brownish liquid—the same shade as the damaged chest in the corner that he uses as a seat. He offers the bottle to Moyo and me. We both decline, though I hesitate.

"Didn't you say you needed to work on your MIT essay?"

Shane shrugs boozily, reaching for his laptop.

"Hemingway said, *write drunk, edit sober*," Moyo says, pacing the room, his hands laced behind his back like a bodyguard.

"Well, I'm not working drunk," I say.

Shane looks at me as if I've committed some vague betrayal.

"So much for old times' sake," he mutters. He takes another swig of whiskey, this one bigger and somewhat theatrical. A few drops of liquid dribble down the side of his chin, and when he slams the uncapped bottle on the wooden chest, a bit splashes on his MacBook. Shane doesn't seem to mind. With his hands free, he digs into his pocket for the key chain.

I'm not sure what to make of Shane's reaction, so I ask, hesitantly, "Is that all right with you? Or . . . do you want to leave?"

Shane says nothing. There's a small Rubik's Cube at the end of his key chain, not much bigger than a die, and he goes to work on it. His fingers move in teensy motions, like he's sewing a Christmas sweater for a mouse, and within fifteen seconds he's got himself six little squares of solid colors.

"If you guys aren't drinking with me, we should hang out in the house," he finally says. "The couches and chairs are comfier there."

And so we move next door, inside the former home of Bill Hewlett and Dave Packard. The living room looks like it was plucked out of a 1950s sitcom, complete with floral curtains and dusty picture frames. Plush leather armchairs and a random oscillator on the mantelpiece. Relics of a simpler time.

Moyo and I claim the couch, and Shane sprawls over the armchair, Jack Daniel's bottle and MacBook in tow. For the rest of the night, we do our work. Shane clacks away on his keyboard, perfecting his MIT application to satisfy his father's high standards, and Moyo and I scrape every comment and "like" from this week's top content, hoping to discover something interesting.

Sometime after midnight, Shane passes out completely, with his bottle of liquor wrapped in one arm and his laptop propped against the base of the chair. The room is quiet for a while, and I move closer to Moyo on the couch to inspect his latest design ideas. It's not until the faintest snore escapes Shane's lips that we acknowledge him.

I look at Shane and wonder: *What's going on inside that head? Was he angry with Moyo and me for not drinking? Is he pissed at his parents? Could he still have feelings for me, even though it's been years since we kissed and stopped talking, and we both swore we'd never do that again?*

Then the wheels in my head spin in a different direction. Because Shane has given me the spark I needed for *Behind the Scenes*— not with private user data, but with the private issues that people never deal with or talk about.

"Think he's okay?" Moyo asks.

"Of course."

"Okay. Good."

I turn, smiling heartily at my friend. I remember the last time we snuck off campus, Shane poured too much vodka into his Coke—three, maybe four shots with each glass. Moyo ended up cleaning up after him the next morning.

"Moyo, don't worry."

And he didn't even complain about it.

Moyo nudges me in the rib.

"You're the one worrying," he says.

We giggle loudly.

Chapter
Twelve

The night before Halloween, I tuck my headset underneath my bed. Power off my PolyWall. Chain myself to my desk. I even go so far as to tell M4rc to shut off the internet connection. (M4rc asks me three times if I'm sure about this, and it bothers me how well he understands my most basic needs.)

I rest my fingers on the bumpy terrain of my keyboard and take a deep breath, my chest rising and falling through the knitted fabric of my Cyber Club sweater.

I read the Stanford essay prompt aloud.

Describe a problem you've solved or a problem you'd like to solve.

Same problem. This stupid essay.

I've solved my biggest problem. *Behind the Scenes* is back, stronger than ever. Our XP is causing a commotion again, now that I'm asking the audience about extremely personal topics: friendship, family, relationships. Topics I know people lie about all the time. I don't think the Livvit boards will ever stop clamoring about the dramatic breakup that went down in our last episode, when a guy's biometrics revealed that he had the hots for his girlfriend's little sister. After the guy zapped out of the XP abruptly, everyone looked at the sisters like they were expecting them to break out into hair-pulling or a catfight, but the girls just waved at his empty seat and went, "Boy, bye." Someone made a holo of the moment and it's been trending all week.

Now that we're breaking a million views again, WAVEcon is back within reach. I'm hopeful that we'll hit Poseidon status in no time. Next week is the presidential election, and we've got a killer post-election episode planned. It's supposed to be a razor-tight race between Martina Alvarez, the Democrat, and Trent Worthington, the Republican, and I'm planning to have a very real, very candid talk about how the winner can heal the nasty divide in our country.

Unfortunately, that leaves little time for things like school, where my grades are slipping. Let alone college apps.

I've tried writing about our success with *Behind the Scenes*, but I can't. Because to talk about our success would be to talk about how we got there, data hack and all, and why I entered Make-A-Splash in the first place.

That night, instead of planning a Halloween costume or writing my essay, I open a folder I haven't touched in a very long time. It's hidden deep in my hard drive, so hidden I can't find it with the search function. I get lost in folders with old homework assignments and screenshots I can't for the life of me remember why I took, until I land on the one I'm looking for. This folder is encrypted, but as soon as I'm prompted for the key, it comes to me like muscle memory.

And there it is.

FIND DAD

My detective folder. I started it after it became clear that no one else was going to try and find him—not the police, not my mother. The folder is split into two subfolders. The first is simply called RAN AWAY, and it contains every possible theory of where he could have gone—detailed maps of Tahoe and the different camping sites we had stayed on, interviews with students and colleagues, the ones who wrote back with bombastic grief instruction manuals. I scroll through the files I'd downloaded from the one phone of his I managed to unlock. The pages he had liked on Facebook. My inventory of his room: he took nothing with him, but I did notice his mud-splotched hiking boots were missing. I figure he was wearing them the night he left, along with his gray windbreaker that smelled like burnt butterscotch.

The other subfolder is much thinner. The theory diagrams and maps are less detailed, just vaguely jotted. I let out a single, sad laugh as I think about how much it pained me to put together this folder yet how I knew it was still a real possibility. How I spent one afternoon jotting notes while reluctantly searching the San Francisquito Creek, just in case this theory checked out.

HOWIE.

Once in a while, a dark part of me—maybe even the logical

part—wonders if Howie Mendelsohn killed my dad. I picture that night vividly in my mind: Howie and my dad on one of their late-night walks along the San Francisquito Creek. Howie telling my dad that he was fired, or that they lost funding, or that they needed to shut down their start-up. My dad telling Howie that he'd sacrificed everything for it—his job, his relationships with his wife and daughter. I see Abba refusing. Softly, at first, and then angrily. I see him threatening to sue Howie if he left him in the dust.

And then, Howie snaps.

I close all the folders and windows.

A deep breath later, I go back and add Amber Donahue's private message to the file. I consider reaching out to her again—she never replied to my email blowing off our call—but I tell myself I'll do it later. I need to get back to this essay.

Halloween comes and goes. Moyo, Shane, and I skip the annual Halloween Extravaganza, where they turn the gym into a holographic haunted house with elevated beds. We spend the evening at the HP Garage instead. We've been sneaking off campus more lately.

The night of November 1st, I'm back at my desk. "Let's write this essay," I say to myself through clenched teeth. I almost expect those words alone to inspire me. Usually, when I tell myself I'm going to do something, I do it. I'm not the type of person to give up easily. Yet here I am, coming up short. Desperately flicking the lighter, but my finger keeps slipping against the metal spark wheel.

No flame. No essay.

I don't end up applying early decision to Stanford. I'm too distracted these days. I comfort myself with the obvious fact that I don't have to apply early decision, that I can submit my app January 1st like everyone else. It even strikes me that by applying regular decision, I could benefit more from the success of *Behind the Scenes*. It's the kind of entrepreneurial endeavor an admissions committee would gobble up.

****

There's one other distraction. This one has been sitting patiently in the back of my mind, the quiet and shy type in a classroom full of loudmouths, showing no sign that eventually it would rise up and cause more noise than the rest.

Moyo.

The night before the presidential election, Shane convinces us to take one shot of whiskey—*"only* one," Moyo assures us—before we go back to work. We fill the ancient porcelain cups with clear brown liquor, clink our glasses, toss them back, and wince. It's been a rough week for all of us. Moyo's soccer team buddies are giving him crap for hanging out less this semester, I missed my second History of Social Media assignment in a row, and Shane's been sort of withdrawn lately. It's like he's with us and somewhere else at the same time.

For Shane this shot is merely the opening fire, followed by a barrage of shots over the next hour until he's passed out on what has become his personal armchair . . . but not before making an observation.

"You guys are always together on that couch," he slurs. An outside observer might have heard the words *geyser* and *end catch*, but Moyo and I know perfectly well what Shane is saying. We have context. "There's another . . . *armcherrrr.*"

I laugh nervously. I'm sitting cross-legged, my oversized sweatshirt creating a small cushion in my lap for my MacBook. At first, I don't look up from the lines of code on my screen. Shane's picked up on something I don't care to acknowledge, and judging from the silence to my right, neither does Moyo.

But then, seconds later, I hear throaty snores rising from Shane's armchair. Drunk people are like amnesiacs: they never remember their last thought. Relieved, I let myself laugh in that carefree, hiccup-hoppy manner you see in bobbleheads and toddlers and people who squirt apple juice out their noses from giggling too hard. I turn into a pinball, falling forward and sideways, victim to a humorous situation. And to my further relief, Moyo is laughing too. The floorboards begin to creak from our bouncing on the couch. I find humor in his laughter, and he finds humor in mine. It's an endlessly positive feedback loop, the kind you expect to go on forever.

Until my arm presses into Moyo's and I don't pull away. And, technically speaking, neither does he.

"Armcher," I breathe.

Moyo looks over his shoulder. He turns slowly, confused and smiling at my choice of words to break the silence.

"You know, I don't think he was talking about that armchair at all," he says. "I think he was saying there *are cherries* in the kitchen."

"Ha."

"That's all I get? The drunk guy gets a standing ovation, and all I get is 'ha'?"

I turn my cheek, determined not to let him see me smiling. "Ha! Ha, ha! You should be a comedian."

"Yes. Maybe I should be the one addressing a million avatars on *Behind the Scenes*. Then we'll hit Poseidon status, Zeus status, all the Greek god statuses!"

"Somehow I don't think your attempts at humor would be as interesting as the fact that literally *everyone* lies in relationships." Without realizing it, I pull away from Moyo, one finger jabbing at the green lines of text on my screen, the other finger on my keyboard, waiting to pounce. "Look here. If you ask anyone, they'll say honesty is one of the most important qualities in a partner. But then *half* of men admit to keeping a secret from their girlfriend or boyfriend. I bet that's even higher if we—"

Moyo snaps my MacBook shut.

"Why don't we give WAVE a break and check out the, um, cherry situation in the kitchen?"

I nudge Moyo playfully, reopening my laptop.

"Something tells me if this house is really such an important Silicon Valley relic, we won't find any cherries in the kitchen."

Moyo looks at me, his mouth opened slightly and his chest ballooned, prepared to say something bold or daring to me, his friend. His friend *for now*. But slowly, for some reason, his face twists and his desire deflates.

I'm not blind. I'm not an idiot. I can read emotions clearly; every magnet, arrow, compass, direction-telling instrument within me shoots toward Moyo Adeola's heart. Blame it on the late nights we've spent together, his unwavering belief in me, his trust in the world's chips falling into place. Blame it on the thousands of times I've stared at his smile for just a split second too long, or all the times he's made me laugh despite not once having told an objectively funny joke in our three years of friendship.

Lean in . . . and pull away. I have my reasons. I cock my head back and smile at Moyo, the kind of smile that says *Here we are. It's been a long, pleasant ride, and we've finally reached our inevitable destination.*

I move to the other armchair.

Chapter
Thirteen

The mood around campus on election day is like a pride parade: colorful, hopeful, ready to show the world we're on the right side of history.

That night, the Democratic and Republican clubs co-host a viewing party in the cafeteria. Moyo, Shane, and I attend, occupying a couch in the lounge area in the back. CNN anchors are projected holographically around the perimeter of the cafeteria. Timothy Hackney and his crew team friends throw pretzel bites at them, laughing like goons.

"My mom says people in Nigeria have been treating this election like a reality show." Moyo laughs. "No offense, but it's kind of ridiculous it's even close."

"It's not close," Shane goes, popping a rolled-up Twizzler into his mouth. "That's just the media trying to get people watching."

"Kind of like us," I say, chuckling.

"Yeah, but our numbers are *real*," Shane says proudly.

"I wonder where they came from . . ." Moyo looks to Shane,

and Shane punches him sideways in the shin, and I'm just grinning to be caught in the middle of this couch war.

The screen directly above us, which usually displays the ever-changing cafeteria menu, rotates through crowds of people in California, Texas, New York. It clearly detects Moyo's presence too, because it shows a quick shot of a viewing party in Lagos.

The analysts are saying there's a chance none of the candidates will win the electoral college, in which case Congress would decide. Trent Worthington, the first gay Republican presidential candidate, has the best shot of winning both sides of the aisle in that case. Talk about a historic endnote to a depressing election cycle.

****

Something is going wrong. It's six p.m., and Pennsylvania is dangerously close. None of the states in the northeast are supposed to be going for Gaby Swift. But with more than 90 percent of votes reported, Pennsylvania is a razor-thin three-way tie. And considering the only precincts left are the ones that still use paper ballots, it's not promising.

Half an hour later, one of the analysts calls the state for Gaby Swift. The cuddle puddle of drama kids boos, and one of them throws a french fry up at the screen.

"Coal country," Shane says reassuringly, though he's fumbling with his pale fingers. "It's fine. Unless Gaby Swift wins one of the big states like Texas or California, it's statistically impossible for her to win."

"It'll probably go into a runoff," says Jez Marshall as he passes by with two handfuls of fries.

****

An hour later, the cafeteria is buzzing with nervous energy. Gaby Swift has swept the Midwest, and even though that was expected—states like Kansas and Oklahoma are peanuts compared to California—each flashing green border overlaid with her face, her searing red lipstick, sends us into a collective panic attack. Rosalind Wu, ever the optimist, has started going around and reassuring everyone that it's all going to be okay. The presidents of the Democratic and Republican clubs have taken over one of the walls and started mapping out the country, plotting the votes necessary for one of their sides to win.

My sweater feels itchy against the couch. Sweat is forming underneath my arms. Somehow, I don't think numbers are going to save us.

****

The puddle of drama kids is now a puddle of dramatic tears. Gaby Swift has won California. My classmates are calling their parents, demanding to know if their older siblings voted, or if their grandma really voted for Swift like she said she would. Shane bolted back to his room—he couldn't handle the stress of the cafeteria—and Moyo is watching like it's an intricate dance number and he has to remember every step.

The screen above us pans to a rowdy bar in Los Angeles.

They're interviewing some older industry executive who doesn't like what virtual reality has done to the entertainment business.

Another screen flips through Luddites celebrating across the country. It shows them bursting onto the streets, seeming just as shocked as we are that their movement has made it all the way to the White House. In Kansas City, they're smashing self-driving cars and destroying self-sorting trash bins. They're literally driving into driverless streets. If ever the Luds were going to feel invincible, it's tonight—and maybe nights in the future. They're chanting their signature chants, the ones we've laughed at and mocked for months: *"Roads, not robots"* and *"Silence your phones, please"* and *"There's no AI in team!"* One of them, a middle-aged white man with a smug face, is holding a sign that reads: BACK TO THE BASICS. Tim Li and I made fun of that one just weeks ago, because BASIC is a programming language.

Half of my classmates are sobbing incoherently. The other half are sitting or standing, stunned, catatonic—like I've been all these years.

Another nail in the coffin.

****

The next morning feels like waking up from a nightmare and finding it was real. I've been in that place before, but never with this many friends by my side. It's pure silence when I enter the Sphinx, the usual energy dampened by the hideousness of the night before.

PAAST has always been an asylum for nerds. For dreamers.

For the kids who wore glasses and got made fun of for dreaming too big and acting different, wanting to do things differently. It's the only place where we fit in.

Now, the Luds want to take us back to that old place—where people like us, the coders and the dreamers, are relegated to the loser table.

****

Days later, I'm standing in front of the green screen. Nearly a million people are waiting in their seats. It's more than we've ever had live. Because in the midst of all the depression, all the shock, one key fact flew over my head: I'm the girl who predicted an election. I called it from the start, even if it's the opposite of what I wanted.

I look at Shane in the control room, his face as expressionless as it was when he stormed out of the cafeteria. My eyes turn to Moyo, his fingers dropping one by one.

Moyo goes, "Action."

PART TWO

GIRL IN THE DEEP END

Chapter
Fourteen

The third week of November, on a particularly miserable rainy day, my mom texts me to ask about Thanksgiving.

> Why, hello, my little celebrity :) :) Coming home
> next week? ;)

I stare at my phone screen while Tim Li solders our motherboard with gumdrop-shaped capacitors. Normally I wouldn't dare check it in the middle of shop class, but Mrs. Fischer's been in an especially good mood lately, ever since the Luds swept the election.

My mom had once said that she'd always be proud of me, no matter what. I'm starting to believe that. Ever since we lost Make-A-Splash, she's been texting me constant words of encouragement, calling me her "rising star" or her "little celebrity." I almost feel guilty, because as far as she's concerned, I'm just doing this for fun. She doesn't know about Neil Finch. She doesn't know there's still the very real possibility that I could meet Howie Mendelsohn at WAVEcon.

Guilt or no guilt, I can't go home. Thanksgivings have been quiet or awkward since my dad disappeared.

Not this year. I'm crazy busy.

Upside: our post-election XP hit three million views. It's not quite Poseidon status, but it does award us a temporary whirlpool icon that implies we're "brewing a storm." I don't need hacked data anymore to succeed on WAVE. And to top it all off, we're getting attention from legitimate news sources now—enough that I don't even notice the crap that Matthew Seamus writes anymore.

Downside: people are afraid. It's not lost on me that my surge in viewers is because they believe I know something they don't. Millions of avatars sit before me because we're charting new territory, all of us. No one knows what this country will look like when Gaby Swift takes office in January. It's an image that's slowly loading, and no one wants to click Open.

Upside: Moyo, Shane, and I are minor celebrities at school now. Seniors we've never talked to high-five us in the Sphinx, freshmen stare, and sophomore and juniors wonder how *they* can achieve something so big, so real, so distinctly Silicon Valley.

Downside: While our names fill awkward gaps in conversation and echo off the lockers in Hell, one name echoes louder than the others.

"Since when has Opal Hopper given two shits about politics?"

"I had Differential Equations with her. She was such a bitch."

"I bet Shane and Moyo do all the work."

"Girls love to take credit like that."

"Kara Lee must want to kill her."

Truth be told, Kara's been spooking me lately. Every time I pass her in Hell or the Sphinx, her eyes flicker with pleasure, like she has something planned. I try not to think much about it. It's Kara Lee—chances are she just got a "likely letter" from Juilliard, or got cast in another Hollywood movie that no one our age will watch in theaters. Or maybe she's just happy that I'm the girl our classmates are bitching about now.

"Opal Hopper is icy as hell."

"The whole 'friendly' thing, it's an act. We had a chem project together and I don't think she said more than five words to me. Stiff as a covalent bond."

"Where'd she apply?"

"Isn't she a shoo-in for Stanford?"

"If she gets into Stanford . . ."

Oh, the casino of college admissions. The timing couldn't have been more perfect, actually, because as November dims into December, our anxiety about America's future is eclipsed by anxiety about our own. All bets are final on Decision Day—and the house is ready to show its hand.

Every year, the December's Blast from the PAAST dance falls on the same day as D-Day. It's less of a coincidence than a mental health and safety measure. A couple of years before I got here, a senior boy took his life after he didn't get into any of the colleges he applied to, so the administration asked the student council to move the dance permanently. College results go up at five, and the dance starts at six. Rejected or accepted, seniors have one hour to deal with the flurry of emotions, pull themselves together, and, some way or another, haul their asses to the gym.

I walk into the Media Room at 4:55 p.m. Shane and Moyo are already there, with their eyes glued to blank screens.

Without uttering a word, I step up behind my friends. Half my face shows in each of their screens. Moyo nods to acknowledge my presence.

4:56 p.m.

Moyo swipes the touchpad to wake up the computer. Shane does not. He continues to stare blankly ahead—his big, worried eyes and messy hair reflecting off the glass.

4:57 p.m.

Passing through the Sphinx earlier, I could feel the stress in the air. Some students choose to check their admissions decisions from the privacy of their dorm rooms, but others want to be around friends. There were about a dozen cliques scattered on the Sphinx floor in their designated spots. I noticed Jacqueline Sharif and Spencer Nottingham, lying on their bellies next to each other in the corner by the water fountain. For once, PAAST's most high-profile couple was neither cuddling nor making out. Jacqueline was twisting her brunette locks—once full of shine and volume, now flat—around her finger like yarn on a spool, and Spencer was biting his stubby nails. Within minutes, the future of their relationship would be determined. Harvard for Jacqueline, MIT for Spencer.

I calculate in my head the odds of them both getting accepted at the neighboring schools. It's less than one-tenth of one percent.

4:58 p.m.

Moyo slowly navigates to admissions.brown.edu, each finger tapping the keyboard with the thrill of a death march.

Shane still hasn't touched his computer.

4:59 p.m.

As if he feels my eyes narrowing on him, Shane swings into manic motion. He swipes at his trackpad and opens a browser, his fingers tapping away at the ergonomic keyboard faster than a concert pianist's. He logs into admissions.mit.edu with his thumb-print and, with no less than fifteen seconds to spare, enters the application portal. Shane refreshes the page exactly once when his admissions decision appears at the center of the screen. Everyone at PAAST knows you can get your decision a few seconds faster on the application portal than by email.

But Shane can't believe the words before his eyes.

Neither can Moyo, who has refreshed at virtually the exact same time. Both of them open their email windows for the official letter.

"Holy shit," Moyo says.

"Holy shit," I say.

"My entire life. . ." Moyo doesn't finish the thought.

Shane doesn't say anything. He's determined to read every single word of the decision letter. His eyes scan each line from left to right and right to left. They search up and down for some hidden meaning, an alternative interpretation.

But college decisions are hard-coded. They can't be hacked.

5:00 p.m.

Dear Moyo,

Congratulations! On behalf of the Admissions
Committee, it is my pleasure to offer you
admission to the Brown University–Rhode
Island School of Design joint program. You
were identified as one of the most talented
and promising students in one of our most
competitive applicant pools ever . . .

Dear Shane,

We have completed our early review of your
application and have decided to hold it for
further consideration in the spring. Please
do not feel discouraged by this decision. The
Application Committee is very conservative in
its early admissions offers. In fact, the majority
of students who apply under Early Action are
deferred. Of those deferred over the years, up
to several hundred have subsequently been
admitted to MIT in the spring . . .

We sit in silence for the five longest minutes of any of our lives.
I don't need to read the emails over Shane's and Moyo's shoulders

to know who was accepted and who wasn't. The flood of joy in Moyo's eyes followed by the look of terror and pity that washes over him when he turns to Shane tells me everything.

Finally, Moyo says to Shane, "Deferred, not rejected—right?"

He nods slowly.

"They'll take you in April. Don't worry."

Shane closes his eyes and chuckles. It's an empty laugh. He hunches over and lowers his chin, letting it teeter like a white flag hanging on a thread. His elbows dig into his lap. He cradles his pale face with the palms of his hands. I can feel Shane's glare through the tiniest slits between his fingers.

The room grows colder.

"I am so fucked," Shane mumbles into his wrists. "My parents are going to kill me. I'm dead. I'm fucked. I am so, so, so . . ." He takes a deep breath. "Whatever."

More time passes. I shift in my hard metal chair, reminding myself that I'm not the reason Shane is angry, or even MIT, but his parents. His grandparents. The long line of Franklins who've attended the university and paved the path for one generation's inevitable failure. Shane looks at Moyo, stares at him, and I see jealousy in his eyes.

But at the end of the day, we're all PAAST students. Our skin is thick, and our school dances are mandatory. Moyo and Shane and every other senior manage to escape the suffocating air of rejection—firsthand for some, secondhand for most—and find their way to the gymnasium for a special edition of Blast from the PAAST.

Outside the gym door, Rosalind Wu, queen of student government, hands out multicolored headsets to everyone who enters.

"What are these?" I ask.

Rosalind smirks and winks in her signature style: mouth open, shoulder dipped, her eyes flashing like they hold every secret of the world. Like she could share a piece of that exclusive knowledge with a singular blink.

"The senior class council has taken some inspiration from your show," Rosalind says.

I don't follow, and I make that clear with a confused, almost offended squint. Rosalind just winks again.

"You'll figure it out soon enough. Don't worry—they're AR goggles, so you can still see." Augmented reality. I've never been a big fan of this wannabe form of VR, since it truly blurs the lines between fiction and reality.

Rosalind finally notices the death glare Shane has been giving her, because she nudges him playfully in the arm. This does nothing to soften the daggers in his eyes. "So, are you guys ready to *break* it *down?*"

Tired of playing coy with Rosalind, I hand a pair of magenta goggles to Moyo, a royal blue set to Shane, and grab a particularly dull pair of yellow goggles for myself. My hand darts past Rosalind's each time I go for the rack, and before I can be reprimanded for not taking the pair I'd been offered, I'm inside the gym. My friends follow behind me, strapping the headsets around their faces.

Everything is white. All the seniors appear as slightly off-white figures, like oddly shaped eggs, so that we don't bump into each other, but otherwise the entire room is devoid of lines and color. I can't make out the bright orange and kiwi green of the concrete walls; or the plasma screens that display motivational quotes during PE and scores, stats, and replays during basketball games; or the space-efficient bleachers pressed up against the north side of the gym. It looks more like Heaven than a gym.

The creamy blobs seem to be shimmying their shoulders and torsos to music I can't hear. Some shimmy in groups while others shimmy alone. It's strange. Not that PAAST students aren't known to bust solo dance moves from time to time—the typically quiet class nerd break-dancing in the middle of a large circle is one of our favorite pastimes—but tonight something feels different. Circles do not form around these blobs, and each one is totally engaged, like they're dancing with an imaginary friend.

Within seconds, a large block of text appears to my right. I assume the same text appears for Moyo and Shane, because they shoot their heads in the same direction.

WELCOME TO A VERY SPECIAL EDITION OF BLAST FROM THE PAAST! LET'S BREAK IT DOWN INSIDE SOME OF THE MOST BEYOND MUSIC VIDEOS OF THE 2000s AND 2010s. SOUNDSPECTACLE™ WAVE GOGGLES COURTESY OF OUR CORPORATE SPONSOR, PALO ALTO LABS.

As soon as I finish reading the text, there's color. Green.

Green hearts flying across the room, green waves rippling between my classmates, who are no longer blobs but vibrant avatars. And the members of OutKast clad in silly green knickers and long black socks, shimmying at the center of the gym to their hit song "Hey Ya!"

And backup dancers! They can't be from the original music video, because they have that flagrant digital hue, that almost-too-perfect bone structure that means they were drawn up by some graphic designer like Moyo. There have to be at least fifty of them scattered throughout the gym, throwing their hands up and pumping their arms, shaking their hips and wiggling their fingers to the music.

When I turn around, I find myself standing inches from Moyo's gorgeously designed avatar. My nose nearly touches his perfect nose, and my WAVE-issued blouse flaps its digital threads against his vibrant Nigerian shirt.

I smirk, mirroring Moyo's smirk down to the last dimple.

"Let's dance," I say, pulling his arm.

****

"Woop! Gangnam style!"

The song opens with Psy, the K-pop superstar in his signature white suit and sunglasses, in the middle of the gym, as tall as a bursting fountain. Halfway through, he multiplies—two, four, eight—and before we know it, there are hundreds of Psys splayed out across the gym. Moyo, Shane, and I—and the entire senior class—are performing the same crisscross-gallop dance move with the army of Psy clones. If you looked down from above, you'd think you were looking at a military parade gone wild.

"This is even better than those old Taylor Swift videos you dug up on your show the other week!" Peter Isaacson yells into my ear—er, microphone. He gallops over mid-song with Gabe and Amrita, his friends from the theater department.

"I like to think we started the trend." I smile, punching the air with my crossed arms.

"I've gotta say," Amrita slurs. Is she drunk? There are rumors that the theater department stores booze underneath the sound-board. "I gave Peter so much crap for writing those scripts for Kara . . . they were cheesy, like, beyond. But what you've done with the channel is so much better. Get it, girl."

"Are you sure we're still at PAAST?!" Gabe yells sarcastically, like the troll he is.

"Ha. It doesn't feel like it," Moyo says.

"No way. Not at all. This is, like, regular high school shit."

"Better," Gabe says. "This is, like, college spring fling level."

"Paaaarrtaaayy," Amrita adds, shooting a finger in the air to emphasize her extremely relevant point. "And bullshit! College is bullshit! Fuck Michigan!"

"And fuck Yale!" Gabe yells.

Amrita and Gabe look at Peter and roll their eyes. Avatars reveal a lot, and Peter's is glowing with a permanent shine that doesn't waver as his friends flick off the colleges that have rejected them. It's the same beneath-the-hood grin that Moyo can't wipe off all night. I don't even need to ask or confirm before I hug Peter.

"*NYU!* Dude! That's incredible!" My cheeks press into his as we embrace, and I feel his face lift with a smile. I quickly remember that Gabe, Amrita, and Shane had all been deferred or rejected just hours ago, so I quickly break the hug and shout, "Gangnam style!"

The song ends just seconds later. Shane retreats back to the corner of the gym where he had spent most of the Blast from the PAAST until "Gangnam Style," when Moyo and I pulled him onto the dance floor. He's been standing with Heather Lowenstein and a few others who I can only assume also got deferred—or worse, rejected—from colleges that afternoon. Not everyone can be as blasé about rejection as the theater kids.

Other than them, nearly everyone is glued to the dance floor. I've never witnessed so many of my classmates letting loose like this. I mean, I'm hardly the type to let loose myself. The head bopping and fist bumping, the shimmying and shaking—in a way, it's all because of me. *Behind the Scenes* is the reason student council thought to let us dance from the comfort of our avatars, instead of in our awkward physical bodies.

"Hey," Moyo says, appearing from behind. "Do you think Shane is okay?"

"Of course," I say. "Well, no. Of course *not.* But he's as okay as he can be after getting deferred from MIT."

"Shouldn't we go try and cheer him up, then? I feel bad, with him over in that corner when we're over here . . ."

"Moyo, come on. Let the kid sulk. Personally, I think it's stupid they make everyone come to this thing right after decisions come out."

I look at him with an expression that calls for validation. Moyo nods.

"Exactly. But that doesn't mean *we* can't have fun!"

Suddenly, the room transforms into the inside of a giant school bus, complete with brown leather seats and dusty windows.

The bus driver: James Corden.

"I can't believe it," I whisper, my eyes wide with delight. "I can't believe it!" I say louder this time. "Carpool Karaoke!"

"No, no. *School bus* karaoke!"

James Corden's avatar does not actually leave the driver's seat, though, because the star of the XP is a young Taylor Swift, "shaking it off" up and down the aisle of the bus. The entire senior class is screaming. And of course, shaking.

"I've got to say," Moyo says, his hip bumping against mine as we flail our arms left and right, our legs side to side. "For once I'm impressed with senior council."

"You think they did this themselves?" I yell. I turn around and wiggle down low, my backside against Moyo's.

"No way. These music video graphics are too polished and high-def."

"PAL?"

"Definitely PAL."

A horde of Swift's backup dancers surrounds us, and Moyo and I move even closer together, our arms having no choice but to touch. It's a truly bizarre feeling—brushing against another person when all you see is their avatar—like the static electricity on your clothes that sparks your finger out of nowhere.

As the song fades to a close, the school bus fades as well and warps into an extravagant jungle. The air turns hazy, savanna trees tower overhead, and giraffes stretch their long necks through the bleachers.

"Good Lord," Moyo says as the pounding drumbeat shakes the floor beneath us, punctuated with slow chants of *"waka, waka."* "The biggest 'African' song of the decade, and they couldn't find an African singer?"

"I'm surprised you even know this song."

"Of course I know this song! It's Shakira. She's a good singer."

"So you admit it's a good song?" I ask.

"Of course."

"But she's not African, so you don't like it."

"That's right."

I push Moyo and laugh.

"That doesn't make any sense! If you think a song is good, you should like it. It's as simple as that."

Moyo peers over at Shane, checking to make sure he's still chatting with Heather in the corner. He looks back at me and clucks his tongue.

"Nah, it's never that simple. It's the principle of the matter."

Truth be told, I don't disagree with Moyo. In fact, I envy him for his principled approach to all things. He's the guy who labors over his group project work before his own homework—"you owe it to your partners," he always says. It doesn't matter what Moyo wants or what he likes. It matters what's right.

For me, it only matters if it makes sense. That's how I'm

wired. And right now, with Moyo so physically close, what makes sense is us.

"Why don't we get out of here," I say, "if you don't-like-slash-like-but-really-*don't*-like this song so much?"

"I . . . don't think I follow." Moyo chuckles.

"Is that a yes?"

He smiles in that way that says he appreciates my forwardness, and I smile in that way that says I appreciate how he's always himself too.

"Sure."

****

We step through the gym doors, tossing our goggles to Rosalind, who, for once, does not wink but looks past Moyo and me longingly. She must be getting tired of standing right on the edge of so much fun. That's the problem with putting on the show: you don't get to enjoy it yourself.

The gym sits at the end of Hell, opposite the cafeteria. Between those large rooms are the Oceanography Lab, Robotics Lab, and the Media Room. Moyo and I walk toward the cafeteria, where there's supposed to be punch and an array of processed snacks from the early 2000s, like Flamin' Hot Cheetos, Cool Ranch Doritos, and sour gummy worms. After your Bluetooth chip has registered your presence at the dance for at least one hour, you're allowed to leave and enjoy the themed snacks. The administration isn't strict about much, but they're strict about Blast from the PAAST.

"Look in there," Moyo says, pointing into the Oceanography Lab to our right.

Tanks filled with marine life conceal the outside of the Oceanography Lab. Vibrantly colored guppies, puffer fish, stingrays, starfish, and jellyfish float among the coral reefs and seaweed without a worry in the world. They create a kaleidoscope of color and light up the end of the hallway with a cozy aquamarine glow. Sometimes, students go out of their way to pass through this part of Hell before a stressful exam.

Through a gap in one of the coral reefs, I make out two small figures embracing at the far end of the Oceanography Lab. I squint my eyes.

"Oh my God. That's Jacqueline and Spencer. How'd they get in there?"

I'm wrong. They're not making out, I notice, when I take a closer look. They're holding each other. It's a tense scene. Jacqueline is whimpering, collapsed and shaking in Spencer's arm. He's standing still with a ghostly expression on his face.

"You think they got rejected today?"

Moyo and I shuffle past the Oceanography Lab; a few steps later, we're standing outside the Media Room. We pause.

"Worse. I think one of them got in, and the other . . . didn't."

Without thinking, I push the massive steel door to the Media Room. To my surprise, the door budges open. It must still be before curfew. I lost track of time at the dance. Moyo and I step inside and collapse on opposite ends of the black leather couch near the back.

"Do you think they'll stay together?" I ask. I notice Moyo's gaze ambling over my shoulder. He's staring at the computers in the control room, almost as if he's searching for some kind of explanation.

Moyo snaps his attention back to me.

"Probably not," he says.

I feel a tinge of sadness at Moyo's answer.

"But what about WAVE?" I say. "There's that XP, Fondr, that lets couples do everything together with their avatars. Watch movies, go on picnics in the park, have sex . . ."

"You know that's not the same."

"Oh really?" I smile; he teed me up perfectly. "Ever since WAVEverse got big, they've done half a dozen studies comparing the effects of the stuff you can do on WAVE with their real-life counterparts. You know what they concluded?"

Moyo clucks his tongue again. He slides down the slippery couch cushion.

"I know," Moyo says. "I just don't buy it."

"People couldn't tell the difference. There was no statistical significance between their pleasure from VR and their pleasure from the real world."

"Studies aren't perfect."

"You're right," I say, self-assured, and my friend raises an eyebrow. "Studies aren't perfect. The VR experience is probably better."

Moyo chuckles, sliding farther down the couch so that he takes up nearly two-thirds of the space. I sit squarely on my cushion at the end with my legs crossed and my fingers laced tightly over my knees.

"I'm serious," I say. "It removes all the real-world crap that gets in the way."

"Like what?"

"Like . . . Movie theaters. No sticky floors, no buttery seats, no kids making noise, no annoying couples making out in front of you. Or picnics. You don't have to deal with gnats or mosquitoes or the heat."

"But those are the things that make movies and picnics fun! Plus, there's food. That's a big hole in your argument."

"You can always switch to AR mode and eat too. You just can't share food if you're not in the same room. But they're working on that."

Moyo turns his head away, resting his chin on the back of the couch. He looks particularly attractive from this angle—older and worthy of esteem, like a military leader or a writer—and with his jaw clenched, his cheekbones steal the spotlight. He resembles his avatar more like this. I relax, unlocking my fingers and draping an arm over the back of the couch.

"You really think it's the same?"

"Better. Once they figure out taste and smell, virtual reality will be so much better than reality. Put on a haptic suit and you won't know the difference."

"Maybe you're right," Moyo says, his gaze still distracted. He rocks his arm back and forth behind the couch, grazing my wrist with every swing. "I guess it'll be a good thing, with me at Brown and you at Stanford."

"I haven't gotten in yet."

"You'll get in. We don't need data to tell us that."

My chest fills with the weight of clashing emotions. The warm satisfaction of Moyo's faith in my ability. The reminder that next year, we'll most likely be thousands of miles apart. The argument I just made that VR might render distance meaningless. Harmless. And the gut feeling that maybe Moyo is right. Maybe sitting next to each other on this physical couch is somehow different, somehow better, than sitting next to each other on a virtual one. Maybe Moyo's real finger touching my wrist transmits a different kind of electricity than his avatar fingers.

As a scientist, I believe there's only one way to test a hypothesis, to prove your instincts right or wrong.

I take Moyo's hand from behind the couch. His eyes shoot up. There's a beeping noise coming from somewhere in the room, and it clashes with the pounding of my heartbeat.

This is the logical thing to do, I tell myself. But it's also what I want. I smile at Moyo, at the perfect intersection of our Venn diagram. But I can't move. I can't set my plan into motion, literally, because the entirety of my body freezes.

Moyo catches on to what's happening. He turns his face sideways, somehow pleased with his friend's inexplicable stumble. His eyes dig deep into mine, planting a stake to mark the moment where our relationship would forever look different.

He leans in, and he kisses me.

Chapter
Fifteen

Since the beginning of time, the laws of energy have been simple. Energy can be neither created nor destroyed. Only transformed. This phenomenon is exactly what occurred that night when Moyo's and my lips touched for the very first time. For three years, a mighty storm of potential energy had been brewing between us, awaiting the moment when it would slip over the edge of the roller coaster into an endless descent of kinetic energy. Finally, it happened. And boy, did our energy change.

Over the next week, we can't get enough of each other. We're still friends, but now, something more—though what exactly isn't clear. We hang out in each other's dorm room after class, cuddling and laughing and rolling around in bed until curfew. We linger in the Media Room after Shane leaves, pretending to fine-tune frivolous design elements when really we just want to satisfy that insatiable craving. We even fool around in the HP Garage, stealing kisses in the kitchen after Shane passes out. I'm happy to have Shane around most of the time, actually. He keeps us focused with school and *Behind the Scenes*.

Exactly one week after the December dance, after Moyo leaves my room minutes before curfew, I feel a pang of guilt. For what, I don't know. The show's been giving me a lot of nebulous anxiety lately—the kind where I worry I'm not doing enough, but I don't know what else I could be doing. I've been engaging more with my fans on Zapp, in the occasional WAVEchat room, with optimally timed posts that tease future episodes. Yet I still feel like something's not right. I shift in my bed, hoping maybe a different perspective will help me figure out what I might have done wrong. Nothing. I twist my elbow into the messy mountain of sheets by my side. I fall into them, close my eyes, inhale the fabric that now smells so distinctly of Moyo's winter-fresh deodorant.

"M4rc, put on a talk show. Anything."

Of course, M4rc isn't going to fill my walls with just anything. He's well tuned to my patterns, my likes and dislikes, the many events in my life. And he has options. No fewer than three competing late-night talk shows are airing live right now, not to mention countless reruns to choose from. Of course he'll choose wisely.

MAGNUS PORCELLI

. . . truly amazing. You've had three exits worth
a total of four-point-seven billion dollars and
you still have the energy for a fourth start-
up.

                        NIKKI WALKER

[Nodding] Yep.

                         MAGNUS

    I would have bought a one-way flight to a beach
    or island by now.

[Audience laughter, zoom in on a teenage girl nodding.]

                         MAGNUS

    Hell, I would have bought the island with that
    kind of money!

I'd nearly forgotten about my encounter with Nikki Walker in
the *Scalleyrag* lobby. Good for her, I think. Finally giving the talk
show circuit another go.

                         NIKKI

    Can I be honest, Magnus?

                         MAGNUS

    Isn't everyone honest on my talk show?

                         NIKKI

    Ah, yes, just the two of us having an intimate
    conversation . . . with millions of live view-
    ers, and many more replays.

[Magnus laughs nervously, looking at Nikki with
growing eyes that strongly encourage her to stick to
the talking points.]

NIKKI

Like I was saying. It's kind of an addiction.
Ever since I was a little girl, I've gotten
off on the *high* of building something out of
nothing. First it was LEGOs, you know. Towers
and cities. By the time I was ten I was making
iPhone apps. Remember those? iPhones? Yeah, I
was obsessed. I've always been a phone girl,
so it feels good to be able to come back to my
roots with Zapp. It feels like a harking back
to the good old days of Instagram and Pinter-
est, but with better interactive features.

MAGNUS

Do you think you'll ever bring Zapp to WAVE?

NIKKI

Sure. Our product team is working on it. They're
all young and super sharp. Those kids just get
the VR trend better than I do.

MAGNUS

You mean the VR *wave*.

NIKKI

Ha.

MAGNUS

And they're getting younger! That one girl, Opal
whatshername . . .

NIKKI

Opal Hopper. Really impressive young lady.

MAGNUS

Do you remember those silly YouTube stars from back
in our day? Paul Logan, Pew Pew Pew, Tyler Oak-
tree, whatever their names were. That's what
Opal reminds me of. She's like a modern-day
YouTuber, but in 3D.

NIKKI

I think she's an entrepreneur, Magnus. She thinks
differently.

MAGNUS

Well, she sure is controversial. Did you see the
show she put on after the election? *Whew*. That
girl knows how to stir the pot. I'll tell you
this: she's a good talker.

[Nikki Walker bites her lip.]

I bite my lip too. Hard.

It kills me, the way men talk about me. Like I'm some naive
girl who just happens to be spewing the right opinions on the right
platform at the right time. Yes, men. It's almost always men who
doubt my ability, the Matthew Seamuses and Magnus Porcellis of
the world. Some of them say I'm too poised, too put together,
trying too hard. Others say I'm a lightweight, too fluffy. Whatever
they say, they never seem to take me seriously.

When I was eight years old, my dad took me to my first national chess tournament. I'll never forget the smug look on my opponent's face when he found out he was paired against me; it was like he had already won. I complained about this to my dad right before our match, and Abba said to me, "Then the boy is not as smart as he thinks he is." He was right. As I played against this boy, took his pawns and rooks, and eventually, his queen, I watched him wipe that smug look off his face. I watched it change from *I'm gonna beat the girl* to *uh oh, I'm losing to a girl* to *holy shit, I just lost to a girl*. His prejudice became my ammunition.

After I won, my dad ran over to hug me. The boy's father ran over to scold him for losing "to the girl," and when Abba heard that remark, he lost it.

"Don't ever talk about my daughter like that."

"Sir, please don't shove—"

"You low-life, redneck piece of trash. She's smarter than your—"

"Mr. Tal, if you get any closer, I'm going to have to ask you to leave."

"Abba, stop!"

Sometimes, I wonder if people are right, when they refuse to treat me or talk to me with equal respect, because I'm a girl. Maybe we live in a world where I'm not meant to succeed. A world that actively fights to limit my success. And maybe, in that same world, my dad really did bring his fate upon himself. I can't deny the note. My mom certainly didn't, when she accepted that Abba was gone forever and sent me into fits of crying and hysteria.

I need to make it to WAVEcon next month. Howie Mendelsohn wouldn't have become reclusive and closed off the walls of Palo Alto Labs if he didn't know something. I don't care if the police say he had an alibi. Maybe he bought them off.

It all comes back to our *Behind the Scenes* numbers. And right now, they're not so hot—hovering between two and three million since the election. I'm seeing loads of pop-ups for Poseidon channels on WAVE, and the fact that I'm so close to joining their coveted club kills me.

I think back to the advice Nikki Walker gave me over email, right after my run-in with Matthew Seamus. *He's hungry for a stepping-stone. Anything that'll give him hits.* Shitty blogs like *Scalleyrag* need shitty articles like his to get shitty hits to survive. More hits, more ad dollars. They have to appeal to the masses.

Use that to your advantage.

I noodle on Nikki's advice—on the idea that I can influence the media, change the way people talk about me, by knowing what they want—as I close my eyes and fall asleep. I've already done it once. I can certainly do it again.

****

"It'll only be for three weeks."

"That's twenty-one days. Five hundred and four hours. Thirty thousand, two hundred and forty minutes . . . One *million*—"

"Congratulations! You can multiply."

Moyo and I are curled up in his bed, half dressed, half wrapped in his white sheets. My bare leg dangles over the edge of the bed. I swing it back and forth, tapping my toes against the rough cardboard that makes up his makeshift drawing board. Moyo clutches my waist with his large hands to keep me from falling over.

"You really have to go to Nigeria? The holidays are going to be prime time for *Behind the Scenes*. All the legit TV programs and news shows take time off. Which is dumb, because that's when everyone is home on their laptops and WAVEs, looking for entertainment. I bet we could break five million like *that*," I snap.

Moyo pulls me up onto the bed and flips me around so that our faces rest on the same pillow—our noses a feather apart.

"I have to see my parents," he says softly. "I haven't seen them since August."

I stack my hands and rest my chin on them.

"You talk to them all the time on WAVE," I say, my head slightly elevated so that I have to peer down to see Moyo. "Your mom chats with you like every other day."

"You know that's not the same."

"You *know* I don't agree with that."

Moyo sits up against his headboard. I wave my hand in front of his Picasso Mirror to check the time. It's ten minutes before curfew.

I add, "Not to mention our viewers. They in particular would disagree."

I hop out of bed and scan the floor for my Cyber Club sweatshirt. It fell atop one of Moyo's sketches. A grand colosseum he's been working on for *Behind the Scenes*.

"Well, regardless of what you or everyone in WAVEverse

think, my parents are old-fashioned. And they're Nigerian. Being home for Christmas is a nonnegotiable."

He looks at me, expecting me to nod in agreement. Instead I pull back my hair and tie it in a tight bun, sighing.

"Well, at least *we* can keep in touch on WAVE."

"It's just three weeks. I think it will be good for us. You'll finally have time to work on that Stanford essay you've been putting off—"

"Actually, I wrote it all last night. Submitted and everything."

"What?" Moyo crawls toward the edge of his bed. "But I was over in your room last night until curfew . . ."

I take his hands and pull him up.

"Now when was the last time I went to bed at curfew?"

"Touché. Well, congratulations."

"Three weeks. Tsk, tsk. One million, eight hundred and fourteen thousand . . ."

"Don't be so dramatic. It doesn't suit you."

"Oh yeah?" I smirk. "Drama seems to be my *soupe du jour* these days, don't you think? *Hello, world! And welcome to another episode of—*"

Moyo covers my mouth, laughing into the back of his own hand.

"I'm not going to miss *Behind the Scenes* at all while I'm gone."

I yank his hand off and place it snugly around my waist.

"Well, I bet you'll miss this . . ."

I push Moyo into the wall by the door and press my lips against his. When I pull away, I catch an odd look fluttering across his face.

I go in for another kiss—this one quick—and when Moyo pulls away this time, it feels as if the distance between us has already grown.

"I'll see you in three weeks," he says, half smiling.

"I'll miss you," I say quickly, almost wishing I could take back those vulnerable words.

Moyo smiles again, wider this time.

"I miss you already."

Chapter
Sixteen

I go home for Christmas Eve. I can't skip this one. Mom always tries so hard, decorating the tree perfectly with a shining star on top and hordes of presents underneath. Abba was Jewish, and he used to tease that she never got this fired up about the menorah. In the morning, I open presents. Cashmere sweaters. An expensive bottle of perfume that I'll probably never wear. Ultra-lightweight slippers. My mom prods me about *Behind the Scenes*, and I give the bare minimum of replies.

After lunch, I post a couple of holos of my presents to Zapp, and another one juxtaposing the Christmas tree with the miniature menorah on my nightstand. Then I head back to campus. It's a ghost town, and I immediately feel a queasy sense of loneliness. Before going home, I missed Moyo a normal amount, but now that I'm back in the empty residence hall, my heart burns for his comfort.

That night, instead of practicing my lines for the upcoming episode, I get an idea. It's inspired by an ad I see on WAVE; I've been getting tons of them all day, thanks to the e-gift cards my mom got me. At first, I think it might be too forward, too ridiculous. But I decide to give it a go. I order two—one for me, and one for Moyo—and select express shipping. They should arrive by New Year's Eve.

****

"What is it?" Moyo asks, box in hand.

We're on WAVEchat, but using the augmented reality feature, I can see Moyo in his clean, minimalistic room. I hear chatter in the background. It's two hours past midnight in Lagos, and his family's New Year's party is still in full swing. Over here, it's only six p.m. We're on different continents, in different years.

"Open it." I giggle.

He looks at me suspiciously, then carefully tears open the package. Parts the cardboard. Peeks inside. "Oh Jesus."

The panicked expression on his face tells me Moyo knows exactly what he's holding.

I show him mine.

"Please tell me you don't think we should actually . . ."

"We need to try it," I insist.

"Opal, I'll be back in two weeks!"

"Yes," I say, "and I was very understanding of the fact that you needed to go home. Spend time with your family. But please, do this for *me*."

Moyo sighs.

Without another second of hesitation, he rips the airtight seal and stretches the elastic, Saran Wrap–like plastic over his arms, chest, hips, and legs. It presses in just tightly enough that he winces.

"FondrFoil . . ."

"Is for long-distance couples like us," I finish. I follow suit and wrap my FondrFoil over my tank top and leggings.

"Now what?" Moyo says.

I smile, move across my half of the WAVEchat room—which looks like my dorm—and into Moyo's half. I reach for his waist.

"Ow!" he snaps.

I jump back.

"Maybe my hand's supposed to go—"

"Whoa."

Suddenly, arrows appear, pointing me to my bed. Confused, I go and lie down.

Moyo appears right next to me.

"How are you—"

"It told me to go to my bed," he says.

"Me too."

Fondr has placed each of us in the other person's bed. From my perspective, Moyo is lying next to me on mine.

We stare at each other, right up against the precipice of the moment. Slowly, I curve my hand around Moyo's ribs, squeezing them between his body and my mattress until I land on the small of his back. It's warm, like real skin. Soft. It gives perfectly. Moyo's trembling, and naturally I go in to kiss him, but that's not part of the experience. So instead, I pull him in closer. He sighs with relief. Ease. And then he moves his hand too, both of them, first over my shoulders, down the sides of my arms. I get goose bumps.

This feels right. Moyo and I holding each other silently, thousands of miles apart but just as close as we were two weeks ago.

"Now what do we do?" he whispers.

"I—I'm not sure, but this is nice, right?"

Moyo smiles. "This," he says.

His hands drop to my waist.

"This," I say back, grinning widely.

Mine drop to his.

"And then—"

Moyo lets go abruptly when one of our doors slams open. His headset tumbles to the floor; from the corner view, I see him falling off the bed.

And in the other corner, his mom.

"Mama! You're supposed to knock!"

"Tsk, you go to school in America for three years and you forget I'm your mother. Privacy is for Americans. What are you doing on the floor?"

I'm holding my breath. I have to remind myself I'm not really there.

"And why are you covered in plastic, my son?"

Say something, Moyo. It's for a project. A new game. Anything.

But Moyo can't lie.

His mom brushes it off and says, "Your aunt and uncle wanted to say goodbye."

"I'll be out in a minute. I'm talking to Opal."

"Opal! Tell your lovely friend I say hello."

She closes the door. Moyo groans. He throws his arm over

the edge of the bed, and I take his hand in mine. Rather, his haptic glove in mine.

"That . . ."

"Was terrible," Moyo says. His headset is on speaker.

He lets go of my hand, gets up, and starts taking off the FondrFoil. It makes a sticky sound as he peels the plastic and rolls it into clumps.

"At least you're starting the new year with a bang . . ." I say.

"Watching the clock strike midnight with my eighty-year-old grandmother was more of a bang than that," he says. "That was a bust."

Moyo and I say good night before he leaves for his family obligations. Later, I watch the ball drop in Times Square on my Poly-Wall. Alone.

****

The red number hovers in the corner of my room, and I'm seriously tempted to jump out of bed and punch it.

732,999.

Those last three digits bug me the most. As if it wasn't bad enough that we're nowhere close to breaking one million views this week, that we lost our whirlpool icon, that Poseidon's trident is slipping out of our grip . . . it's our smallest audience since Hailey Carter. People don't want *Behind the Scenes* for the holidays. They want XPs where you cozy up by a virtual fireplace, or where you play the romantic darling in an old Hallmark classic. Anything to escape reality. Shane and I tried getting Moyo to design something new for us along those lines, but his family is demanding too much of his time in Lagos.

A week before Moyo returns, I get another email from Neil Finch asking if I'm free for a quick meeting. I think about texting Shane and Moyo, but they've been hot and cold about WAVEcon. Especially Moyo—it seems he just wants to stay in Palo Alto Labs' good graces until graduation. Probably best if I don't bother them.

We meet again at Philz. This time, Neil gets there first. He's sitting at the same table outside the front door when I arrive, his face buried in his phone. He's clearly on Zapp, I notice as I get closer, allowing the latest *Behind the Scenes* holos to dance in his palms. I watch myself "throw" an audience member into Taylor Swift's mouth, and in the last second of the holo, we dance happily alongside Taylor.

I clear my throat; Neil looks up at me with those piercing eyes.

"Why, if it isn't our little star. Happy new year."

Neil motions for me to take a seat. He shakes his phone twice so that the extendible screens slip back into the body, and he sets it down on the table.

As soon as I sit down, I experience a vague feeling of regret that I can't shake. It bothers me when guilt crawls under my skin like this. Maybe I'm finding myself sinking deeper in his slimy pool of quicksand.

"How are you, Mr. Finch?"

"Neil. *Please*. Call me Neil. I'm not your teacher."

Neil bows his head, a gesture that seems to imply that he and I are equals at the table of entrepreneurship.

"Terrible," he says, chomping a large bite out of his blueberry scone. "I've been terrible. Gaby Swift is going to be inaugurated soon, and she might as well take a flamethrower and burn down this entire town. Have you seen her one-hundred-day plan?"

I shake my head. I'm slightly embarrassed that I haven't read up more about the new administration.

"You should be worried, Opal. Gaby Swift and her party pose an existential threat to us all. She's proposing a bill that would limit automation and give jobs back to *people*. Factory jobs. Healthcare! Just when we've got robots taking care of our sick parents, diagnosing disease and treating illness, removing bias from the medical process . . . she wants to put our lives back in our own hands." When he says it like that, it doesn't sound so crazy. "And her robot tax proposal. Dear God. 'Companies can be more efficient, but they'll have to pay the price.' The only thing that's going to do is drive up prices for everyone."

Neil continues, "And don't get me started on Hollywood. That's how she won California, you know. She's blaming us for their struggles. Because of WAVE and all the other lovely entertainment options we've given the world, *that's* why they're failing."

Neil Finch winks at me. What is with everyone winking at me these days?

"I did hear about the human driver lanes," I say.

Neil smiles approvingly. It's an unusually bright January day, and the sun has chosen to shine strongest upon our table. Any sliminess I felt just five minutes ago seems to have been washed away entirely.

"Brilliant, right?" he scoffs. "Just what we need, Gaby Swift. Take us back to those high accident rates, and for what, a little thrill?"

A soft breeze passes.

"It all boils down to comfort with the old way of doing things," Neil says. He leans back in his chair and stretches his arms above his head. The way the light hits his face, it brings out the lines around his eyes. Slowly, he cradles his hands behind his neck and holds that position, like he's relaxing on a hammock. "It boils down to nostalgia. To *you*, Opal."

"I don't follow," I say, puzzled.

"We have data that suggests you played a not-insignificant role in getting Gaby Swift elected president," Neil says.

The way he looks at me, like he'd been building up to that final accusation—déjà vu slams me in the chest. Neil Finch: King of Burying the Lede. Master of Dropping Bombs at Philz. Destroyer of My Sanity.

"But we only had two million viewers before the election," I blurt defensively. "Two million out of a country of four hundred million."

"Have you heard of paper?"

My heart is pounding. "Is that a rhetorical question?"

"Gaby Swift's campaign is known for their flyers. The one they printed just before election day highlighted your stunt on WAVE— how you suggested many people may have secretly wanted to vote for Ms. Swift," Neil explains.

"I didn't see anything on the news, or the forums . . ."

"Our team has been working diligently to keep the story out of mainstream media," Neil says. His focus drifts down the sidewalk, to the end of the block. The metallic shine of a passing Caltrain flickers through the trees. "It's a bad look for the platform. For you."

"I— What can I do to fix it?" I realize I'm shaking my leg intensely. I try to stop. I might as well stop breathing, from the sheer magnitude of what Neil is saying.

"That's what we're working on."

Neil Finch turns his head to the side, his expression flat and cavernous, erasing any notion that the two of us are equal. His mind is still somewhere else. Part of me wonders if he's actually bluffing, and if that bluff is part of some grand scheme of his. Of Palo Alto Lab's. Of Howie Mendelsohn's.

He darts his attention back to me.

"I want you to meet Howie, Opal. I really do. But you have no idea the amount of stress he's under right now."

"But WAVEcon is in less than two weeks, and you said . . ."

"With the state of the country right now, WAVEcon is the least of our concerns. I can't even guarantee it's still going to happen, let alone that Howie will be there to meet and greet creators like you."

"But you said if we hit Poseidon status . . ."

"I understand where you're coming from, Opal. I really do." Neil looks down at my quivering leg, and he moves his hand closer to mine on the table. "When I was younger, I lost my parents in a car accident—"

"My dad's not dead."

Neil Finch and I both jerk our hands back.

"I'll tell you what," he says. "You keep working on *Behind the Scenes.* Keep exposing the truth and making yourself heard. Though I recommend avoiding politics, at least for the time being. I'll work on WAVEcon and Howie. He's always had a soft spot for his Poseidon channels; I'm sure we could work something out if you earn yourself that golden trident."

A devilishly handsome grin escapes Neil Finch's lips, exposing a mouthful of pearly white teeth. He smiles so widely it practically wraps around the back of his head and pats himself on the back.

I ask, "Do you have any advice for us?"

"Hmm." He scratches his chin. "You could always spruce up the XP design. You've had the same one for, what, an entire month now?"

"Our designer, Moyo—"

"Interesting name. Where's he from?"

"Nigeria."

"Interesting."

"He's working on this epic colosseum," I say. "Our numbers show that little changes in venue don't seem to affect audience growth very much. But a big change—that will be worth talking about, both on the XP and in the comments."

Neil waves his hand in the air, as if brushing off everything I've just said.

"There's that old adage," he goes, leaning across the table, getting a bit too close. "*Sex sells.* I'm not saying you need to get naked or anything. But change up your avatar. There's a start. Reveal a bit more. Open up."

Whether he's talking about my body, my personal life, or my past, I honestly don't know. That's the scariest part.

Chapter

Seventeen

It occurs to me that night that I might never find my dad if I put all my eggs in one basket, especially when the White House could pulverize that basket by Easter, so I reach back out to Amber Donahue. I'd tried emailing her just before Thanksgiving, but that was her dad's birthday and she said it wasn't a good time. I emailed her again in December, but she was busy with finals. Maybe she didn't want to talk to me. Maybe she'd made a mistake. I mean, a *friend* of my dad's? My dad barely tolerated his own colleagues in the computer science department. I just couldn't picture him skipping across campus for a friendly lunch with Amber's father, who taught political theory.

Still, a lead is a lead. And with Neil Finch and Howie Mendelsohn jerking me around harder than a sinusoidal function, I feel an urge to put my detective hat back on and hear what she has to say.

This time when I email Amber, she responds right away. We hop on a video call.

"Hello!"

"Hi, Opal."

"I'm—it's nice to meet you. I have to say, I was surprised when I got your message back in October. I didn't think my dad had any friends at Stanford," I say, sitting at the edge of my bed with my back straight.

"I didn't either. About my dad, that is." Amber scrunches up her button-shaped face, which is blown up on my PolyWall. I notice the light blue scarf draped around her neck and the lion teddy bear tucked into the pillow on her bed. She's a Columbia student, but I already knew that from the internet. "Sorry, it's still hard talking about my dad after he died."

A chill runs from my tightly wound fingers to my toes.

"Do you mind if I ask . . ."

"Suicide," Amber says quickly.

"Right. I remember. I'm so sorry."

"I always assumed he took his life because of his depression. He'd had it under control for as long as I knew him, but we moved to Estonia and all of us were a little lonely there . . . But after I read about you in *Scalleyrag*, I remembered something. Howie Mendelsohn had visited us the year before my dad took his life."

My eyes pop out of my head. "Howie Mendelsohn *visited* you?"

"Yeah."

"Like, real-world visited? He got out of his office and took an actual plane and showed up at your doorstep in *Estonia*."

"Yes," Amber says, and her expression is a combination of annoyed and hurt. I let her talk. "It was three years ago. I was working on my college apps and went into Papa's office to ask if he had any connections in the admissions world. He was with this man who kind of looked like a washed-up opera singer. He was wearing a black suit with a white dress shirt, collar super unbuttoned, and he had a virtual reality headset tucked underneath his armpit. I didn't think much of it, until I saw the picture in the *Scalleyrag* post about you. That was the guy. He had a beard back then, but I still recognized him."

"You never asked your dad—"

"I was too busy with apps," Amber says, her voice strained.

"How long ago was this?"

"Three years ago. We had moved to Estonia four years before that."

I do the math in my head. "You moved right when my dad disappeared."

Amber nods. "That's the weird part. After I read your story, I went back to my dad's calendar. He wasn't a big computer guy, but he kept a detailed log of his daily schedule in this leather-bound notebook. He had met with your dad and Howie Mendelsohn twice the summer before we moved."

My chest rises and falls slowly. If Howie and Neil had jerked me around before, then Amber Donahue was throwing me an inverse function.

"What do you think all this means?" she asks.

"I don't know yet. But I appreciate you telling me."

I hold my breath and take a good look at Amber Donahue. We've endured the same loss. She's telling the truth. Yet not a single corner of my brain is able to do the math and solve for x in this complicated equation.

On the second-to-last day of winter break, I find myself sitting alone on the bench I usually share with Moyo. The wind whips my hair, tossing and twisting it in funny ways. Delivery drones whiz through the air en route to the post center, probably with late Christmas gifts or holiday shopping spree purchases.

I crane my head backward, looking up at my windowsill. Just three months ago, Neil Finch had sent one of those drones with a present to help me. I think to myself, *He wouldn't mess with me. He's direct. He's on our side. Right?* Or is there something bigger going on, more dangerous, that has to do with why Amber and I both lost our fathers after they'd crossed paths with Howie Mendelsohn?

Over in the street, I notice a sophomore from my shop class getting out of a sleek black car, hauling his suitcase and duffle bag. People are starting to come back to campus. Moyo will be back tomorrow.

****

The next morning, I'm at the Picasso Mirror, exploring some of the more intricate makeup options, when my phone buzzes.

MOYO (1:12 p.m.)
Good news! Landing in an hourish.

SHANE (1:13 p.m.)
W00T! Finally! I was getting sick of spending all
this time with Opal.

I wonder if Shane even has an inkling about our romance. He said something over winter break about how "refreshing" it was, spending time with me. Sometimes I forget that I was friends with Shane long before I'd even met Moyo.

As I lean in closer to the mirror to apply the tiniest dash of black eyeliner, my phone buzzes again. I should ignore it. I should focus on the fine details of my makeup. But out of habit, I swipe it off the table.

MOYO (1:13 p.m.)
Bad news. Totally forgot about my big AP Government project this week. Group's been working on it all day. Have to join them as soon as I land.
Ugh.

SHANE (1:13 p.m.)
All good, Moyo-dude.

SHANE 1:15 p.m.)
HP House tonight?

MOYO (1:15 p.m.)
Why?

SHANE (1:16 p.m.)
To celebrate the new year . . . And work . . . And celebrate . . .

I check my private thread with Moyo. Nothing. I refresh it four times, in case the connection went bad or something. (Not like that ever happens.) I flutter my eyes and shake my head. No. I won't be the type of girl to worry over Moyo not making concrete plans to see me when he lands. I won't be the type of girl to wonder why he texted the group thread and not me, individually, about his group project. I won't let my imagination run amok with excuses for how Moyo, the most responsible member of any group project, could have possibly forgotten about this meeting.

I set my phone at the base of the Picasso Mirror, finish applying the eyeliner, and calmly instruct M4rc to text back my friends.

OPAL (1:18 p.m.)
Let's do it! Whenever your project's done, Moyo.

****

New year, same Undetectables.

We scurry away just minutes after midnight on an abnormally balmy January night. Northern California's microclimates have that effect. The weather warms and cools as it pleases—unfazed by seasons or what the weather looks like thirty miles away. For all I know, it could be snowing in San Francisco.

Something is off with Shane at the HP House. When Moyo and I take our usual seat on the ancient living room couch, he snaps at us to be careful with the upholstery. Since when does

Shane care about some tattered, knockoff floral print from the 1950s? Then, when I'm quizzing Moyo about his three weeks in Lagos—the bustling streets, the peddlers who still sell selfie sticks, the Nigerian mothers and grandmothers who continue to carry baskets atop their heads in the most modern city on the African continent, a city that was the first outside America to embrace driverless cars . . . Shane just completely loses it.

"We get it! Lagos is cool!" His eyes bug, and he balls his fists tightly. "It's, like, San Francisco in Africa! Why don't you two just strap on your headsets and go for a walk on Ozumba Ma, Maba . . ."

"Ozumba Mbadiwe Avenue," Moyo corrects, eyeing Shane like he's holding a ticking time bomb. "It's, um, not actually such a picturesque road."

"I don't care."

Silence balloons in the room. It's the awkward kind where we're all sitting around waiting for someone to pop.

"Forget about it." Shane finally surrenders, slumping in his seat. "Why don't we just get back to *Behind the Scenes*."

"Shane, chill. We'll get to work soon, promise." I twist my face. "But weren't you the one saying we should relax and celebrate tonight?"

Moyo chuckles. "If Opal's all right with chilling—"

"I know about you guys."

My pulse freezes. I clench the wooden arm of the couch, digging my fingers into the upholstery's ropey roots. Moyo's eyes grow big with fear and confusion.

"Come on. How much longer did you think you could keep it a secret?" Shane inches his chair closer. "To be honest, I didn't even figure it out on my own. Heather Lowenstein told me. You two are so blind you didn't even notice when you were hugging in the cafeteria the day before winter break. In a *very* friendly way, she made sure to add."

Moyo and I have grown so tense we can't even speak. Shane rolls his eyes, pulling his Rubik's Cube key chain out of his pocket. As if ending the one-sided conversation, he tucks his head down and starts solving. Of course, this isn't his first Rubik's rodeo, and in no fewer than fifteen seconds he has six bright colors on each side.

"I'm just saying. I felt like an idiot when Heather told me. She assumed I already knew, that you guys had the courtesy to tell me first . . . even if you wanted to keep it a secret from everyone else, for whatever reason," Shane mumbles.

He jams the key chain back into his pocket. I swallow dry air. It's like Shane just lodged the Rubik's Cube right in the depths of my throat.

"I should have known, right?"

I look to Moyo, whose expression has morphed from fear to a mix of regret, apology, and honest shock. Not from Shane finding out, but from the way Shane is expressing how he feels about finding out, in such an elaborate way. This monologue is the most Shane has ever said to us—from his heart—since the three of us became friends.

"Are you guys going to say something?" Shane shakes his head. "Look. I shouldn't have to read your minds like you're one of those people on WAVE. If we're going to keep lying to each other like this, then I'm out."

Typically, whenever problems arise in my life, I deal with them head-on. I reason things logically. From the fairness of my brain. But my relationship with Moyo, just like my search for my father, and how it oscillates depending on the day—it's not like they're illogical. After all, I think about them often, deeply, rationally . . . but the feelings come from somewhere else. I don't know. I guess it's my heart.

My heart doesn't know what to say to Shane here.

"Guys. Come on. Say something."

My heart wants this conversation to be over, to be swept under the rug. For an earthquake or natural disaster to make it all go away.

And there it is.

"What was that?"

"Holy shit."

A knock on the door.

Chapter
Eighteen

"What do we do?"

"Just ignore it. It's probably a lost homeless person or something."

"There aren't homeless people in Palo Alto."

Three more knocks in quick succession, each one pounding the old, wooden door harder than the last. And then, a flat-palmed *whack*.

"That doesn't sound like someone who's lost," I whisper. "It sounds like someone who knows exactly where they are."

Shane shrinks into his seat. It can't be his parents on the other side; they would have simply unlocked the door. But that means it's someone who could *tell* Shane's parents—leaving him royally screwed. The intruder keeps knocking and knocking, using both hands now, an urgent drumbeat that vibrates through every bone in my body.

Soon, a muffled voice shouts over the knocking.

"*Let me in!*

"*Opal, Moyo, Shane, I know you're in there.*"

Moyo stands up to face us, crouching for no reason.

"We have to let them in."

Before Shane and I can object, Moyo tiptoes over to the door, twists the lock, and cracks it open an inch.

Stunned, he takes a step back. The door swings open all the way, nearly hitting the wall.

"Finally. Jeez."

"Kara?"

Before the pitch-black curtain of Palo Alto at night, Kara Lee looks more villainous than ever before. Her arms tremble by her side—the aftershock from all that knocking—while she huffs and puffs like she's blown the house down. And yet her face is totally calm. That has to be the creepiest part.

"How did you . . ." I begin.

Kara cocks her head.

"You think you're the only ones who can sneak out?"

"That's not what I meant," I say. I do notice that Kara isn't dressed in her usual wardrobe of expensive leather jackets and snakeskin boots. She's wearing a black hoodie with tight leggings. And Kara Lee never dresses down. Even around the dorms, she makes a point of wearing her bathrobe from the Ritz-Carlton. "What I meant was . . . How did you find us?"

Kara steps inside, shutting the hefty door behind her. She takes a moment to survey the inside of this historic house: the polished cherry of the dining room table and its ten matching chairs, the landscape painting hanging on a single nail, the faded oscillator on the mantel above the fireplace.

"People talk."

"They sure do," Shane grumbles, eyeing Moyo and me on the couch. The two of us couldn't be sitting farther apart.

Kara doesn't get the reference, nor does she care.

"Whatever. It doesn't matter *how*, only that I heard about these off-campus meetings of yours. Doesn't make sense, if I'm being honest. A bunch of VR nerds want to hang out after curfew and they can't just use WAVEchat? Come on, people. It's not 2020. I figured there had to be some kind of logical reason, so I—"

"You followed us."

"I *tagged along*, Opal. Don't be so accusatory." Kara steps closer. "Last I checked, nobody was allowed to leave campus after curfew."

My heart sinks.

"Now—we've talked about this before, haven't we? How I'm so, *so* impressed with all the work you've done on *Behind the Scenes*? I mean, gosh. I never would have expected it to take off the way it did."

"Cut the crap, Kara. What do you want?" I ask.

Drama has always been Kara Lee's preferred route. But just as she was willing to forgo a glitzy outfit for the evening, she's more than capable of cutting her act a little short.

"I want back in."

"Shocker. And no."

Kara stomps a foot and balls up her fists. Her jaw becomes tense, and she appears to swallow something. Maybe gum. Maybe her pride.

"Opal."

"Kara."

"You are *beyond* impossible."

"If I'm impossible, then you're Fermat's last theorem."

"See! That's exactly why you need me!" Kara digs her fingers in her hair, its sheen less glossy than usual tonight, more like the surface of a chalkboard. "Weren't you saying back in August that you had *zero* interest in getting in front of cameras? That you were doing this for the, what did you call it . . . the technical thrill? Honestly, you might be a better actress than I am. Your whole 'Hello, world! I'm Opal Hopper' act that you put on each week?" Kara harrumphs. "Everyone at school knows you're the brainy, nerdy type."

Even with the air quotes around "brainy" and "nerdy," I'm actually flattered by Kara's rant. I've always prided myself in my intelligence. Everyone at PAAST does. The way I'm talked about in the media these days, even in Hell, I was starting to wonder if I still come off smart.

Kara continues: "Look, Opal. You don't want to be doing this alone."

I roll my eyes. "Funny of you to say that. Remember freshman year, when they seated us by middle school at orientation and you completely ignored Shane and me? You left us hanging. I know we were never the best of friends, but as soon as you got to PAAST, you had your eye on the Silicon Valley crown, and you got it."

Even without peeling my attention away from Kara, I can feel the curious looks from Shane and Moyo darting in my direction.

"It's more complicated than that," Kara says, her eyes dropping.

That word stings when Kara says it—*complicated*. I had confided in her about my complicated past once, and she listened.

"Okay, yes," she admits, "I came into PAAST with other *goals*, and I got them—but I didn't always have full control over them. Which is why I'm telling you that what you're doing is only going to get worse with all the extra attention."

"And you don't think I can handle it?"

"I don't think you *deserve* it. Me?" She shrugs. "I'm superficial. Good attention or bad attention, it's all the same to me."

I roll my eyes. Kara, who's been standing on the border between the dining room and living room, steps fully into the latter.

"Look, Opal. You're smart. *Beyond* smart. We both remember AP Chem, how you nearly died when the bot paired us up." Kara rolls her eyes. "You literally didn't let me touch a single beaker all year. And we got an A+."

"Yeah, because half the time you were Hyperlooping down to LA for some audition."

Kara opens her mouth to defend herself. *It was, like, five days total! I got called back for the Chazelle movie! I couldn't not show up!* I've heard these excuses already, back when I gave Kara a poor rating in our lab partner evaluation.

But she stops herself.

"We're not in chem lab anymore," Kara says firmly.

"I know."

"You're building a media empire."

"I know."

"You need to share the beakers."

From the desperation in Kara's eyes, I'd almost think someone else was putting her up to this. I look to Moyo and Shane for relief, but they clearly have no intention of getting involved. Moyo's taken out his phone, the ultimate symbol of neutrality, and he's half-heartedly scrolling through old Zapps, while Shane—who already got his fill of confrontation—is now curled up in a ball.

"I *know*."

I want nothing more than for Kara Lee to leave. But if there's one thing Kara knows how to do, it's stay. And talk.

"Do you, really? I'm not sure if you remember, but our country is about to be run by some anti-tech dimwits. Now, I know my dad didn't help us out the way we were expecting when I was on the show. But he's powerful. You can't deny that. And if Gaby Swift and her crew come after WAVE, you want someone like him—like *me*—on your side."

"What are you saying, Kara? You want me to just give you the show?"

"Don't be ridiculous," Kara scoffs. "You're the face of *Behind the Scenes* now. You're Opal Hopper. But that doesn't mean you can't go a little vintage with an old face."

I consider the idea, but before I can make a verdict, something rustles in the corner of the room and startles everybody.

"It's not such a terrible idea, Opal."

"Seriously, Shane?"

"Sure," he says shyly. "It would be nice to have another person on the team."

"Plus it's only fair," Kara adds quickly.

Without realizing it, I explode with laughter. I look at Moyo, whose face has turned stone cold, and I cover my mouth right away—an attempt that ends up backfiring with snot all over my hands.

"Fine!" I say with an exaggerated expression of defeat. "Not because you followed us out here and have dirt on us now. Or because your dad is literally the twenty-seventh richest man in the country. But because of *fairness*."

The way Kara smiles nervously—like she's just won a steep, uphill battle—gives me exactly what I wanted. Schadenfreude.

With Moyo and Shane, I've been the unequivocal leader of the pack. I wasn't about to let that change with the intrusion of a rich and popular drama queen. Besides, I was thinking earlier today about inviting Kara and some of the theater girls onto *Behind the Scenes*. If we have any chance at becoming a Poseidon channel before WAVEcon, we're going to need to pull out all the stops. More segments. More faces. More work.

I was just showing Kara Lee who's boss.

****

It turns out having Kara around isn't so bad. Our first day as a team, she waltzed into the Media Room singing a sexy love ballad she heard on WAVE; the next day it was a Gregorian chant. This is a version of Kara Lee we didn't see earlier in the school year, when we were her minions. Her antics have even been making Shane smile, which is no small feat.

Kara doesn't just sing her mind; she speaks it too. She has no filter. When Moyo shows off his latest designs for the colosseum, Shane and I applaud him for his effort. But Kara asks why he's drawn modern theater seats for the audience, rather than more authentic stone benches. Clearly not for comfort. In a VR venue, you wouldn't feel the difference.

Though I'm more concerned about filling the seats.

"Stop worrying so much," Shane says as we wind through Friday morning traffic in Hell. We never resolved our fight from the other night, but that hasn't stopped me from complaining to Shane about our channel's numbers all week.

"I feel stuck."

"Have you been looking at your comments?"

"Of course I have. I've been sifting through them every night, trying to come up with another edgy topic for—"

"Opal, I mean the ones about *you*. People really like you."

"Then where are those people?" I widen my eyes. They sting, bloodshot from all the hours I've been staring at screens this week.

"Waiting in the wings for you," Shane chides, turning in at the Oceanography Lab. He tips his head back around. "I don't know if you realize this, Opal Hopper, but you have fans. And they want to know more about who you are."

****

That weekend, I search my name. I've been avoiding this particular form of narcissism on principle—not because I don't have an ego like everyone else, but because of how viciously it affected me seven years ago.

The search bar takes over my PolyWall, a soft white rectangle awaiting my query. I croak my name. I'm expecting the auto-fill suggestions to populate with words like "opal hopper dad" or "opal hopper howie mendelsohn." In my mind, people are hunting for "opal hopper grope replay," or maybe they're looking to take me down with "opal hopper privacy is it legal."

But that's not what floats to the top of the list.

opal hopper boyfriend

I'm reminded of what Neil Finch had said the other day. *Sex sells.* He must be searching my name more than I have.

I'm reminded of what Nikki Walker said about Matthew Seamus.

He's hungry for a stepping-stone. Anything that'll give him hits. Use that to your advantage.

I get an idea.

Sunday night, after I steal away from Moyo's room just before curfew, I decide to email him about a topic we've been discussing on and off.

Moyo,

I get what you were saying. It would be messy if people found out. Relationships are hard, but they're even harder when one party is a minor celebrity and the other party has to find a way to tell their more culturally conservative mom who doesn't want him dating until he's 30.

But wasn't Kara a reminder that people are going to find out anyway?

I haven't been able to say this to you in person, and I know we've only been "dating" for a month. But you've been my best friend for a lot longer than that, so here goes nothing.

I love you. There, I said it. I love you, Moyo Adeola.

Ok. I just needed to get that off my chest. When you see me tomorrow . . . Well, no pressure. Just wink once if you love me too, and wink twice if you want to pretend I never wrote this email. I'll understand.

—Opal

If there's one thing I've learned over the years, it's how to channel my passion to get what I want.

"Send to . . . Moyosore," I say to M4rc.

Something's wrong. M4rc knows it. I haven't used Moyo's full name since we first met, and I hesitated before uttering his name.

I mumbled the word, *Moyosore*, almost unintelligibly.

"Send to Moyo?" M4rc double-checks.

"No."

At this point, I have three options. I can choose to hit Send on this spur-of-the-moment email to Moyo. I can choose to delete it from existence.

Or I can choose to follow through on my original idea, duplicitous as it is.

"Send the email to . . . Matthew Seamus."

M4rc does not respond immediately.

"Are you sure you would like to send the email addressed to—"

"Yes."

I bury my face into my sheets. I grab a pillow and cover my head, pressing down so hard my ears hurt. I remind myself of the logic behind this wicked scheme. How if people are really interested in my life, then they'll salivate over a story about my secret relationship with my co-founder. How dropping this kind of news the morning before an episode could inject new life into *Behind the Scenes*. How it doesn't matter if you're dealing with Silicon Valley or Hollywood, Capitol Hill or high school. Sex always sells.

I tell myself it will distract from any gossip about "Opal Tal." Her past. The girl I was before I'd met Moyo.

In all my years, I've never done anything so categorically wrong. I can even sense the judgment in M4rc's tone.

I'm betraying the one person who would never betray me.

But sooner or later, the truth is going to come out. It always does. Matthew Seamus already dug up that old gossip about my dad; it's only a matter of time before he gets to my boyfriend. I might as well beat him to the punch. For once, I'm controlling my story—the way I wasn't able to control it all those years ago.

Better to control the truth and get something out of it.

"Email sent."

Chapter

Nineteen

Well, here's a juicy start to the workweek! Opal Hopper, the Princess of Palo Alto, seems to have found her prince.

And get this: She plucked him from within the kingdom.

Yes, Ms. Hopper is said to be dating **Moyo Adeola**, her co-founder and chief design guru. The two are seniors at the Palo Alto Academy of Science and Technology. Mr. Adeola is one of the school's prestigious Musk Scholars, awarded annually to five international students. Don't get too impressed. Since PAAST is a full-scholarship high school for all students, the "scholarship" is just a name, covering up the fact that they only accept five students from outside the US each year.

But enough about Mr. Adeola's credentials. *Scalleyrag* has learned that he and Ms. Hopper have been dating since as early as December, when the two were spotted dancing verrrry intimately at a Blast from the PAAST dance. (Don't ask.) (Actually, do. Because then you'll understand how truly weird nerds can be. And, like us, you'll scratch your head wondering how these socially inept beings may, someday, take over the world. If the robots don't beat them to it.)

Where were we? Ah, yes. The dance. Ms. Hopper and Mr. Adeola were spotted dancing in a special Palo Alto Labs–sponsored augmented reality environment to old hits such as "Hey Ya!" and "Shake It Off." Notably missing was co-founder Shane Franklin.

This reporter, for one, is happy to hear there's at least one start-up that is willing to "shake" things up beyond their product.

Step it up, Silicon Valley! Have some fun. Date your co-founders. All the cool kids are doing it. Literally. The kids.

More updates on the Prince and Princess of Silicon Valley to come.

In the meantime, make sure to snag a seat for the newest episode of *Behind the Scenes*, airing today on WAVE.

****

It's not just *Scalleyrag* this time. Every journalist with the slightest interest in Silicon Valley, every news bot running off a half-decent algorithm, picks up the story.

BUZZFEED: *Behind the scenes . . . on this hot, young WAVE couple*

DAZED: *Viral teen sensation dating behind-the-scenes set designer*

RECODE: *High School Never Ends: Start-Up with a Side of Budding Romance*

News of our relationship reaches far and wide—much farther, and far wider, than any story about the show since the election. We contain multitudes now. We're not just mind readers and invaders of privacy; we're human beings with our own secrets and drama. That's what people want right now—something to take their minds off the impending doom of inauguration.

When M4rc reads the pinnacle aloud, just minutes after it was posted, I fully expect Moyo to come running into my room. But he never comes. As I step out into the chilly January morning and cross the lawn, slippery and damp under my feet, I keep an eye on my phone. But it never buzzes.

Then I see him from across the Sphinx. He's towering over a sea of freshmen who are sitting in the corner by the water fountain, where Jacqueline and Spencer used to lie on their bellies and cuddle.

Moyo looks anything but cuddly.

I weave my way around bodies, backpacks, and laptops. For once, I don't consider the most efficient path through the Sphinx. I move along the sides of invisible rectangles, not the diagonals, getting stuck behind people because, for once, I have absolutely no desire to reach my destination as quickly as possible.

"Hey."

What feels like an eternity later, I'm standing across from

Moyo. There's at least an arm's length between us. Freshmen take turns peeking up at us from the floor. I think I see one pointing nosily.

Moyo steps closer.

And he kisses me. Quickly, but publicly.

"Whoa," I say.

Moyo leans in closer. "This is completely nuts," he whispers into my ear. "I can't believe Matthew Seamus posted that pinnacle. What an opportunistic pig."

I hold my breath.

"Are you all right?"

"I was livid half an hour ago. But I'm fine now. It was bound to happen, right?"

"Mmhm. Yeah." I peek down at the freshmen out of the corner of my eye. One of them has strapped on his WAVE headset and is "watching" Moyo and me, the red recording light on the front of his goggles flashing.

"Hey," Moyo says, pulling away. He looks at me with tender eyes, with the same genuine concern he had for Shane right after his MIT rejection. "Hey. Don't look so sad. You didn't do anything wrong. It's not so bad, I think."

I turn my back so I'm blocking Moyo from the peeping freshman.

"Lunch in the Media Room?" I say softly.

Moyo nods. I swivel around and scurry off. My legs are trembling, my stomach's twisted, and I want nothing more than to barge into a bathroom stall and bawl my eyes out over the cold toilet seat.

Instead, I head straight to first period.

****

"You guys, I'm getting Zapp'd so hard I think I'm gonna die of electrocution."

Moyo closes his eyes and sticks his tongue out, and without any warning, he shakes his arms and legs spastically. His body goes limp while Kara and Shane die of laughter. We're all sitting around the table nearest the steel doors of the Media Room, a table we never touched before Kara joined the team. We've been meeting here since she joined; with four of us, the control room was starting to get cramped.

"Seriously," Moyo continues, waking up to grab another slice of the pizza that Kara ordered from Z's. "One of them even sent me a death threat! He said he had this grand plan to meet Opal and marry her someday. Creepy, right? But apparently he's a big fan and has been watching since day one."

Kara lifts her chin, impressed.

"Day one?"

"Yes, ma'am. I cross-checked his Zapp profile with our audience data. He's been watching since the first episode." Moyo chews and swallows. *"Live."*

"Damn," Kara says. "You pissed off one of the O.G. viewers."

"It wasn't a very good death threat, if you ask me. Even for a holo. One second I was holding hands with Opal, and the next second I was a splattered tomato."

"You and this pizza have that in common," Shane says, bringing the slice to Moyo's nose before taking a giant bite.

The three of them laugh.

I haven't uttered a single word since we sat down. I'm resting both my elbows on the plasma-screened table, taking minuscule bites out of the same slice of pizza. I focus all my energy on eating. Make a system of it. One bite from the left side, one bite from the right. Two left. Two right.

I feel like a robot—all my emotion, drained. The entire morning I've been dealing with one surprise after another. Surprised with my own reaction to this publicity stunt I chose to pull. Surprised with Moyo's positive response. Surprised with the way Moyo texted Shane and Kara about it on our group thread:

> Now all we need is for the two of you to strike up some romance, and we'll literally dominate the news!

Surprised with how he's embracing the scandal, enjoying it, even joking about it.

Surprised with Shane's nonchalance about the world finding out just days after he did. Surprised with the pizza Kara ordered for the team. Surprised with Moyo's open-mouthed chewing. Usually he has manners.

I should feel relieved, not surprised. Right? My first major betrayal, and I'm coming out unscathed. But somehow, the outcome feels wrong. Like I'm to blame for this Moyo I don't recognize. Because the Moyo I know isn't even ready to reveal our relationship to his family and friends, let alone to millions of strangers on the internet.

"Can you believe it?" he says, showing off his Zapp profile. "Now I understand how Opal feels every single day. Before this morning I had, what, one hundred? Two hundred followers? Check it out. Almost ten *thousand*."

This is a Moyo drunk on fame. I know how it works. Soon enough, the hangover will kick in, and his real feelings will follow.

I know what I need to do. I need to be honest first.

"Guys."

Whatever joke they're laughing about, they stop. The holos continue to roll from the center of the table on Moyo's phone, but Moyo's, Kara's, and Shane's heads all turn to me.

"It's my fault."

I'm going to tell them the truth.

"I wrote a private email last night that I meant to send to Moyo, but I accidentally sent it to Matthew Seamus instead."

Sort of.

As soon as the words spill out, I realize I've dug myself an even deeper grave. I try my very hardest to play it cool. I suck in my lips. My eyes dart from Moyo to Shane to Kara and then to nobody at all, because I can't bear to look at their speechless faces. Playing it cool means acting guilty. And I'm guilty, all right—in ways my friends don't even realize.

The first person to speak is Shane. He doesn't use words. He begins cracking his knuckles, loudly, and tapping his foot at a rate of approximately a million taps per second. He raises his eyebrows as if he's sucking on the sourest lime in the world, and then he tilts his head as if to say, *Well, shit happens.*

Kara looks across the table at Shane, and, with a singular nod, she agrees with his sentiment.

The last person to chime in is Moyo.

"What did you write in this private email?" he finally says.

"It's not important," I mutter, pressing my thumb into the inside of my wrist. I stare at the white around the fingernail.

"How in the world did you—"

"It was late. I was tired. Last night, after I got back to my room." I look up, knowing that Moyo will remember exactly why I was up late last night. Where I was before I wrote that email. The conversation we were having about our relationship: *What* are we? Those are the secrets we shared, just the two of us. I look at him intensely, and I feel him trusting me again. "I got back and I *needed* to email you about . . . well, us. I was just completely emotional, and when I started typing your name, the drop-down—"

"Moyo. Matthew." He sighs, rubbing his temples. "I understand."

I go back to my warm wrist.

"So it could have been avoided," he says to himself, glaring at his reflection on the table. "But . . . I don't know. Maybe, maybe not."

"Moyo?"

"Don't worry about it, Opal." He forces a smile. "Shit happens, as they say. Even Opal Hopper makes mistakes. Right?"

I smile back, dimly.

"Right."

Maybe Kara wasn't kidding, I think to myself as Moyo steers the conversation back into lighthearted Zapp fare.

Maybe I really am the better actress.

Episode 020

From the darkness of my Invisigogs, I hear Moyo counting down: *"Three, two, one . . ."*

And there they are, like a chaotic flash before my eyes.

The newly designed colosseum lights up with the precise shade of honeysuckle yellow recommended by an algorithm. It's a glowing stadium—modeled after the Roman landmark. Fifty thousand seats are filled to the brim, the rows stretching around and beyond my line of vision, topped off with crumbling arches.

It strikes me that this audience before my eyes is merely 2 percent of the total number of people watching right now. I can flip through fifty other colosseums. The avatars in this colosseum are just the ones who had "arrived" earliest. Some of them might have camped out in WAVEverse for hours. Maybe all day. The ones who didn't pay for SpotSaver must have entered our channel and left their headsets alone for a long time.

We've never had anywhere close to this many live viewers. Not that our numbers even matter at this point—the golden trident appeared next to our channel just after lunch, and as I was walking to the Media Room, I got an email from Neil Finch with our official invitation to WAVEcon. The buzz must have been enough to cinch our spot.

I was holding Moyo's hand a minute ago, squeezing tight, when Kara came up and swiftly karate-chopped our hands apart.

"I don't care if you guys are in love," she snapped. "This is my first show. A lot is at stake. This has got to be the best episode yet."

For the first time since starting *Behind the Scenes*, I get cocky about our success. On-air.

                  OPAL

Hello, world! And welcome—

I look straight into the camera.

                  OPAL

To our biggest—

Get inside their heads.

                  OPAL

Episode—

And steal their hearts.

                  OPAL

Yet.

Chapter
Twenty

The morning of WAVEcon, I'm waiting for my friends on a couch in the residence hall lounge when a girl comes up to me. She's short and pretty, and I recognize her as one of the overeager freshmen who signed up for every club the first week of school. She stands a few feet back, underneath an elaborate light fixture.

"Hi," she squeaks. "I'm sure you're constantly getting bombarded with attention from underclassmen like me—"

"People have actually been pretty cool about it," I say.

"Oh." She blushes.

"Sorry, that wasn't, like, a hint or anything."

"Oh! In that case, I just want to say that you're my role model."

Now I'm blushing too.

"I'm trying this thing where I'm more direct with people," she says, cracking her knuckles, "and I thought I'd start with you, since you're officially, like, the most honest and direct person ever. The *queen* of directness. Anyway, I watch your XP, and I think you're just so strong, so smart, so unapologetically fierce."

"You really don't have to . . ."

"I'm from Ohio and my parents want me to become a bioengineer, but I don't know how to tell them I don't *know*, you know? Like, yes, we're smart, but we're so much more than our brains. Like you! You're getting recognized—"

"Opal, are you ready?" Moyo appears at the entrance, the sun glowing strong behind him. "Everyone's waiting for you outside."

****

We take a car to San Jose, and as soon as we step out, I hear angry chants from a protest. I look across the street from the convention center and see a crowd of men and women with wacky haircuts and American flag shirts, holding signs with phrases like THERE'S A NEW WAVE COMING and BEHEAD THE HEADSET.

"They already won the election," Shane mutters. "Can't they let us have this one thing?"

The mood is completely different on the other side. Hundreds of people have spilled out of the convention center, and as we cross the pavilion, the excitement drowns out the protesters' noise. We're swallowed up by what can only be described as a fangasm. Clusters of WAVE fans have gathered out here, and they're all hugging and shaking hands like they've known each other forever. Like they've waited their entire lives for this day. I spot a couple of Timmy shirts in the mix and steer clear of those groups. There are even reps from Palo Alto Labs outside, wearing dimpled smiles and showing off the latest equipment.

My eyes bounce around like crazy. They jump from a boy in a

full haptic suit hopping off a short ledge to a rainbow-haired girl twirling in circles with her arms spread wide to a group of Star Trek fans decked out in headsets performing some sort of chant.

It crosses my mind that Howie Mendelsohn might be standing among one of these groups, and the possibility alone gives me goose bumps. My throat goes dry, like I'm about to take a test I haven't studied for (though I wouldn't know from personal experience). Because ever since I spoke with Amber Donahue, I've realized I'm ill prepared to meet him. I don't understand why he would leave the Palo Alto Labs campus and visit her dad in Estonia, and I don't see how that fits in with my own dad's disappearance. As I look around the pavilion at this boisterous community, this multibillion-dollar world Howie created, I wonder if he would really sacrifice it all to harm someone. Maybe that trip to Estonia was for business. Maybe Amber and her dad have nothing to do with me.

After all, her dad is dead.

My dad is missing.

"I love this," Shane says. I snap my attention back to my friends, who are still ogling the scene around us. "I love everything about this. It's like a big 'screw you' to the Luds. Like, 'You may have won, but we're going harder than ever.'"

"It's not like they're going to snatch all technology away," Moyo says. "They just want to set proper limitations."

Shane and I roll our eyes. Ever since Gaby Swift won, Moyo's become a low-key Luddite sympathizer. He's always trying to understand how the other side thinks, but this takes it too far.

"False," Shane says. "If they could take us back to the 1800s, they would, and you know it."

"I don't know. Maybe things are getting out of hand," Kara says.

Shane snorts, and I shoot Kara a look.

"Kara, your dad is literally a Silicon Valley billionaire," I say.

"That's the problem! He made all his money from technology and became, like, totally absent. Well, no, not completely. He's really involved in my future as an actress. Which is obviously what I want, but see what I mean? He's just obsessed with stuff that shines."

"That's kind of sad," Shane says.

"The Luds are evil," I say. "End of story."

Last night, I went back into my old files—RAN AWAY and HOWIE. But there's a third folder that I never made, one where my dad might have met a fate similar to Amber's dad. What if that's the secret that Howie Mendelsohn is hiding from me, the reason he's so afraid to tell me anything? What if he showed up in my dad's life like some kind of deadly plague and infected him, the same way he showed up in Estonia?

I shake off my paranoia and follow my friends.

****

It's like extrovert camp inside the convention center. People have no shame whatsoever about whom they approach or how. I learn this pretty quickly when we're climbing the curved stairs in the lobby and I'm ambushed within three steps.

"Oh my God. Opal Hopper!"

To be clear: I don't know this girl. She's wearing avatar art on her shirt—thankfully not mine—and practically pushes me against the railing. My heart begins to race. But I remind myself she's a fan, not a paparazzi drone.

"Hi," I say. "Nice to meet you."

It's times like this when I realize I'm actually an introvert at heart, despite the half hour I spend with millions of strangers on WAVE each week. I still need time alone to recharge. And I still get overwhelmed by people like—

"My name is Felicia and I'm your biggest fan," she bursts out. The many bracelets on her arm jingle as she jumps up and down. "I've been there for *every* episode of *Behind the Scenes*. I even left school early once for—" Felicia turns and notices Moyo. "Ohmygosh. You're here too! Can I get a Zapp with the two of you?"

We do as she asks. Shane holds back his laughter, and Kara looks understandably jealous, but soon we're off to explore the convention center. Our meeting isn't until three, leaving us with plenty of time to melt into the chaos of WAVEcon.

Upstairs, we start with the sports wing. Holographic athletes are scattered around the turf, shooting goals and practicing pitches. They're programmed to turn their heads and greet us as we wander through this scene straight out of an Olympic training center. Shane finds himself an immersion rig in the back, and after he slips his arms and legs through the Velcro bands, he's an Olympic gymnast in no time, off on a joyride of flips and turns. Moyo and I opt for a game of tennis, and it turns out my boyfriend's got a mean serve. I keep swatting at air when his serves come hurling at me, and I end up losing two games to none. We take off our headsets and burst into laughter when we see Kara. She's put on some kind of FondrFoil-like wrapping that has her in a fit of giggles. Apparently she is swimming in the ocean.

We rush through the education and productivity corner—who wants to think about schools and offices on a Saturday?—and find ourselves in a Brooklyn alley. There's graffiti sprayed all over the brick walls, and upon closer inspection, it seems the fire hydrants are not solid but digital. This is the arts corner. Moyo lights up like a kid, and within seconds, he's talking to a WAVE rep about how the studio XP could be *vastly* improved to mirror the drawing experience.

The rest of us find a room where we're given titanium brushes and instructed to "go crazy." Shane flicks his hesitantly, and virtual paint comes splattering out onto the wall. Kara waves hers across the room, and a glorious streak of pink appears. We keep whipping and turning and snapping and bending our brushes until the room is covered in our abstract expressionist masterpiece.

After observing a casual heart transplant in the healthcare corner, we make for the entertainment wing. It has the usual immersion rigs and holograms, but roaring in the back is a giant concert. We move as close as we can, though there have got to be at last five hundred people sardined in here.

"Doesn't make any sense," Kara complains. "Isn't the whole point of virtual reality that you don't have to deal with hordes of people?"

I narrow my eyes on the man who just jumped onstage, small as a speck of dust from where we're standing. "Give it up for DJ Wanton Destruction!" His voice booms through the speakers, and the crowd booms back. "Waddup, folks! I'm so amped to be here today. Now I know this is super IRL, but you can catch me on WAVE soon . . ."

"Let's keep moving," Shane says, leading the way out of the crowd. "I want to spend some time at GameWorld before our meeting."

****

People recognize me throughout the day. Some walk right up and hug me without warning, some blubber and cry, some just stare from afar. The ones who manage to string together sentences ask me things I've never thought about, like if Hailey Carter and I are friends, or if Gaby Swift is telling the truth about video game addiction. One girl asks, point-blank, how Moyo and I can possibly trust each other when I'm so distrusting of the internet. These strangers approach me like I'm their friend, and while it's jarring at first, I warm up to their sincerity. There's a community around WAVE that I'd never appreciated before, that's just as comforting as the blanket of code I've been hiding under for years.

The shameless energy, the fangasms, the virtual worlds—it's all getting to me. I feel like I'm part of something. A different kind of family.

****

The centerpiece of GameWorld is a holographic field. Avatars enter two at a time to compete in a melee tournament where everything but your opponent is shifting—your setting, your weapons, your hiding spots. The first to get three kills wins.

We're standing around the field, basking in the final round of a match where a centaur-inspired avatar smashed a coconut over his opponent's head. The coconut morphed into a hammer at the last second and knocked the other player out with a loud ring.

"That ended faster than we were expecting!" snorts the announcer, and everyone watching laughs and cheers. I notice the two players dismounting the immersion rigs behind the field; from their expressions, it seems the winner is an elderly woman with wild locks of white hair, and the loser is a boy my age, wearing a "1337 h4ck" shirt.

"Any volunteers for the next round?"

Shane takes my hand and raises it in the air. "She'll play!"

A scattering of applause breaks out as I shove Shane. Someone hollers, "Go, Opal!" I smile, shrug, and walk over to the immersion rig.

The announcer says, "We need one more brave player."

"I'll go," another girl says.

I turn to size up my opponent and—oh my God.

The girl is wearing a tight-fitting Madonna T-shirt, the shoulders draped with her messy brown curls. Her eyes are as blue as the sky on the day I last saw her.

"Hailey."

As people recognize what's going on, the audience claps. I

even see a few people in Timmy shirts applaud reluctantly, and Hailey Carter smirks at one of them as if to say, *Yeah, sucker, your fandom got exposed.*

Hailey steps up next to me and smiles. She extends her hand. "I've been looking for you all day!"

"I had no idea you'd be here."

"Well, when I heard you were coming, I—this sounds stupid, but I honestly just wanted to come and say thank you."

Stunned, I shake her hand, but Hailey pulls me in for a hug so tight I can feel her heartbeat against my collarbone. The audience cheers and claps, and as soon as we break apart, the announcer leads Hailey and me to the immersion rigs. Hailey grabs the metal sidebars and lifts herself up, and in two fell swoops, she slips her arms and legs in. She's ready to go. I follow suit quickly, stumbling with the Velcro as I lock myself in.

I turn to Hailey. "Are you sure this is a good idea when we've just met?"

"We're fighters, Opal. It's what we do."

The clock reads ten seconds until start. I take this time to assess my surrounding—an arctic lake, frozen over, with a shack on each side—and process the weight of this full-circle moment.

A loud beeping noise goes off in my ears.

I run over to my shack and find exactly two weapons in there: a rusty knife the size of a pencil, and a fat club. I choose the knife, because I feel it might transform into something stronger. As soon as I leave the shack, I hear the sound of feet slapping the ice, so I turn back inside. I grab the second weapon—there's no reason I can't carry both—and crouch behind the wall near the opening.

Hailey's footsteps get closer, showing no sign of slowing down. Whatever she's holding, it's apparently stronger than what I'm holding. I can hear the cockiness in her stride. But as soon as she enters the shack, the tomahawk in her hand morphs into a candy cane, and my pencil knife becomes a full-on machete. I stare at Hailey's avatar, glowing purple with snakeskin accents—it's funny, I've encountered her so many times in virtual reality but have never actually seen her avatar. She stares at mine, emerald green. In that split second she runs out of the shack.

I snap back into motion and chase her. All those years of track meets and practice come in handy, because I catch up quickly. As the distance between us shrinks, I yank my hand back and hurl the machete straight into her back.

Game one, Opal Hopper!

The lake shakes, and her avatar is back. This time she's holding a bow and arrow, and I've got ninja stars. I flick one in her direction and miss by a long shot. Hailey's face fills with a smug grin, and I wonder if she let me win the first game as a courtesy and is only just getting started. She sets the bow in place and pulls. As soon as she lets go, I crouch—but her shot hits closer to the shack than to me.

She grunts and comes racing toward me like a ravenous hyena. I jet to the right to hide behind a thick shard of ice, and just when I think I'm out of sight, I hear a loud crack. Hailey's fallen into the lake.

Game two, Opal Hopper!

When they broadcast my name for the second time, I suddenly realize: Hailey was right that we're fighters, but we're also partners in war. I stand perfectly still. The field changes into a desert, sand blowing off towering dunes and blinding me. I see her outline trudging toward me, carrying a weapon that shimmers in the desert sun. Hailey Carter and I share a common wound: for so long, we've let others determine our self-worth. This girl, like me, has endured.

I let her stab me with her sword.

Game three, Hailey Carter!

The desert shakes, and now I'm the one holding the sword, staring into the face of an innocent girl.

I stab her back.

Game and match, Opal Hopper!

Chapter
Twenty-one

The boardroom smells like citrus. It's an intimidating space in the basement of the convention center, erected out of nothing but finely polished glass, expensive gadgets, and screens. Screens for walls, screens on the table, even little screens on the arms of the white swivel chairs for reclining your seat and adjusting its warmth. The table itself is a long, never-ending touch screen. You could steal every table out of every house in Palo Alto, line them up end to end, and still fall short of this table's sheer length.

But when I take my chair, two seats away from the head of the table, which Howie Mendelsohn is sure to occupy soon, the first thing I notice isn't the sleek design or the size of the boardroom but the bitter smell of citrus.

Not a minute later, Neil Finch and four other men file in through the door, one after another. The two men directly behind Neil are tall, dressed in slick expensive suits. Neither of them is Howie Mendelsohn.

The third man is much younger than the suits. He's wearing

all the latest fashion crazes. Teal sneakers with thunderbolt accents, leather pants that open up around the knees, and a crinkled polyester T-shirt. His hair is messy on top and short on the sides, with "lawn mower cuts" just above his sideburns. I recognize him from somewhere, though I can't put my finger on where. The last man is dressed fashionably as well, but in a more understated sort of way. He's wearing all black, as if he needs Undetectables to escape wherever he came from.

There is no fifth man.

"Hello, Opal." Neil smiles. He grabs both arms of the chair at the table's head and lowers himself steadily, as if performing an exercise.

"Ah!" His eyes lock on Moyo. "And hello, Opal's boyfriend."

Moyo clears his throat.

"It's nice to see you again, Mr. Finch."

"Please. Neil. Oh—no! Sit, sit!" Neil slaps the edge of the table and points a finger at Moyo, cocked like a gun, waiting for him to react to his joke.

Moyo lets out a single, charitable laugh. "Hah. *Kneel.*"

"How's your father doing, Kara?" Neil Finch leans deep into his chair like he's going in for a dental examination, then shoots back upright. "Always hungry, eh?"

"Still delivering food," Kara says shyly.

"Yeah, half a billion dollars' worth a year," Neil says with a twinge of jealousy. "So how are you kids liking this whole extravaganza? Pretty beyond, right?"

"We're all thrilled to be here," I say shakily. God, the stench of this room is making me dizzy. "Is Howie running late?"

From the way Neil Finch cocks his chin and frowns at me, I already know the answer. "Unfortunately, Howie is busy meeting with members of Congress who've flown into Palo Alto for an emergency," he says. "In a matter of days, Gaby Swift will become *President* Swift, so you can imagine the situation is quite dire."

I try to blink myself out of my stupor, but it's no use. Neil Finch tears into a lofty speech about "embarking on a united journey" and "reaping rewards," none of which I process.

"Maybe we can meet with him next week," I interrupt. "We're all in Palo Alto. We're local. We could stop by sometime."

Neil sighs. "That's not going to be possible."

"Or we could even just email."

"Howie's very busy, Opal."

"But you said—"

"I know what I said, Opal." Neil slams his hand down on the table. He draws in a sharp breath and bites his lip. "Sorry. Things are tense with Howie right now, so you'll have to excuse me."

Anger loops around my mind like a Möbius strip. *I did everything right.* I did exactly what I was told. I've spent all of high school doing what I was told: study, socialize, code. Run. Forget. I became the perfect PAAST student, and the one time, the *one goddamn time* I see a chance to make ten-year-old Opal happy and pick up the last piece of her puzzle, I keep getting screwed by this company and their shady technicalities.

"As such," Neil says, and he clears his throat. "We have decided to invest two million dollars in *Behind the Scenes*."

"I'm sorry, *what?*"

I break out of my daze.

Neil looks straight at me, demanding my attention. "My team provides support for Poseidon channels, especially innovative ones like yours. We believe in your message. The way you fight for the truth. As such, we would like to invest significantly in the channel's growth."

My chest tightens and explodes all at once. I'm not sure whether to interpret this news as salt in the wound or something less vindictive.

"Neil," I breathe. "I—I don't know what to say."

"You could begin with 'thank you.'"

I choose my next words carefully. "I'm not saying we were planning to quit. But I don't know if we can commit . . . for the long haul."

"Nonsense! An opportunity like this, well . . ." Neil turns to Shane. "It looks good on college applications." Then Kara. "It impresses parents." Then Moyo. "And it couldn't be more perfect for aspiring entrepreneurs such as yourselves."

Slowly, my friends nod. Neil's right. Two years ago, a group of juniors raised half a million dollars for their artificial intelligence start-up, and now they're PAAST legends. They went on and dropped out of school to focus on the company full time. It would be idiotic for people like us to pass up an opportunity like this.

Neil Finch careens his attention back to me. "If we want to take our country back after that upsetting election, we all need to be on the same side." He adds pointedly, "After that *blip*, Opal, it's important that you show America where its *true* heart lies. You need to fight for the future your dad wanted. That's what Howie would say."

If Neil Finch is blaming me again for the Gaby Swift episode— well, I'm afraid it's working. Because some nights, I do lose sleep thinking about it. But as uncertain as that correlation is, I know this: Howie Mendelsohn can't ignore me forever. Not if I keep growing on his platform.

The Palo Alto Labs lawyer, one of the tall, suited men, informs us the two million dollars has been wired into a corporate bank account they created for *Behind the Scenes*. He also explains that once we legally incorporate—Kara chimes in to say that her dad's lawyers can handle that for us—Palo Alto Labs will own 25 percent of our show.

"Any questions?" Neil looks around the room for a split second. "All right. First order of business. Meet Stephan over here."

He points an open palm at the boy wearing all black.

"He's your new design guru."

Stephan waves earnestly. But nobody waves back. Instead, the boardroom goes completely silent as we exchange glances. My eyes ping-pong between Neil and Stephan, and then to my friends; Shane's go to Moyo, sussing out his candid reaction, before they drop to the table; Kara stares right into my eyes, attempting to glean some understanding of what is going on here; and Moyo's eyes lock upon mine too, growing in size.

"Stephan is one of our best designers. We plucked him out

of Stanford, and he's been designing WAVE environments at Palo Alto Labs for more than five years. And get this. He's a PAAST grad! You guys will have so much—"

"I'm sorry to interrupt," Moyo says, far more politely than I would have expected. "But I thought I was in charge of design."

Neil flinches.

"Oh. I didn't realize that was an official *role*. In fact, I didn't realize anyone except Opal had roles yet. That was on our agenda for today."

I do remember Neil mentioning that we could do more with design. But he never specified what. Or did he? I can't quite recall . . .

"Consider Stephan a partner, Moyo." Neil nods, satisfied with his choice of words. "As you all know, Congress is clamping down on legacy content on VR—Gaby Swift and the Luds want to back-pedal to 1989, and they're starting with us. What that means is that your show, *our* show, needs to be just as stupendous, just as entertaining and high-quality as decades of film and television." He looks to Moyo. "Starting with design. Opal and I agreed when we met the other day that you could use someone with Stephan's *illustrious* experience."

Neil Finch locks eyes with me, his gaze twisting and stabbing me in the back. I freeze. I'm unable to look at Moyo, who must be livid that I met with Neil without him.

"Hi, Stephan," I say. "Welcome." I feel the words coming out calmly—but inside, they sputter like hot oil out of a deep-fry vat.

"Wunderbar!" Neil exclaims. He knocks the table twice.

"Next order of business . . ."

As Neil dives into another speech, Moyo, Shane, and Kara, and I discuss what just happened among ourselves, in the sly language of glances.

Did you know about this?

I swear I didn't know.

You're sure?

No, I can't remember.

Two million dollars!

That means we're worth . . .

Ka-ching.

People are going to freak.

Just so you know, I had nothing to do with that, Moyo.

Okay, Kara.

Me neither.

You never have anything to do with anything, Shane.

"Next order of business!"

The messy-haired boy stands up and smiles. It's not your typical smile. It's the effortless smile of a model mixed with the hungry grin of a vampire, although that may have more to do with his pale skin and the cliff-like bones under his cheeks.

"Hey," he says. "I'm Constantine."

"Your *new co-star*," Neil says, looking to Kara and me. "Constantine's a legend on the rise. He's too humble to tell you himself, but he's one of the biggest Zappers, and you may have seen him up on stage earlier—"

"That's why you looked familiar," I say.

Neil smiles. *I wasn't finished.*

"We worked every connection possible to poach him from Zapp. You guys get a lot of traction on Zapp, I'm sure you've noticed. There's a lot of overlap between your audiences. But let's be honest. Zapp is finished. It's yesterday. Any tech company that takes that long to come out with their WAVE XP . . . you know they're a dinosaur. We convinced Constantine he needed to move to the next big thing."

"So here I am." Constantine shrugs.

"We ran the numbers and found that nearly eighty percent of Constantine's followers aren't watching *Behind the Scenes* yet. But they're exactly your target audience. You could literally put him in the corner of the XP and your numbers will skyrocket," Neil says, gesticulating wildly. "But you're smarter than that."

For the first time since I took Kara's place and nervously croaked the words "Hello, world," I'm starting to think I might have bit off more than I can chew. I've dug myself into a hole with Moyo, and now we've got two new team members, investors who pretty much own the school we attend, and two million dollars to burn.

I look around the boardroom. Neil and Stephan are bouncing around ideas about magical elements and props we could incorporate, but everyone else is staring at me—even the new guy, Constantine. They trust me. They expect me to guide them through this, all the good and the bad, to great new heights.

An electric surge runs through my veins, and it takes me back to those seconds right before the first time I got on WAVE. That surge is responsibility. I owe it to myself to keep chasing after what I want. To the strangers who give me their time and attention every week. And now, to my friends—to the nth degree, multiplied by infinity.

I can't get intimidated.

PART THREE

GIRL FULLY LOADED

Episode 021

OPAL

Hello, world! Welcome back to our colosseum.
We've fixed every crack, polished every blem-
ish, touched up the fading façade of this historic stadium. Go ahead, make yourself comfortable. We're going to get real today. I have
something I need to get off my chest, and I
should warn you, it's hot.

I hold out my palms. And wait.

Usually, when I'm wearing Invisigogs, I lose myself completely
in this virtual world, forgetting that I'm actually inside the Media
Room. The moment I appear onstage and take one look at the sea
of avatars screaming before me, I convince myself that this reality
is the only one that matters.

But sometimes, my mind wanders to the mechanics—to what's
going on in the control room. I'll imagine Stephan cueing Shane
with his flat, authoritative hand. Shane twirling his fingers over the
trackpad. Kara going over her lyrics on the couch for the millionth
time, next to Constantine, who didn't even bother rehearsing for his
first show. And Moyo, in the middle of all this, probably standing
over Stephan's shoulder, watching listlessly. Feeling useless.

That's one reality. But it's not where I am now. I look to my
left and right, and in the palm of my hands are two fireballs, glowing orange.

I throw the fireballs into the audience. They catapult far past what any normal human could throw, even the best NFL quarterback. And they multiply, into hundreds of fireballs, dropping into the audience like meteors.

OPAL

That'll teach you guys to meddle in my private life!

Even as the crimson embers shower over them, the audience bursts into roaring laughter.

Moving forward on the half-moon stage, with my arms crossed and a cocky smirk on my face, I dive into my opening monologue.

Today's topic? Moyo.

Over the last week, public interest in our relationship has catapulted. People can't get enough of Opal Hopper, rising starlet, and her partner in crime. My fans are creating more holos on Zapp than ever before; they're hypothesizing how Moyo and I met, how our love developed, how we eat, kiss, hug, sleep; they even write fan fiction about our dates, our working relationship, our every interaction on and off set.

There's a simple explanation for this new level of obsession: moms. A disproportional number of my most recent fans are middle-aged women who grew up following celebrities like Taylor Swift and Kim Kardashian. Celebrities who weren't ashamed of their relationships with men but flaunted them, reflected on them publicly.

Poking inside the heads of strangers has been fun. Uncovering the ways they think and feel—what they're really looking at, and ultimately, how they lie—it got us this attention in the first place. But sometimes you have to get inside your own head. Otherwise, people will get inside it for you.

So I'm taking a page from Taylor and Kim. I want to control the narrative. There's no stopping fans from posting theories online. There's no stopping the internet. So why not double down on the attention? I brought it up with Moyo in the morning, and his face curdled as I tried convincing him it could be the best path forward for me—for *us*—to tell our side of the story.

"I suppose that makes sense," Moyo finally said, planting his hands in the pockets of his perfectly fitted sweatpants. "If it makes you feel better, then talk about it."

And it's working. For the first time on *Behind the Scenes*, I'm sharing *my* biometric data with these strangers—how my heart is racing, how my lips hesitate every time I say Moyo's name. I tell them about our friendship, how it started in freshman calculus—when I was the only girl and he was the only black kid in our nine-person class. How we were always destined to grow into something more. How he's intelligent and kind and loyal and empathetic. And like the balls of fire I just threw at them, the audience's attention skyrockets. They're on my side.

OPAL

Now enough about me.

I throw aside all the holos and props I had used to talk about my relationship.

> OPAL

Kara's got a brand-new song for you folks this
week.

I look off to the side.

> OPAL

No? Oh, I'm sorry. I'm being told she has a MED-
LEY of songs prepared!

I turn off my Invisigogs.

"I knew that Moyo segment would work," Constantine says, running up and slapping me on the back. "Personal shit is the best shit."

"Profound," Moyo says from the control room.

"Was that okay, Moyo?"

"You made me sound pretty good," he says from his seat next to Shane, his head turned only halfway toward me. "Nice job."

I smile.

A minute later, Shane warns me that Kara's segment is about to end.

> OPAL

Brava! Wunderbar! *Magnifique!*

Kara's avatar dissolves offstage as my avatar appears next to hers.

OPAL

And how did you like that K-pop bit? Just kidding. I *know* you loved it. Your faces were
dancing like a drunk girl at karaoke.

Slowly, I take a step back onstage.

OPAL

But we're not just emotion-punching wizards over
here. You, my lovely audience, need lighthearted fare more than ever, don't you? The
world is falling apart. Our future is uncertain. And your friends at *Behind the Scenes* are
here to help.

My avatar begins to shrink, as if dropping slowly through the
stage, and at the front of the proscenium, another avatar appears.

OPAL

Our next segment is a real treat. Because we've
brought on board one of the world's biggest
Zapp stars.

CONSTANTINE

Whaaaat up, dudesies!

The audience fills the colosseum with thunderous applause,
cheering, screaming. Some of the avatars break down into tears.

Others begin sprinting down the aisles to fill up every inch of space in front of the stage.

                           CONSTANTINE

    Dayum, this totally beats photoshopping cool shit
    together for three-second holos. This is the
    real freaking deal!

Constantine runs along the base of the stage and high-fives a group of teenage girls. One of them actually passes out.

                           CONSTANTINE

    You know, I never thought I was drop-dead any-
    thing until . . . that. Anyway, what I really
    want to do today is take you all on an adven-
    ture.

He puffs his chest and looks across the entire colosseum. His eyes twinkle like shooting stars, a swoon-inducing effect designed by Stephan.

                           CONSTANTINE

    Let's go skydiving.

Chapter

Twenty-two

A deep and gloomy depression has settled over campus now that Gaby Swift is President Swift. It's like someone poured a bucket of water on our hard drives, leaving just soggy parts and dying sparks. It doesn't help that the day after her inauguration, she dives headfirst into her Luddite agenda, signing an executive order banning any American company from employing robots when a human could perform the same job.

The first week of February, Neil Finch asks if I'd like to join him for a PR meeting in Los Angeles. I'm tempted to say no. Even with fans clamoring about Moyo and me, I've had trouble taking my mind off the situation in Washington. It seems like every day, another Lud comes out of the woodwork—like they were always dubious about technology, but only now can they stand up and say it. As if he's reading my mind, Neil follows up and says this firm has ideas for how we can use *Behind the Scenes* to fight back against the Luds. I agree to go.

I'll admit, I'm a bit nervous when I leave for LA after my last class of the day. PAAST is my safe haven. My utopia. It's where I'm allowed to be a tech nerd and test new versions of myself, but at the same time, dig deeper into my old self.

As I'm crossing the street in broad daylight, I feel something strike against my body. It's hard, sharp, and it grazes the skin between my jawbone and ear.

"Ow!" I scream.

I whip my head around. Hovering twenty feet above me is a drone—beady and black, regaining its balance midair. I recognize this particular type of drone from its flashing red eyes, from the worst days of my childhood. From the Hailey Carter meltdown.

It's a paparazzi drone.

I turn my face the other way and hurry down the sidewalk. To my relief, the drone doesn't follow. My fingers and legs are trembling; I pick up the pace and run, swinging my arms wildly. How long was that thing waiting there, just off campus? What kind of footage was it trying to gather? It came so close. I've never in my life seen a drone get so close to a human.

Nearly out of breath, I bend over my knees outside the Palo Alto Hyperloop Station and close my eyes. I haven't felt this scared in a long time. Not from the Zapps, not from the thousands of private messages I've been receiving in my inbox. *Marry me* this, *fuck my* that, *you're a stupid fucking goddamn* thingamajig. I can laugh off all the comments. Treat WAVE avatars like they aren't real people.

But this drone is different.

I feel a tap on my shoulder. Without looking up, I register the polka-dotted tights, the frilly pink tutu, the HoverSneaks, the school-issued tablet. This girl is in middle school.

I stand up.

"Oh my God, it's you! Opal Hopper!"

I smile. The girl does a little dance, flapping her hands in the air and spinning in a circle so her tutu floats like a pink cloud.

"Will you—"

The girl swipes the side of her tablet and snaps five selfies with me, making a different face in each one.

"Are you old enough to be riding Hyperloop?" I ask, gesturing above at the skeletal dome of the train station. "By yourself?"

The girl giggles. She shakes her head and points at a small crowd that's formed by the doors to the station. There are three other girls her age, all clutching identical school tablets, along with a teenage boy and two middle-aged women. One of the women looks like she had rushed over from the office, still in her pantsuit.

"Oh," I say, taking a step back. "How did you . . . ?"

"It said on Livvit that you would be here."

I take another step back and nearly stumble. I smile politely but then pivot on my back leg and bolt through the Hyperloop station doors in two long strides. With just a minute left to spare, I board the three thirty p.m. Hyperloop, recline the leather seat all the way back, and wait for the train to zoom forward and take me away.

****

The heat waves sting as I step off the smooth-stopping train. I'm sure as hell not in Palo Alto anymore. Los Angeles is scorching. I rip off my jean jacket, wrap it around my waist, and crack my neck. There's already a small pool of sweat at the base of my spine. From the heat, from the nerves. The ride down was only an hour long, but with the anticipation of meeting with Neil Finch, it felt much longer than that.

As instructed, I board an orange Tesla that's waiting for me outside the Hyperloop station. The car navigates through the traffic-less streets of Los Angeles until we reach a pristine white building just off Venice Beach. As soon as the car door opens to let me out, I'm greeted by a familiar face wearing Ray-Ban sunglasses, topping off Bermuda shorts and fat brown flip-flops.

"Talk about a warm February day!" Neil Finch bellows. "Did you get here all right? Good, good. Now come inside! We have plenty to talk about."

He leads me past the office assistant—a living, breathing woman, far more beautiful than anyone I've ever laid eyes on in Palo Alto— and into a conference room not unlike the one where we met at WAVEcon. Another man is waiting for us at the head of the table. He's wearing shorts and flip-flops like Neil Finch, though his frame is significantly lankier. He talks so fast that I miss his name the first two times he says it. I catch it the third time: Tommy Kazinsky.

"As I was telling Neil," Tommy says, scrutinizing his bitten fingernails, "our team has been crunching your social clout numbers, Opal. They're resoundingly positive. People trust you. Perhaps you've noticed similar stats on your end, but we've found that between your defense of Hailey Carter, your foretelling message around the election, and your openness with your love life, you've gained a level of trust not unlike Ellen DeGeneres and

Oprah Winfrey." He looks to Neil as he references those names.

"That's amazing," Neil says, beaming with excitement. "Exactly what we want."

I sit up in my chair. "Why is that amazing?"

"Trust is an undervalued asset in these backward times," Tommy says. "When people think of Silicon Valley—of tech—they think of stodgy men like Neil and myself. But you, Opal. You give off a different impression."

"How does that help us reverse what Gaby Swift's doing?" I ask. I purse my lips. Part of me was hoping this PR firm would have scored us an interview with Senator Worthington, or some other big name in politics.

"Just keep being you," Tommy says, as if I know how to be anything else. "Keep building that trust. Our team is exploring a number of ideas."

Neil Finch rests a calloused hand on my wrist. "I know things aren't looking great, but be patient. The resistance is just getting started."

For the next hour, Neil and his publicity wizard shepherd me around the office, introducing me to various analysts and account managers. One of them shakes my hand appraisingly and then asks how I'm liking the spotlight. "I like it," I say after a pause. She smiles as if I passed her test.

****

After I get back to campus, I take a quick shower and run over to the HP House in my track jacket and army khakis. I move quickly through the dark, quiet streets of Palo Alto—keeping an eye out for paparazzi drones and fans. When I tiptoe up the creaky front steps of the house, I see one other person waiting on the porch.

"Shane's not here yet," Moyo says.

"Oh! Hey." I nudge him with my elbow. For two very serious high schoolers, Moyo and I like to nudge and poke each other for no reason. Some of our latest nights and laziest mornings in bed have been spent competing to see who could jab the other the most sneakily, the most foolishly. We still kiss and cuddle and fool around doing normal teenage things. But our poking contests are particularly special.

Maybe he's just comfortable where he is, leaning against the door with his arms crossed, but Moyo does not elbow me back. His gaze drops; I take his hand and bring it close to my waist, thumbing the inside of his palm.

Moyo looks up.

"What were you doing in LA today?"

"How did you—"

I drop his hand.

"Right. Livvit. It was a meeting Neil set up for me a while ago, with this public relations firm." When I visited *Scalleyrag*, I was too embarrassed to tell Moyo what I was doing. Now, it's something else. A different kind of pride.

Even through the veil of darkness, I see Moyo's eyes narrow on me.

"When were you planning to let us know?"

"I don't know."

"What did he want to talk to you about?"

"Nothing!"

Moyo sighs. He opens his mouth to say something, but both our phones buzz at the same time. Stephan and Constantine are texting to say that they're running late.

"Caltrain delay," Moyo says, reading off his phone. "Probably another . . ."

"Yeah." These days, the trains are never delayed for technical malfunctions. It's always because someone jumped.

"Hopefully no one from PAAST," Moyo adds quietly.

"We would have heard if it was someone we knew," I say without any trace of emotion. "Maybe it was a Paly or Gunn kid."

These incidents always thrust my mind into the darkest rumors about my dad. What he might have done to himself. All the ways Abba might have been suffering—not physically, but inside his head.

I hate myself for even thinking it.

****

None of us have the courage to tell Constantine his ideas suck. After pretending to entertain at least half a dozen of them, from "SurviVR" to an Easter egg hunt, we manage to convince him that our best bet for retaining viewers is for him to continue as he is, an irresistible heartthrob.

At the end of the night, Constantine and Stephan take the train back to San Francisco. Apparently, they're testing the new Caltrain dating app, where you have access to all your fellow passengers' profiles. Shane, as usual, claims he's too tired to walk back to campus. "I'm just gonna crash here," he slurs, and I roll my eyes. Recently, I figured out that means he's drinking himself to sleep. I know this because he's been drinking during meetings, and I notice each time he pulls out his whiskey or rum bottle that the line of liquid is lower than it was at the end of the last meeting. I've been meaning to confront him about this. But I don't want to embarrass Shane in front of the rest of the team, and I can't seem to find a moment alone with him.

When we reach the dorms, Kara quickly peels off from Moyo and me, turning left at the lobby. Technically all of our rooms are in the right wing. But Kara is clearly taking the long way for a reason. This leaves me with Moyo to walk quietly through the dorm's halls, until he stops outside his room.

I bump him with my hip.

"It's been a while since we . . ." My eyes flicker. I tilt my head.

Moyo pats the side of my arm.

"It's pretty late," he mumbles absently.

I reach for Moyo's hands, leaning forward to press my chest against his, but I feel the cold skin under his fingers pulling back.

"Not tonight, Opal."

"Why?"

"I have a lot of work to get done for tomorrow." Moyo doesn't seem convinced by the words coming out of his own mouth.

A wave of heat flushes over my face.

"Like . . ."

"Like the designs," Moyo says, swiping his thumb over

the doorknob. He steps inside. Without looking back he adds, "Stephan wants more shooting stars for the next episode."

Moyo takes another step into his room and the door swings shut. I know it's not his fault—the doors are automatic—but I get the message, loud and clear.

He might as well have slammed the door in my face himself.

Chapter
Twenty-three

It is a truth universally acknowledged that when your boyfriend blows you off without explanation, refuses your advances, and closes a door on your face, there's trouble in paradise. Over the next few weeks, Moyo will say hello in the Sphinx and Hell, make as much eye contact with me as with anyone else in the room, even smile back when I smile at him. By normal standards he's not being mean at all. But it isn't our normal rapport.

I hear his message loud and clear, but I don't try to do anything to fix the tension. It's fine. I tell myself Moyo is just reacting to all the big changes—to being forced to take a back seat to Stephan. I'm busier than ever these days anyway, trying to juggle our growing team with constant feedback from Neil Finch, not to mention the new level of attention from fans. Many of them are still hammering me about Moyo. As I'd expected, hurling fireballs at the audience and asking them to stop meddling in my private life only upped their interest. Fortunately, I have plenty of old photos and videos of the two of us from sophomore and junior year, which I ration carefully across my social media channels.

Times are awkward, but I'm confident that the awkwardness will blow over. Growing pains. Every start-up—every human—deals with them.

Three weeks after my trip to LA, I join Shane, Kara, and Moyo at yet another mandatory Blast from the PAAST. Ever since the December dance, the student council has decided to keep the AR headsets. This time, they're playing 1950s music.

In the middle of "Hound Dog," Moyo weaves through a grid of hundreds of Elvis Presley copies—er, "impersonators"—to find me.

"Let's go somewhere private," he yells over the music.

I take a second to come down from the whirling thrill of being totally immersed in a rock 'n' roll music video. Then I see Moyo's face. His typically bright eyes are heavy and serious.

Without saying a word, I tear off my AR goggles and follow him out of the gymnasium. Nerves boil under my skin. He probably wants to discuss our relationship. That should be a good thing; we're overdue. And I've always said I prefer to tackle problems directly.

Most problems. I've always suffered from the exceptions.

We park outside the Media Room. Just as Moyo curls his fingers over the steel handle of the door, I push it back. I rest my hand on the cold, galvanized metal, and my heart goes racing. As much as I would like to blame it on my animated dancing, on the temperature inside the gymnasium, I know better.

"I could use some fresh air," I say, my mouth dry as sand. "Maybe we could go outside? For a walk?"

We march side by side through the Sphinx and out the main building, passing other seniors who'd put in their required time at the dance and are now lying on the lawns, rolling around the fresh grass, laughing, making the most of their last semester at this wacky, incomprehensible gem of a high school. Without uttering a word, we agree this isn't the vibe we want for the conversation we're about to have. We continue walking off campus till we hit University Avenue. I twist my head, admiring all the popping lights, the ancient awning of the old movie theater turned Blue Bottle Coffee. Families and Stanford students mix on the sidewalks, drones buzz overhead, cars drift down the street in perfect sync.

I can't remember the last time downtown Palo Alto served me so well—the perfect backdrop to the night. Not since my tenth birthday, when I roamed these streets with my dad, who broke his silent streak one last time to take me out. It's just the right distraction from the silent boy walking next to me.

Eventually, we hit the Palo Alto Caltrain station. The underground tunnel that connects northbound trains with southbound trains emits a dim orange glow. Moyo and I slip into the passageway; we still haven't said a word to each other. Maybe he intends to make it to the other side, but the silence is so suffocating I need to lean against the curved wall.

"Are you going to say something?" I venture. A light flickers overhead.

"This is very weird."

"No shit, Moyo. It's late and we're hanging out underneath the Caltrain station."

"I'm not talking about right now. I'm talking about lately."

My eyes cut past Moyo, following a tall, lanky boy with a messenger bag. He's probably two or three years older than us.

"Yeah," I say.

The boy adjusts his glasses and turns his head. He's walking by slowly, rubbernecking, watching us. Maybe he recognizes me. Maybe he's just wondering what two teenagers are doing late at night in this underpass. Whatever the reason, soon enough, he disappears. I swing my attention back to Moyo.

"There you are," he says, mockingly.

"What?"

"You were distracted. You're distracted a lot these days."

"I've been focused."

Moyo inhales sharply.

"That's what you're calling it? *Focus?*"

"We're a real company now, Moyo. Isn't that what we always wanted? We're a real company with investors and employees and—"

"I know," Moyo snaps. "But we're also real people. Teenagers."

"What's that supposed to mean?"

"It means we need to figure out *us*. As people. You can't keep cracking jokes to your millions of fans about us—'Oh, don't go stealing my man,' all that stuff. You can't keep posting old photos of us if we're not . . ."

"If we're not what?"

Moyo's stare sums up every feeling that's been brewing inside him for God knows how long.

"You're my best friend, Opal. I think the world of you. You know that. It's scary to think how much you're capable of, which is why . . ."

The rumbling of a train overhead drowns out the rest of Moyo's sentence. We stand still, waiting for it to pass.

"We both know how much you're capable of," he finally says.

"And?"

"And . . . I'm confused—and I hate to say this—but I'm confused how your exceptional abilities have failed to benefit me."

My expression simultaneously drops and turns dumbfounded.

"You never used to make mistakes," Moyo says. "Not big ones. And I know it's only human, but it's also been convenient."

"What do you . . ."

"The email to Matthew Seamus. Matthew, Moyo—I kind of got it. But then, you met with Neil Finch by yourself, and the Stephan thing happened. I just . . . I find it hard to believe that Neil forgot to mention it to you. Or that the girl who obsessively checks her WAVE stats, who I met in freshman calculus, just wasn't paying attention. Especially when your 'mistakes' have benefitted *Behind the Scenes*."

Another passerby. My eyes wander once more, afraid of revealing too much.

"Unless . . ."

Moyo's face fills with terror, with doubt, with the weight of undesired answers, with the taut tension of all the dots he's just connected, the string between them twisting tighter and tighter and digging under his skin. He's figured it out.

And me? I . . . I can't do it. I can't look my best friend, my boyfriend, directly in the eyes. I can't tell him the truth, but I can't deny his accusations either. I can't lie anymore. I'm done. I'm tired of a lot of things these days, but most of all, I'm tired of feeling shitty toward Moyo. So I keep my eyes squarely, neatly focused on the opposite wall. On the curvature. On the gaping holes. On its stiff, simple complexity.

This is all the answer Moyo needs.

Chapter
Twenty-four

I cry that night. Not right away. Somehow, I manage to hold myself together while Moyo and I walk back to the dorms. Maybe it's because he doesn't dump me right away. He doesn't say much at all. He passes plenty of judgment with his scornful expression, but I can tell that Moyo, like any rational person, needs to think first. And so I swoop in with apologies. I'm sorry for emailing Matthew Seamus. I'm sorry for taking our relationship for granted. I promise to stop talking about it publicly once and for all.

But it makes no difference. At the end of it all, after we enter the lobby of the dorm building, Moyo picks up my hands and whispers: "I'm sorry too."

He shakes his head and drops my hands. They fall listlessly, swinging by my sides like rusty old pendulums.

Moyo turns around. I watch his shoulders rise and fall, once, before he takes a step and marches toward his room. I count to thirty. Check my surroundings for any classmates. And I break down.

I cry myself to sleep. I cry until my eyes are red, until my pillowcase is soaked, until the bitter smell of saltwater permeates every corner of my room. M4rc picks up on my sadness and asks if he can help—if he can play a late-night talk show interview or tell me a funny story. But it's no use.

For the first time in a long time, I come undone.

But the next morning, I pick up the pieces. The sun comes up and I wake up feeling numb. Refreshed, almost. It's as if a robot overlord has snapped his mechanical fingers so that I could move on with my life.

And I do.

I stop posting about Moyo or discussing him on *Behind the Scenes*. I discover that there is, in fact, a way for M4rc to help. I instruct him to filter out any messages that contain Moyo's name, or phrases like "boyfriend" or "relationship." This works wonders; the less I hear about him privately from my fans, the less I feel obligated to discuss him publicly.

The people in my life are harder to filter. The morning after the breakup, Kara and I are running to English class to nab seats in the back—Mr. Gladstone is a relentless spitter—when we walk right past Moyo.

"What was that about?" Kara asks.

"What?"

"Moyo. I saw you look at him, but you didn't say hi."

I grit my teeth. "You didn't say hi either."

Rosalind Wu waves at the two of us. Kara returns the wave, her smile coated with artificial sweetener. She turns back to me.

"Are you and Moyo fighting? Because the other day on *Behind the Scenes*, you were talking about him like he's your everything, and now you're acting weird."

I don't say anything, hoping that Kara, the actress, will pick up the cue.

"Or did you . . ."

"It's none of your business," I snap back.

The conversation ends there. But it *is* Neil Finch's business. Literally. He owns 25 percent of *Behind the Scenes*, so it seems he feels entitled to 25 percent of my time and personal life. We haven't met at Philz since the end of winter break, but the two of us spend plenty of time on WAVEchat in Neil's gorgeous chat rooms—courtesy of Palo Alto Labs. Grand palaces, serene jungles, amusement parks, and museums that put Pete's Arcade to shame. He always calls at odd hours of the day and night, leading not with a "hello" or "how's it going?" but with bursts of spontaneous inspiration.

"So now that you and Moyo aren't dating, I was thinking—"

"How did you find out Moyo and I aren't dating?"

It's Tuesday night, just a minute shy of two a.m., when M4rc wakes me up with his usual *Ding! WAVEchat request, from Neil Finch.* Not that I was sleeping. I'm incapable of sleep before at least three in the morning, especially now. But after the breakup, I've spent hours each night in that half-conscious, half-catatonic state, lying in bed with my eyes closed but not even close to REM cycles. Begrudgingly, I reach for my goggles and accept Neil's request like I always do.

Tonight, Neil's wearing periwinkle blue-striped pajamas. This is already quite the contrast from last time, when I somehow found myself discussing audience-viewing optimization software with a shirtless Neil Finch in Brazil. Tonight, he's brought me into his bedroom.

"Isn't it obvious?" he answers.

I step to the right to get a full view of Neil in his four-poster bed. He's lying there casually, his back leaned against the palatial headboard as if he were reading a book or chatting with his husband.

"First of all, you stopped posting on social media. Cold turkey. Which is bizarre, considering all the hullabaloo around that viral Priyanka Collins video with the legless lizard. Secondly, yesterday's episode. No boyfriend jokes. That's a first for you. Thankfully your first-twenty-four stats look fine. You can afford a hiccup, especially with Constantine and Kara carrying the show these days. But I was thinking—"

"I'm sorry," I blurt. I find myself standing inches from Neil, at the side of his bed but crouched against the wall. I'm feeling dizzy, like someone spiked holes in my head and the air is leaking out.

"As I was saying," Neil says, waving his hand to deem my apology unnecessary and unimportant. "Now that you and Moyo aren't dating, I was thinking you could air a sort of *public* breakup."

"I'm sorry, w*hat*?"

"It sounds crazy, but hear me out. What if you let your fans into your breakup the same way you let them into your relationship? You know better than anyone else that full transparency is the only way people will empathize. Show them your biometrics. Heck, bring Moyo on and show how he really feels too. It would be an entirely new way of looking at *grief*, and I think you'd get the point across better than ever. It would be disruptive."

"I'm not grieving."

Neil looks at me, disappointed.

"Opal, I've been there. We've all been there. You can be strong and vulnerable at the same time. It would be great for the show *and* great for you. I'm telling you, it's the perfect two-plus-two-equals-five situation."

I don't exactly know how to respond to my sole investor. I know how I feel. Disgusted, helpless, grimy, like a terrible person for even entertaining Neil Finch's idea. For reminding myself of the very logic that pushed me to betray Moyo. But I can't say any of those things out loud, so I stick with the facts.

"Two plus two equals four, though."

Neil laughs, and he leaps out of bed. Literally. His avatar bounces no fewer than ten feet in the air and lands on the far end of the room like an Olympic gymnast. He leaps again, standing directly in front of me so I'm looking at his chin.

"Consider it. Play around with the numbers. I know you want to move on, that you're hurting, but the only way to overcome pain and heartbreak is to be honest about it. It feels good to open up. You'll see."

Chapter
Twenty-five

There's still one person who refuses to move on from the breakup.

Matthew Seamus.

As the official "breaker" of the relationship news, he's built quite the following around his coverage of the subject. Nikki Walker was right: Matthew Seamus is a hungry journalist, and he finally got the story he wanted. He brought more attention to me, and I brought more attention to him.

This positive-feedback loop broke down, however, when I stopped wanting the attention on my private life. Every day for three weeks straight, Matthew Seamus has been pressing and pressing with new pinnacles. *Where did Opal Hopper's boyfriend go? Why did she stop talking about Moyo all of a sudden? Why won't she address her fans?*

Why, why, *why*.

By the third week of March, I'm undeniably sick of it. Even with the boundaries that M4rc has set up around my messages and news alerts, I can't help checking Matthew's pinnacles. I feel the same urge to confront him directly that I felt back when he first started posting about me. But I know better than to waltz into the *Scalleyrag* office again. This time, we meet on WAVEchat.

Entering Pete's Arcade is like revisiting my old preschool. It's been months since I set "foot" in this place we abandoned for the Media Room, for the HP Garage, for grand studios and theaters and colosseums. For once, Pete's feels right. I wanted to meet Matthew somewhere familiar—on my own turf—but without the bells and whistles of *Behind the Scenes*. Without a reminder of all that makes me newsworthy.

"Opal!" Matthew Seamus's avatar is exceptionally simple. Not much more than a stick figure with a little pink meat. "How kind of you to grace me with your . . . *presence*."

"This is all off the record, Matthew," I say.

"Well, of *course*. What happens on WAVE stays on WAVE, right?"

"Something like that."

"You were very cryptic in your email when you asked to meet. I would have been delighted to host you at *Scalleyrag* again, but from what I understand, you're quite busy these days. So busy that you can't seem to bother addressing the silence around your boyfriend."

"I need you to stop posting all those pinnacles."

"Or is it your *ex*-boyfriend?"

"His name is Moyo. And yes, we're over. You know it. I know it. Everyone else knows it, which is why I don't understand—"

"So why don't you say it, then?"

I grit my teeth.

"Some things are better left unsaid."

"As a journalist, I don't agree with that statement. And considering your claim to fame, I'm surprised you would take that stance."

"Really, that's what you call yourself?" I spit. "A journalist?"

Matthew Seamus flutters his eyes, pretending he didn't hear me discredit his career. "So tell me: Why did the two of you break up? I thought he was your best friend, your confidant?"

So much for an off-the-record conversation. I ignore Matthew's question and instead busy myself with the old-school pinball machine. I fumble with the plunger. My heart steadies as I touch the slippery curve of the sphere-shaped pixels through my haptic gloves.

"Could it have anything to do with Amber Donahue?"

I pull and let go abruptly. *Ding! Ding! Ding ding ding ding!* My heart clamors with similar pandemonium.

Matthew Seamus smiles.

"You've been liking her Zapps quite enthusiastically since January," he says. "I think you might have a keen interest in her."

I catch my reflection in the glass of the pinball machine—jaw clenched, eyes growing wide. The only interest I have in Amber is in getting more information from her. She told me she'd go through the rest of her dad's leather-bound notebooks and files when she was back in Estonia after graduation, and would let me know if he wrote anything about his meetings with my dad and Howie. I've been liking her Zapps to stay in her good graces until then. I can't believe her profile is public.

"She's just a friend," I say in a flat tone.

Matthew Seamus walks over to the pinball machine.

"A friend whose dad also taught at Stanford? Who met a tragic fate, like yours? My intuition tells me it's part of a bigger story."

Stay cool, I tell myself. *Don't let him intimidate you.*

I let out a nervous laugh. "Intuition?"

"Intuition, yes."

This time, I manage a snort.

"You've got to be kidding me."

"I'm not sure I follow . . ." Matthew says.

I keep staring at the glass screen of the pinball machine, counting and considering all the paths a ball could take once it shoots through the hole.

"Intuition is just pattern-matching over time," I say. "If *Scalleyrag* cared about intuition, you'd be using algorithms to do better reporting. Instead, you post stupid XPs of reporters trying to bludgeon their way out of unbreakable cubes. You post pinnacle after pinnacle about my private life when everyone else has moved on."

I jerk my attention away from the pinball machine.

"You want to be intuitive?" I stare Matthew Seamus straight in his freckled face. "Look at the data. People stopped caring about my relationship eight days after I stopped talking about it. And yet you kept going."

I take a deep breath.

"Maybe you don't care about decency," I say, and I narrow my eyes on him, making it abundantly clear that Moyo and Amber are no longer up for discussion. "God knows nobody's perfect. But if

you really gave two shits about your job, about your hits, your goddamn readers—you would have stopped."

With the slightest twist in his face, the smallest jump in his
cinnamon brows, Matthew Seamus shows that he's done playing
games with me. Silicon Valley has enough gamers and players. It's
an industry that suffers from an abundance of games and a lack of
actual depth, where virtual reality trumps reality itself. As a *Scalleyrag* reporter, Matthew's job is to perpetuate that culture. He's
created a snarky character who lives to inform and entertain. But
right here—right now—for whatever reason, it's clear to me that
he's ready to drop his act and bring out the Valley's rarest unicorn.

Real talk.

"Do you honestly think I want to rack up page views for the
rest of my life? You think *this* is what I want to do for a living?"

I jerk my head forward. *Then what?*

"Novels," Matthew says quietly, the word clipped. "I want to
write novels. *Scalleyrag* is just my day job."

I raise a brow, and Matthew reads between the lines.

"Let me guess," he says. "You don't read novels."

"Not anymore," I say.

Now it's Matthew's turn to jerk his head. "What made you
quit?"

"That's a highly personal—" I stop myself. If Matthew can be
honest with me, then I can be honest with him too. "I dunno. My
dad used to make me read novels when I was growing up. But you
know what happened there."

I grow quiet.

"What's the point of made-up stories, anyway?" I ask.

As soon as the words come out, I regret them. They're honest. Too honest, to the point of being mean. But Matthew doesn't deluge me with an emotional defense like I expect.

Not right away.

He looks at me intensely. He's analyzing me. Reading every pixel of my expression, every muscle that shifts nervously. He watches me twitch. He's making me sweat.

"I get it," he finally says.

"What?"

"I understand what you think. But you're wrong."

"Um—"

"I know your type, Opal. I went to Stanford, remember? Majoring in humanities at a school like that was a constant battle. It was like being an atheist in a room full of evangelical Christians."

I shift my weight to the balls of my feet. That's the most my body allows me to move; I'm all but frozen in place.

"You believe in numbers," Matthew goes on. "The power of algorithms. You have no doubt in your mind that artificial intelligence is the future, and that robots should take over our lives, our jobs, until we achieve singularity—that frightening moment when they're as smart as us, for a split second, when they have every bit of intuition and instinct and emotional capacity that we do, and then, the next second, they're smarter."

"I should have known you're a Lud," I say.

"Better than the alternative," Matthew says.

I throw my hands in the air. "Oh, so there's the solution! We should all sign up for the backward society that Gaby Swift is selling, right? We should give up on decades of innovation and live like the cavemen, right?"

"Better to have President Swift," Matthew says, "than a robot president."

As I hold his condescending gaze, I remember a picture I drew in elementary school and showed my dad just before he disappeared.

"A robot president. What an interesting concept."

"You don't like it, Abba?"

"It's not that."

"Then what?"

"Balsa, it wouldn't be very practical to put computers in charge."

"But Abba, you're the biggest computer nerd I know."

"Yes, which is why I'm right. Artificial intelligence, virtual reality—these are all wonderful things. But they were invented by humans. They will not save us, nor will they destroy us. They are tools. There must always be a human touch."

"You look down on people like me," Matthew finally spits. "People who read and write and appreciate art. Who enjoy irrationality and inefficiency. Who don't live optimized lives."

"That's not true," I fire back.

Matthew Seamus raises an eyebrow.

"For starters, I think I asked a fair question," I say. "What *is* the point of made-up stories?"

"Humans are a storytelling species."

"Okay. That makes sense. I like stories. Everyone likes stories," I say. Matthew nods, and I take this as an indication that he's willing to listen. "However, I *do* think we could use artificial intelligence and numbers to tell them more, well . . . effectively."

"Like you're doing on your XP."

I sense a bit of resentment in Matthew's statement.

"I'm just being smart."

"You're manipulating the public," he accuses.

"I'm taking *information* that's already *out there* and I'm *giving people what they want.*"

Our avatars are standing inches from each other. I can almost feel Matthew's nonexistent breath on my lips.

"Someday your job won't exist," I spit harshly. "That's a fact, Matthew. It honestly baffles me how human editors still exist. Why should we trust your so-called *intuition* when an algorithm could come up with better headlines and magazine covers? When they could write better articles and author better novels?"

"You can't possibly think an AI bot could write a novel."

"I *know* they can. Remember *Josie's Creek*, that big-budget Hollywood flick from last summer? Total bot script. They scraped a billion screenplays and novels for all the perfect topics, themes, dialogue, phrases, everything. And it was a hit."

"But computers don't have personalities, Opal. They're not *human.*"

"So?"

"So maybe it worked for a Hollywood script. But when people read my pinnacles, they see it was written by me. It has my personal flair."

"Bots can mimic 'personal flair.' "

"Or novels—when an author writes a novel, he's making a story out of his personal, *human* experiences," Matthew says, blinking nearly as fast as he is speaking. "And when he publishes that novel, he has fans. Fans who want to understand the fictional story in the context of his life and experiences. Who want to write letters, have convers—"

"Bots can do all of that," I say.

"Readers like unpredictability. Twists and turns. Surprises!"

"Bots can learn to be unpredictable."

"They like mistakes. Authenticity. Imperfections."

"Bots can learn to make mistakes too. Don't you see, Matthew? The whole point of artificial intelligence is that it can learn anything."

Matthew Seamus sighs. "But why should we let it?"

Silence.

"What you tech types need to understand is that *humans* are the dominant species. We're storytellers. We don't just want to listen to perfect stories. We want to create them out of our imperfect lives." Matthew walks toward the door of Pete's Arcade, and I'm tempted to tell him it makes no difference if he leaves through the virtual door or just logs off. "So I'll continue writing my own novels, thank you very much, even if robots might do a better job someday. And I'll keep writing pinnacles."

"I'm just saying, you could do a better job with—"

"Numbers. I know."

"I'm thinking about the end reader . . ." I say, my words trailing off.

"Ah yes, just like your viewers."

"Exactly."

"You know—I actually like you, Opal. You've got your own authentic story you're burning to tell. It's clear as anything. But be careful."

"Careful with what?"

Matthew Seamus smiles.

"With the power you give numbers to change your story."

Chapter

Twenty-six

Humans are hardwired to create conflict. We thrive off pointless controversy, petty arguments, silly little reasons to disagree with each other. Thousands of years ago, it was man versus wild. Hundreds of years ago, it was man versus man. Now it's man versus idea, man versus technology, man versus woman versus gender-nonconforming person. We hate, and we fight hate, and hate fights back, and most of the time the good guys win. But not always. You can't always count on the good guys winning—but you can count on conflict.

I learned something in AP Psychology the other day. Study after study proves that if you drop a group of little children onto a desert island, they'll split into warring factions and get nasty. It's *Lord of the Flies*. It's *The Hunger Games*.

It's Matthew Seamus. I'm worried that he might dig even deeper into my relationship with Amber Donahue, so I text her.

Hey, if you hear from a reporter named Matthew Seamus, just ignore him.

Already did. He found my Columbia email and asked some questions about our dads. Sounded like a real asshole.

Textbook definition. Thanks. I'm about to leave it at that when I think, maybe I should do some digging myself while I have Amber's attention. Hey, I hate to make you talk about it, but did your dad ever leave a note?

Nope. No note. Did yours?

Yeah. I think about those lines that Abba left us with. *The world is complicated.* Does the word "complicated" ring a bell?

Amber doesn't respond for a minute. It says she read my message, but she's not typing. Maybe she has Text Preview off. Most people our age would. I'm asking M4rc for the millionth time if the internet's gone out—that's only happened twice in PAAST history, and the second time a freshman freaked out and pulled the fire alarm—when her reply comes in.

Actually, yes. That's weird. A week or two after Howie Mendelsohn visited, my dad came inside from our balcony with this pale look on his face and said, "I have complicated the world." My mom and I were sitting at the breakfast table but he wasn't talking to us. It was like he saw a ghost. I asked what he meant and he just shook his head and said his meds were acting up. I gave him a hug and went back to my college apps. Why?

My heart rate picks up as I'm reading Amber's message, but I don't waste a second with my reply. What was he doing on the balcony?

Amber doesn't respond right away. Crap. I messed up. Her dad died by suicide; that was insensitive of me. I try not to think about it, she writes after a couple minutes, but honestly, he might have just been on a phone call. He liked to take phone calls on the balcony.

Do you know who he was talking to? I write back without thinking.

Nope.

I stop there. This discovery, the possibility of a connection between Amber's dad and mine, sends a painful chill down my spine, one I don't have the time, the will, or the mental strength to explore right now. With everything else going on in my life, it's the last thing I need.

I should try not to think about it, too.

****

It's *Behind the Scenes.*

The six of us are sitting tensely around the pewter table by the Media Room's steel doors. Exactly two months have passed since Constantine and Stephan joined our group. But nobody is celebrating. Instead, we're divided down an invisible line at the table. On one side: Kara, Shane, and Moyo. And on the other side: me, with Constantine and Stephan, my unlikely allies.

"It's not like all the other media requests," Stephan says, fumbling with his visitor badge. "This one is a *national*, late-night talk show."

"And not just any late-night talk show," I say. "*Seth Meyers.*"

"We gotta do it," Constantine whoops. "This is going to be huge for Opal and me . . . and for the XP."

Maybe it's a by-product of my sudden breakup with Moyo. How quickly I got over him, or at least, how quickly I told myself to get over him. Maybe it's all the newfound attention from fans. The nonstop requests for interviews from reporters like Matthew Seamus, bloggers, other VR channels. Or maybe, just maybe, like we learned in AP Psych, it was only a matter of time before our team of six brilliant minds would split into two factions.

"Seth Meyers is kind of old-school, though," Shane protests, the last person I expect to chime in. "Maybe we should try for a different talk show?"

"Shane, he's a *legend*. Besides, they don't just all come calling at once," I mock.

"I also don't understand why Seth Meyers only invited the two of you," Kara says, flipping her hair.

"These shows never bring on more than two people at a time," I say with a laugh. "It's nothing personal, Kara."

"Uh huh. Yeah."

"Come on, guys. Think practically here," Stephan says. "We've been struggling to really grow lately. We've neglected interviews and media requests for long enough, which has been fine until now because we *are* media. But this is different. The whole talk show thing—it's in our DNA."

"Do it," Moyo says.

Everyone turns their head. They're looking at Moyo, but his eyes are fixed across the table on me. No one was expecting anyone to back down, least of all me or him. It's our fault these factions were born in the first place.

"Do it," Moyo says again. "Go on the show. You're right, Stephan. It'll be good for us. Our numbers could use the boost."

Kara opens her mouth and croaks an unintelligible sound. I almost see the unspoken words escape from her mouth. *What the hell, Moyo.*

"Besides," Moyo adds, his gaze dropping to the table, "I think it's safe to say Opal has been preparing her entire life for this."

To everyone else at the table, it means nothing. They probably assume Moyo is referring to all those months I've spent addressing millions of live viewers. But I know exactly what he means. Moyo and I speak the shared language of people who have spent thousands of precious hours together. Who, despite weeks apart, still share so much. He's talking about my love of talk show hosts, how I idolize these fatherly figures. I see it reflected in his eyes: the late nights we spent together watching veterans like Jimmy Fallon and up-and-comers like Tan Hamid. The pretend interviews he would conduct. He remembers.

"What's next for you, Ms. Hopper?"

"Well, Mr. Adeola, chances are I'll say good night to the fellow in my bed."

"I was asking about your career, ma'am."

"Right. World domination, of course."

". . . But speaking of the fellow in your bed. How did a stunningly beautiful and intelligent girl like yourself end up with such an average specimen of the male species?"

"I think you answered the question with the way you asked it."

"Are you calling me . . . recursive?!"

"Recursion is sexy."

Moyo doesn't give a crap about the numbers. That's not the real reason he jumped ship in this debate. Moyo started working on *Behind the Scenes* because of his friends, and he kept working on it—despite the hiccups, despite the breakdowns—because of his unwavering loyalty to us.

Everything isn't lost, after all.

SETH MEYERS

. . . Next up, the girl you can't stop talking about! Those of you stuck in the real world might not have heard of her, but if you've spent any time in WAVEverse, then she's probably your best friend. She's a viral sensation, a virtual superstar, and she's here in the flesh . . . Ooooopppaaalll Hopper!

OPAL

Hello, Seth.

SETH

Anyone else you'd like to say hello to?

I blush. My gaze is glued to Seth Meyers. I peel it away slowly, like gum off a shoe, forcing myself to make eye contact with the hundreds of people in front of me, seated stadium-style in the chilly TV studio.

My voice becomes thin as thread. I wave.

OPAL

```
Ha. Hello, world.
```

I can't believe it. Where I'm sitting, how I got here. All those years spent falling asleep to the voices of middle-aged men on television. Comforted by their stories and conversations. All those showers where I lingered under the warm stream of water pretending it was *me* in that interview seat. Answering questions about my made-up future. Pretending I'm successful, clever, and intelligent. Winning over the hosts, the audience, everyone.

And now. Something's happening inside my chest. With my heart. I should be a pro at this, but it's different, sitting in front of a real audience. Those hundreds of physical bodies make me more nervous than the millions of avatars who watch *Behind the Scenes*.

SETH

```
Now, we're doubling down on WAVE talent with an-
   other treat. Say hello to your favorite Zapp
   star turned Behind the Scenes co-host, Con-
   stantine!
```

Constantine runs across the stage, waving with both hands, and leaps into his interview chair.

CONSTANTINE

Yooooooooooo!

SETH

Now, Constantine, I understand you skipped college altogether after your Zapp career took
off. But Opal, you're still in high school?

OPAL

That's right. I'm a senior.

SETH

Don't you have school tomorrow?

OPAL

I do.

SETH

So you're skipping . . .

OPAL

Actually, I have permission to be here. I took
Hyperloop down after my last class today and
I'm taking the first tube back in the morning.

SETH

Aw, come on. You deserve to skip a day of school.
You're busy!

I smile; I was expecting this line of questioning.

OPAL

I'm sacrificing a little sleep, but I'll just
sleep when I'm dead.

SETH

I'm sure you're running quite the sleep tab for Dead Opal. Anyway, you know what they say. Sleep, school, *fame*. Pick two.

CONSTANTINE

That's not fair! I feel like I only got one.

Laughter erupts from the studio audience. A few of the younger girls are holding up their phones with all the side screens out, capturing the perfect holo.

In reality, I don't need to sacrifice any more sleep to be here. When I told Neil that we'd agreed to the interview, he nearly burst with excitement. Opal and Constantine! Together at last! He wanted to make an entire spectacle of it. Have us meet and greet fans at the Grove, ride bicycles along Venice Beach, hike up to the Hollywood sign and watch the sunrise . . . all while sharing the experience on WAVE with viewers from around the world. He was prepared to call Principal Frasier's office—arrange for me to miss two full days of school—when I shot down the idea. Constantine and I were being interviewed as co-stars. Nothing more.

I surprised myself with the words that escaped my lips. How they shattered Neil's proposal like a vase hitting the floor, sudden and sharp. I'm proud of myself for how instinctively I refused to consider his scheme, no matter what the numbers or data say. Because Moyo—he's been through enough. There's a limit to how far I can push people. If I have any hope of reeling my best friend back into my life, I can't deceive him again.

SETH

Now let's talk about *Behind the Scenes*. I have
to admit, I thought this was just another
fifteen-minutes-of-fame situation at first.
But you've really come a long way since the
begining, when—what was that young woman's
name again? The one who threw a steak at
Timmy?

CONSTANTINE

Hailey Carter! That crazy girl.

OPAL

Now, that's not very nice.

Constantine slaps his leg, laughing. He makes a face and points
at me, mouthing, "Can you believe this girl?"

SETH

Which part?

The audience roars with more laughter.

OPAL

I can fend for myself. But Hailey Carter . . .
  She had real mental health issues that she's
taking care of now.

CONSTANTINE

Opal's right. The whole reason we made it big is

'cuz Opal convinced everyone to empathize with
that chick.

That's a big word for Constantine. So, of course it was planted.
We'd talked to Seth Meyers's producers earlier about using it as
a segue into . . .

                              SETH

All right, you got me. Speaking of empathy, I'm
    just completely fascinated and, if I'm being
    honest, kind of boggled by the virtual reality
    craze these last five or six years. It came out
    of nowhere.

                        CONSTANTINE

Yeah, and I thought *I* was late to the game.

                              SETH

Call me old-school. I'm just a television guy.

                        CONSTANTINE

VR is hot, it's sexy, it's the shiny new thing
    that everyone can't stop talking about.

                              SETH

Kind of like you!

I cringe inside as Constantine's fans shriek.

                              OPAL

Everyone my age just wants to be totally immersed

in WAVEverse. They want to be inside it all the
time.

> SETH

Again . . .

Constantine's fans might actually cause the studio to collapse
with their screaming.

> SETH

But seriously. Tell me, Opal. What makes virtual
reality so sexy and important?

> OPAL

Well, it's two things. The first is what Constantine was saying. With VR, you can literally
put yourself in someone else's shoes. Twenty
years ago, if you were online, you'd see all
these articles about war and poverty and human suffering and you'd think, *Man, this is so
depressing!* So you open up a new browser, fire
up YouTube and watch something lighthearted.
Like skydiving videos, or epic stunts, or a
dude trying to ask out ten girls in a minute.

> SETH

That's a strangely accurate depiction of my
single years.

> OPAL

But you couldn't really know how any of those

experiences felt. Now you can. Because WAVE can send you to that war-torn battlefield. In a split second, it can transport you into a poor family's house. You can know exactly what it feels like to jump out of a plane and drop thousands of feet, or, if you want, you can put yourself in the shoes of that guy who keeps getting turned down.

CONSTANTINE

I'll pass on the last one.

SETH

As if you have any problems with girls.

OPAL

So it puts you in other people's shoes. And that's great. But the second thing is access. These people in your audience—they probably had to take a car to get here, or maybe they even flew across the country to see you, Seth. And I'm sure they were lucky to get tickets in the first place.

I flash a smile at a family in the front row wearing matching sweatshirts. If I had to guess, I'd say they had camped out overnight.

OPAL

With *Behind the Scenes*, it doesn't matter if you're in LA or Tokyo. We're all neighbors in

>   virtual reality. And everyone's invited! Our
>   show is never at capacity. So that's—

> ### SETH

>   Okay! Okay! No need to steal my audience away.

> ### OPAL

>   I rest my case.

> ### SETH

>   One last question. What's going on . . . here?

He points at us. Seth Meyers's producer had failed to mention this part of the interview. If I wasn't on live television, maybe I would have kept my cool. But alas.

> ### OPAL

>   Oh God.

I bury my face in my hands, and the audience loses it.

> ### CONSTANTINE

>   Let's just say she's playing hard to get.

> ### OPAL

>   Rest assured, Seth, there is nothing to *get*.

Constantine winks at the audience.

> ### CONSTANTINE

>   That's what she says now.

OPAL

I'm seventeen. You're old.

CONSTANTINE

I'm not even twenty yet . . .

OPAL

This is getting awkward.

CONSTANTINE

All I'm saying is, I can be persistent. How many
girls do you know who are wicked smart and
drop-dead gorgeous?

More than you think, asshole.

SETH

Let's leave it at that, folks. We're almost out
of time, and we haven't even gotten to the best
part yet. Look under your seats . . . Yep,
everyone is going home with the latest WAVE
headset, courtesy of Palo Alto Labs. Now let's
explore the Milky Way!

Chapter

Twenty-seven

After the show, Constantine and I stick around to record holos with some of our more rabid fans outside the studio. It's kind of heartening, how Constantine constantly embraces the impact he has on them. He goes in for hugs. He listens to their stories. When it happens to me—when young girls, their brothers, their mothers appear in my face and gush about my weekly dose of "real talk"—I feel . . . less deserving, somehow. I'm used to gushy comments on Livvit, Zapp, all the blogs. But other than WAVEcon and the Hyperloop station, I never encounter my fans in the real world. The PAAST bubble protects me.

Sometime after one a.m., we say goodbye and take a stretch limousine to our hotel in West Hollywood. We're silent the whole ride, sitting on opposite ends of the passenger compartment. The streets of LA are dark and empty—except when they aren't. The city installed new motion-activated digital billboards a few years ago that light up only when you drive by them. Not that Constantine and I can see. Our attention bounces between the screens that line the windows of the car—flooded with real-time reactions to the show—and our phones, which we've placed on the floor to roll through Zapp after Zapp.

The next morning, I leave my hotel room painfully early to catch a seven a.m. Hyperloop back to Palo Alto. But I never make it to the station; my phone buzzes as soon as I step out of the hotel with a text from Neil Finch.

> Don't leave LA yet

Jesus Christ. I start to tap out a reply, though I haven't quite made up my mind if I'll shoot for diplomatic or full-on WTF, when another text comes in.

> Surprise meeting for you. Remember the PR office?
> Be there at noon. I think you'll be happy. You can
> head back to school after.

If Neil is implying what I think he's implying . . . I look around the sleepy LA sidewalk outside my hotel, my heart racing faster than the Ferrari that blazes down the street, and I press my balled-up fist to my chest. I try to convince myself that I'm ready for this. I'm ready to meet Howie Mendelsohn.

But a small part of me doesn't want it anymore.

Moyo was right when he broke up with me: I *have* been distracted lately. Like my application to PAAST, *Behind the Scenes* may have started as a plan to get closer to Howie Mendelsohn, but it's evolved into something else. A distraction. A new life. But instead of changing my name this time, I got famous. Instead of making a new friend, I've made millions of fans. I'm not sure I'm ready to go back again.

Not that I have a choice. Last night, as I was falling asleep, I wondered to myself: If Abba is really out there, wouldn't he have seen me on *Seth Meyers*? Wouldn't he have heard about my meteoric success by now?

Another text from Neil Finch.

Talked to Dr. Frasier about classes. You're all set.

Well then.

****

I'm back at the same beach-chic office building, sitting in the same boardroom with sky-high ceilings, white and stripped of any real personality. Neil wasn't here to welcome me personally this time. I entered myself, checking in with the sexy receptionist in the lobby, and was led to the meeting room.

Denise, the receptionist, pops back in and asks me to sign a nondisclosure agreement. Standard procedure, she says with a smile.

As I'm signing the paper document, I see myself in the spotless reflection of the table, the self-conscious stare of a teenage girl sitting on eggshells. My eyes remain fixed on that face, even after Denise leaves. That face becomes younger, a little girl, and I smile, because I realize

I still want what I've always wanted. Those files are still imprinted in my mind. The questions are still itching to be answered.

"Opal!"

I turn around.

My face drops.

Laini, Felix, and Hailey Carter march in together, dressed like they've just stepped out of hair and makeup.

"I—um, hi, Hailey. I wasn't expecting you."

"It's so lovely to finally meet," Mrs. Carter says.

Mrs. Carter is wearing a red blazer, crimsoned at the collar, and her hair is tied in a tight bun with two metallic chopsticks crossed through. Holding her hand is Mr. Carter, in an expensive-looking suit, probably from one of those Italian designers. Hailey slides out from behind them and hugs me.

"You look stunning, Hailey," I say when she pulls away. And she does. Her skin glows under the harsh conference room light, unblemished and healthy. The orange and purple tulips on her sundress seem to be dancing as she taps her feet.

"You look surprised," Hailey says, nudging me.

"Sorry," I croak. "I thought it would be . . . someone else. Anyway, how's rehab? I read somewhere that your new place is working a lot better."

Hailey eyes her mom sweetly.

"Opal," Mrs. Carter says, giving weight to both consonants. She sits down across from me. "Hailey is healthy."

"I can tell." I beam, my eyes wide. "I'm so glad the rehab is working. I wasn't sure, since it's been so long—"

The Carter family exchanges glances.

"What I'm saying, Opal . . ." Mrs. Carter reaches across the table and places both hands over mine. "Hailey has been healthy . . . for a while."

I raise an eyebrow.

Hailey looks to her mom with an expression that reads: *Tell her.*

"I don't understand," I say.

"You know about Hailey's childhood. Those years she spent struggling with her mental health, in and out of rehab. It's been all over the headlines. We've been working closely with this PR firm to mold Hailey's image in such a way that her *insecurities* work in her *favor*."

"Sure," I say. "Every celebrity needs PR."

Mrs. Carter gives her daughter a sidelong glance. "You're sure about this, honey?" Hailey nods.

"It's more than that," Mr. Carter says, growing frustrated that I'm not reading between his lines. "The route we chose to take was more—"

"It was staged," Hailey says flatly.

"What was staged?"

Hailey looks to her mom one more time, all the sweetness wiped off her face. *Do your fucking job.*

"The breakdown," Mrs. Carter says. "All the breakdowns, really. After the first one."

"I—I don't under . . ."

"Hailey's first public *faux pas*," Mrs. Carter goes, "was very real.

Surely you remember when she was young, when she got angry with one of her friends at a sleepover and left the apartment with her sleeping bag, sobbing. One of the girls came chasing after her, and, well . . . the rest is history. There weren't many paparazzi drones at the time, but someone caught it all on camera. That's New York for you. The next day, the video was all over the internet."

"I remember," I say, my gaze unfocused, in a sort of stupor. I'm still chewing on Hailey's words.

"A couple of years later, the PR team here noticed something interesting. Not only did downloads of my husband's and my music skyrocket after Hailey's incident, but they discovered exactly what you discovered. People *felt* for Hailey. Yes, the internet trolls came out and left nasty comments. But if you look deeper, you'll find a different narrative. Tommy Kazinsky reached out and showed us the data. You've met Tommy, yes? He walked us through what people were watching after they saw Hailey's video. How it made them feel. And instead of letting that incident ruin our daughter's life forever—her future prospects—we seized the moment, and we made lemonade."

Hailey Carter's face lights up with the smile of a popular girl who's just been crowned Homecoming Queen.

I'm speechless. I cling to my seat, because I imagine it's going to disappear any moment now and I'll slip through a trapdoor. That's how I feel. Tied to an iron anvil, my body light and weightless as I plunge toward some bottomless peril. I look down. It's still there, the seat underneath my ass. I *feel* like an ass. I feel like the biggest fool in the world, for I had blindly assumed.

"So you lied," I spit.

"I didn't—Mom, just tell her the plan."

"Opal, we see a win-win scenario. Hear us out. This could be a massive turning point for both your careers."

"People love an underdog story," Hailey toots.

"Hailey," her dad snaps.

"What I'm suggesting is an interview. Fifteen minutes on *Behind the Scenes*. You and Hailey. An exclusive conversation. Talk about how she's feeling healthier than ever, how rehab helped, how she's going to begin her acting career. Go back to your *roots*, Opal. Can you imagine what that would do?" Mrs. Carter says, beaming. "Everyone would be talking about it. Even Lud supporters."

Hailey's dad chimes in: "It's true. I hate the Luds as much as the next guy, but they're still human. Did you hear Gaby Swift's latest proposal? I mean, shocking *children* with *electricity* for spending too much time on their phones . . . It's inhumane! The polls say even her own supporters think it goes too far. Thank goodness they draw the line—"

"There's nothing humane about staging breakdowns!" I stand up and pace along the side of the table. "This is ridiculous."

"No more breakdowns," Hailey's dad says.

"That chapter is over," Mrs. Carter follows up. "September was the last straw. End of season one. Now, it's season two. Hailey Carter is coming out untroubled, fixed, stronger than ever."

"Mom says I could win an Oscar someday," Hailey boasts.

"You will, honey," Mrs. Carter says, rubbing her daughter's arm.

"The bar has been set so low for Hailey that now, anything she does will be trumpeted as an unbelievable comeback. She's going to *kill it*," Mr. Carter says, slapping the table. "The sky is the limit."

"She's been through so much," Mrs. Carter coos sincerely.

"Are you people nuts?!" I stomp a foot on the floor. "Let me say it again. You're *lying*. This is morally reprehensible."

"Everyone who lives in the public eye has to lie a little," Mr. Carter defends.

"That's the truth," Mrs. Carter says. "The key is who can lie most intelligently. Take yourself, Opal. You didn't honestly care about Hailey's mental health. You saw an opportunity and you grabbed it."

"You gave the people what they wanted," Hailey says proudly, looking at me like a sister.

"I wasn't lying," I say, turning my back on her. I think about my initial connection with Hailey, how I believed we had both been unfairly scrutinized as kids. Caught out of the shower with our hair wet, our towels still wrapped around us. "I sifted through the data and made an observation that I thought people would care about."

"And Moyo," Mrs. Carter says.

I freeze. "That was *not* a lie."

"But the way you publicized it, Opal."

"What you're doing, Hailey. What you've done . . ." I grit my teeth. "It's a slap in the face to anyone who's ever really suffered."

"That's not fair!" Hailey cries petulantly.

"Opal, be nice," Mr. Carter says.

"Sorry. I take that back," I say, turning around sharply. "It's a slap in the face to your own fucking dignity."

The two of us glare at each other from across the table. Hailey breaks eye contact first, huffing and sinking into her chair.

"Just consider it," Mrs. Carter says.

I have my sights set on the door when I turn back around and ask, "Why did you tell me this? Couldn't you have kept it a secret?"

Mr. and Mrs. Carter sigh deeply.

"Hailey insisted that you know," Mrs. Carter says. "The two of you aren't so different. At the end of the day, you have the same goal."

I take one last look at these people.

"Screw all of you," I say.

I barrel out of the boardroom with the sky-high ceilings, out of the beach-chic office building, out of this paper-thin city of angels and demons. I leave LA stunned. Frazzled. Enraged. Conflicted. I board the first Hyperloop back to Palo Alto. I don't speak to anyone, nor do I look at a single screen.

****

"What the hell, Neil."

I make it all of three steps into my dorm room before my rage manifests itself into something more tangible. Actionable.

For once, I'll be the one to surprise Neil Finch with a call.

My goggles feel colder than usual against my bare skin. Shockingly, Neil is available, and I invite him to WAVEchat.

"Greetings, Opal!"

I look around.

"Are we inside . . . ?"

"Yes, ma'am. Kind of nostalgic, isn't it?"

A paper factory. Neil stands before a giant row of printers, clunky, cream-colored boxes that spit out sheet after sheet of dead trees.

"Can I ask why . . . Never mind," I say, shaking my head. "I need to talk to you about Hailey Carter."

"So you've met," Neil says, bending to pick up a stack of papers. He hauls the weightless pile to the other side, where there's a ladder.

"Met? I'm *disgusted*," I say. "Everything—I feel like everything I've done until now has been a lie. I helped a liar!"

"Oh, Opal, *everyone* in the entertainment business knows her whole 'poor girl' act is staged," Neil coos from two stories up. For some reason, he's carrying the fat stack to the top shelf. "You said it yourself—everybody lies, right?"

"But what Hailey did was wrong, Neil."

"It's her choice. She's giving the people what they want," he says, his voice muffled. He digs his head around the shelf. "A show. Same as you. Now, I have to say, I'm surprised you didn't jump on the chance to interview her."

I bite my lip.

"Why would you set me up to interview her?"

"Your public profile, Opal! Your trust! We at Palo Alto Labs are all about helping you soar to the highest level of admiration. We want nothing more than for you to feel beloved by America, for your star to shine."

"Is that what *Howie* wants?"

Neil pokes his head out of a box.

"Howie would want you to be strong."

Once again, I feel like I'm being strung along. The old Opal wouldn't have let anyone gaslight her like this, not even Howie Mendelsohn's henchman.

"No," I say, shaking. "I'm done. I've helped a lying narcissist win more attention. I've helped an evil woman win the presidency. You know why I entered Make-A-Splash in the first place, Neil? Of course you know. I wanted to meet Howie."

"And you will, Opal!" Neil jumps at least five stories to the ground. "I want you to meet Howie too. Believe me, I do. I want you to have answers, the truth, so you can move along and accomplish even greater things. But nobody was expecting this election, and things are so tricky with the Luds, which is why we need you to keep—"

"Keep what? Lying?"

"No!" He licks his lips, searching for the right words. *"Entertaining."*

I shake my head. "I want to be honest."

"That's what your show is all about! But it's also a show. There's a fine line between honesty and entertainment."

"But we can build—"

"Just stick with entertaining," Neil says, short-tempered. "You've built enough. Leave the building to the big boys."

Fire burns in my eyes. If my goggles could transmit heat, I have no doubt I would have blown Neil into virtual smithereens.

Instead, I grab a sheet of paper that flies out of one of the printers.

"The *big boys*?"

I look Neil Finch squarely between the eyes.

"What I—what I meant to say—"

As if closing a book, I fold the sheet squarely in half. I keep staring at Neil, narrowing my focus on his massive rock of a nose.

"No, I heard you the first time."

I fold the paper twice, thrice. Sharp folds.

"Come on, Opal. I didn't mean—"

"I know what you *didn't* mean to say. My answer is no. No, I won't stop building. I understand I've been more of a talker lately, but I can still build whatever I want. You own twenty-five percent of *Behind the Scenes*. I own a lot more than that," I say, my voice cool and collected. "I can build software, hardware, monologues, dialogue . . . even airplanes."

I toss the paper airplane, sending it gliding through the air and crashing into Neil's smug face. Directly into his nose.

"I can build anything I damn want."

Chapter
Twenty-eight

Twenty minutes later, there's a knock on my door.

"Come in," I say sharply.

The door swings open. Outside stands Shane, his mess of brown hair all over the place, the strands curling and twisting in every which direction. He looks nervously excited. This is not a normal look for Shane.

"You were amazing on *Seth Meyers* last night," he says, stepping inside the room and waiting for the door to close. "Really."

"Thanks, Shane."

"The way you talked about what we're doing—the importance of it—especially compared to Constantine. He doesn't seem to care about anything but himself . . ." Shane presses his eyes closed, collects his thoughts. "You were awesome."

"It's not that important," I mumble, rolling over in my bed. I bump into my headset and it tumbles over on the floor.

"What do you mean?"

"We're not—never mind," I say.

"I didn't see you in class today."

"It's been a long day." I grab a pillow and hug it tightly. "A long freaking day."

Shane's attention lingers on the empty space where the pillow lay just seconds ago. He takes a step toward me.

"Want to talk about it?"

We're silent for a moment. The air is sharp to breathe, like every oxygen molecule cuts like a knife.

"Not now," I say, forcing an exhausted smile. "Maybe later."

"Okay," Shane says. He looks at the door. His face is lost in thought as he dips his chin, sucks in his cheeks. He takes a deep breath.

"I wanted to tell you something, Opal."

Honestly, I'm not in the mood to talk. Not after the meeting with Mr. and Mrs. Carter, with Hailey. Not after Neil Finch blew off my moral qualms. And certainly not after he told me to lay off on *building* and leave that to the *boys*. But Shane doesn't want to talk often. I come to my senses and reply, "Sure."

"We've been friends for a long time, right?"

"Sure."

"Since, like, the fourth grade. We were best friends in middle school, and then when we got into PAAST, you met Moyo and we became a trio."

I smile. "Yeah," I say longingly.

"And . . . It's no secret that you and Moyo got close, after we kissed at that party freshman year."

I drop my hands into my lap. I don't know what to say.

"Which is fine," Shane says quickly. "I've been fine. I'm lucky to have you guys in the first place. But . . ."

"Shane?"

"I like you, Opal."

He blurts the words and clenches his jaw, his chest filled with air, waiting for me to say something.

My heart stops. A long time ago, I liked Shane too. Not because we both preferred puzzles and riddles to sports or because both our dads had instilled in us an obsession with Weird Al Yankovic, or any of the other nerdisms we had in common. Those brought us together, sure, but I grew to like Shane because he saw me the way I wanted to be seen. When everyone around me treated me like a fragile porcelain doll after my dad went missing, Shane treated me like a normal person. And when those same people expected me to be normal, to have moved on, Shane let me cry on his shoulder. He entertained my detective work. He covered for me when I ran off to Tahoe. He hacked into WAVE when I needed it most.

But then we kissed. And when our lips touched, it was like all those old feelings I decided to get rid of in high school . . . it was like they came rushing back. The wrong ones. I couldn't bear the sight of him for months, because looking at Shane was like facing a past I was desperate to leave behind.

How could he possibly like me? There's nothing to like about the division in our team, and Moyo and me acting weird around each other, like bickering siblings.

"You can't," I finally say.

Especially now. Shane doesn't even know the full extent of things. I don't deserve to be liked. I'm a fraud. To my friends, to the millions of people who tune into *Behind the Scenes*.

"But I do."

"You *can't*," I say again, my eyes closed, shaking my head.

"I've liked you for a long time," Shane says. "I just never thought—I never wanted to ruin our friendship after we made up the first time. I didn't want to ruin our dynamic with Moyo. But then you guys started dating, and it was like none of the rules mattered anymore. And now that you and Moyo are over, I don't want to miss my chance again. I mean, watching Constantine badger you like that on *Seth Meyers* last night, I just—"

"What, you thought you would just swoop in and date me?"

Shane crumples his brow and frowns.

"I didn't mean it like that," I say. "I—you know I couldn't do that to Moyo, so soon after we . . ."

"Yeah," Shane says.

"Believe me," I say, still avoiding eye contact. "It's not a good time. There's so much going on. Beyond."

Shane goes quiet. He shifts his legs, turns his chin, and disappears into himself.

"Shane, are you still seeing that therapist?"

I realize my question is born out of suspicion, rather than concern. I'm wondering, did his therapist put him up to this? One of those exercises in being honest with the people around you? And in realizing that, I'm disappointed in myself. Because I should have asked the question months ago, about Shane's drinking problem.

"What?"

"I remember in eighth grade, when we both started seeing someone. After Tahoe. I was just wondering if you still . . ."

"Do you still see your therapist?" he asks, glaring.

"No. I stopped after freshman year," I say.

"Well, then don't worry about it."

"Shane."

"Opal. You said it yourself. It's not a good time."

Another heavy silence. I can't even begin to understand the chronic depression that Shane was going through. My therapy sessions were different; Mom made me go back as my only consequence for running away. I got better with high school, with my many activities, with Moyo and my revived spirit. But Shane suffers something less fleeting. It's the way his brain is wired. He's always been like this and always will be—that's what he told me the last time we talked about it, a long time ago. Shane seems to hate discussing his mental health as much as it pains me to bring it up.

"Okay, Shane," I say.

This is why the Hailey Carter bullshit stings so much. People like Shane genuinely deserve sympathy, but it's the attention mongers who get it.

Shane walks toward the door.

"I'm not saying I don't like you," I blurt out. "You're my oldest friend, my co-founder. None of . . . *this* would have happened without you." I throw the pillow over the edge of my bed. "I just don't *like* like you like that. I can't."

"I get it."

He leaves the room, and the door slams shut, automatically, and I can't help but wonder if he really does. If Shane really understands the full extent of what's going on.

If any of us do.

I don't see myself as a cold, emotionless monster. But over the years, I've learned to suppress my emotions. Kick them in the gut and bury them under a heavy pile of dirt. I've taught myself to ignore feelings in order to move on with the plans I've made for my life. For better or for worse, it's the only way to survive.

Nikki Walker once said in an interview that no one is truly fearless. Everyone is afraid of something. We all experience fear, but some people control it better than others. It's how you control fear that makes you fearless.

And so despite the whirlwind of emotions I experienced in Los Angeles, despite my discomfort with Hailey Carter, the way she smugly promised that she would win an Oscar someday—despite the shock of Shane admitting his long-standing crush on me—I decide to keep moving forward.

It's the only way I know how to move.

Besides, after the Seth Meyers interview, there's no turning back. M4rc informs me that twenty thousand people have lined up outside the colosseum for our next episode. *Twenty thousand.* I pick up my headset off the floor and check out the scene for myself. He wasn't kidding. A line of avatars wraps around the stadium, waiting for the doors to open so they can rush in and claim the best seats.

Behind the Scenes isn't just about me anymore. It's not about

Neil Finch or Howie Mendelsohn, or my friends. It's about the fans who believe so fiercely in what I have to say and show to them that they're willing to park their avatars out here for days. The ones who still believe in a techie future—a future where online communities are just as important as the ones you may or may not have in real life. We put on this weekly, half-hour mind-reading spectacle for parents, teachers, sons, daughters, gamers, nerds, hopeless romantics, all the dreamers who are fed up with the world.

My mind is so crammed with reasons and fears, shoulds and should nots, that I almost forget about Thursday.

Thursday is D-Day.

Chapter
Twenty-nine

"How is it already April?"

"If Harvard rejects me, I'm just gonna reply, 'April Fools!'"

"Can you believe Rosalind applied to twenty-five schools?"

"What a prestige whore."

"Will she get in?"

"Maybe. One for every extracurricular on her beyond-padded résumé."

"One. I just need one Ivy."

"My parents will kill me if I don't get into CalTech."

"Berkeley."

"Amherst."

"Harvard."

"Harvard."

"MIT or Harvard. Boston or bust."

****

It's an otherwise cheery Thursday afternoon. Freshmen and sophomores fill the lawns, throwing Frisbees and tripping and slipping around on the school's newly purchased hovercrafts. As I cross the lawn, I nearly get pummeled by one of the Patel twins. They're practicing their somersaults in glittery unitards, the sun glowing off the silvery fabric. Juniors sit scattered on blankets and towels, flipping through their SAT books. Physical books. A beautiful day like this calls for real pages.

But not for us. Not the seniors. Today, we're bogged down by the real world and the fact that it's about to determine the rest of our lives. All day, we're counting the minutes until five p.m. A lot of people pretend they aren't, of course. They busy themselves with every fidget imaginable. Pencil twirling. Foot tapping. Knuckle cracking. Peeling wrappers off soda bottles, twisting old cords that should have been replaced decades ago. We refresh web pages and lose ourselves in the most mindless environments on WAVE. We swing our arms left and right and up and down in Tetris. We beat pumpkins to pulp in Pumpkin Smash.

Shane finds comfort in his Rubik's Cube.

Twist. Twist. Twist twist twist flip twirl twiiiiist. Tw-tw-twist.

He solves it over and over and over. We're back in the control room, with Kara this time. Just the four of us. No adults.

Kara, Shane, and I—the three of us, the nervous applicants—sit before a row of computer screens, with Moyo watching us as a lifeguard of sorts.

"Does anyone else's mouth feel like the inside of a dust storm?" Kara says dryly.

"Juilliard will be so lucky to have you, Kara." Moyo smiles.

"Shut up, Moyo," she snaps, tapping at the trackpad. "Holy shit. It's 4:59. One more minute. Oh my God, oh my God . . ."

In this minute, my confidence teeters. I tell myself I'm a shoo-in; there's no way Stanford could reject the star of the moment. But I should have applied early. I tell myself I worked hard, scored good grades, and padded my résumé with all the right activities. But Stanford's 3 percent admissions rate doesn't guarantee anything. I tell myself I go to one of the best high schools in the country. But seventy-two other PAAST seniors applied to Stanford this year, and everyone knows they never take more than five of us.

I tell myself to check my email when the clock strikes five.

Dear Ms. Hopper,
Congratulations! It is with great pleasure that I
offer you . . .

I lose my mind and shriek. At the same time, Kara bursts out into an ear-piercing screech, and our noises blend in a dissonant sort of way. The two of us jump up and slam into each other, hands locking, fingers fumbling to cling to the other, and we bounce giddily. We swing our arms left to right, wildly, still screaming. Kara starts to cry, but I keep swinging our arms left and right, left and right—

I look to my left.

Shane.

****

The whole room goes quiet. It's like a metal tray fell to the ground in a crowded cafeteria.

We wait for Shane to check his other emails. An acceptance from anywhere else with an engineering program—Virginia Tech or Olin—would be a saving grace. But Shane's fingers don't move. They hover over the trackpad, shaking, as his face goes ghostly white. MIT didn't just reject Shane; it sucked the life out of him.

I put a hand on his shoulder.

"How about . . ."

"I didn't apply anywhere else," Shane breathes.

Without meaning to, I gasp. I cover my mouth.

"It was MIT or nothing," Shane says, his eyes bulging. "That's what my parents told me."

Kara stands to the side, her arms crossed. She looks at Shane not with disgust or pity but with sympathy. I've never seen Kara like this before; her head hangs low, humbly. Her big brown eyes, sincere.

"But Shane," Moyo says. "Does that mean . . ."

"I don't know what it means," Shane says, "except that my parents are going to be so pissed. They're going to kill me."

"Why didn't you—"

"Why don't you shut up, Moyo," Shane snaps. "You wouldn't know the first thing about not getting what you want." He looks at me, and I look at Moyo, and we agree with our worried expressions not to push Shane any further than he's pushing himself.

Than his parents push him.

"Fuck," Shane says. He's still sitting, though his hand has moved off the trackpad to the Rubik's Cube, clenching it tightly. "They're already so pissed about . . ."

Shane looks to Kara, and she tilts her head, like they're sharing a secret. I wonder if Shane has been confiding in Kara all these months I've been absent. Come to think of it, I remember seeing Kara and Heather Lowenstein talking in the Sphinx the other day.

"It doesn't matter," Shane finishes. "Fuck."

He pushes his chair back so that it clatters to the floor, and he hurls the Rubik's Cube across the room. It slams into the green screen.

"FUUUUCK."

"Shane!" Moyo says, running over. "Calm down."

"Fuck you, Moyo," Shane says. "Enjoy the East Coast, thousands of miles away from—"

He charges out of the room before finishing his sentence.

Chapter
Thirty

We stand there, stunned, staring at Shane's empty, fallen seat.
None of us have ever witnessed him lash out like that, so ruth-
lessly, so devoid of happiness. He's had his outbursts before. He's
thrown things. And he yells at his overbearing mom all the time.
But never at his friends. Shane is usually a gentle giant around
us. But this time, with the rejections—from MIT, from me, from
whatever other corners of his life—it seems every last page of the
Book of Shane has gone through the shredder.

"I'm worried about him," Moyo says. "Maybe I should—"

"Don't," I say. "You're clearly the last person he wants to talk
to right now."

"I don't understand," Moyo says.

"I'll text Shane," Kara says abruptly. "No, no. He won't want
to hear from me after . . . I'll text Heather."

"Since when have you and Heather Lowenstein texted?"

We stare at each other, and a confused emotion washes over
our faces. Just minutes ago, Kara and I were jumping around the

room like someone had set off dynamite in our hearts. Our past didn't matter. It got swept under the intoxicating rug of acceptance. But now . . . Well, fuck. Pleasure and pain don't always mix so well—especially when the pleasure is yours and the pain is someone else's. Now we feel guilty.

Kara swallows. She closes her eyes and twists her neck.

"Shane's going through some shit, Opal."

"Like what?" I demand.

"Like what," Kara repeats, scoffing. She looks at Moyo, who shrugs. "Don't worry. Everyone understands how beyond busy you've been lately. Especially Shane."

"I *am* worrying, Kara. And since when have you been such an expert on Shane?" I say. "Let's not forget I've known him the longest out of everyone in this room. Just tell me what's going on with him."

"Maybe you should talk to him yourself."

"Oh, you've got a lot of nerve, Kara Lee—"

"You guys." Moyo looks up from his phone. "Blast from the PAAST."

I let out a groan. "Right. That's tonight. And we can't be late to this one. Constantine's making an appearance, remember?"

"God, what shitty timing," Kara says.

"At least we know Shane will be there," Moyo says, "since it's mandatory. They're especially strict about this one."

We run to our dorms to get dressed. I throw on a red romper—the same muddy red as the Stanford mascot—and tie my hair back. I finish a few minutes before the doors to the gym are scheduled to open, so I stop by Shane's room to check on him. I knock, but there's no answer. I want to text him, but it'll only make Shane angrier to hear from me. Hopefully he's with Heather, or loitering outside the gym.

But he's not at the dance. I know because the four of us are supposed to introduce Constantine as the MC of the dance, the last one before senior prom. The student council thought it would be a perfect way to unwind after the most stressful day of our four years, with a heartthrobby superstar.

After we introduce Constantine, he leads the goggle-clad senior class in a jumpy rendition of "99 Red Balloons." I swing to the corner of the gym to catch Heather Lowenstein, but Moyo pops up from behind and grabs my arm.

"I already talked to Heather," Moyo says. "She hasn't seen him. I don't care if I'm the last person he wants to talk to right now. I'm worried. We need to look for him."

I dig my chin into Moyo's shoulder.

"I'm worried too."

****

Moyo and I bolt through the doors of the gymnasium. Rosalind Wu tries yelling at us to stop—we haven't put in our mandatory hour—but to hell with student life. We check every lab, every classroom in Hell, every inch of the Sphinx, but Shane is nowhere to be found. He's not answering texts or picking up phone calls.

By the time we're standing outside the dorm building, hands

on our knees, panting, I allow my imagination to go somewhere I'd only considered in passing.

"Moyo," I say, breathing heavy. "What if . . ."

I motion diagonally, toward the southwest corner of campus, toward Alma Street—toward the Caltrain tracks.

"No way," he says. "No, no, no. Shane wouldn't."

"But what if?"

The two of us look at each other intensely. I've never seen Moyo's eyes bulge like that before, the veins popping with agony.

We sprint off campus—Detectables and cameras be damned.

****

I have a very specific memory of Shane. It plays in my head while Moyo and I race through downtown Palo Alto, like a song to the rhythm of our pounding feet.

Junior year. We're sitting together in the back of AP Physics—Moyo and Shane, with me in between. Topic: quantum mechanics.

"Quantum mechanics tells us," Dr. Delaney drones, "that an object does not exist independent of its observer. The mere act of observing an object causes it to be there."

Moyo raises his hand.

"Yes, Moyo?"

"So you're saying a quantum object is basically . . . invisible until it's been observed? Or it doesn't exist without an observer?"

"Quite the opposite. A particle exists in what we call a 'superposition'—in all possible states—until it is observed in one specific state. Take light. Most people would describe light as a wave. But under observation, light waves are forced to behave like particles. That's quantum mechanics at play."

"So all these quantum particles are basically faking it," Moyo says.

The entire classroom laughs. Especially me. I lean over in my seat and nudge Moyo playfully. Then I look to Shane, expecting him to join the banter, but he doesn't seem very entertained. He'd been like this all summer, I realize. Not reacting to jokes, to good news. Not acting the way people are supposed to act around other people.

"You could say they're faking it," Dr. Delaney says. "Or you could say they're full of surprises."

****

"Oh, thank God," Moyo says, letting out a sigh of relief.

We reach the Caltrain station and all is calm. Just the usual clusters of students and tech employees waiting to board the next northbound train to SF or southbound train to San Jose. Moyo and I weave between kids with backpacks—my future classmates—and tired, middle-aged engineers and marketing gurus. No sign of Shane.

We take the underpass to check the other side; once again, no sign of Shane.

On the way back through the underground passageway, Moyo stops to lean against the curved wall. He closes his eyes. The significance of where he's standing, under the same flickering light where I stood the last time we met in this tunnel, isn't wasted on me.

"What now?" I say, poking Moyo in our old way. "You know you can only break up with me once."

Slowly, Moyo's face creeps up to reveal his bloodshot eyes. His jaw is tense with rage.

"I can't believe you have it in you to joke right now," he says.

"What? Because this is all my fault?"

"I'm not saying that."

"Well, maybe *I'm* saying that," I say, leaning against the wall next to Moyo. "If I just—if I hadn't been a dick to Shane this whole time. Ignored him, ever since you entered the picture. God, it's all our faults."

"What are you saying? You're sounding crazy."

"Don't call me crazy."

We pause, each taking a deep breath. A train rumbles overhead.

"And what are you saying," Moyo goes, "about me entering the picture? That's . . ."

Another rumble. This time from our phones.

Moyo and I read the first line of the text message from Shane and hear the train's rumblings choke to a screeching halt.

We skid across the concrete floor of the tunnel and pounce up the stairs, our faces already horrified at what we're expecting to see.

PART FOUR

GIRL REDEEMED

Chapter
Thirty-one

Three days. I don't leave the dorms for three straight days. I hole myself up inside my room, skip my Friday classes, and subsist on stale snack bars and Red Bull for the entire weekend. Every now and then, M4rc asks if I want to hear a message from Moyo, enter a WAVEchat with Neil Finch, and I give the same answer. No. People knock at my door, but I don't answer. The only person I want to talk to is Shane, and that's not going to happen.

If I thought Shane could so easily take his life, why hadn't I done something about it sooner? His drinking problem was front and center. I knew deep down that Shane was dealing with a lot of stress this year, with the spikes of failure and the tight grip of pressure, yet I did nothing. I said nothing. I was so absent that he went to Kara Lee with his problems. Only when he disappeared did my better sense kick in, because I knew, I *knew*, he was that close to the edge. What kind of friend does that make me?

It doesn't matter that the Caltrain was just screeching to its natural halt. Nor does it matter that Shane's cryptic text was asking for "space" for a *little while*, not forever, as I had horrifically imagined when I read it in the tunnel. Shane locked himself in his room after he got rejected from MIT and skipped the Blast from the PAAST dance. He needed time to himself; he didn't want to talk to anyone for a while.

My imagination was wrong.

I spend the weekend wallowing in bed, clutching my pillow, flipping through environments on my PolyWall. I let the infinite blackness of outer space and the royal blue ripples of the ocean become my surroundings. Anywhere but here—anywhere but reality—because the possibility of losing real-world Shane shook me to my core. I realize it doesn't matter how impressively we design our avatars, or how many millions of views we have in the virtual world. This life is all we have. I could replicate Shane's consciousness, his personality, his shaggy hair. Sit across from his perfect avatar in Pete's Arcade. But none of it would be the same.

I spend the weekend staring into the lifeless pixels on my wall and questioning everything. After a stint in Tokyo, I ask M4rc to take me somewhere else, anywhere, and he does exactly that. The high-rises and city lights fade out, replaced by tall trees and dirt roads. An orange fire crackles by my side.

He's taking me to Campfire.

You are my everything, Opal, Abba texted me just weeks before he disappeared. I know I've been busy, that I haven't been around enough lately. But that will change soon. We will have an entire universe to ourselves.

I re-created our campsite out of pixels and spent hours inside that world, smiling at Aaron Tal's avatar. But the summer before eighth grade, I remembered the little song he used to sing for me—*you are the stones and the trees and the waterfall / you are my Opal, my balsa, my Tal.* How he would always sing those lyrics with gravity. What if my answer was right there beneath the California sun and the dirt roads? What if Abba had left clues in our private getaway, or had even escaped there himself?

So I showed up. I hopped off the bus with my drawstring bag full of water and snack bars, and I hiked all over Tahoe. I waited patiently at our campsite with the acorn-red house off in the distance, surrounded by pine trees, and I dipped my feet in the lake where we never once caught a fish, and I slept in my sleeping bag under the stars. I was too busy re-creating our private universe to notice the drones overhead that eventually spotted me. I was too lost in my memories to object when the police car rolled up.

Those flying cameras had exposed me again. My mom had come to my rescue again. And I still didn't have my dad.

Maybe the rumors were right. Maybe he jumped off the Bay Bridge, like everyone says behind my back—from the pressure to succeed, to win over investors. I'm already learning the kind of shady tactics it takes to be successful, with morals as gray as the foggiest day in San Francisco.

I've never considered myself a quitter. But the toll this school year has taken on me—on my friends, on my conscience, on my privacy—and with the odds stacked against me . . . it might be in my best interest to move on.

Maybe it's just not worth it.

****

All my life I've comforted myself with memories of my dad. I thrived on the closeness I still feel with this man who was once my everything. But it strikes me profoundly, now, that I've had a physical part of him with me all along. Wherever he is, my dad will always live in my mind. But my mother is right here, on the opposite side of town, in real life.

By Sunday evening, I feel lightheaded. I need a real meal—something warm, and preferably not wrapped in shiny plastic—but I don't dare set foot in the cafeteria. Maybe that's why I leave the dorm building for the first time in seventy-two hours, why I go where I go. Maybe I'm craving something else too.

I shield my face from the paparazzi drones that follow me, occasionally swatting at them like flies. Within minutes, I'm standing at my front door.

I knock.

The Tesla is parked outside in the driveway, although that's no guarantee my mom will be home. I haven't forgotten how dedicated Dean Tal is to her job, to the freshmen at Stanford. She could be at a student life event, or—

The door opens. Across the gap stands my mother. A mess of tears already streaks down her tan, rosy cheeks. Her knees are shaking and her arms extend awkwardly, hesitant, unsure if after more than three years of stiff interaction with her daughter, if she can . . . Yes. She will. We both will, in fact.

My mother and I hug fiercely, and she begins blubbering.

"I—I saw you in the PorchCam, back in my office, and I—I just, couldn't believe. I thought you were a holo, or . . ."

I pull away.

"I've missed you," Mom blurts.

"I know."

She pulls me in for one more hug, quick and affirmative like I remember, and brings me inside. We settle on the high chairs by the kitchen island.

"I never asked you why you replaced the marble," I say, tapping on the clear glass surface. Just like the boardroom tables.

"Oh yes." Mom blushes. "I know I was against having screens in the kitchen, but, well . . ." She gulps. "It was getting lonely here, eating meals alone."

She straightens her back, smiles, and reaches out to take my hand, pulling it closer.

"But *you*. I've been keeping up with all your success, young lady. Gosh. You've grown into such a smart and poised adult, Opal." My mom's eyes fill with pride, and I see myself not just reflected in them but tattooed. She never gave up hope. Not for her daughter.

"Mom, I'm not that—"

"No! No, I won't accept any humility. Not today. Not after you got yourself into *Stanford*! That was all you, honey. I'll admit, I was worried when I saw you didn't apply early. I thought maybe,

maybe you didn't want . . . Well, you had plenty of reasons not to apply. But Dean Narendra, she was telling me your application was so stellar it was worth the wait. And now, with this XP—"

"Mom—"

"You've really got a pulse on exactly what people care about. It's so commendable, what you're—"

"Mom!"

She collapses her head and laughs.

"I'm sorry. Can you tell you've been on my mind a lot?"

I should be laughing too. But instead, I'm dying a little inside, and it takes everything in me not to collapse into an ugly puddle of tears. How could my mom be so happy, so genuinely thankful to have me home for the first time since winter break? Why hasn't she yelled at her daughter? For acting selfish, unappreciative, for abandoning her mother? And what kind of person does that make *me*?

"Thanks, Mom," I eke out.

"I just wish you didn't have to take that PAL investment," Mom sighs, checking her perfectly manicured nails.

"What?"

She looks up. I forgot how pretty my mother was.

"When you were young," she says with a faint laugh, "I was so worried you'd either never stop looking for your father, or worse, turn out like him. I didn't want you going down those rabbit holes. And now that you're in it, I feel like I can't pull you out."

"You could have just said that," I say.

Mom sighs, rubbing her eyes. "I wanted to . . ."

"I know."

"Protect you."

My heart drops. "I know."

We look at each other honestly. I dangle my feet, kicking under the seat.

"Well. I imagine you're very stressed these days," Mom says as she pops out of her seat. She takes out two green bottles from the refrigerator, handing one to me. "Drink this. Lots of electrolytes. Are you handling everything okay?"

"Of course, Mom." I consider filling her in on the total mess I've made with my friends, but I don't want to ruin the joyful rhythm of our reunion. "I'm fine."

"Good," she says, taking a long gulp of her drink. She keeps her eyes glued tight on me. "Honey, I know things haven't been easy for you. And if I had to venture a guess, I'd say they're not perfect right now either."

"Mom, I can handle—"

"No, no. Let me finish. I *know* you can handle anything that gets thrown your way. I'm your mother. I know you, Opal." She closes her eyes, takes a deep breath. "I'm happy to give you your space. Always have been, always will be. But I'll always be here for you too."

Sip after sip, my mother and I finish our green drinks and start our relationship afresh. We roast chicken and sauté kale, and we eat and talk and laugh about silly things. We dream up my life at Stanford, play out our awkward run-ins, how we'll pretend to be strangers on campus. Mom doesn't ask about *Behind the Scenes*. She doesn't ask why I still applied to Stanford, knowing very well that she works there. We'll get to those things, eventually.

For tonight, what the two of us need most—what I need to feel the ground beneath my feet again, and certainly what my mother has craved for a very long time—is to slip back into place as mother and daughter.

****

The next day, I leave the house before the sun has fully risen. Clouds ripple across the morning sky, masking the yellows and oranges and crimsoned reds that are begging to burst out of the background. As the world above me works to extract its daily dose of color, I scurry back to PAAST. I tiptoe down the dorm hallway and around the corner to my room—but someone is sitting outside my door.

"Kara?"

Kara snaps her head up.

"There you are," she mumbles, shaking herself awake.

"How did you know I was coming?"

"I heard you left campus alone last night," Kara says, propping her arm against the wall behind her to stand. The bottom of her robe gets caught in one of the sensors on the floor and she stumbles. "Ow. I saw it on Livvit, so I camped out here so I wouldn't miss you when you got back. Where have you *been*?"

Between her hair, which seems to have lost a hard-fought battle against static electricity, and her bloodshot eyes, Kara is an utter mess. She raises her nose to sniffle and lets out a roaring sneeze instead.

"I was home," I say, resisting a smile. "Kara, are you all right?"

"Ugh, I've been sick all weekend."

"Now who's the girl gone viral?"

"You're terrible. Anyway, I'm glad you're—" Kara sneezes again, wiping the snot with her Ritz-Carlton robe. "*Ekh*. I'm glad you're back. We were all worried after you locked yourself in your room all weekend." She pauses. "Ready for today?"

"Today?"

"It's Monday."

I open my mouth to speak, when I hear someone else's door open at the other end of the hall. Jacqueline Sharif. She must be up early for gymnastics practice. Or maybe she's going to see Spencer. They're still together, against all odds.

"Kara," I say, my eyes following Jacqueline. "I . . . I need a break."

"Nope. *That's* not happening."

Kara snaps her fingers right before my nose. Twice. Loudly.

"Kara!"

"Look, I get how the other night freaked you out, like, beyond. Moyo filled me in on everything," Kara says. "But trust me, Shane's gonna be all right. His parents suck; we've all been there."

"I just don't understand."

"Understand what?"

"How all of a sudden you're like, best friends with my friends."

"I think you've been a bit busy lately, Opal."

Blame it on exhaustion, but we break into laughter—until Kara lets out a crescendo of sneezes. Then I really lose it. We step into my room.

Kara inspects the mess of Red Bull cans and wrappers at the

base of my Picasso Mirror. "Do you remember when you came over to my house in middle school?"

"I remember the self-pushing swings in your backyard. Takes all the fun out of swinging, if you ask me."

"At least we had swings at that house." Kara sighs. "My dad thought they were too tacky for the mansion."

"At least you have a mansion . . ."

"He wasn't happy, you know," she says. "That I invited you over. I told him it was for our COMET project—collect, observe, measure, whatever the rest of it stood for. But my dad was all, *I don't want you talking to Opal Tal.*"

Kara clears a space on the floor and sits down with her back against my dresser, clenching a fistful of her robe. If she vomits right now, we can pretend she never brought up the fact that her dad didn't want me around. It would also give me an excuse to clean up my room.

"Sorry," Kara says after a long silence. "What I meant to say is that my dad believed certain things about your past, about your dad, and he didn't want me hanging out with you. And so I didn't. That's why I ignored you when we got to high school. You know that's when his business took off too, right? My dad was always a loser in high school and college and growing up in general. He was a loser at *Harvard*. Pretty sad, right? And so once he became cool by Silicon Valley standards, he realized I could be cool too, in a daughter-of-a-billionaire sort of way . . . He wanted me to throw the parties he never got invited to. He wanted me to be the center of attention he never was."

"I would say I'm sorry, but—"

"No, I get it," Kara says. "I'm not looking for an apology. It's not like I was abused. Honestly, I think I like the attention. Nature or nurture, it doesn't matter. But Shane's been feeling the same pressure from his parents lately, to be more *present*, more *noticed*. And you know him. That's not his style."

"Of course," I reply tersely. I'm gutted. Why didn't Shane ever tell me this? I glare at Kara, my eyes one-upping hers in what I perceive as a friendship competition. "Shane hates the spotlight. That's why he's so pale."

Whether or not she means it, Kara chuckles at my poorly timed joke.

"His parents have a harder time accepting that," she says. "Especially after he got deferred from MIT. You know the Franklins."

"But he's the whole reason we went viral in the first place! The reason we kept going after we lost!"

"Yeah, and *you* got all the credit," Kara says. "Honestly, I think his dad's a little sexist. That's how it started. *How come* Opal's *making all the headlines?* You think Shane would have wanted to admit that to you?"

Silence.

"And then I joined the team," Kara continues. "Then Constantine, and then you and Moyo became a thing and made Shane, like, the fifteenth wheel. His parents have been smashing it over his head all year. And then the MIT bomb . . ."

"That's so stupid," I sigh. For some reason, my mind wanders to Palo Alto Labs, the PR firm, and Hailey Carter's conniving family. "Whatever. All the more reason to put *Behind the Scenes* aside for a while."

"Are you joking? If you throw this away—this thing we've built, all of us together—you make it worse. None of it will have been worth it."

"It's more than just Shane."

"Oh, really? Enlighten me."

"I can't."

"Why?"

"Because it makes me look bad!" I say. "It's all been a lie."

Kara takes a deep breath. She looks at me curiously, wondering what on earth I could be hiding.

"Look, I'm not going to pry," Kara says. "But I'll say this. You've been airing *Behind the Scenes* for more than six months now. *We've* been airing it. You, me, Moyo, Constantly-Into-Myself, and Stephan . . . and Shane. If you give up now, you're giving up for all of us." There—*there's* the melodramatic Kara Lee we all know and love. "If you're saying it's all been a lie, do something about it. Be honest."

"What if the truth hurts?"

Kara lifts her chin, about to sneeze, but she stops herself. Instead, she smiles.

"Come on, Opal. If Shane can fight past pain, so can you."

That's when it strikes me that Kara is right. I don't need to take off a few weeks. I don't even need a day. Pain shouldn't get to win, ever, for any of us. At the end of the day, our show is about exposing the truth. The anger I feel about Hailey Carter, the pain I feel for Shane, they should only make me stronger. Push me to do better. I realize the magnitude of this odd situation, the opportunity at hand, and I figure out how I can make good again.

I'm going to make ten-year-old Opal proud.

****

"I'm fine, I'm fine, I'm fine."

Because my plan involves Shane, I give myself an excuse to knock on his door again, and to my surprise, he opens it.

"I know," I say. "I'm just pissed you didn't talk to me sooner."

"You were busy."

"Yeah, but I still *care* about you, Shane. So when I saw you Thursday and you freaked out, obviously I freaked out too, and— anyway. That's not the reason I woke you up."

"Good," he says, "because let me say again, I'm *fine*."

"That's up for debate," I say, reminding myself of Shane's drinking problem, how I want—no, need—to address that. But for now: "Are the comm links ready for action?"

"Um, what? Yes?"

"You know what I'm talking about, right? We discussed it way back in October, how I might need to share some stuff with the audience and they might need to share some stuff with me."

"Yeah, I'm pretty sure I built that when I was bored over winter break," Shane says. "Or after a therapy session or something. I can't remember."

I smile. That son of a bitch *is* still seeing his therapist. I can't believe I'd ever doubted him.

"Good."

"So . . . You want me to activate it for today's episode?"

"Yes!" I yell, jogging back to my dorm room. I won't be attending any of my classes today. I won't be following any of the rules. I've got a monologue to write. "It'll help both of us," I sing, my feet switching to a skip. "Promise!"

Episode 032

OPAL

```
Hello, world.
```

The colosseum flickers with artificial spotlights and yellow sparkles. I used to hate all this light because it made it harder to look—really *look*—at the tens of thousands of avatars in my live audience. So I'd sweep my eyes over the crowd like they were one giant blob. But this time, I make a concerted effort to register this collection of tiny dots as individual people, just like myself. Each outrageous outfit, each perfectly crafted avatar, is a person putting out the ideal version of themselves.

I smile.

Stay calm, I tell myself. Stay calm. They're not just avatars; they're people. Their emotions aren't just numbers; they're feelings.

OPAL

```
Today, we have a different show for you. No
   tricks. No simulations. No face tracking, no
   performances. And, sorry, no Constantine.
```

Confused murmurs ripple through the crowd. I can hear the muffled popcorn sound of avatars zapping out of the XP.

OPAL

```
Today, I'm getting honest.
```

New avatars fill their places. Whether they're from one of the alternate audiences—we've filled the colosseum one hundred times over with live viewers—or avatars that had chomped on LiveTags, I don't know. Nor do I care. I feel destiny tugging at my strings, recklessly, showing no concern for what's strategic or clever.

Just what is right.

OPAL

The other day I told Seth Meyers that virtual reality takes empathy to the next level. It lets us experience someone else's suffering, thrill, fear, even love, and it puts us in positions we never in a million years would have imagined. But I learned shortly after that VR can be manipulative too.

I take a deep breath.

OPAL

I learned that our show is rooted in a lie.

Gasps from the audience. Out of the corner of my eye, I notice our live view count creeping up.

OPAL

Hailey Carter never had a mental breakdown. It was a publicity stunt. And when I came up here and threw

```
     you into that XP, accusing you of lying . . . I
     had no idea that she was the real liar.
```

More people gasp. They begin to chatter amongst themselves. I have to hush the crowd twice before I can keep going.

                              OPAL
```
     Listen! Publicity stunts happen all the time. But
         this—this one hit close to home.
```

The lights grow out of control. People must be taking screenshots, recording holos, Zapping like there's no tomorrow. I imagine the Livvit boards going nuts, and I can picture Matthew Seamus drooling with this juicy scoop. But I have to keep going.

                              OPAL
```
     I saw myself in Hailey. In her very public pain.
     And it—it comforted me to know that people out
         there genuinely felt for her.
```

I gulp. Squeeze my eyes tight. Then, I open wide, prepared to tell the truth, my truth, unattached to algorithms and attention.

                              OPAL
```
     Put yourself in these shoes: ten-year-old girl, a
         total dork in the classroom, constantly raising
         your hand in math and science, a rising star in
```

the local chess league. Annoying curly brown
hair that can't seem to tame itself.

A smile tickles my face.

And a dad who pats your back for raising your hand.
Who cheers a little too loud at your chess tour-
naments and brushes your hair even when your mom
says it's no use. And then the next day, he's
gone. He leaves a note, but you look for him
regardless, even if that "complicated" world he
wrote about might have been you. You sift through
everything he left behind: his tablets, drawers,
even the old receipts he kept. You get in front
of cameras and beg for him to come back.

My breaths get short, difficult. Sometimes, when it all feels too
heavy, I'll pretend my tragedy happened to someone else. I imagine a ten-foot pole between the girl who experienced all that pain,
that trauma, and the girl I wanted to be.

That girl is still me.

OPAL

That's pain I'd shoved away for a long time. When we
started *Behind the Scenes,* I didn't intend to become a star. I had my own motive. I wanted to meet

Howie Mendelsohn, the inventor of WAVE, because,
as some of you know, he did business with my dad.
I thought Howie Mendelsohn could help me understand what happened to Abba. And in a messed-up,
collision-course sort of way, I ended up here.
For the last seven years, not a moment has gone
by when I haven't wondered what happened.

Another deep breath.

OPAL

People talk. Some say Howie Mendelsohn did it.
Some say my father ran away. Some say he killed
himself. The pressure, his desire to succeed,
that it all got to him. That he was a nutcase
anyway. However, I'm not convinced. That's why
I want your help.

I look at the view count. I don't need Howie Mendelsohn anymore. Six months ago, I heard from a girl named Amber Donahue
because I put myself out there on this stage, and she had information I never would have learned otherwise. There have got to be
more Ambers out there.

OPAL

The millions of you who've stuck around. Will you
help me?

A white line flashes through the audience, like a TV screen gone black, and suddenly my entire view curls into a tornado. The next second, there are hundreds of small, flat squares hovering on a screen in front of me. Shane has given me a comprehensive view of everyone. Each little square contains fifty thousand audience members. He zooms out so that I can see all of them, the millions of avatars sitting with me. What's more, he's split them up by location. Two squares for California, three for New York, two for Tokyo, even a square for Hungary. I stand before all these strangers, waiting for them to answer.

Of course, they do—all at once. A thundering round of yeses. The colosseum is bursting with the echoes of their excitement and support.

OPAL

All right, then. Now Shane Franklin, our resident
genius—

For the first time on air, I touch the Invisigogs, quickly fluttering my fingers over the side to activate the recording feature—which takes me out of the colosseum . . . and into the Media Room. I'd expected there to be more gasping, more WTF reactions from the audience. But their murmurs are more out of curiosity than anger. I scurry away from the green screen, past Kara and Constantine on the couch—that must have given the audience a squeal—and focus on Shane. He's shocked at first. I see the screens in front of him showing the audience, and they're somewhat confused too. But then he smiles, chuckles, even waves.

I scurry back to the green screen and return to the colosseum.

OPAL

Well, that was fun. Sometimes it's refreshing to see how the sausage gets made. And we're all about honesty today. So. Shane's set up a super-sophisticated communication channel, where I will dump a wealth of information.

I pull a sub-XP, Dropbox, out of WAVEverse. In it is my file. The one that's been sitting there, waiting, since long before we started *Behind the Scenes*. The one with every piece of evidence, every lead, every journal entry, every theory or hunch I've managed to come up with. This file contains . . .

OPAL

Everything. This is my relationship with my dad. But it's incomplete, and that's where you come in. Aaron Tal would have interacted with hundreds of people before he disappeared. All types of people. I need your help to make sense of these files. If you so much as emailed with him, speak up. If you met him at a conference, have any security footage, did his taxes, were his student. I've tried hard over the years to

figure out what happened to my dad. But I don't
have all the data. You do.

I drop the physical manifestation of the file, and it shatters
into millions of little pieces that disseminate into the audience.
And with it, pride. I feel my chest swell with the excitement of
the moment. I built *Behind the Scenes* with one team, and now,
maybe I'll uncover what happened to Abba with another. My eyes
sweep across the square panels and land on the stage under my
feet, which lights up with the other side of the comm channel.
All the information being blitzed back to me. It's a bonanza of
knowledge, but I've already got my loyal partner, M4rc, shuffling
through the crap for the most relevant bits.

It's nearly three forty-five p.m. in San Francisco. Dinnertime
on the East Coast. Our British fans are up late, and our Korean and
Japanese fans must have woken up early. I had nearly forgotten that
we'd picked the perfect time for the entire world to come together.
Suddenly, I feel a special kinship with these strangers who've been
with me. Who offer snippets of information about their lives—the
precise moments in which they crossed paths with Aaron Tal:

"So, I work the night shift at the London Convention Centre. Your
dad's calendar puts him at an EECS conference here, and if you think
it would be helpful, I'm happy to go through the security footage . . ."

"We emailed two years before he disappeared, about . . ."

"I was his thesis advisor in grad school. I don't have anything
of particular use to your mission, but I can say that your father was
a magnificent . . ."

"I was his student two semesters before . . ."

"We emailed every spring. I'm a plexiglass salesman. I tried selling him a ton of shit, but your dad, he's all *Get with the times! It's all about . . .*"

Avatars fly in and out of their seats, go still, start talking to each other. It's utter commotion in the colosseum, and I couldn't be happier. *This is the power of VR*, I think. To make sense of life. To provide a space where you can share your experiences for the better. I already can't believe some of the anecdotes people share about my dad, how they're letting me into their lives: teachers, security guards, customer support reps. Real people, not numbers. For the last six months, they've been like family to me—stepping into my living room, listening to me crack jokes and discuss what's happening in the world. Of course they were going to help me when I needed it.

The amount of information coming through is astounding. The floor of the stage lights up like a work of psychedelic art, just dazzling and manic and full of color, and it strikes me that it might take all summer to sift through everything.

I won't deny that one name still swirls in my head with painful clarity. I won't deny that as I watch the incoming messages on the stage, as my eyes pool with tears of happiness and hope, each time his name pops up, I flinch. He's undeniably linked to my dad. And for seven years, he's cornered me into action: led me right into his house, right here. I may not need his help anymore, but it doesn't mean I'm safe from him.

The murmurs from millions of on-screen avatars drown out

the unsettling hammering sound that fills my head. Slowly, I raise my chin. I continue lifting my gaze until it lands on the top-right screen. San Francisco. I squint my eyes, and I can almost see Howie Mendelsohn somewhere in the crowd, watching me carefully. Maybe even furiously. Holding back his piece of the mystery.

Chapter

Thirty-two

They show up within minutes. I can hardly remember how I ended the show because the stage begins teetering beneath me. Something's wrong, and when I whip off my goggles, I check inside the control room and see my friends' stunned faces, staring past me. I turn around to find four Palo Alto Labs employees, dressed in the company's soulless fleece vests. One of them locks eyes with me, and just like that, I know why they're here. Neil Finch wants to see me. These are his henchmen.

My friends and I march silently behind the men through Hell. I would have expected a car to take us to headquarters, but instead, the employees guide us through Palo Alto. Immediately, hordes of locals gather around, flooding us with questions about Hailey Carter, about the search for my dad, about what had come out of it, about, about, about. Paparazzi drones swoop through the crowd like falcons. Why would PAL subject us to this? Every step I take upon the spotless pavement feels heavier than the last, crushing my high spirits.

Before I know it, I'm inside another citrus-stained boardroom. Neil Finch barges in within seconds; his entrance sends chills down my spine.

"Well, *that* was a show," Neil snarks, taking one last sip of his coffee before tossing the paper cup into the bin.

Moyo, Kara, Shane, Stephan, Constantine—they all look to me. I say nothing.

"I can only imagine all the chatter in WAVEverse right now. Oh, and Matthew Seamus must be having a field day!" Neil says.

The way he hits every word with the invisible hammer of subtext, I get Neil's message loud and clear. The question is, what next? Punishment? Divestment? Surely they'll get the PR firm to cover up . . . well, everything.

"You've taken this very far, Opal. Farther than I ever thought you'd go. My colleagues and I have already discussed what action we might take, were such a seismic event to occur, and now seems as good a time as any to make our offer."

Here we go, I think.

"To acquire *Behind the Scenes*."

The chills in my spine melt into warm blood, and I finally speak.

"Excuse me?"

"Now, it won't be a massive offer—you don't have any revenue yet, so we can't justify hundreds of millions of dollars, but we were thinking something to the tune of $12 million should be plenty—"

"Neil," I burst. "I'm sorry. I don't understand. What part of the show that I just put on makes you want to acquire us?" I think for a second, remembering the very first time we met, when Neil Finch threatened us for hacking their user data, and I shudder. "Why would Palo Alto Labs . . ."

"We see a great deal of potential in a closer relationship." Neil smiles, his crooked nose wrinkling with delight. "As you can imagine, PAL has so much to offer beyond an investment."

My friends look to me desperately. I roll my eyes. What am I, their collective microphone?

Well.

I gulp.

"Don't—don't all PAL employees live on campus?" I ask nervously. "As you know, some of us are going to college next year . . ."

"Details, details," Neil says. "We'll have you for the summer and figure the rest out as we go along."

I look to my friends, their eyes wide with confusion.

"It's too early," I say. "We can't. I'm sorry."

Neil Finch taps the table.

"You know, Opal, you should think hard about the kind of relationship you want with your sole investor," he says. "After all, it would be a *shame* if we weren't on the same team, considering how you outed Hailey Carter just now. The last thing you need at your age is a multimillion-dollar lawsuit."

I freeze. Neil drops his eyes to the table, upon which he pulls up an electronic scan of my signature. That's when I remember.

"Breaking a nondisclosure agreement is a serious offense," Neil chides. "Especially in Silicon Valley."

For a split second, I remember the beachy PR firm boardroom, the human secretary who nonchalantly prompted me to sign . . .

Now I'm the one looking desperately at my friends. We're all experts in eye contact at this point, and mine cowers in the helplessness of being cornered.

I think about Shane, who doesn't have a college to attend next year anyway. I think about Kara, whose father does business with Palo Alto Labs and would ensure our safety. I think about Stephan and Constantine, whom I never fully trusted anyway. And I think about Moyo. My best friend—whether he admits it or not. I think about all of us together, spending the summer inside the world's most powerful, opaque tech company.

And then I think about my dad. He wouldn't want me to back down in fear to Palo Alto Labs. Not like this.

"We'll consider it," I say firmly.

Moyo turns and looks at me with a grim expression. "Opal," he half whispers. "We should take the offer. We have no choice."

The others nod in agreement.

"We're not going to let them bully us like this," I say, raising my voice. "People are watching now. If it comes out that a giant corporation is suing a bunch of teenagers—well, we can let the public decide for themselves. WAVE doesn't just belong to you, Neil. Not anymore. It belongs to all of us."

Neil Finch takes a sharp breath. His eyes narrow on me like tweezers, looking to pinch out the slightest hint of doubt.

I don't give.

Our staring contest is interrupted when a young woman enters the room, marches up to Neil, and whispers something in his ear. From the way his face relaxes, and then becomes surprised, and then surges with delight, you'd think the man was just promoted to be CEO of the whole company. And then it hits me— Howie Mendelsohn is involved.

"Very well," he says, clearing his throat after the woman takes off. "The rest of you may leave now. Opal, please stay behind."

A moment passes as everyone looks around the table. Another moment passes before Constantine rises slowly from his seat, followed by Stephan, and the two file out of the room. Moyo and Shane and Kara stare at me, their faces twisted with concern. As much as I wish they could rescue me, throw me a life ring, I remind myself that I'm the one who sank this ship in the first place. I take a deliberate breath and nod at them.

They leave, and the door shuts.

Neil sits still. He puckers his lips, presses them until they turn white.

"Do you want to know something, Opal?"

"I'd like to know a lot of things," I say shakily. If confidence could walk, my voice would be teetering on crutches right now.

"I planted that data," Neil says, "on Shane's computer. I wasn't supposed to, but I did, and now it seems my plan is working."

My eyes widen. Narrow. Explode in utter terror. I search Neil Finch's face for a sign that he's bluffing, but I find no such sign. All I see is a man, stone-cold serious.

He gets up and moves toward the door.

"Let's go for a walk," he says.

****

Neil leads me briskly through a dimly lit hall, wide as a highway and long as a football field. He doesn't utter a single word. Employees march by in their drab corporate attire, which they undoubtedly purchased from the company store, staring with big eyes like they recognize me. There's not a drop of color—not in the walls, not in their expressions. Even the hanging lights seem to emit grayness. As we turn a corner, one of the steel doors swings open, and I peek inside—there's a beautiful, holographic cityscape projecting from the floor, with red laser beams attacking it from every angle.

"Three layers deep," Neil says sharply. "Six sides. This building is a hexagon within a hexagon within a hexagon."

In ninth grade, I almost went on a field trip to Palo Alto Labs. But that was the year I wanted to hit Reset and start over, so I opted out. Now I understand what my classmates meant when they said it gave off creepy prison vibes.

We turn another corner, crossing diagonally this time. I think we're cutting through the hexagon layers. As Neil and I march silently, I consider the potential motives: why Neil Finch would plant the WAVE data, and why he now wants to acquire us. Every conclusion I reach is less than ideal for my safety.

He stops in a quiet hallway, before a steel door that looks different from the others. This one's set with eight thick bolts instead of two. A harsh yellow light scans Neil's face, and the door slides up to reveal another door.

"We're on the same team, Opal."

I shake my head.

"No we're not," I say. "You're dangerous. This entire company is."

Another light flashes over Neil's face, opening a second door. We enter a small courtyard with dozens of topiary sculptures scattered across a green field.

"Look over there," Neil says, pointing a finger.

Across the field, a frail man emerges from behind a lively penguin topiary. His face is one I know all too well and not at all.

Familiar.

Stranger.

Villain.

Howie Mendelsohn.

Chapter
Thirty-three

My mind goes blank. Bucket-of-white-paint-poured-everywhere blank. In that split second, I don't even remember why I'm standing here. Why did I ever want to meet this man in the first place? What do his billions have to do with me? My heart accelerates. My jaw is hanging in a daze. Neil Finch steps back and leaves through those steel doors. They beep shut, and when I hear the last bolt slide into place, a chill washes over me. I remember exactly why I'm standing here.

"It's about time," I say.

Howie Mendelsohn frowns.

It's not a big courtyard; there's about fifty feet between us, the entire length of the lawn. Howie strolls past a line of topiaries—android, alien, one-eyed ghost—and takes a seat on a stone bench. As I slowly approach, I take inventory of his every inch.

Tired eyes.

Thin shoulders.

Fists, small but mighty, clenched like shriveled walnuts.

He's wearing the gray Palo Alto Labs vest, though his particular version is more stylish than the ones worn by employees. Velvet instead of fleece. Buttons instead of zippers. It's got a ribbed collar, with the company logo—PAL—sewn into the flap, the letters thin and overlapping.

"This is my private courtyard," Howie says. I'm hovering over this bench, where he must expect me to sit next to him. "It's the humble heart of this sprawling campus. Only my office and eight other executive offices have views of it, including Neil, whom I understand you've met. One for each division of the company. Full transparency."

"So it's not very private," I say.

Howie half smiles for just a beat too long. "The topiaries are a nod to different mascots in the history of modern technology. The penguin is for Linux. Android for Google, Alien for Reddit, the ghost for—"

"Snapchat, I know."

Another awkward silence. I notice Howie looks older. Much older. His face is longer, the skin coarser than it was the last time I saw him, late at night when I stumbled into the kitchen during one of his impromptu meetings with my dad.

My dad.

Abba could have grown older like Howie too. His face could have hardened and wrinkled, and the fringes of his hair could have grayed just like Howie's. Maybe it did. But I wouldn't know.

"Opal, I'm so sorry for your loss," Howie says gently. It pricks my skin. "I knew all those years ago, when you were little, how it affected you. But until today, I didn't realize—"

"That I'm still looking for him?" I snap. "That I'll be looking for forever?"

Howie bites the edge of his lip.

"Truly, I, I thought you'd moved on," he stutters. "With PAAST. With WAVE. You don't understand what a delight it's been to watch you grow on our platform. It's just as much yours as it is mine. Your father would have been so proud—"

"Who are you to tell me about my father, when you gave up like everyone else?" My voice cracks. "When you wouldn't even talk to me? When you acted suspicious as hell, went radio silent, then you went off and got Amber Donahue's dad killed, and you—"

"Excuse me?"

"It's a gap, Mr. Mendelsohn! It's a fucking gap!" I kick the foot of the bench. The anger bubbles up and surprises me, like an old friend. "I never bought into the idea that my dad was gone. I kept his seat warm. He was on his way back. Taking his time to show up for my next birthday or to pick me up from school one day. That's what I wanted. And if he taught me any-thing, it was to chase the things I wanted, so I did. For years. And nobody listened, least of all you. You could have filled that gap, told me he loved me and that he never would have left me. You

370 Arvin Ahmadi

could have lied. I've realized that now, that it was more about me than anything else. But you ignored me, Mr. Mendelsohn. You ignored me."

His eyes dim.

"The world is complicated, Opal."

My eyes grow wide, fearful, with the pain of that word from Abba's note. The one I doubted all along.

Complicated.

"Do you know the story of Elijah?" Howie asks.

I shake my head, scanning my mental files for an Elijah. No one with that name had ever come up in my investigation.

"From the Bible," he clarifies, blinking fast. "Everyone knows Sodom and Gomorrah, David and Goliath, but not as many people know of Ahab and Jezebel, let alone Elijah."

"I don't see the connection."

"Ahab was an Israelite king who married an evil woman named Jezebel. Evil in the biblical sense. She was a beautiful, commanding, ambitious woman; nothing like the other wives you'd see back in those times. But she also murdered prophets and framed innocent townspeople. Elijah stood up against Jezebel, warning the king that his wife's wicked misdoings were not in the name of the Lord. He accused her of bringing false idols into Israelite society, of contaminating its purity. She was a woman wreaking havoc on social order. As you might expect, Jezebel did not take well to opposing forces. She threatened Elijah. And so he fled to the woods."

I notice Howie twisting his fingers in his lap. For whatever reason, I sit next to this nervous man.

"But Elijah had a fire inside him too," Howie whispers, his head hanging low. "While he was away, he slaughtered four hundred and fifty of Jezebel's followers. He and Jezebel had the same religious fervor, just different loyalties. They were both fiery. Determined. True to their beliefs.

"Each time Elijah left, he came back stronger than the last. Ahab died eventually, and so did Jezebel. They were supposed to take care of God's people, but they abused God's trust. And they both suffered violent deaths in the name of the Lord, just as Elijah had predicted."

Howie's voice is wobbling now, like an out-of-tune trumpet. A pen that's low on ink. "The Bible paints Jezebel as evil and Elijah as the martyr. It condemns Jezebel's rule of order, her passionate reign that defied the values of society. I don't believe it's so simple."

"I still don't understand," I say.

"I didn't expect you to. But I can show you."

My eyes narrow.

"What do you mean?"

"I know what happened to your father, Opal. But I have to warn you—it's a dark and ugly truth, and just because you want the truth doesn't mean you deserve it. Are you *sure* you want to know? I read the emails you sent when you were a little girl. I did. And now I see your determination has no limits. Still, I'd hate to drag you into a past that might hurt you, so I must ask one more time . . ."

My mind is swimming in theories, but theories are useless without the full set of facts.

"I want to know," I say.

Howie Mendelsohn leaves the courtyard and returns with a shining headset.

He slips it over my eyes.

****

I'm walking through a deep, dark wood.

Tree branches rustle as I twist my head. Leaves blow softly in the wind, whispering secret stories and portentous warnings, though it all drowns out when my eyes land on a figure to my left.

"—maybe we hold off on town halls until we have more data."

Abba. I panic at first, suspecting I might be inside a hacked version of Campfire. But this isn't Tahoe; this is the park behind our house, the one that follows the creek. I register my dad's windbreaker and the muddy brown boots he was wearing that September night he went missing. I register a trail. I also register the outline of a smile on his face. That smirky grin when he's making a point.

A point about town halls and data. This is the first I'm hearing about his work with Howie Mendelsohn. I listen carefully.

"Aaron! Come on!" It's Howie's voice, coming from me. The avatar I've inhabited. "I was hoping you'd come around since our last walk."

"Howie, I haven't *slept* since our last walk."

"How many times must I tell you, town halls are a crucial element of any early stage democracy."

"The issue with the town halls—"

We hear footsteps approaching from behind. My dad perks his chin up.

"What was that?" Abba asks.

I catch a glimpse of horror on my dad's face, and then nothing. His face is gone. It's swallowed by a brown sack. I check over my shoulder and a masked man snaps a brown sack over my head too, but for some reason, I can still see. My view switches to waist level, and the next thing I know, I'm being dragged, my legs and arms slamming into tree trunks. Part of me wonders how I went from seeing through Howie's eyes to Howie's waist, but it doesn't matter, because the rest of me can't breathe. All my nerves have gone numb. My vision is a blur of twigs and starry sky, thick hands and masked faces.

The sound of water rushing over rocks.

"Aaron Tal." There are five masked men, tall and built like the trees around us. The shortest one is speaking, though the hum of the creek muffles his voice. "We've been told if there's one man who will change the face of technology—the face of the future—it is you."

"I can't fucking see," my dad garbles through the sack. Two of the men have pinned him down against a mossy rock. "Who are you? What's going on?"

"Which VC do you work for?" Howie asks.

"You're with Sigmund Lee, aren't you? We told him twenty million times, we're not joining his silly food delivery start-up just because they use drones—"

"Enough!"

I can't tear my eyes away from my father. Despite my mind telling me to study the surroundings, the group of masked men, the leader of the pack—despite knowing there's nothing I can do to help my dad, because even though I'm here, I can't change what happened—I cling to him.

"The real question is, who are *you* to attempt to construct the future of democracy?" the masked leader spits.

Silence. My dad stops thrashing around.

"How do you know about that?" Howie says quietly.

"Of course we're aware of what you're building," the man responds tersely, "or, rather, destroying. The fabric of society."

"Jesus Christ," my dad moans.

"Aaron," Howie snaps. "I apologize, he's delirious."

"*Apologize?* I think these men need to apologize for COVERING OUR HEADS AND DRAGGING US INTO THE WOODS."

The leader grunts, digging his bare knuckles into the bark of a nearby tree. "Do you think this is a joke, Aaron? This is not a joke. Technology has been the downfall of society for decades now, ever since Ted Kaczynski's brilliant manifesto, and we're only shooting ourselves deeper and deeper in the foot."

My dad inhales.

"And what would you like us to do about that?" he asks calmly. It's the same restrained tone he used whenever I interrupted him at his desk. Dripping in faux politeness.

The leader of the pack adjusts his ski mask, and I make a mental note to return to this part to try to catch a glimpse of his face. He begins pacing. "Smartphones ruined our attention spans. Self-driving cars took away our freedom. And now, artificial intelligence and virtual reality will take us the rest of the way in rendering humans obsolete. It will make us ignorant. Weak. This technology you're building will corrupt us further with narcissism and greed, alienate us further from our best selves—"

Abba snorts. The masked leader glares at him, not saying a word.

"You consider this your best self," Abba mutters.

Every organ inside me twists. I want to beg him to stop.

"We wanted to *inform* you," the man says, growing agitated, "of the harm you'll inflict if you take this project of yours any further. On human lives. Last year, a classroom of children was killed in Japan because they were wearing cheap virtual reality headsets that exploded." He looks at the other men. "On *jobs*. You wouldn't believe how many Americans have lost their jobs to software and robots. Soon, it will take our very livelihood. Our freedom. Our choice."

"How do you—" Howie begins.

"Technology is a *pox* on society," the man finishes.

"You fucking cowards," my dad spits. "Idiots like you would be the first weeded out in a smarter society. That's the irony of whatever is going on here."

"I'm sorry, he hasn't slept in days," Howie says frantically. "He's delirious."

"Robots would weed *all* of us out!" the man screams.

"No they won't! There won't ever be a robot president!" my

dad shouts, and chills run down my spine. "There must always be a human touch. But don't you understand we're not perfect?" Abba is lecturing through his sack, even with his hands held back. I recognize those lectures. I've been given those lectures. I miss those lectures. "In the real world, we're stirred by our vices. We're impulsive. We make choices that aren't in our best interest, short-sighted—"

The man lunges forward and rams my dad in the face with his elbow, and I hear a *crack* as the back of Abba's skull smashes into the moss-covered rock.

Abba's face drops.

I whimper.

The men all look at their leader.

His eyes widen.

He hesitates.

And then, he pulls off Abba's sack.

I crumple into a ball.

"What's happening?" Howie says.

The leader inspects Abba's eyes, takes his pulse, and grunts. He slaps Abba across the face, over and over, and then he mutters a series of expletives.

"Aaron? AARON?" Howie is panicking.

I surrender. I'm past goose bumps. Past chills. Past knots in my heart and churns in my stomach. My entire body has turned inside out, given up, sirens wailing.

"We weren't supposed to kill him," one of the men says.

"What the hell—"

"Quiet." The leader of the group cups his face in his shaking hands, lets his fingertips melt over his cheeks. He takes a deep breath. "Listen carefully, Mendelsohn. Here's what's going to happen. We could frame you for this. But we won't. We'll make it look like an accident—you'll see, and believe me, when you do, you won't want to mess with us. You're going to pretend tonight never happened. Understood?"

Howie gulps.

"Understood."

PART FIVE

GIRL WITH THE TRUTH

Chapter
Thirty-four

My dad is gone.

Was that real?

My dad *might* be gone.

Do I want it to be real?

I'm stuck inside a world of pixels. The screen goes black, but I don't unwrap myself from the fetal position; I don't stop rocking back and forth or peel my sweaty palms off my knees. Howie Mendelsohn lays a hand on my back, and I shake it off violently. I try to remove the headset but it gets stuck in my hair, so I yank it off and fling it hard. It makes a soft thud as it lands in one of the topiaries.

"I'm so sorry, Opal," Howie whispers. "I've been dreading this day for seven years."

My vision blurs. I look up at the blue sky, and I'm overwhelmed by how enormous it is.

The man in that scene was my dad. I know it intuitively, from the little signals no one else would ever pick up on—the way he bobbled his head when he lectured, down to his mentioning the robot president. I'd drawn that picture for him just weeks earlier.

The man in that scene was killed.

I always thought when I found out what really happened to my dad, if he had really died, that I wouldn't get bogged down by the loss. I told myself I'd clear my head and focus on the cold, hard facts. After all, I'd already lost so much these last seven years—I should be an expert in loss by now.

But I'm realizing I never stopped stretching that rubber band of fairness. I was hoping for the best, objectivity be damned. I wanted my dad. I never really moved on.

Maybe now I will.

****

"How did you get that recording?" I eventually ask.

I must have sat there silently for minutes. My mind knew very well what questions I needed to ask, but my heart demanded I keep mourning. It was torturous, how my heart clobbered inside my chest, my stomach, my ears—until by some miracle I managed to sedate the damn thing. I bit my bottom lip and focused intensely on one of those stupid topiaries. The penguin one.

"I'll tell you," Howie says, "but the NDA is for real this time."

"That NDA is the last thing on my mind right now."

"Opal, please."

"Okay, fine," I reply.

Howie takes a sharp breath.

"Your father and I were building a virtual society," he says, kneading the two buttons at the base of his vest. "It was going to change the way people lived. By the end of that summer, we had a prototype—a democratic, VR world where you and I could raise families, build meaningful relationships, work and play."

I look down at my hands. They're shaking.

"Still, we needed data from the real world, in order to emulate the nuances of everyday life." Howie glances at my fingertips digging into the bench. "We started with ourselves."

Howie leans in closer to me, his face drifting out of the shade.

"We embedded cameras in our clothes that summer," he says. "To track our every step, conversation, interaction. We surveilled ourselves."

"But you never—"

"I never showed it to anyone, yes."

Bile rises up in my throat. Howie Mendelsohn had been sitting on the truth for all these years.

"The note," I croak. "You let me believe the note they found . . . That note was a lie." My voice breaks as I think about those words. *The world is complicated. The future even more so. I don't wish to complicate it further.*

"They planted it." Howie's voice drips with resentment. "Watching those men kill your dad, learning what they were capable of doing—I was terrified, Opal. I thought they had infiltrated the police investigation. Little did I know those men *were* the police. Little did I know that in just a few years, those disgruntled bastards who lost their jobs to software would grow into a damn revolution."

I remember, now, how the police had closed the case quickly, as soon as they found that note. How they apologized because they were short-staffed and couldn't look for someone "who didn't want to be found."

I didn't blame them, not once, because you're supposed to be able to trust authority figures. The system is supposed to be on your side. People may be flawed, but systems are supposed to work.

Goddamn it.

"I wish you had told me," I say, swallowing tears.

Howie shakes his head. "No you don't."

"I was looking for him!"

"And what was I supposed to do, shatter your hope?" Howie yells, standing abruptly. "That fucking night had already taken your father. Broken me. I wasn't going to break you too. I wanted to forget that nightmare had ever happened. Erase it into oblivion, like a faded pencil mark. I stayed in bed for days, deleted every line of code, every file I had ever worked on with your father—"

"You went back to PAL," I say bitterly.

"The only place where I felt *safe*," Howie defends, rubbing his temples. The wrinkles on his forehead are tense and deep. "At first, I thought about disappearing. Moving to Australia, maybe some Scandinavian country. But that would only have made you more suspicious, wouldn't it, Opal? I was suspicious to everyone. Anywhere I went, I'd carry that history with me—the man whose co-founder *disappeared*. At PAL, I could be my old self again. At PAL, I felt protected. It was like coming back home to family."

I push myself off the bench, and when I stand upright, I get woozy. Howie catches me before I can fall. He squeezes my arms, and when I look up at his face, I see him searching mine.

"You got to move on," I say.

Howie lets out a single, sad laugh.

"Have you seen the news lately, Opal? Nobody's moved on."

****

If there's any silver lining to Howie's version of events, it's this: Abba never left me. He never abandoned me. I wasn't a burden, or a distraction, or a complication in his life. He loved me, and he wanted to stay.

All those moments we never had—he wanted them too. He wanted to link arms with me at the father-daughter dance in the eighth grade. He wanted to teach me integrals. He wanted to help me debug my code. He wasn't running away from any of it.

My dad never gave up on his life.

His life was taken from him.

****

Howie Mendelsohn shattered my past, and in those glass shards, I saw glimmers of a future I could have had with my dad. But now, I'm clenching the pieces. My hands are bleeding with anger.

"How did they even find out about you and my dad?" I ask, weaving between the topiary sculptures. "The Luds barely existed seven years ago. Why would they target you?"

"After the incident, it took everything I had to forget about that night. Those men." Howie trails behind me. "I hoped they would go away. But three years ago, the Luds began picking up steam with their laptop-smashing protests. I had flashbacks to that night in the woods, the things they said about the downfall of society, about greed and corruption . . . it kept me up for weeks. I remembered Elijah and Jezebel. Those men were back."

Three years ago. Right when I stopped looking, went to PAAST, tried to move on—Howie was just getting started.

"I needed to know who they were," he continues. "Your dad and I had met with numerous engineers that summer, but we'd been intentionally vague about the purpose of our technology. The man who killed your father specifically brought up the 'future of democracy.' Only one other person had knowledge of the politics of our project."

My eyes grow, and I spin around and nearly knock Howie's nose off.

"Professor Donahue."

"I showed up at his doorstep in Estonia," Howie says, his eyes going blank. "He insisted I was just being ridiculous. 'There was a note, Howie. The man disappeared. You're making up conspiracy theories.'"

The rest of Howie's face loses color too. "I showed him the XP. His daughter walked into the room when he took the headset off, and his expression was completely aghast. Poor girl. She ran out immediately. Donahue denied it at first, said I was making it all up, but I cornered him. Did you notice that split second where the man who killed your father adjusted his ski mask? I told Donahue

I could use facial recognition and voice recognition to identify the guy—as if I hadn't already tried—but I made him sweat, and he cracked. He admitted to telling the chief of the Palo Alto Police about our work, after the police chief had given a guest lecture for his summer justice course. Donahue was *curious* if there was any role for human police officers in a digital society, and he wanted an expert opinion. The man in the mask was the goddamn police chief."

I'm still doing the addition in my head. "Professor Donahue killed himself," I say slowly, solemnly. "Because the guilt got to him."

Howie nods.

"That's the truth," he says.

I think about Amber. About my dad.

"We all deserve better than the truth," I say.

"We do." Howie pauses, giving me a tentative look. "The man who murdered your father is one of Gaby Swift's key advisors now. He's untouchable. The Luds are moving quickly, Opal—but so are we." A flash of hope overtakes his face. "That virtual society I told you about? After I returned from Estonia, I decided to bring it back to life, here at Palo Alto Labs. They're not going to stop us from achieving our dreams—your dad's dreams. We've been working twice as hard since the election in November. We launch this summer."

****

Howie walks me through the room with the holographic cityscape, with the red laser beams, and it's a wonder. The technology is beyond description; it makes headsets look like typewriters. In those few minutes, I experience a world that is perfectly optimized for me and only me. I sample ice cream flavors that taste like my favorite outfits, listen to music that sounds like purple wildflowers, consume images that transport me to my happiest memories.

I don't see how anyone could be opposed to this.

No one.

This is magic.

****

"You're tracking us at PAAST, aren't you?" I ask Howie in the car. We're in the back seat of a tinted SUV, rolling down a quiet Palo Alto street in the direction of my school. "Those Bluetooth chips in our clothes—they're not *just* Bluetooth, are they? You've tracked my daily routine, the nuances of my existence, just like you and my dad were tracking yourselves, and that's how you created such a perfect world."

He's quiet for a minute.

Then he pulls up the Palo Alto Academy of Science and Technology terms of agreement on the car window, and highlights a passage:

I hereby agree and consent that my personal data may be collected, used, processed, and disclosed by Palo Alto Labs.

"You of all people should understand the power of data," he says.

The air in the car gets heavy as I realize what he's insinuating. As Howie Mendelsohn compares himself to me. That's what this is all about, isn't it—that he and I are on the same team. He lured me in with Make-A-Splash by planting data that I eagerly took, because it was a means to an end.

"This is the future you and your classmates want," Howie says. "It's the future everyone wants. The future being threatened right now by the Luds."

"Why didn't you tell me any of this in September?" I ask. "Why did you have to lure me in with Make-A-Splash?"

Howie turns to me and half smiles.

"I understand you've gotten to know Neil Finch."

"He said he planted the data on Shane's computer for you."

"For *me*?" Howie chuckles, shaking his head. "Neil is my best friend. He was my assistant for years—I hired him straight out of college, and when I returned to PAL, not only did he make me feel welcome but he took a serious demotion to be my assistant again. He controlled my inbox and saw every single one of your emails. I insisted that I knew nothing, that your dad seemed fine to me. But even so, Neil egged me on. *Why don't you just tell her that? Why don't you write her back?*"

A queasiness lurches in my gut.

"The truth is a funny thing, Opal. It festers. But it also frees." Howie gazes out the window and, I can only assume, into the past. "Neil's parents were victims of a terrible car accident when he was a boy, but his mother didn't die right away. She was in a coma for seven days. Waiting by her side, not knowing if she would make it or not—it was the longest week of Neil's life."

The SUV turns a corner, and I flinch. My eyes flicker at the front seat, the empty driver's seat. That accident would never happen today.

"After I finally confided in him about the night your dad was killed, Neil told me two things: that none of this was my fault, and that even after all these years, you deserved closure. I told him you'd moved on. That I didn't want to drag you down with me, with all I knew about the Luds."

"So what changed?"

"Nothing, except that I was wrong." Howie tips his chin and looks at me. "You persisted. Neil noticed that you were entering Make-A-Splash, and he went behind my back and gave you an extra push. He saw himself in you. He saw himself in that uncomfortable hospital chair, waiting until the bitter end, even when the doctors told him his mother was all but gone. I was livid when I found out he had meddled like that, compromised the company—but I didn't fire him. Because some part of me was impressed with you, Opal. You kept going. You made yourself *seen*." Howie clears his voice. "Everything changed in November. What I just showed you—the virtual society we're building at Palo Alto Labs, the work your dad and I started—it's more important now than ever. It's how we get back at the Luds."

"That's why he kept pushing me," I say. "Why he invested and offered to acquire us. Neil wants me to be a part of it, doesn't he? My dad's legacy."

"Only if that's what you want."

I gaze out the car window as we approach the PAAST campus, and I think of Schrödinger's cat. One foot in, one foot out. Stuck in the past, but over it. Juggling fact and fiction. Truth and lies.

Howie Mendelsohn must sense my doubt, because he adds, "I'm trusting you, Opal. I wouldn't trust you like this if I wasn't telling the truth."

The SUV parks outside the Sphinx, and in that final moment as I glance over my shoulder for one last look at Howie, I think of the roller coaster this man has taken me on. He's pushed me out of my comfort zone, yet comforted me. Been absent, yet present. Shared history with me. Disappointed me. Enraged me. Enlightened me.

There's a strong, inexplicable piece of me that wants to believe him.

Maybe even join him.

Chapter
Thirty-five

The funeral flashes through my head quickly and repeatedly. But with it, the thunder of deep paranoia. My clothes. Those little chips. Palo Alto Labs can see me grieving in my dorm room. They can see me curled up in a ball on my bed, hyperventilating, trying to physically fill the gaping hole in my chest with my fists. They have front-row seats for the moment I realize my dad is actually dead, and even if it wasn't my fault or his fault, the new default in my life is that he's actually gone. This funeral is open casket, open everything.

I consider ripping every Bluetooth chip out of every article of clothing in my closet, but that would disable so many of the features that make life easier at PAAST. Personalized screens and automatic doors and the fact that teachers don't have to call out attendance in class. I hate it that amenities like that even cross my mind. My dad tried to make the world a more amenable place, and he got killed.

The tracking is bad, but I'm angrier at the Luds. I look up

old news stories and discover that the police department was, in fact, going through cuts at that time. They were being replaced by software. Because they were biased, because they were inefficient, because they were making mistakes—like every other human job that robots have taken over. The world Howie and my dad were working on would have had room for both.

I think about spilling what I've learned to the world. Another *Behind the Scenes*, where I tell the truth about my father's death and the Luddite Party. But that would compromise Howie's project, my dad's vision. Besides, Howie Mendelsohn has already showered me with the truth; if I spill too much, I could slip and fall.

****

I'm back on the wooden bench under my dorm room, staring at my reflection in the glass exterior of the Sphinx. It's been raining all week, though the sun is finally breaking through this morning. Moyo is sitting next to me, and squeezed beside him are Kara and Shane. It was Moyo's idea to meet out here before first period, since it's early enough and wet enough that no one will be around.

After my eye-opening conversation with Howie Mendelsohn, I found the three of them waiting in the residence hall lounge. They rushed up to me and hugged me and held me tighter than I'd ever been held in my life. My arms went limp by my side. I didn't feel like I deserved their love, because I hadn't decided yet what to tell them. I needed the rest of the week to process everything I'd just learned, to carefully weigh what it would mean to pull my friends in even deeper.

I've been circling them like strangers around campus this week. Now that we're together again, I still don't know what to say. Do I tell them the truth? I'm tempted to keep it to myself—this hideous history—because in their eyes, we have no choice but to accept Palo Alto Labs' offer. Why let the sharp thorns of the past dig under their skin when they've already accepted the present? Don't we all lie to ourselves already?

I look over at my friends. Shane, squishing a leaf into the mud with his white shoe. Kara, who would have never sat on a wet bench like this before. Moyo, who had the heart to reach out and ask if I wanted to meet here, at our old spot. I'm done lying. I'm done stretching the truth like it's some kind of toy. It's not fair to them.

I'm not lying to Palo Alto Labs, either. We're all wearing our Detectables. If they want, Howie and Neil can watch me be honest to the people I care about most.

First, I come clean about the planted data.

Shane says, "I knew that data was too good to be hacked. I just knew it! Not that I'm not capable of hacking, like, anything, but . . ."

Kara says, "So *that's* how you came up with the Hailey Carter idea. You already knew everyone would lie! Not that I wouldn't have done the same thing . . ."

Moyo says, "I'm so sorry, Opal."

My chest is in a permanent state of tightness before I even get to the difficult part. Where I tell my friends, for the first time, that my dad didn't take his own life. Nor did Howie Mendelsohn. That the Luds murdered him.

A painful symphony rings in my ears, but my lips still manage to move, and before I know it, my friends' faces are all turned, staring at me in disbelief. Jaws ranging from slightly open to fully dropped. Eyes wide as the ocean.

Shane says, "Fucking Luds."

Kara says, "I can't believe all the crap my dad said about your dad over the years. He was wrong. I was wrong. Everyone was wrong."

Moyo says, "I'm so sorry, Opal."

Twelve million dollars is a lot of money. But it's not enough money to get roped into Palo Alto Labs' web of vengeance. My friends want to back out of the deal—especially now that we have this knowledge. We have leverage. I pause and consider pushing back, but I realize that urge is coming from the selfish person I've become lately.

We get up and cross the field together. Puddles glimmer beneath our feet, and the smell of fresh grass fills the air. There's something comforting about the early morning, like it can lift the gravity of any decision.

Heads turn as we step into the Sphinx, because now we're not just the kids who went viral but the kids who've risked everything. The rumor mill has been busy guessing why Palo Alto Labs demanded to meet with us. Our heads veer somewhere else, though: to the giant screen along one of the slanted glass ceilings of the Sphinx. Gaby Swift's face is all over it. Her bob of blond hair, her cake of pale foundation, her harsh gray eyes—and the audio caption. *Our great nation used to be a simpler place. We used to be happier without all this techie smut.* She's just signed a new executive order that places the selling of all electronic goods under government control. All of it. Including WAVE.

President Swift's blood-red lips curl into a smile as she makes the announcement, and the Sphinx goes silent. Moyo, Shane, Kara, and I look at each other, and I see the invisible lines between our eyes. Lines connecting my dad's murder with Gaby Swift's crusade to eliminate technology in America—to bring us back to the Stone Age. I see my friends reconsidering their decision to back out. I see the four of us, all of a sudden willing to fight with Palo Alto Labs for the future that Aaron Tal never brought to life.

Chapter
Thirty-six

My mind is so bogged down these days that I nearly forget about Ask Week. One might assume that prom is just an afterthought at America's nerdiest high school, but when you think about how seriously we take our monthly dances, it should come as no surprise that our prom is a giant extravaganza—starting with Ask Week. A month before the dance, the senior class puts on a full week of shows and spectacles for the other classes, with the most outlandish prom asks imaginable. In the past, I've seen trapezes in the Sphinx, light shows and robots and thousands of tennis balls arranged outside on the main lawn in PROM WITH ME? block letters. It's a go-big-or-go-home affair.

By Friday of Ask Week, I accept that I'll be going stag. Which is fine. The topic has hardly come up around my friends, since we're all knee-deep in anxiety over the upcoming summer. If anything, I've been savoring every last minute I have to myself. I've taken to eating lunch alone these past couple of weeks, on the lawns, just outside the door to the Sphinx. Today is a particularly quiet day, the wind blowing softly, like the whole school—the entire city of Palo Alto—is taking a collective breath.

That's when something tumbles before my feet. I don't see where it came from, since my eyes are glued to my phone. But it taps my ankles.

I look down. It's a Rubik's Cube.

My heart skips a beat. Surely this doesn't mean anything. It's a coincidence.

I pick it up anyway. Fiddle with the layers, the little cubes. Some of the squares have letters on them. It takes a few minutes— I haven't solved one in years, not since middle school with Shane— but I keep at it, and I get it. That's the thing about Rubik's Cubes. There's always a solution.

On the yellow side:

S	P	H
I	N	X
H	2	O

Sure enough, I find another Rubik's Cube underneath the water fountain. Again, I twist all the colors in place. The green side directs me to a specific locker, where I find another cube. Now I'm beginning to worry; this has to be Shane's doing. What will Moyo think if he asks me to prom? Has Shane forgotten about our conversation before D-Day? Ever since that last episode of *Behind the Scenes*, he's been getting inundated with job offers from tech companies. Hopefully he hasn't gotten too cocky.

I solve the third Rubik's Cube faster, and the fourth and fifth one, and finally, with the sixth little rainbow block, I know I've reached my final destination. There are no more colors left, not to mention that this last cube brings me to a place I know well:

M	E	D
I	A	R
O	O	M

Outside the Media Room, I find a friend.

"Kara?"

"Opal?"

We exchange puzzled looks.

"How did you—"

"Rubik's Cubes?"

"Yeah."

Before we can say another word, the steel Media Room doors swing open, and standing there are not one but two more friends, each holding a bouquet of fresh orange tulips.

Kara and I gawk for a moment. Then we see the way the two boys look at us. Their eyes full of love. Not the romantic kind, but a stronger bond. One of friends who've been through so much together, who have carried each other and will continue to carry each other. They extend their arms with the bouquets, and I smile at how close we've all become. Moyo looks at me, fully aware of my missteps but proud of me in the end, more in love with me for my strength, I hope, than ever before. And Shane looks at Kara, grateful for her compassion, for her friendship, for being there when he might have otherwise felt alone.

"Ladies," they sing together, in syncopated unison. They

aren't actors, but they've clearly rehearsed. "Will you go to prom with us?"

A small crowd forms around us. I meet eyes with Rosalind Wu, who shoots a wink—and I wink back. For a small second, I'm quiet. I want to take in the moment, this slice of pure happiness, and savor every last crumb. I want to remember how everything feels right and everything is real, and I feel safe and hopeful and proud of myself.

And loved. It doesn't make sense, this desire for love, unattached to numbers or logic or clear and definite goals, but I crave it anyway. A pattern, a habit, a rock. Whatever it is, I need it. We all need it.

My pals and I, we'll survive.

Acknowledgments

Writers are known for googling weird things from time to time, which is why I'm not embarrassed to admit that I just googled "number bigger than infinity." Obviously that number does not exist. Infinity is infinity. But in writing these acknowledgments, I decided I *needed* that number. "Infinite thanks" just wasn't going to cut it. I need more than "infinite thanks" to thank Tina Dubois and Alex Ulyett, for example, for the tremendous work they put into editing this book. They helped me find the heart of this story. They believed in it from the beginning. They deserve so much more than infinite thanks.

Well, as we all know, mathematics is a cruel and uncompromising field, and at the end of the day there is no number big enough to represent just how grateful I am for people like Alex and Tina. So I've decided we are calling it exactly what I typed into Google: Number Bigger Than Infinity. NBTI.

NBTI thanks to Kendra Levin and Maggie Rosenthal, for championing this book in so many ways. I feel very lucky to have you on my side.

NBTI thanks to the engineers and entrepreneurs who so kindly agreed to speak with me when I started writing this book: Tracy Chou, Ayna Agarwal, Samantha Wiener, Estefania Ortiz, Dana Yakoobinsky, Marie Hepfer, Eline van der Gast, Erin Summers, and Zainab Ghadiyali.

NBTI thanks to Lauryn Chamberlain and Nava Ahmadi, for reading multiple drafts of this book. And to my writing friends: Adam Silvera, Patrice Caldwell, Laura Sebastian, Mark Oshiro, Jeffrey West, Jeremy West, Emily X.R. Pan, Cristina Arreola, Dhonielle Clayton, Zoraida Córdova, and MJ Franklin.

Infinity-squared thanks (take that, math!) to everyone I worked with at Yext, especially Howard Lerman, for showing me the positive side of the tech world. And to my high school, Thomas Jefferson High School for Science and Technology. There would be no PAAST without TJ.

Infinity-cubed thanks to everyone at Penguin: Lily Yengle and Marisa Russell, you deserve so many more thank-yous than I could ever give; Felicity Vallence, the genius behind Penguin Teen; Ken Wright, our fearless Viking captain; copyeditors, I appreciate you very much and apologize for this semicolon-heavy paragraph; and everyone on the marketing, sales, and school and library teams. It's because of you this book is being read. Full stop.

Infinity-to-the-infinity-power thanks to all the readers, booksellers, librarians, and teachers out there.

And, lastly, a simple *merci* to my family. Maman, Baba, Neeki, Arman, and Nava—I love you beyond numbers and words.

5